DREAMERS IN HELL

Perseid Press
P.O. Box 584
Centerville Massachusetts 02632

Dreamers in Hell

A Perseid Press Original
First Perseid Press Trade Paperback Edition, June 2013
First Perseid Press ePub Edition, June 2013
First Perseid Press Kindle Edition, June 2013

 This book is a work of fiction. Names, characters, places, and incidents either are the products of the author's imagination or are used fictitiously, and any resemblance to actual events or person, living or dead, is entirely coincidental.

Book design by Sarah Hulcy; cover design by Sonja Aghabekian
Cover art: Cover image copyright (c) Perseid Press, 2013.
Cover and title page art: Artist: Unknown, Detail from Aeneas and the Sibyl

TRADE: ISBN-10: 0989210022, ISBN-13: 978-0-9892100-2-7
KINDLE: ISBN-10: 0989210030, ISBN-13: 978-0-9892100-3-4
EPUB: ISBN-10: 0989210049, ISBN-13: 98-0-9892100-4-1

Published in the United States of America

10 9 8 7 6 5 4 3 2 1

ACKNOWLEDGEMENTS

Nancy Asire, The Unholy Hole
Yelle Hughes, Essence Helliance
Sara M. Harvey, Barefoot, on Brimstone
Shebat Legion, Ophie and the Undertaker
John Manning, Just Dessert
Michael A. Ventrella, Hell I Must Be Going
Bill Snider, Head Games
Tom Barczak, Blood and Ash
Sarah Hulcy, Hellexandria the Great
David L. Burkhead, The Knife-Edged Bridge
Deborah Koren, The Wager
Bettina S. Meister, More Light!
Jason Cordova, In the Shadow of Paradise
Richard Groller, Zero Sum Game
Jack William Finley, And the Truth Shall Set You Free
Michael H. Hanson, The ITTT
Petra E. Jörns, Siegfreid's Blade
Edward McKeown, Stairway to Heaven
Larry Atchley, Jr., Knocking on Heaven's Gate
Chris Morris, Fools in Hell
Janet and Chris Morris, Alms for Oblivion
Janet Morris, Hell Bent

RELATED WORKS:

Heroes in Hell

The Gates of Hell

Rebels in Hell

Kings in Hell

Crusaders in Hell

Legions in Hell

Angels in Hell

The Little Helliad

War in Hell

Prophets in Hell

Explorers in Hell

Lawyers in Hell

Rogues in Hell

DREAMERS IN HELL

created by JANET MORRIS edited by Janet Morris
by Chris Morris

with the diabolical assistance of their damnedest writers

Sara M Harvey • Nancy Asire • Larry Atchley, Jr. • Tom Barczak
Jason Cordova • Jack William Finley • Richard Groller • Michael H. Hanson
Yelle Hughes • Sarah Hulcy • Petra Jorns • Deborah Koren • Shebat Legion
John Manning • Ed McKeown • Bettina Meister • Janet Morris • Chris Morris
Bill Snider • Michael A. Ventrella • David L. Burkhead

TABLE OF CONTENTS

DREAMERS IN HELL

FOOLS IN HELL

Chris Morris

> Now will I show myself to have
> more of the serpent than the dove;
> that is, more knave than fool.
> – Christopher Marlowe, *The Jew of Malta*

"I still say 'they that love not tobacco and boys are fools,'" Christopher Marlowe told William Shakespeare as they slid into their seats in New Hell's Old Rogue Theatre. The auditorium smelled of rancid butter, stale popcorn, and sweat. Lights were low, the production's rehearsal about to start.

Sometimes they played this quote game too long, too hard, Marlowe knew.

"'Love me little, love me long,' you also gave us in *The Jew of Malta*, Kit," Shakespeare quoted his friend, leaning back in his sticky seat: "But unlike your Malta play, boys in hell are few and vicious, and tobacco tainted. And I'm loving you as little as I can manage, now that I've seen the Devil in his true glory. 'It lies not in our power to love, or hate/For will in us is over-rul'd by fate,' you said in *Hero and Leander.* So since you well know it, forgive me now. I must find Satan and feel those creamy wings against my burning skin."

Will Shakespeare was Kit Marlowe's greatest sin: beloved beyond measure, tender-hearted and in constant need of Kit's protection – an obsessive distraction. Kit rejoined, "'So lust, though to a radiant angel link'd,/Will sate itself in a celestial bed/And prey on garbage'? Am I garbage to thy love-besotted eye?"

"No, but these here are, Kit: Machiavelli directs this travesty of *Hamlet* to get back at you through me. *'Damnedlet'*: even the name of my tragedy this Italian cannot leave alone."

"You'll hate it. I told you. They've women playing women; all the electronic paraphernalia of hell is in this production – and most lines are bowdlerized."

"So we're here why, then? Poor plays in hell are nothing new. As for basing all on me – or you – theft is a hellish excellence."

"We're *here,* Will, because Satan plans a great festival, lasting weeks, to celebrate the reopening of the Hellexandria Library. Entertainment will include *some* production of a play of yours, and one of mine, staged with great fanfare. So we must see what's on offer. And then you can try rubbing against the legs of your fair-fledged fiend, and make a plea for which renditions of our plays should be allowed, and which not."

"Satan thinks naught of me." Shakespeare sighed, so deep ensorcelled by the Devil that he'd missed Kit's point.

"Think you so?" said a voice like a viper as someone moved to take a seat behind them and the house lights dimmed still more. Marlowe could smell the femaleness of this speaker before he turned: pungent, musky, and ancient.

A second tangy distaff slid into a seat beside the first and said, "So you are the two, Marlowe and Shakespeare. Which is Shakespeare? – I've a bone to pick with thee." Whisper as dangerous as rocks settling; fetid breath that made Marlowe gasp.

"And I," said the first female, whose skin had a greenish glow against the shadowed dark.

Shakespeare turned and put both arms on his seatback, squinting in the dimness: "And you are? I've enemies in hell, but all males, I'd thought..."

"Sin, I am called," said the first. "The selfsame snaky sorceress your time vilified – and this play's executive producer."

"I am Hecate," said the second. "Up from Hades to make sure that if *MacDeath,* rather than this *Damnedlet* play is chosen, my name will be removed from it: 'witch'? 'weird sister'? How durst you scratch such denigrations upon a page? Now we'll remove all that...."

"No, you won't. Not even 'when the hurly-burly's done/ when the battle's lost and won.' Never shall my lines about the three witches be rewritten," said Shakespeare. *"Not* 'in thunder, lightning, or in rain.' What are you, the vilest editor in hell? I've fought more battles on paper and onstage than you can dream of. And won."

"Satan, Son of the Morning, Prince of Hell, is my father," said Sin. "Surely you don't think to prevail against *my* versions of your damned plays?"

"Or against me," said Hecate, "a goddess, not some weirdy crone of a silly witch. You failed to do your homework, Shakey, when you took *my* name in vain."

This is not good, my love: a spat to end in tears.

Kit Marlowe had a mission to accomplish here for interests among the Devil's Children, an army of intriguers who worked infernity's most secret designs: simply bring Machiavelli down a peg. Kit didn't know or care why Machiavelli was his target; the Romans and the Italians and their antics held no fascination for him. In life, he'd taken on a raft of covert enterprises such as this and never needed, or wanted, explanations. It paid well. He'd kept at it till one had killed him. But this was hell itself: no feud here was ever over; every enemy you made drew a bead upon your very soul.

Now the stakes were getting too high. Bad enough that his Will was enthralled by Lucifer at his most beautiful. Now these two harpies – powers beyond Kit's control – wanted a piece of the only soul in hell that Marlowe loved. "Sisters Sin and Hecate," Marlowe soothed, "we had just been saying, if only we could see a clear blue sky, a sunny day, the stars at night – *one* time more – we could write a new play together for the Library's reopening, glorifying all infernity. And you two could make that happen: give us a glimpse of Elysion, Hecate; fly us there, Sin, as only you may; you are easily among the most powerful forces in all the newer hells."

"Too cute, Marlowe. I'll fly you to deepest damnation first, where your breath will freeze your lungs," Sin said dangerously. "My father Satan requires your presence at the Library as His plans for torments unfold."

"Aye, and I'll show you Tartaros, not Elysion," added Hecate, "unless you two can write this play and finish it and prove it's more suitable than Niccolo's *Damnedlet,* better even than the original."

Now a tumult broke out upon the stage, and Sin said, "Hush, look what we've made of your humanizing drivel."

Next the curtain lifted and Niccolo Machiavelli, the very model for Kit's Jew of Malta, strutted back and forth before the footlights, his face caked with powder; on his lips a parody of the opening lines from *Hamlet.*

Shakespeare shot upright before Marlowe could stop him: *"No!"*

Kit grabbed his friend by the arm lest Will cause a fuss that never could be expunged. And held him tight.

Sin giggled like dice in a cup.

"Call me a crone, will you, in your silly little play?" Hecate reached beside her and from under her skirts pulled a greasy bone that stank of garlic and dripped blood, chanting in Carian that sounded Greek: "Tell *me* what *you* want, Marley? Fly you *where?* Show you *what?* Take care what you wish for in hell, writer boys."

"Damn," Marlowe muttered, just before a whirlwind issuing from the greasy bone caught him and Shakespeare up and sucked them round and out of the theatre and away.

All Marlowe could remember was the wind whipping him and his cloak slapping him and wrapping up his head, and his hand digging into Shakespeare's shoulder as they were buffeted and blown where witches go.

Then the whirlwind died.

They fell. They fell together. They fell grabbing onto one another; embracing one another. They fell a thousand years. They fell through wars and pestilences and flights of angels falling faster.

And landed hard, on a heath more blasted than Marlowe could have imagined. Yet he still held Shakespeare fast.

"Will, get up. Are you hurt?"

"Deeply – in my pride," said Shakespeare, ogling the ruddy vault above. "Is that New Hell in the far distance?"

Marlowe tried his limbs and looked where Shakespeare pointed: at the black and belching smoke, the low brown clouds of filthy fog, the spires pointing to a Paradise that none could reach. "I think it is. Or is today."

Marlowe was helping the bard to his feet when a small and winged and furred and bright-clawed beast came yowling at them, its black tail lashing.

It pounced on something among the rocks, not an arm's-length away: a snake, five feet long or more. The bat/cat shook the serpent in powerful jaws until the snake hung limp and lifeless.

If the snake ever had 'life' to lose in hell.

The victor (part bat, part cat, part worse) spat out the snake and growled at them, its tail bushing wide. Then it reached between its leathery black wings and pulled out two rolls of parchment, two feathery quills, and a pair of inkwells with a very red liquid visible in each one.

These it laid before them. Then it howled, "Nnn-naaaooowww," and turned, and bounded off.

"Are we to write? Is that what it wants? Here? Now? Or perhaps to follow it?" Shakespeare guessed as he picked up the parchment rolls, the quills, and the jars of blood-red ink. "That's Satan's very own familiar, is it not: the famous 'Michael?'"

"Write as we go, I'd say, Will," Marlowe answered. "It's a long walk back, but the route to New Hell is difficult to mistake."

And, of course, it was. Kit Marlowe had made his own deal with Satan, and that deal had no escape clause: Marlowe could shelter Shakespeare, to a point, if Kit would serve the fallen angels, spy upon the damned as he'd once spied upon the living. If he did his job well, in the view of those who ruled the hells, he'd not lose his friend to the Undertaker's table.

Kit eyed Will, still far too tender a soul after centuries in perdition, and racked his brain for a bracing quote or two, to start the play's dialogue and ease their trek across this lifeless landscape beneath the brooding vault: some words, some inspiration to begin this play, which he'd promised the hags they'd write together. But no clever turn of phrase or shrewd observation came immediately to mind. At last Kit sighed. "'Honor is purchased by the deeds we do,'" he reminded Will. His had been bought and paid for long ago.

Shakespeare looked at him puffy-faced and said, "I know. 'Where hell is must we ever be.' But we have a new patron, now... the Devil himself. And a new play to write: that's the thing."

And it was, for Will.

Shakespeare did not, would not understand that rending such a fragile soul as his was mere amusement for the Father of Lies. But Kit Marlowe understood, and wondered how in all infernity he could free his beloved from Satan's black intentions now that Will was in the Devil's thrall so completely – ambition, pride and all.

Marlowe replied to his friend, "From *Faustus*: 'Fools that will laugh on earth, most weep in hell.'"

As if to prove that nothing would avail, Shakespeare took Marlowe by the arm, then hugged him tight. Will kept one arm around him as the two of them followed the Devil's furry familiar toward their well-earned fates, Satan's hot embrace, and a new play to bring to light: a tale to tell writ in the bowels of hell.

ALMS FOR OBLIVION

Janet Morris and Chris Morris

"Time hath, my lord, a wallet at his back,
Wherein he puts alms for oblivion,
A great-sized monster of ingratitudes:
Those scraps are good deeds past; which are devour'd
As fast as they are made, forgot as soon
As done:"

– Shakespeare, *Troilus and Cressida*

Satan flew through the past, the future, and the present of infernity, thence alighted on the highest parapet of his lordly seat in Pandemonium.

There he raised his fists, spread whitest wings, and bellowed at the blood-red vault above while Paradise mocked him, shining, forever out of reach. "Leave me in hell then. But leave my hell to me!" he screamed. "Call back these crude enforcers from Above, auditors who punish both innocent and guilty with such glee: only with subtlety does torment last!"

On high, an omnipotent ear pricked, but no more. Overhead, the light from Paradise flickered, reminding Satan that even reflected grace could be withheld.

Damned he was, beyond hope, beyond redemption; imprisoned here – cast down with his faithful, so far at first that not even a glimpse of the heavens could be seen: in the dark, in the cold, in the deep between knowingness and oblivion: fit punishment for him and his, who'd risked all, and lost it.

It had taken forever for the hellfires to kindle: he and his banished cohort had flown aloft in total darkness, until the underworlds were named and souls came here to suffer dreams of redemption. Now he reigned in this hell and its vast dominions, over the most disbelieving of the damned.

This teeming multitude of dead – repenting, keening, sobbing, overweening souls – had more chance of deliverance than did Satan's once-mighty army, all the banished sons of glory. He and his were starshine on a sunny day, nothing more. Insignificant. Rulers of naught. Lords of noplace. Banished. Shamed. Nearly forgot....

For eons the Son of the Morning and his troops had presided over the worst of souls; forever and ever, the meting out of torture and torment had been their province. Reigning nowhere but the country of the lost, Satan had nursed his rage, studied his trade, and shared the netherworlds with all the downcast gods: lords of mankind's hells were many, from ancient Sumer and Babylon and Asia and Greece and times before and after; they ruled their damned, he ruled his. So it had always been.

But no more.

Now came auditors from Above to hell: all the hells had been adjudged too comfy; not horrid enough for the satisfaction of the heavens. These auditors number only eight: the symbol of infinity. They are everywhere, everywhen, pitiless and terrible enough to make hell-scapes quake.

Here they wreak vengeance as decreed on high, stalking the netherworlds, striking panic into condemned souls, shattering hopes and destroying wantonly – as if Satan could not do so... should he ever wish.

Infuriating slight: the newer hells were his by dispensation and the Word.

Although banished from the heavens, he, Satan (sometimes Lucifer, sometimes the Adversary, the Deceiver), is still lord supreme of his domain. His hell is all around him, his to hold.

But the cosmos is not as bespangled as once it was: as above, so below. With Satan fell a third of the stars from the sky: his loyalists. When war sweeps the heavens, the firmament and the fundament both are losers. Satan dared to fault mankind, decry flawed humanity; to show what foul clay was the human being. So from that day to this he tends his damned, with whom he is free to do his worst. Or was...

Now crude Erra, god of plague and mayhem, and his seven personified weapons, the Sibitti of ancient desolation, tramp through the fields of damned souls and pillage among all the hells, not only Satan's underworld. These destroyers roam unfettered, unchecked, spreading anguish and woe wheresoever they should go.

Adamantine and fiery was Satan now, hot with wrath, standing on his parapet, his palace all around, whose stones drove down into the chill deep and up as high as infernity's reach. But not high enough.

Once he had been mighty and more beautiful than any. Once his angels had battled the very phalanxes of the heavens. And may again.

He would call them all together, his warriors from the past, present, and future of man's self-inflicted pain. Akkadians and Danaäns and Macedonians and Arabs and Spaniards and Huns and more... all who died for glory and waked to an afterlife of infamy would he forge into a new army to do away with Erra and his Seven, foul destroyers: one minor, ancient god he must defeat – only *one* – and seven soulless weapons, sons of heaven and earth, creatures without remorse.

Satan was the Trickster, the Deceiver. He had been cast down once; he would not risk falling lower. Too cold down there. He would spark his war, not fight it – not this time. He would incite his damned; he would whisper in the ears of the greedy and the lustful and the hateful and the ambitious and the vile. Irredeemables. He had enough of them to overwhelm the scintillating ramparts of all the heavens.

If truth be told, he had more than enough of them – to confuse, to abuse, to turn to hideous purpose. For humankind had brought this fate upon the Father of Lies: when man was created and favored above all other beings, jealousy ignited in Satan's breast, and burned there still.

Satan's gut churned with the fury of a demiurge deposed. He could fly to the gates of the heavens and shield his eyes and beg; repent, but he would not: he'd been right, was right, would always be right: humanity was flawed, an unworthy impulse. Else why would so many bide here with him, and so few ascend to the paradisiacal light? A killer species like no other: they killed their brethren, every animal and plant and insect and everything that lived on the wide Earth made for their pleasure.

As Satan bestrode the battlements of his citadel he made a shining plan. And that plan was a plan for humankind to prove itself unworthy even of hell and deserving of oblivion. Thence the netherworlds would be less crowded, and in future there would be no need for auditors from Above to run amok in Satan's domain.

The archfiend waxed wroth. Black he became, and fearsome, with burning eyes and forked tail and leathern wings to suit his mood, and went sojourning in the streets of New

Hell City, to find a dupe or two, to give humanity the first, soft push toward dissolution.

With him came his angel of death, Samael, to mark the souls he'd choose: Satan rode a blood-bay hell-horse, hot between his knees, the color of the vault above; Samael rode beside him on a bone-white horse with eyes of unremitting doom. Into the midst of the depraved they thundered, a squadron of banshees going on before, heralding their coming; a retinue of demons shredding souls and chortling in their wake. The Old Dead gave way. The New Dead covered their heads with their arms.

Doomed souls wailed, paled and scattered. The young screeched and the old howled and everywhere in New Hell the cry went up: "The Devil rides the streets! Take care, take care!"

Their path cleared before them; everywhere, doomed souls dropped to their bellies, their faces to the ground.

Into New Hell's stinking center they rode until they reached a pavilion that scraped the sky with stone and glass and metal, wide-stepped and presumptuous in design, where illustrious dreamers of the afterlife were convening. Before broad stairs of ruddy granite, the two fallen angels waved away their banshees, their horses and their demons. Then Satan said to Samael, "Now we shall entice them, seduce them, and inspire them. So be you beauteous."

Thus they both remade their shapes, no longer snaky and fearsome, but exquisite as they had been on the day the heavens first expelled them: white winged, flawless and long of limb; faces like creation itself: they could still do that, be that. Then up those stairs and inside they strode, more beautiful than man or woman, like unto the godly host on high, with alabaster pinions wide.

Before them in a corbeled foyer, an obelisk announced in English, Greek, Chinese and Akkadian: *'New Hell Visionaries' Conference: Dreaming A Greater Tomorrow'* and a blinking red arrow pointed down a hallway.

Along that hall of granite they found door after closed door, each clearly labeled: *'Architecture,' 'Arts and Letters,' 'Biology,' 'Computer Sciences,' 'Engineering,'* but found no souls wandering there. They went on, through corridors echoing and empty, until they came to the last doors, that read: *'Creativity: Workshop in Progress.'*

Satan inclined his head. Samael, as tall as he with hair sparkling of flames and wings folded about him, threw both doors open wide. The double doors flew inward, banging against the inner walls.

Samael bowed Satan inside.

Now voices raised, then died away amid a seated audience; now five men behind a table on a dais sat back, silent. Before each was a placard: *'Leonardo, inventor'; 'Shakespeare, playwright'; 'Marlowe, dramatist'; 'Aristotle, philosopher'; 'Byron, poet.'*

Behind his placard, baby-faced Marlowe leaned into a microphone and spoke to the assembly: "To quote my humble self: 'Hell hath no limits, nor is circumscribed/In one self place, for where we are is hell, –/And where hell is, must we ever be.' Welcome the Prince of Darkness and the Angel of Death to our midst." And clapped his hands.

The audience applauded too, reticently. Some made to rise; some squirmed in their seats. The hall buzzed with their consternation.

Now Samael swept his coruscating glare across them and said from the aisle: *"Silence.* Bow you down, sinners. On your knees, doomed souls. Your lord Satan is among you."

All scrambled to obey; chairs screeched and bumped in their rows; yet the five speakers were slower to abase themselves, staring at Samael and Satan, transfixed.

These were the ones whom Satan had come to collect: "You five," he said to those on the dais, "come with me."

Shakespeare and Marlowe were off the riser like a shot, bold in doublet and hose; Byron offered a red-velveted arm to help linen-robed Aristotle, then Leonardo, to their feet: Leonardo and Aristotle were too dangerous to be reborn young in hell, so infirmity was their lot.

"We shall have a short intermission, worthies." Leonardo smoothed his russet sculptor's smock before he took Lord Byron's arm. "Whilst we are absent, remember these words of mine: 'knowing is not enough; we must apply. Being willing is not enough; we must do.'"

By then, Satan's plan was in motion: these conferees of perdition would set jealous hearts alight and stoke the enmity of the good for the great among all the lesser damned. Behind them would come armies of their admirers, impersonators, imitators, and detractors, each hoping for an ort from their feast, a role in whatever might be stewing.

These anointed five clustered around Satan and Samael as the others filed out, casting covetous glances at the chosen few.

Samael preened his wings and Leonardo trembled, so much did he crave to touch those feathers fledged in heaven: he'd painted wingless angels, once, long ago. As Leonardo reached out a palsied hand, Byron caught and held it, saying to Samael, "Angel, are we honored? or worse doomed?" Mad-eyed Byron was a club-footed warrior, and a lover of warriors, a would-be hero and a singer of glories.

Samael entranced him with the slightest smile, locked eyes with him and said, "As my lord Satan wills, so shall ye do, Man."

"We will, O Angel," replied Byron, stretching out his arms to encompass Leonardo, and Aristotle, and all those filing from the room. "We will."

Aristotle, cannier than any, shook his head and in his turn stayed Byron's arm. "Unprecedented acts have unprecedented consequences," warned the wise old Chalkidian who'd taught Alexander of Macedon how to war.

Kit Marlowe, cherubic and sly, hid a frown, his hand on Shakespeare's shoulder as the bard of Avon gazed moonstruck upon Satan with such hunger as would eat a world.

"You are my poets, my architects, my metaphysicians, my exemplars," said Satan. "I have chosen you five from all hell's teeming damned to spread the word, wake every soul from apathy: we shall resist the depredations of Erra and his Seven, pitiless champions. You will make weapons. You will write plays. You will pen songs and sing them. You will spread this word among your fellows: The heavens are not unconquerable. Salvation is not out of reach, if all the souls in hell but storm the gates of Paradise. Its fastness can be yours. Redemption favors the bold."

Shakespeare licked his lips. He cleared his throat. His eyes were huge as he said, "Lord, I must study at your knee. I must learn your thoughts, your feelings, your passions... to write what will please you."

"Write what will light the fires of striving in the doomed and the damned. They can save themselves, if they but do as we bid. But yes, Shakespeare, you may come to me."

Kit Marlowe squeezed his eyes shut; then opened them, crestfallen. This one, of all five, was the most mischievous, the most inured to blandishment; this one was careful when he spoke: "Devil, I shall labor with my friend Will, to write poems and plays to teach your message. But will you tell me why, show me how, one so great as Thee can need us?"

"Quiet, impertinent soul," said Samael, not a subtle angel, but so powerful, "or I'll start your afterlife anew."

"No, he may ask," said Satan, feeling joy upwelling in his groin now that the game was begun and Shakespeare gazed at him, yearning. "And I will answer you, Marlowe, whose 'Faustus' did amuse me: I am not a man, nor the doomed relic of a man, his immortal soul. Were I a man's soul, I would not be Satan, nor would I be in hell. And if I were not Satan, and not in hell, then I would not exhort my damned to rise up against the scourge from Above. Were there no scourge from Above, punishing all the souls consigned to me, then I would not come to lowly men to raise their mettle and fight back. And were I not calling all the souls in my hell to battle, then I would not need Shakespeare, nor Marlowe, nor Aristotle, or Leonardo, or Byron to exhort their brothers to arms and their minds to service. But there is a scourge abroad in hell, and I am Satan, and you are the souls to cry foul and wake your brothers to storm the gates of Paradise, one by one and altogether."

"So be it," whispered Shakespeare, a man transfixed.

"At your service," seconded Byron, who would always dream heroic dreams.

"I think I can design a tool or two, to reach high enough to scrape the vault of heaven," offered Leonardo, pulling on his beard.

"Good. To your labors, then, souls," said Samael. "It is decided. I will watch over you."

Only Aristotle had not volunteered.

So Satan said, "You, who inspired a boy to conquer the entire world of men, can you call the vast forces of hell to order, from every age, and create concord out of discord?"

"I can," said Aristotle, always logical. "But I shall need wherewithal. Provide it, and I can bring you even Alexandros."

Then Shakespeare said, "Alms for oblivion... what we have done in life, gentlemen, is but a puny shadow of the deeds we'll do here. Forget the past; what we have done before is dust. Look up. Free all the souls in hell...." Wistful, eager, passionate Shakespeare sought Satan's approval: a glance, a word, a ratification of the chance of love, or even the tide of lust.

"Will, start by freeing thine own self," warned Marlowe softly. But it was too little, too late.

"Tell me, Will Shakespeare, of your idea, your plot, what your glimmering mind can apprehend," said Satan softer still. "But be you careful: these dogs of war, once loosed, will battle till the end of time." And Satan unfurled one wing, enough to curl it round Shakespeare's shoulders, enough to put that wing between the bard and Marlowe's touch. "And you, Marlowe, who wrote so much about my glory, are you willing? To aid all souls and aid your friend, if only to keep him safe – as safe as a soul can be in hell? Will you risk yours, beside us? Or sit and watch, as damned and hopeless as the least renowned, and be carried along by the whirlwind that must follow as we remake what destiny we all can share?"

Now, Marlowe straightened up. His frown softened. His handsome face relaxed as Satan offered him a place among this august war council called in hell.

"'Safe as a soul can be'? In my bones, there are too many shocks; in my heart, there are too many breaks; in my flesh, there are too many hungers: how can I refuse? Harness my fury? Put my mind to revenges? How not, once I have heard it can be so? Here stands the angel of death; here stands the lord of hell: come to recruit my childish soul, foolish beyond measure. I will assault the shining gates of heaven all alone, if peace of mind can be won by force of arms. Here am I, a wisp of thought, a creature of habit that thinks itself a man, grieving for a lifetime long forgot. Me, I'll write the doom of ages, succor sin – to prove I can. And Time shall spin me where She wills: 'Come live with me and be my love.... 'Tis Rage who loves me and lives with me. Take rage and love from my breast and put them to work? Yours I am, yours I've always been. What difference?"

To set the hook, Satan said: "All the difference: give me the soul of you, the heart of you, and the dreams that make your soul sing. The rest is what you'll make it, now you sleep with eternity for your bedmate. Yes, Marlowe, you are mine, and the mountain will not fall upon you... yet."

Crack!

Perfect timing: The building around them shook from its foundations to its highest tower.

Boom!

Air slapped windows; ceilings creaked; dust and dirt and insects drifted down.

Shiver!

Aftershock shimmied through the air, along the walls. And every soul among the crowd in the antechamber and the hallway (and those yet lingering to overhear whatever they could as they filed out) dove for cover, grabbing their hell-phones or fingering communications leeches curled around their ears, asking everyone: What? Where? Who? How?

Roar!

A final blast, a shocking gust of vacuum; reverberation...

Wordless shrieks, growls and shouts rang out as the damned in the foyer and the hallway pushed and pulled and fell and shoved, milling with no thought but to flee.

The blither of the affrighted damned bathed everyone, licked them like surf, ebbed and swelled in quick succession until some Roman legionary bellowed, "Caesar's villa. It's been hit. Erra and the Seven have destroyed it. All's lost. All's lost!"

Now come sobs of fear and misery. And screeches. And curses falling like rain from incautious lips. Despite the Roman, every soul in New Hell was yelling and calling to each other, demanding comfort of whomever their voices could reach, seeking news about the blasts.

"Best get out of here. Don't push. I'm Sulla. I'm in charge until we hear from Caesar's household. Romans, to me: we form up a rescue party. Single file...."

Hearing this, Samael chuckled like lava invading seawater. Around Satan, his five victims stood firm, watching him.

"Rescue?" Aristotle echoed.

"In charge?" Byron scoffed.

"Sulla. I'll need to speak with him," Leonardo mused, unerringly fixing on a countryman of power and influence.

Neither Marlowe nor Shakespeare had moved. Shakespeare, still in the shelter of Satan's wing, had hardly flinched. Now the playwright said, "If Erra and the Seven have pillaged Caesar's villa, all New Hell's souls are ours for the taking: the play's already taking shape in my mind's eye, full of sound and fury." The homely bard grinned so wide his goatee thinned: "Flames and devastation incense the masses like no other fuel."

Samael's gleaming stare caught Satan's eye. Samael nodded. Satan took back his pinion's shelter from Shakespeare and the bard took one, then another, unsteady step toward Marlowe. These two intimates had written together; and more, together.

Christopher Marlowe said, "Is this luck, Father of Lies? Fate? Surely not coincidence? Or did you know this was coming? Help it hence?"

"Did I know? How could I not? Did I help my enemy? Do you care? When our cause is so aptly served by bodies ripped asunder, tears wetting infertile ground, and grief howling up to bounce off the uncaring vault of heaven?"

Even Shakespeare cocked his head: "Great Devil, did thy machinations put this whirligig on destruction's track? You show no surprise...."

"Raise thy sights, mortal laborers," advised Samael before Satan could reply. "I have deaths to mete out among the fallen, entrails to squish underfoot, limbs to kick from the bloody path of our Lord, Satan, who is about his own revenges. And though you may not kneel again today, be you warned: you will kneel again tomorrow before His Satanic Majesty. And for a thousand tomorrows."

So Satan said then, "Surprise? Why should I? I know my enemy, and his name is Erra. If anything is surprising, it is that the privileged in New Hell have escaped the Seven's notice for so long. Now blood will spill like wine until the smoke of roasting souls blots out the light of Paradise – and for a brief moment, the true character of heaven stands revealed. Will Shakespeare, Kit Marlowe: you shall tell the tale of heaven's rage in hell. Shall we go together, and view the carnage, smell the shit of death, the cooked flesh, splash in the gore that marks heaven's dreadful judgment of the damned? And whilst we do, wonder why humans pray to such a deity as will pile insult upon injury, time after time, and never stop?"

Beyond the five gathered round Satan and Samael, Sulla's Romans were forming up ranks and calling for work details among the bravest souls attending the conference. Others sat sniveling, backs against walls, or whining that they must not be conscripted. Sweet chaos reigns for the briefest while, among those who'd dared to think their fates could not be worse.

Satan folded his snowy wings, and so did Samael, and they strode back the way they'd come, five great souls clambering along in their wake.

So it begins, the battle joins, and against heaven's cruel despite, all of hell will soon unite.

The irredeemable will make war upon the highest heavens: a battle that will rage in every soul and every heart among the damned and reach down into every crevice of the darkest underworlds and up to the glistening pylons on high.

And if behind him, Shakespeare smelled of lust and want, and Marlowe of caution and cunning, and Aristotle of deepest thought, and Leonardo of eagerness to invent new tools for a new war, and Byron of the effort it took for a lame soul to keep pace, then Satan found the stench a rarefied perfume.

When the damned stink to high heavens, change is on the wind.

THE UNHOLY HOLE

Nancy Asire

"Would you look at this, would you?"

Napoleon, once Emperor of the French, glanced up from a particularly virulent weed he was attempting to remove from his front yard. His neighbor, Wellington, stood at the end of the hedge that separated their two houses.

"What?"

"It's my hedge! My damnable hedge! I'm beginning to think it's out to get me, that's what!"

Napoleon stood, the invasive plant held in one hand. "Out to get you how?"

The Iron Duke, former Prime Minister of England and celebrated victor at Waterloo, waved a hand. "It's growing extraordinarily long tendrils that sway in a nonexistent wind. It's almost like they're sentient!"

"Let's take a look." Napoleon dropped the weed and joined Wellington at the end of their driveways. He was fairly certain when he returned it would have rooted itself and grown to twice its original size. "You haven't insulted it lately, have you?"

"My hedge? Surely you jest. But when I go after it with the clippers, the tendrils draw back as if they know I'm going to –"

The earth *moved.*

Wellington's face turned white. "What the bloody hell?"

Napoleon grabbed Wellington's arm; the two of them swayed as the ground beneath them rose and fell like an earthen wave.

A cacophony of shrieking alarms filled the neighborhood: house alarms, car alarms, all set off by the sudden movement of the earth.

"Napoleon!" Marie Walewska, Polish Countess and Napoleon's lover in life and afterlife, stood on the porch, the front door held open by one hand.

"Marie," Napoleon shouted, "get out of the house! *Now!*"

She ran across the front yard, the ground now vibrating beneath their feet.

"What's happening?" Marie asked, her eyes gone wide.

"I don't know," he replied, letting go of Wellington's arm. "But I don't want you in the house if a stronger shock comes at us."

A tremendous explosive sound swept over them and a wind tore across Decentral Park, tossing the tops of the trees in its passing.

"Oh, for the love of... look, Napoleon, *look!*"

Napoleon turned and followed the line of Wellington's finger that pointed to the east end of the Park. Above the trees rose a dirt-colored cloud that grew in height as they watched.

"What in all the hells is *that?*" Napoleon grated. "It looks like it's coming from Caesar's villa!"

"What, indeed?" Wellington straightened his British general's uniform. "And who? And why?"

The ground had ceased to move; the trees were still now. And, as they watched, the dirty cloud began to slowly dissipate.

"Victoria!" Wellington exclaimed in a choked voice. "My queen! What if –"

"I don't think it's close enough to have harmed her," Napoleon said quietly. "She's some distance from Caesar. Go see if your house suffered damage. I'll check ours."

As the Iron Duke hurried around the end of the hedge, Napoleon led Marie into their living room. She grabbed the key fob from the dining room table and silenced Napoleon's car alarm. The large window had a crack in it that ran from one edge to the other; several pictures had fallen to the floor. Upon further inspection, a few fine cracks ran across the walls and three other windows were damaged.

"What could have done this?" Marie asked, picking up the pictures.

"I have no idea." Napoleon opened a closet and reset the house alarm. "Whatever it is, it's trouble. And if Caesar's villa has taken a hit, it must have been a big one."

Wellington burst through the opened front door. "Bloody hell! Bloody, bloody hell! I've got cracked windows, things knocked off…" He paused and looked around the living room. "Oh. You've got damage, too."

"Did you think you were the only one?" Napoleon asked. "What next?"

In hellish fashion, he was answered:

An imp, holding an envelope, appeared out of nowhere and extended it to Napoleon and then, as suddenly as it had manifested, disappeared with a little pop of displaced air.

"What… *who* was that?" Marie stared at the envelope.

"Oh, shit, shit, shit," Napoleon muttered. "This is getting worse by the instant." He glanced at Wellington and then at Marie. "HADES: Hell Automated Delivery Executive Service."

Wellington shook his head. "Worse and worse."

Napoleon opened the envelope, took out a folded piece of parchment and quickly read it. "Quadruple worse. We've been reactivated."

Wellington closed his eyes briefly, then lifted his head and stared at the ceiling. "I say," he commented in a distracted tone of voice, "you've got a crack up there, too."

"What do you mean, you've been reactivated?" Marie questioned.

Napoleon extended the parchment. "Wellington and I have been called back to active duty. We're to go to the other side of the Park and, as it says here, 'keep a lid on things'."

"By whom? Can they do that?"

"Anyone with the rank of major and above in Satan's armies is never really retired. We can be called up at any moment, for any reason. Or for no reason at all. Since Wellington and I hold the rank of general, we're fair game."

"I thought Caesar had us under some kind of protection from just such an event," Wellington huffed, trying to look at the notice of reactivation. "Who signed the damned thing?"

Napoleon lifted the parchment. At the bottom, in letters that were flames but didn't burn the paper, was the signature.

"His Satanic Majesty, himself."

Wellington bowed his head. "Oh, shit."

*

Brakes screeched from the street. Wellington was first out the door, coming to a halt at the edge of Napoleon's porch.

"Attila!" he called. "What the bloody hell is going on?"

Clad in his warrior's leathers and fully armed, the king of the Huns jumped out of an Armored Personnel Carrier and walked up the driveway.

"Don't have a fucking idea," he said. "All I know is that whatever happened, it was huge!"

Wellington drew a quick and furious breath. "Napoleon and I have been reactivated. Signed by Satan himself."

Attila's face went blank for a moment. "The hell you say. Just now you find out?"

"HADES," Wellington replied, as he sensed Napoleon approaching.

"Oh, shit."

"That's a popular word right now," Napoleon said, his voice gone grim. "You haven't heard a thing about what's going on?"

"No. I'm not on duty right now but, horse turds to sheep shit, I'll be finding out."

A mental image of Queen Victoria filled Wellington's mind. "I *must* get to the other side of the Park. Victoria. The English –"

"We're going there," Napoleon pointed out. "Even if we didn't want to, we've got our orders. My French are over there, too, you know."

Wellington bowed his head. "Damn, damn, damn!"

The sound of a pulsing phone jolted Attila. "And there it is," he said, returning to the APC.

The numbness of shock began to fade; Wellington watched the Hun pick up a field phone. "Wish we had one of those," he said, glancing at Napoleon.

"If wishes were fishes," Napoleon quoted an old saying. "This *is* hell, remember?"

Attila stood silent, staring at the field phone in his hand, then carefully set it back. Wellington tried to read the emotion on the big Hun's face, but couldn't. Attila slowly walked up the driveway to the porch.

"There you go," he said. "I've been ordered to accompany you." He shrugged. "*My* orders. Guess it's because someone somewhere knows I have the APC today. If we're going to make it across the Park, we'll need it."

"Bloody, bloody hell!" Wellington managed, his fists clenched. "If we're crossing the Park, where are the Vietcong?"

"Gone to ground," Attila said. "If I was in the Park, that's where I'd go."

"In the tunnels, you mean," Wellington inserted, making a mighty attempt to erase Queen Victoria's image. "The whole Park is honeycombed with them."

"That could pose a problem for the Cong." Napoleon stared into the Park. "When the earth shook, it could have collapsed a number of those tunnels."

"When are we leaving?" Wellington asked. He was rewarded with Napoleon's totally disgusted expression.

"Since you and I have been reactivated, I'll have to put on my damned uniform. Stupid piece of shit scratches like hell."

*

Marie stood in the bedroom watching Napoleon don his uniform. Memory flooded over her: he looked so much like he had when they first met in 1807 on the outskirts of Warsaw. She knew how much he hated to dress up; his usual worn jeans and denim shirt were far more comfortable. Besides, the uniform jacket he shrugged into now brought back memories of his life before death and his sentence to hell. Memories, she knew, he made an effort to keep at bay.

He sat down on the edge of the bed and pulled on his boots.

"Damned things," he growled. "At least they're broken in." He stood and stomped down, fitting his feet into the tight boots. "Marie."

She met his eyes. "Don't say it, Napoleon. I'm going with you."

He sighed. "I won't argue. I know I can't keep you here. But, for all our sakes, let's make sure we're armed." He lifted his sword from the bed. "This isn't going to help much at all."

She opened the drawer of the bedside table and drew out her 9 millimeter, checked the clip, and took out two more. "Yours is on your side. I made sure it's loaded and you've got backup clips as well."

He threw her an amused look. "You're prepared, as always." He skirted the bed and retrieved his own pistol and additional clips. "Cursed uniform doesn't have room for a gun."

"I'll take both of them." She went to the closet and took down a small soft-sided carrying case. "What do you think we'll find when we get there?" she asked, extending her hand.

"Damned if I know." He gave his pistol and clips to her. "But one thing's certain. I'm not going to enjoy wearing my hat."

*

The narrow road ran straight through Decentral Park, intersecting several other smallish streets and lanes that crisscrossed the area. Napoleon sat next to Attila who was cursing softly in Hunnish; it was probably best that Hunnish was not one of the languages Napoleon was familiar with. He glanced over his shoulder at Marie who was situated so she could see between him and Attila. Wellington, in the seat behind Attila, was chewing on his bottom lip, a nervous habit he displayed when he was upset.

So far, they hadn't seen a sign of the Vietcong; not to say that at any moment they couldn't materialize from bushes, undergrowth, or from behind trees. "Gone to ground," Attila had said. Maybe. In all probability many of them had been entombed in their tunnels when the shock wave hit. Whatever the reason, the way to the north side of Decentral Park lay open.

Attila drove the APC at full speed, totally unconcerned about meeting any other vehicles that got in his way. Napoleon kept one hand on the dashboard in case some fool tried to cross the road in front of them. He'd stuffed the reactivation notice under his vest on the way out of the house. Satan's signature had burned a great deal hotter as he, Attila, Wellington and Marie had left Hellview Estates, but had gradually cooled, as they came closer to the other side of the Park. Obviously, their haste pleased His Satanic Majesty.

Keep a lid on things. Well, that could have a multitude of meanings. Napoleon stared forward, running through a mental list of everything he would need to keep the lid on. Whatever the "lid" might be. He had Duroc and the French at Louis XIV's palace: he assumed it stood far enough from whatever had hit Caesar's villa to have suffered minimal damage. However....

"Attila. Can you contact any Huns who might be able to meet us at Caesar's villa?"

The king of the Huns nodded slowly, reaching out for the field phone. One-handed, he punched in a number. "Yanush has a phone. He can contact the others."

"What about the Mongols?"

"Them, too, if you need them." Attila spoke quickly in Hunnish, then disconnected. "They'll get here as soon as they can. They're down by the Armory, so it shouldn't take them long since they'll be mounted." He set the phone down. "Damn! We've got to get the horses out of there before –"

"Horses?" Wellington exclaimed. "What about the people?"

"Before what, Attila?" This from Marie, who leaned forward in her seat to look at Attila.

"Before whatever hit the villa comes back."

Napoleon rubbed his forehead. "We don't know if there will be a return strike."

"And we don't know there won't," Wellington said in a tight voice. "Queen Victoria isn't all *that* far away from Caesar's villa. I'm going to try to convince her she needs to evacuate."

"To where?" Napoleon asked. "If it *is* Erra, that Babylonian god of mayhem, no place is safe. And would she go? You know her best, but the way I see it, you're going to have a tough time convincing her to leave."

The APC emerged from the Park onto the boulevard that ran on its north side, up and down the frontage property of what ordinary folk called "Crowned Row." Gathering his bearings, Attila yanked the wheel to the right and floored the APC to the east, headed toward where Caesar's villa stood.

Or used to stand.

*

A fine filter of dust still filled the air as Attila turned up the drive toward Caesar's villa. Marie leaned forward, trying to make out *what* they were approaching. Large trees that lined the drive had been blown down, their trunks snapped about a foot or so from the ground. She drew a deep breath. This did not look good. In fact, it seemed about as bad as she thought it might.

She unzipped the small carrying case and touched the two 9-millimeter automatics: safeties were on, one round was chambered, and each held a full clip. Wellington carried his own pistol, and Attila never went anywhere unless he was armed to the teeth.

Attila slammed on the brakes, throwing her forward.

"By my ancestors' hairy balls!" the Hun exclaimed. "Would you look at that!"

She stared. Wellington cursed softly but Napoleon remained silent. Where the expansive villa had stood was nothing but a gaping hole.

A giant, enormous hole.

And not much else.

*

Napoleon jumped down from the APC, leaving his sword by the front seat. From the looks of things, such a weapon wasn't going to help matters. He stood motionless, hearing his three companions join him. No one said a thing. Silence gripped the surroundings: a heavy, oppressive silence.

Something indescribably horrific flittered by, flying in jerky circles and headed toward the back of the property. Off to the left, a slimy nightmare inched its way in the distance toward what was left of a bush. Whatever the hellish creatures had suffered, their natural comings and goings had been disturbed.

Napoleon straightened his shoulders and started toward the edge of the hole. From his vantage point, he could tell it wasn't circular. It seemed to be wider on his side, narrower on the other.

Nothing stood. He scanned the area: broken statues, snapped columns, gardens ripped asunder. Twisted remnants of vehicles had been tossed around. A few weapons, *gladia* and spears, lay strewn about, along with dented helmets, all probably belonging to Caesar's household guards. Aside from that, there was hardly anything left of what had once been a Roman showplace.

"Oh," Marie said in a choked voice. "What could have done this?"

"It's anyone's guess," Napoleon replied. He sniffed the air. "I don't smell explosives."

"But I smell something smoldering," Attila offered.

"What's left of electrical wiring, I suppose," Wellington said in a hushed voice.

"I thought Augustus didn't like electrics." Marie moved closer to Napoleon.

He reached out and took her hand. "He wasn't fond of them, but he used them. Julius required modern utilities and equipment, and the very best of both. I want you to stay here by the APC. Keep an eye out for anything that moves. If it doesn't look friendly, shoot it."

She started to reply, then nodded.

"What should we do?" Wellington asked, his dark eyes even darker against his pale face.

"Poke around," Attila suggested. "See if anyone survived."

Napoleon nodded, took the pistol Marie extended. "I doubt anything could have withstood this."

He led the way toward the edge of the hole. The hole was deep, revealing where the basement once had been. That was full of water, what was left from the swimming pool. A few crumbling remnants of walls gave evidence of large rooms, but hardly anything remained that could tell him what had stood where.

More toppled statues, more crumbled pillars, broken bits of what must have been furniture, and more shredded rose bushes.

"Look." Wellington pointed off to one side. "A pond."

Napoleon followed the Iron Duke to the side of a large reflecting pool full of fish: dead, floating fish. Caesar's prized hell-koi. Belly up, fangs bared, and freshly dead.

"Now that's odd," Attila said, squatting down on his heels to get a better look. "You'd think they could have survived an explosion. Even losing water, this pool's deep enough."

"I don't know," Napoleon admitted, as Attila stood. "There's something about this that makes me nervous."

"You don't think it was Erra and the Seven personified weapons, do you?" Wellington asked.

"It doesn't look like his work. From all I've heard, he would have taken out the whole row of palaces, not just one."

"Maybe he's coming back," Attila said, glancing upward.

"Don't *say* that," Wellington cautioned. "You know the old adage: don't speak of the Devil lest he appear."

Napoleon walked away from the pond, hands behind his back. He couldn't figure out what had destroyed Caesar's villa. It didn't make sense. The gaping hole didn't make sense. The dead hell-koi didn't make sense. Nothing he saw made any sense.

And what didn't make sense posed a nightmare of possibilities.

*

Marie stood by the APC, pistol in her hand. She had wanted to accompany Napoleon and at first felt frustrated that he would leave her behind. Now, she thought better of it. He trusted her to stand guard, to let him know if anything or anyone approached.

She shivered slightly. Whatever had destroyed Caesar's villa was powerful indeed. And, so far, they'd found no signs of life. Who had been in the villa when the strike occurred? Caesar could have been out on maneuvers. Augustus? More than likely he'd been in the villa, since he was not one known for accompanying the Legions around the countryside. As for the rest of the residents, hell's self-anointed elite? Where were Kleopatra, Hatshepsut, Sargon, Dante, Machiavelli? And the two boys, Caesarion and Brutus?

If they had been in the villa....

She swallowed heavily. Blown to bits. Everyone.

Unless some of them hadn't been present when the villa was hit by whatever destroyed it.

The noise of someone approaching alerted her. She walked to the back of the APC, her pistol ready, and looked down the long drive.

"Napoleon!" she called. "Come quick! We've got company!"

*

Napoleon sprinted toward the APC, Wellington and Attila close behind. Company? Who the hell could that be?

He arrived at Marie's side as a shiny, upscale SUV pulled up a few paces behind the APC. The door opened and a man climbed out.

Napoleon cursed inwardly. Exactly what and who they didn't need at this juncture in time.

Following the red-haired, ivory-skinned man, clad in a silver- and gold-plated cuirass, came fifteen Romans, all dressed in khaki uniforms; some sported arm patches with the "X" of the Tenth Legion, and others with the "XII" of the Twelfth. The ten men behind them were a motley crew, some moderns, some of indeterminate heritage. The Romans and the assorted others arrived on ancient motorcycles and in beat-up vehicles that might have passed for someone's inflated notion of classic cars.

Napoleon glanced over his shoulder, then back at the Roman general. Marie, Wellington and Attila stood silent, weapons held at their sides.

"Napoleon!" the Roman general said. "What are *you* doing here?"

"Lucius Cornelius Sulla," Napoleon responded in polite greeting, remembering proper Roman etiquette, briefly nodding his head. "I ask the same."

His use of Sulla's full name seemed to momentarily deflate Sulla's aggressive attitude. "Napoleone di Buonaparte," he responded, acknowledging Napoleon's noble birth. "I am here because, in Caesar's absence, I'm in charge of... of what's left of the compound." He glanced at the crumbled ruins, then back. "I would have brought more men with me but didn't have time after the explosion. Our rescue mission –"

"As you can see," Napoleon said, gesturing, "there's nothing left to rescue."

"And *you* have no authority to take charge," Sulla snapped.

"Oh? I believe I do."

Sulla's nearly white eyes narrowed. "I see four of you. I have fifteen armed Romans and the willing souls I conscripted to come with me. You're slightly outnumbered, if I still have my math."

The Romans stood waiting behind Sulla, but their faces betrayed confusion. They were fully aware of Napoleon's connection to Caesar and, now, uncertain who to believe.

"Caesar," Napoleon said, "is a friend of mine. And, with all due respect, you're no Caesar. The two of us have worked together many times, and he has placed his trust in me." He shifted his pistol to his left hand and lifted his right. "On this hand," he said, his voice gone cold, "I have worn the signet ring of Julius Caesar. Can you say the same?"

Sulla stared, the muscles tightening on his jaw.

"Hey, Napoleon!" a rough voice interrupted the silence. "Where do you want my men?"

Sulla spun around. Fifty Huns and Mongols sat their horses in a semicircle around Sulla and the twenty-five men who had arrived with him. Bows at the ready, the horsemen glowered at the Roman general and his companions.

"Stand where you are, Yanush," Napoleon said. "General Sulla and I are having a civilized conversation, aren't we?"

Sulla licked his lips. "We are."

"Besides," Napoleon continued, reaching inside his vest, "I have authority granted me to be here. If you would be so kind as to look."

He unfolded the reactivation notice and hid a smile as Satan's signature flared on the page. Sulla drew back, his pale face going even whiter.

"Wellington and I have been given control of the area north of Decentral Park by His Satanic Majesty. If you feel so inclined, you're more than welcome to take it up with Himself."

"Uh... no." Sulla looked up from the notice. "It seems to be in order."

"Then your arrival is beneficial," Napoleon said, folding the notice and tucking it back under his vest. "We don't know what happened here."

"It's Erra!" one of the Romans got out. "It *must* be! Look at the damage!"

The other Romans scanned the ruins, their features etched by shock and sorrow.

"We don't know that," Wellington said, stepping forward. "We have no idea who or what did this."

"Lucius Cornelius," Napoleon addressed the Roman general. "You're absent from the Island of Pompeii, are you not?"

"Attending the Conference," Sulla acknowledged shortly.

"As I said, your arrival is fortuitous. We're going to face a problem here. By now, rumor of the destruction of Caesar's villa will be spreading around New Hell City. Guess what happens next."

"Looters?" Sulla hazarded.

"And people who will be arriving to gawk at the damage. It's necessary to keep the crowds out of this neighborhood. Can I count on you to deploy whatever Romans you can rouse, to blockade any entrance to this area?"

Sulla's lips thinned, but he nodded. "I'll go back toward the City and station whomever I can call to duty." His shoulders straightened. "No one will pass us. I give you my word as a Roman."

"That will be sufficient."

"But if it *is* Erra and he comes back, we're all dead men."

"We're all dead men if *whoever* did this returns," Napoleon stated. "Now go, Lucius Cornelius. Fortuna guide you."

Sulla nodded briefly and returned to his vehicle. "Follow me," he said to the Romans who had accompanied him and the hardy souls he had lured from the city on a fruitless rescue mission.

Napoleon stood silent as Sulla's SUV backed down the drive, herding the other vehicles toward the boulevard.

"Close one," Attila said. "Never liked that bastard. Way too full of himself."

"Thank you for the Huns and Mongols. I think they put the fear of something in Sulla."

"And now?" Marie asked.

"Now we make one last sweep of the compound. Then," Napoleon said, looking down the drive, "we need to see if anyone else on this side suffered damage."

*

Wellington watched the Roman general and his followers disappear. His pulse began to race: images of Queen Victoria filled his mind once more.

"Napoleon," he said. "I *must* see if Queen Victoria is all right... if she and the other English have made it through this attack."

"We'll stop there on the way to Louis' palace." Napoleon's grey-blue eyes softened. "I know you're worried about her, and I understand. I'm concerned about my French."

"What about the other residents? Maria-Theresa and the Austrians? Richelieu?"

"Richelieu's not on the boulevard. We can see if anyone else is in good shape on the way."

Wellington frowned, holding his urgent need to see his queen in check. "So, what next? You suggested another tour of the ruins."

"On second thought, I doubt we'll find anything. Total devastation doesn't lend itself to survival."

What was left of Caesar's villa was more than enough to underscore Napoleon's observation.

Napoleon turned to Attila. "Have Yanush and the horsemen follow. I'm not certain what we'll find and their assistance might be needed."

Wellington rounded the APC, taking his place behind the king of the Huns who was issuing brief orders to the assembled Huns and Mongols. He made an effort to slow his breathing as Napoleon and Marie climbed into the APC. Napoleon was correct: Queen Victoria was far enough from Caesar's villa that she might have escaped major damage.

Bear up, man! Can't let anyone see how worried you are. You have an image to protect, if nothing else. Victoria must *be safe!*

But hell was hell, and nothing was ever certain.

Survival being one of the top ten outcomes most desired.

*

Marie placed her automatic alongside Napoleon's in the carrying case and wiped sweaty hands on her jeans. Her eyes threatened to fill with tears. The total destruction of Caesar's villa was bad enough, but the loss of life nearly overwhelmed her, though she knew Reassignments returned anyone who died to continued existence in hell.

All those people… gone in an instant. People she knew. Though she didn't have much to do with most of them, when an angel had given her the chance to leave hell and ascend to Purgatory, her penance for adultery with Napoleon done, she had shared some intense moments with Kleopatra.

And then there was Hatshepsut: the Egyptian Pharaoh was harder to know. The hardness about her came from being revered as a living god, leading her armies in battle, feared and worshiped in her kingdom. Marie had witnessed a somewhat softer side to the Egyptian the few times they were left alone, but recognized the Pharaoh was one not inclined to sentimentality. Those two women, queens in their own right and each in their own way, had given her courage to choose to remain in hell, simply because she couldn't bear the thought of being separated from Napoleon.

Hell with Napoleon; Purgatory without him?

The choice had been more difficult than any she had faced before. “I can tell you nothing else, Marie,” Kleopatra had said, “save to go with your heart. What you really long for the most will well up from deep inside it.”

Marie pushed the memories aside. She had made her choice. Napoleon had told her she was one of the few innocent souls in hell when she had made her own decision to remain. But afterward, she’d done things she never could have contemplated in life. Killing was one: a grave sin that would have ultimately condemned her to hell anyway.

But existence without Napoleon? She looked between the seats at him as Attila drove down the boulevard. He held his hat in his hands, periodically contemplating it with a deep frown.

“Dammit,” he growled. “I hate this hat! It makes my head too hot. And since I have to stay in uniform, I don’t know if I can get away not wearing it.”

She smiled. “I think it makes you look distinguished.”

He glanced between the seats in her direction, one eyebrow lifted. “Distinguished? That’s a load of bullshit if I’ve ever heard it.”

Wellington was adjusting his own hat. “Oh, come now. It can’t be *that* bad.”

“Said the man who most likely sleeps in his uniform.”

*

The driveway to Queen Victoria’s palace appeared untouched. Wellington leaned forward, willing Attila to keep the APC at speed. The sight of red-coated soldiers stationed on either side of the entranceway released some of his pent-up anxiety. If those house guards kept to their places, showing no signs of agitation, then the destruction of Caesar's villa had done little to disturb the routine of Victoria's residence.

Attila stopped at the head of the curved driveway. Smothering what was left of his nervousness Wellington descended from the APC. He turned, rapped on the door to get Attila's attention.

"I'll be in touch if I can," he said. "If not, give me about an hour and I should be ready to leave. With any luck, I'll be taking Queen Victoria with me."

Attila's frown told Wellington that he would probably be the only Briton riding back across the Park.

Damn! I've got *to do something! Whatever, whoever took out Caesar's villa could return.*

The two soldiers saluted smartly as Wellington entered the great hall. Immediately, a neatly clad butler approached, bowing a welcome.

"Is the queen in residence?" Wellington asked, protocol for any arrival, even those favored by the Crown.

"She is indeed, Your Grace," the butler replied. "Shall I announce you?"

"If you would be so kind. I'll wait here."

Wellington looked around the hall. There was damage to be seen: small cracks in the marble floor, paintings hanging slightly askew. A squad of servants bustled about, but nothing seemed beyond minimal repair.

"The queen will see you now, Your Grace," the butler announced, gesturing to a side room, "if you'll be so kind as to follow me."

Wellington nodded and drew a deep breath. Napoleon had the right of it: it would take some doing to convince Victoria to leave.

She sat in one of two chairs by the window, her black mourning dress a splotch of darkness in the well-lit room. Wellington removed his hat and bowed deeply.

"We are not amused," she said, her chin lifted in defiance of whatever might threaten her. "Please, Wellington, take the adjoining chair."

He gingerly sat down, adjusted his sword, and turned sideways so he could face her.

"What news?" she asked.

"None of it good, Majesty," he replied. "I must first ask if you and the household are all right."

She sniffed. "We suppose you must. We will carry on. Now, we repeat: what news?"

Wellington drew a deep breath. How much to reveal? What exactly to say? Knowing Victoria, she would want the truth.

"Something, or someone, destroyed Caesar's villa. There's nothing left of it, Majesty. Nothing at all."

Victoria inhaled sharply, then her face hardened into a mask. "Nothing, you say? No survivors?"

"Not that we could find."

"We?"

"I've been reactivated: Napoleon and I, on orders from Satan. We've been put in charge of keeping peace on this side of Decentral Park. Attila drove us to Caesar's villa. When we arrived, we found nothing but a gaping hole."

Victoria closed her eyes for a long moment. When she opened them, there was a glint to them Wellington had seen before. Any hope of her seeking comparative safety on the other side of the Park was quickly dimming.

"Do you know who, or what, did the deed?" she asked, folding her hands in her lap.

"No, Majesty. The most common supposition is that it was Erra and the Seven."

Victoria drew in her chin, glanced out the window, then back. "That Babylonian god and his living weapons. We wouldn't doubt it." Her eyes narrowed. "We can, however, assume you haven't placed too much credence in the supposition."

"You'd be correct in that assumption," Wellington replied. "Napoleon and I discussed it. If it *was* Erra, one would think you and anyone else along the boulevard would have been destroyed as well. This destruction was focused on only one place: Caesar's villa. We don't know who or what singled Caesar out, or why, but we can't be certain that a repeat attack won't be made."

"Humpf." Victoria lifted a fan from her lap and opened it. "Nothing, my good Duke, is assured in hell."

"And this is why," Wellington said, gathering courage, "I would be most pleased if you and the household would remove to the opposite side of the Park until we can be somewhat sure the destruction won't recur."

"Ha!" Victoria closed the fan with a loud click. "You, of all people, counsel *me* to leave?"

"I'm merely thinking of your safety, Majesty." Wellington kept his voice even, trying to radiate calm. The royal "we" had disappeared. "I stand ready to make certain you and the rest of the household are given –"

"No!" Victoria snapped. "I shall *not* leave. Nor shall any of the household. We are British and we don't... we *won't* cower in fear." She leaned forward. "And you, my dear Duke? Do you fear?"

"I've seen what has been done, Majesty. I would be a fool if I *wasn't* afraid."

The hint of a smile touched her lips. "And you were never the fool, were you, Arthur? But you can't talk me into leaving. I'll stay here and I'll keep in touch with you. Right now, the most advantageous place for you is at Napoleon's side. Between the two of you, I am confident order shall be reestablished."

Wellington strove to keep the disappointment from crossing his face. "Majesty," he said, bowing his head. "What you will, you will."

Victoria nodded. "You may go now, my dear Duke. Doubtless Napoleon will be wanting your good counsel."

Accepting his dismissal, Wellington stood, bowed deeply, and slowly exited the room, leaving behind a British monarch who had reigned for an astounding sixty-three years. A monarch who refused to surrender before whatever danger faced her.

Pride and disappointment: strange bedfellows.

*

Attila chewed on one side of his mustache, realized what he was doing, and spat it out. His peripheral vision showed Napoleon staring straight ahead.

"Attila. What do *you* think happened?"

This from Marie who leaned forward from her position in the rear seat.

"I don't know, hey?" he responded. "Could be Erra."

The recurring thought had surfaced of the Babylonian god descending with his seven weapons in tow. Attila remembered conversations he'd shared with Napoleon about the god of pestilence and the indiscriminate destruction he could bring.

He shifted slightly in his seat. Erra. Bringing an end to everything he knew, had grown to know, after Satan had plucked him out of his torment to establish him as a go-to man in the Infernal National Guard. By his ancestors! He wasn't going back, not if he had anything to say about it. Even being saddled with his two wives and his brats was better than wandering around in a nebulous afterlife, pursued by spirits raised out of a Hun's darkest nightmares.

"Napoleon," he said, slowing the APC and meeting Napoleon's eyes. "Who do *you* think took out Caesar's villa? *I* think it was Erra."

"It might have been," Napoleon conceded. "But it might have been anybody. We're all so on edge with Erra and the Seven running rampant through the hells we could jump to that conclusion."

Attila cursed in anatomical detail. "If not him, then who? And why Caesar?"

"Why not?" Napoleon raked a hand through his hair. "You know the rumor: hell has become too comfortable. We're not being tormented enough. Satan's falling down on the job. Therefore, we end up with Erra."

"But Caesar was in control of so much, hey? He held enormous power."

"That he did, and he used it. But my observation remains the same. Look at us, living in Hellview Estates. We've been rewarded, to a certain extent, because we serve Satan: you in the Guard, and Wellington and I in Satan's armies. We have food that tastes like food, water and wine we can drink without puking our guts up. Look at the properties we're passing. Way above our level of existence, don't you think?"

"Too big, too – what's the word – ostentatious for my liking."

Napoleon laughed. "Been doing crossword puzzles lately? Ostentatious is one way to put it."

"Don't you think," Marie offered, "that the souls trapped in New Hell City – and here I'm not talking about the government workers, the lawyers and such... don't you think they see the glaring difference between their existence and that of everyone on this side of the Park?"

Attila frowned. "Well...."

"When I worked at the License Bureau, I heard it all the time. And these weren't slum dwellers, mind you. 'Oh, look at those snobs in their palaces. What gives *them* the right to have everything handed to them on a silver platter when we're condemned to our rundown apartments?' There was real and deep envy there, Attila. Given half a chance, I'd wager even they dreamed of assailing Crowned Row to set those noble blue-bloods right."

"Huh." Attila started to lick his mustache into his mouth again, caught himself in time. "Then why would Erra strike at Caesar first?"

"That's the question, isn't it?" Napoleon asked. "There are a number of entities I can think of who could have done the deed. It could be Erra, it could be anyone. And if whoever it is comes back...."

Attila nodded, still not convinced. "At least we can get the horses out. You've got cavalry there and what I wouldn't give to mate some of those studs to my polo ponies."

"Always on the field, aren't you? I know, I know... a Hun without a horse is a poor excuse for a man. Besides, I don't think we're going to be leaving this side of the Park anytime soon. Let's concentrate on people first, Attila. *Then,* if things settle down, we might be able to round up some horses for you."

*

Géraud Christophe Michel Duroc, Duc de Friuli, High Lord Steward of the Empire and Marshal of France, stood on the front steps of Louis XIV's palace. Napoleon breathed a sigh of relief to see his close friend again. He'd left Duroc in charge of the French on this side of the Park, having confined Louis to the back of the opulent structure. Not that Louis was roaming around his old residence: he seldom ventured out of his rooms, and only then heavily guarded by soldiers Napoleon and Duroc trusted. The Sun King had been driven to the edge of madness when Napoleon had assumed command of the French, an edge that now and then he angrily crossed.

Napoleon helped Marie from the APC, noting she still carried the pistols. "Attila, could you wait here before going back to see if Wellington has convinced Victoria to leave?"

"Har!" Attila leaned his head back against the seat. "That old warhorse isn't going anywhere, if I'm a judge of things. Too damned stubborn. Wellington'll be pissed for sure." He shrugged. "I have to give orders to Yanush. Then, if you don't need me, I'll drive back that way. But I'll probably return with only one lone Englishman, and an irritated one at that."

"Understood." Napoleon grasped Duroc's hand in greeting. "Géraud, dammit, it's been too long. What's going on here? Has there been any damage?"

"Some, not much. What caused it? Whatever it was, it happened to our east." Duroc bowed to Marie and kissed her hand. "Come. Let's go inside."

The grand entry appeared in good condition. A few windows were cracked, but the rest of the palace seemed relatively untouched. All, that is, save the Sun King's attempt to replicate the Hall of Mirrors at Versailles. Napoleon winced. If Louis saw his precious mirrors now, he'd stroke out.

Duroc led the way to a small room off to one side of the spacious reception hall. He gestured Marie and Napoleon to chairs, then took one himself.

"Can you tell me what happened?"

"Caesar's villa is gone."

"Gone?" Duroc blinked in surprise. "You mean 'gone,' as in 'not there anymore'?"

"That's exactly what I mean. There's a giant hole where the villa used to be. And nothing else. No one alive that we could find. Dead hell-koi in a pond. Arms and helmets scattered around."

"But, who? Who could do such a thing?" Duroc asked, his eyes wide.

Napoleon looked around for somewhere to put his offending hat, then dropped it to the floor at his side. "Any number of suspects come to mind."

"Erra?"

"That's one. Then there's the dissidents, but I'm not convinced they have that kind of firepower. Maybe the Devil's Children. I'm not leaving anyone out. We don't know who and we don't know why. All we *do* know is that the villa's gone."

"We even suffered damage on our side of the Park," Marie added. "It was like an earthquake."

"We felt the same here." Duroc rubbed the bridge of his nose. "We just didn't think someone or someplace was being attacked."

Napoleon met his friend's eyes. "And we don't know if whoever it is will come back. There's something wrong here, something that doesn't make sense, but I can't put my finger on it. Listen to me, Géraud. Wellington and I have been reactivated, by Satan's command. We're to keep things as peaceful as possible on this side."

"For how long?"

"That, I leave for Satan to decide. I had a little set-to with Sulla, but convinced him to guard any possible ways someone could find into this neighborhood. How many French are here?"

"Right now, including the cavalry, fifty."

"And the DGSE men? They're still with you, aren't they?"

"Anbec, Mirabeau, Barré and LeFlore? Yes. They've been helpful, especially riding herd on Louis. Though he tries not to show it, he's terrified of modern French commandos."

"Good. With their connections, perhaps they can find places for the civilians. I want all the noncombatants out of here. All six of them." Napoleon did a quick calculation. "That would leave, what, thirty horse, ten guards and four DGSE? In the meantime, I'm going to need them all, except for the civilians. I'll ask the soldiers for volunteers, though I don't think I'll need to. As for the rest, I don't care where we take them; I don't want to lose any of you."

"Attila's not going to be happy," Marie said. "He'll drown in tears if anything happens to those horses. He wants to breed them to his poly ponies."

"Horses?" Duroc grinned. "That damned Hun. Where's *he* going?"

"To Queen Victoria's. We left Wellington there. He's going to try to convince her to leave."

"He'll need luck for that. She's one stubborn woman."

Napoleon spread his hands. "This is going to be pain in the butt, I know. Right now, I can't think of any other way to deal with what's happened."

"What about Louis? Should we send him away?"

"Oh, shit. I forgot about him." Napoleon glanced up in the vague direction of Louis' gilded prison. "Leave the idiot here, for all I care. If we're next on the destruction menu, *he* won't be a great loss."

*

"I hate this place!" Napoleon groused, looking around at one of the gaudy bedrooms that overlooked the long driveway to the boulevard.

Marie smiled and sat down in a chair that proved somewhat comfortable. "It *is* a bit much, isn't it?"

"If there was any more decoration on the walls and ceiling, it would strike you blind."

She reached out a hand as he came to her side. "What are we going to do, Napoleon? How long do we have to stay?"

"As I told Duroc, that's up to Satan."

"You do realize we could be destroyed as well," she said. "Just like the villa."

"I'm constantly reminded of that. I can't get the image of that hole out of my mind."

She let him draw her to her feet. They stood close together, hands clasped. "If it *does* happen," she said, "if we're attacked, what will become of me?"

His startled reaction brought tears to her eyes.

"I'm not supposed to be here," she rushed on, her voice trembling in spite of her effort to keep it under control. "You, and everyone else, will go to Reassignments. And where will I go?"

"Oh, Marie." He drew her into his embrace. "I don't know *who* will make that decision, since you chose to stay in hell. But I *do* know that I can't think of eternal existence without you."

"Then," she said, laying her head on his shoulder, his epaulet scratching her cheek, "we'll have to hope nothing will happen to us. And if it does, that Satan will reward you for your service and allow me to stay at your side."

*

Wellington stood on the steps to Victoria's mansion, fighting the urge to pace. He knew there was nothing he could say or do that would prevail upon his queen to leave. A cold dash of reality reminded him that no place in hell was safe if Erra had destroyed the villa. Maybe the god of mayhem was having a little sport with residents of Crowned Row: take out one of the largest compounds, leave, let the other neighbors assume the worse was over, and then return to destroy everything in sight.

Victoria had said, in no uncertain terms, she was not leaving. He knew his queen well enough to be certain none of the British who attended her would drift away, concerned for their own safety. She commanded unswerving loyalty, even here in hell.

He glanced up nervously, almost as if he expected to see Erra and his seven weapons descend, lightning and who-knew- what -else at their disposal. Few things gave him what some moderns called "the creeps," but destruction meted out by that god was one. Another thought, equally creepy, was waking up on the Undertaker's slab, a fate he earnestly wanted to avoid.

So. Satan had reactivated both him and Napoleon: they were to keep things under control on the north side of De-central Park. He had no idea how long they were to stay, or even what exactly they were expected to do. Unless Ma-hell's landlines and the hellphones were rendered useless, he supposed the neighbors on Crowned Row could stay in contact with each other.

He glanced up at the sound of an approaching vehicle, expecting Attila. But, no… it was one of the dilapidated cars that had accompanied Sulla to the villa. As the two guards stationed at the entranceway came to immediate alert, Wellington lifted a hand and approached the newcomer.

A pale Roman face looked up at him.

"Sir," the Roman said, "Sulla sent some of us back to the villa. He wanted us to make absolutely sure there was no one left alive."

"And you found what, legionary?"

"No one, sir. Not a soul. However, I *did* find this. It was in what was left of a bush, probably blown away from the villa. Sulla instructed me to bring it to you. He reasoned you could be found at Queen Victoria's." The Roman reached over to the seat beside him, lifted a large, somewhat dented package and extended it through the open window.

Wellington accepted the box. It was heavy, and he thought he could feel some liquid moving in it. "Thank you, legionary. Inform Sulla I've received it."

"Yes, sir." With a grinding of gears, the Roman slowly drove his jalopy away.

"It's all right," Wellington said over his shoulder to the two guards. He turned the package over, rewarded again by the sensation of moving liquid. There was an address on the top of the box, but no indication as to the sender.

To: G. Julius Caesar, it read. And under that: *Or Current Occupant.*

"What the devil?" he asked of no one in particular. "What was Caesar expecting? And what an odd addressee."

Another vehicle started up the driveway, this time Attila in the APC. Wellington turned to the guards.

"I'll be with Napoleon at Louis' palace," he said. "Her Majesty knows how to find me. Chin up, lads! We'll come through this all right."

He climbed into the waiting APC, wrestling the large package onto his lap.

"What the shit is *that*?" Attila asked, glancing sideways and heading down the drive.

"I haven't the foggiest idea. One of Sulla's Romans found it in a bush at the villa. It's addressed to Caesar, or current occupant. Whatever that means."

"Well, open it," Attila growled. "At this stage, I don't think Caesar will mind."

Wellington inspected the box. "Be a good man and lend me your dagger," he said. "My sword won't be of any use here."

Attila pulled his dagger from his wide belt and extended it, hilt first. "Watch yourself," he said. "I can't guarantee what will happen to you if we hit a pothole."

"Then do your best to avoid potholes, if you please."

Wellington ran the tip of the dagger down the taped openings on the top of the package. Returning the weapon to Attila, he pried the top of the box open.

"So?" Attila demanded. "What's in the fucking thing?"

Wellington sat speechless, gazing down at the contents of the package.

"I'll be damned," he sputtered, still stunned by what he saw.

"You're already damned," Attila shot back. "What the shit's in the box?"

Wellington brought out a clear, heavy plastic bag and held it up for inspection.

"Leeches," he breathed. "That sneaky Roman found someone to send him leeches." He met Attila's eyes. "And I'll wager *these* are the ones that work!"

*

"Where the hell did you get this?" Napoleon asked, lifting a bag of leeches from the package that now sat on a finely-appointed desk in Louis' study.

"From one of Sulla's lads," Wellington said. "He found it in a bush at the villa."

"Shit. Look here... there are three more bags. All of them appear to contain... a guess now, twenty communications leeches."

Attila stood to one side and let loose a long whistle. "Hey! That's a damned big bunch of leeches."

"And I bet they're the good ones, too," Wellington snapped. "Damn Caesar! He *knew* we were hunting some kind of untraceable communications."

"Maybe he was going to share," Attila ventured, then lifted his hands in apology. "Sorry. Wasn't thinking."

"Can you be sure they're the real thing?" Marie asked. "You were scammed once."

"We were, but I highly doubt anyone would screw around with Caesar. The question remains: who sent them?" Napoleon closed the lid, looked at the address, and shook his head. "Yet another hellish mystery." He reopened the box. "And here's a piece of paper. Instructions, it looks like."

"What does it say?" Duroc asked, leaning forward.

"It's in English and Greek," Napoleon replied. "Let's see. 'Keep hydrated, preferably with stagnant water. When communications end, return units to fluid.' Units? Sounds more like you're buying frogs from a bait store." He looked up from the paper. "We've got to test them. This could be an answer to one of our problems."

"Hey?" This from Attila, a puzzled expression crossing his face.

"The civilians. They need to get to the other side of the Park. Our orders are to stay here. Attila, I want you to send Yanush, the Huns and Mongols around the west end. We don't know what's going on there, or in our neighborhood. This means we can't communicate since you and Yanush have the field phones."

Attila sighed loudly. "Oh, I get it now. You want *me* to take the civilians through the Park."

"Who better? Besides, you've got the APC, and going close to New Hell City isn't the best idea right now. I trust you. But you'll need to stay in contact with Yanush. If we use leeches to talk to you, we can make sure everyone's being evacuated to safety."

"If there is such a thing," Wellington muttered. "The British won't be leaving if Queen Victoria has her say. I don't know about the Austrians, and I'm totally disinterested in what happens to Tiberius. Or Richelieu. Or, I assure you, Mithridates, if he's back in residence. *Or* to any number of crowned asses living around here. Who else would be interested in sending civilians to the south side of the Park?"

"Let's start by trying these leeches. If they're good, then we'll make some phone calls to the neighbors." Napoleon looked at his four companions. "Who wants to go first?"

*

The leeches passed several tests. Communication was clearer if the little bloodsuckers were attached to a human ear. Why that was, Marie couldn't guess.

She wasn't overjoyed to participate in the experiment, but her queasiness paled beside Wellington's reaction. The Iron Duke had posted himself on the second floor, a leech attached to one ear, while Napoleon tried to send his thoughts via his own leech. She had all but laughed as Napoleon had grimaced and then removed his leech.

"Damn! Loud and clear. And loud is the word for it!"

A disgusted exclamation echoed off the marble walls.

"Wellington?" Duroc asked, looking toward the sweeping staircase that led to the second floor.

"Who else?" Napoleon said, returning his leech to the bag.

Hurried footsteps sounded on the stairs and the Iron Duke burst into the study, a leech carefully held between two fingertips.

"Bloody hell!" he got out, dropping it into the open bag and wiping his hand on his breeches. "Slimy, detestable things!"

"But I heard you," Napoleon said, "if that's the term. I assume you heard me."

"Oh, I did. It's the thought of this nasty thing feasting on my blood that turns my stomach."

Marie hid a smile. Fastidious as always, Wellington busily scrubbed at the ear he'd attached the leech to. "You're not bleeding," she said, looking closely. "You'll be fine."

"Now what?" Duroc asked.

"Now we start making phone calls." Napoleon looked at his watch. "We're running out of time if we want to get the civilians out of here. But knowing Attila, I'm sure he'd enjoy a little nighttime drive across the Park."

Attila made a rude noise, followed by an even ruder gesture. "Says you. All right, all right. I'll contact Yanush and get him and the rest headed around the west end. Then what should they do?"

"Patrol up and down. Our side needs some kind of protection."

"Do you think we'll have looters?" Wellington asked Napoleon.

"With the grand prize on this side? No. But we can't take that chance. After what happened to the villa, there's bound to be unrest in New Hell City. Face it: hell's bad enough and now it's turned worse. *Someone's* going to be blamed."

"There's the strip mall, the Unsafeway, the Club, our houses... there are plenty of places a mob would love to hit," Marie said.

"They'd probably try to eat my damned goats," Attila growled. "I'll make a call to Yanush."

"And you'd better get on the phone, Napoleon." Duroc gestured to a fancy example of baroque splendor sitting on the desk. "We'll have to find cars for everyone who's going."

Marie glanced at the four men. Leeches or no leeches, let the evacuation begin.

*

The long driveway to Louis' palace was occupied by vehicles; Attila's APC was parked at the entrance to the boulevard. Despite their protestations at being instructed to leave, the French civilians who served at the palace had been joined by five women and men who had left Maria-Theresa's. Not one Briton was to be seen, a tribute to what must have been Queen Victoria's orders. All in all, the little caravan included ten French and five Austrian civilians.

And one determined Hun.

Napoleon had found a heavy plastic bag in Louis' kitchen and gave Attila four leeches in some of the swampy water.

"I don't know how long communications will remain open," he said, "so don't slap one on your ear immediately. We'll take turns waiting to hear from you. That way, there will always be an open channel between us, and we won't exhaust our leeches."

"Huh." Attila looked at the four cars parked behind his APC. "They're quiet, those people."

"Suitably frightened, I should think," Wellington commented. "I know *I* would be if I had to cross the Park at dusk."

"Or, for that matter, during the day," Duroc added.

"Thank you for your confidence in me," Attila said. "Makes me feel all warm and fuzzy inside."

Napoleon grinned at the sarcasm. "Anbec's riding with you. And Barré, LeFlore and Mirabeau will be with the civilians. They're armed, and that should help."

"Has Yanush reached the south side of the Park yet?" Marie asked.

"Last time I called him, he was nearly there."

Napoleon set a hand on Attila's shoulder. "I meant what I said earlier: I trust you. You'll do better than anyone else I can think of."

"Ha! Now *that* makes me feel all warm and fuzzy." He sobered. "I won't let you down. The word of a Hun isn't broken easily."

"Besides," Marie said with the hint of a smile, "you need to protect your wives and children from any looters."

"Huh. My damn brats? I'd feel sorry for the looters." Attila opened the door to the APC. "Anything else?"

"No. Try to keep your speed up. We still don't know what the Cong are doing."

"As if I needed that reminder. I'll keep in touch if anything happens. You're staying?"

"We don't have a bloody choice," Wellington complained. "Until we hear otherwise from Satan, we're stuck here."

Attila shrugged. "I may be back. I don't know what orders *I'll* receive. I could be called to duty, too." He climbed into the APC, slammed the door, and stuck his head out the window. "See you around!"

Napoleon, Marie, Wellington and Duroc stepped back as Attila led the way out onto the boulevard, followed closely by the four vehicles filled with civilians and three DGSE men.

"Do you think he'll make it all right?" Duroc asked. "The Cong aren't known to welcome anyone in their territory."

Napoleon stared after the departing caravan. "Exactly how many of them are there? The Park's a damned big place. We can only hope they're as shaken by what happened as we are. And some of their tunnels could have collapsed on them. Reassignments might be full of Vietnamese."

"Let's hope Reassignments isn't visited by a Hun, five Austrians and ten French," Wellington said. "I have to admit, that Attila's one brave chap."

"The DGSE men are going along, too. Did you notice what was in the back seat of the APC?" Napoleon asked. "Attila's got some serious fire power of his own. Helps with the bravery factor."

*

Despite his outward nonchalance, Attila felt a fine sheen of sweat on his forehead: this was going to be one chancy ride. Usually, no one in their right mind ventured into the Park, even though the streets and lanes were passable. The Vietcong roamed at will through the brush, undergrowth and trees. As far as anyone knew, they avoided the small lakes that dotted the Park. With any kind of luck, they wouldn't be near the street he and the following vehicles took.

He checked his rearview mirror, and saw the four cars close behind. Fear made people do things they otherwise would never contemplate, and the destruction of Caesar's villa was enough to strike terror into anyone.

It was over a mile from the north side of Decentral Park to the south side. At his present speed, barring any trouble, he should arrive in around ten minutes.

"Anbec," he said, glancing at the silent DGSE man. "Keep an eye on your side of the street. I'll watch mine. Those damned Cong can jump out of anywhere."

The Frenchman nodded, one hand caressing his laser-sighted rifle. Attila glanced over his shoulder: his own guns were on the back seat, and his pistol holstered under his left arm. Unless the Cong had mined the road, any attack would be mounted with hand-held weapons.

The street made a long, gentle curve that would let them out close to Hellview Estates. Attila rolled his shoulders, trying to relax. He didn't like the overhanging trees on this curve, or the encroaching bushes. He licked at a corner of his mustache, spat it out, worried that Anbec could sense his nervousness.

And then, the shit hit the fan.

*

"Damn!" Napoleon stiffened, one hand on the ear that had the leech attached. "It's the Cong! Attila's sending. Quiet! I need to hear!"

Marie moved closer; Duroc and Wellington hitched themselves to the edges of their chairs.

We've got Cong in front of us, Attila sent. *About twenty of them. Armed with... it's hard to tell* what *they're carrying. AKs for sure. But all the little fuckers have something.*

Napoleon rubbed his chin. *You're at a stop?*

Damned bastards poured out of the bushes and are blocking the street. They're just standing there, staring at us. I'm going to try to call Yanush.

Is he close?

Don't think so. Hold on. I'm calling him now.

Napoleon rose to his feet and began pacing. "The Cong are blocking the street," he explained. "Attila's contacting Yanush on the field phone."

"How near is Attila to the south side of the Park?" Duroc asked.

"If he was traveling quickly, he's nearly there." He stopped his pacing. "It's Attila."

Yanush isn't close enough to help, Attila sent. *So far no one has moved. Wait... one of the Cong is approaching. He looks like he wants to talk.*

Do you speak Vietnamese?

Hell, no. But I bet he speaks English. The Cong always do when they want something.

That's the truth, Napoleon replied. *Let's hope they're rattled enough by the explosion to want whatever news you can give them. Be nice, now.*

Screw you! Wait. Yanush is calling.

The contact went dead as Attila answered his field phone. Napoleon met three pairs of eyes that silently asked questions. He shook his head; he had to be ready to concentrate when Attila employed his leech again.

All right. I'm getting out of the APC. Anbec has me covered, for what good that *will do. The Vietcong who approached appears to be some kind of officer. The way they run amok, I didn't think they had those. I'll try to send my thoughts to you as I talk, but don't know if I can do that.*

Do what you can. If you can't talk and send at the same time, I'll understand. Be careful, Attila.

Didn't you know? Careful is my middle name.

*

The Vietcong who stood somewhat apart from the others looked up and down the small caravan and frowned.

"What you do here?" he asked. "Park is ours. You trespass."

Attila met the shorter man's eyes. "Oh? I'd think you'd be glad to see us."

"Why you think that? We no like people here. Just us."

"And who provides you with ribs, hey?"

"You?"

"You've got a short memory," Attila said. "*We* do. My neighborhood. That's why you leave us alone. My house is close to red-coat's."

"Ah." The hint of a smile; a flash of possible recognition. "Ribs." The smile disappeared. "But what you do now? I see no ribs."

"What about the explosion? You felt it. Everyone else did, too."

The leader briefly lowered his eyes. "Some died here. Tunnels no good." His face hardened. "You got no ribs, you no go on."

"If we don't go on, you won't get any more ribs."

That threat caused the other Vietcong to raise their weapons.

Impasse. Attila hoped the sweat on his forehead wasn't visible.

"We only want to get out of your damned Park," he said, trying to sound reasonable. In any other situation, he would have welcomed a fight, but he was responsible for the civilians, who would certainly be slaughtered.

"If we let you go, you bring ribs?"

"Where do you think I can get them? Hell's going to hell right now, hey? Can't you understand? That explosion rocked everyone around, including you in the Park."

The field phone pulsed; the officer lifted his AK and assumed a crouched position.

"Let me answer," Attila asked. "I'm not calling in a strike."

"You lie."

Attila was having trouble keeping his anger in check. He drew a deep breath. "You can't be serious! You think *I* want to die? A strike will take all of us out."

The phone kept pulsing. The leader locked eyes with Attila, then nodded.

"You keep talk brief."

"It will be."

Attila returned to the APC, feeling the eyes of the gathered Vietcong focused on his back. Moving slowly, he reached in and grabbed the phone. If Yanush, the Huns and Mongols were close, he might be able to stall long enough for them to come up behind the Cong.

If, if, if.

*

"What's happening?" Wellington demanded.

Napoleon stood motionless in the center of the room, his pacing forgotten.

"I don't know how these damned leeches work," he admitted. "I could hear Attila as clearly as if he stood next to me. Now, I'm picking up some of his emotions, too. Not much, but some."

"He's in big trouble," Duroc said, "unless he can talk his way out of this."

"He's not bad at talking," Marie inserted, "only at holding his temper."

"He's maintaining. Don't underestimate him," Napoleon said. "A long time ago, I used to think he was trouble on two feet, but I learned better. If it means anything, Caesar and the Romans trusted him."

"Let's hope you're right." Wellington still rubbed at the ear his leech had been attached to. "I don't like the odds. Too much can go wrong."

*

Attila carefully replaced the field phone and nodded to Anbec. "Stay alert. Maybe I've found a way for us to get out of this, hey?"

The DGSE man shrugged, but didn't loosen the hold on his weapon. Attila drew another deep breath in an attempt to achieve a semblance of calm. Enemies were similar to beasts in the forest: if they scented fear, they would act accordingly.

"So," he said, approaching the leader. "Conversation was brief."

The officer made a throw-away motion with one hand. "Brief," he acknowledged. "What you give us to let you go?"

"I thought you wanted ribs."

The armed Cong blocking the street started talking rapidly in Vietnamese, their conversation growing louder by the moment. Their leader turned, made a cutting motion, and was rewarded by silence. Once again facing Attila, he scratched his head, puzzled.

"Ribs? Where you get ribs? You give us ribs, we let you go."

"I know where to find them," Attila said. "You and your men come to my side of the Park, and I'll give you ribs."

Suspicion sharpened the Vietcong's face. "You lie. You try to trick us."

"Listen, you little shit," Attila said between clenched teeth, feeling his control beginning to fray. "You can keep your aim on us at all times. We aren't tricking you."

For a long, agonizing moment, the leader seemed to consider the offer. Finally, he nodded.

"Hoh-kay. You be telling truth, or you die. All of you."

"We're telling the truth," Attila said. "But if *you* start something, you'll die, too. Maybe not all of you, but we *can* fight back."

"Then we go before and after. Make sure you speak true."

*

The procession moved forward again, black pajama-clad Vietcong in the lead, the other half taking up positions behind the last vehicle filled with civilians. Since they were on foot, it took longer than Attila was comfortable with to reach the south edge of Decentral Park.

Hellview Estates stood silent. In the distance, he could see his house, Napoleon's and Wellington's. Nothing appeared to have changed since he'd left earlier in the day. The ruddy dusk was deepening: soon visibility would degrade, making them more vulnerable to surprise attack, a situation Attila wanted to avoid at all costs.

The Vietcong leader stalked to the APC, his weapon held so he could raise it and fire instantly.

"Where ribs?" he demanded.

Attila jumped down from the APC. "Follow me and I'll get you ribs."

"You tell truth, you live."

"We'll live. Anbec," Attila called, "all the cars stay here on the street. Try to keep everyone calm. They'll leave a few Cong behind to make sure I'm telling the truth."

And so they set off, Attila beside the Vietcong leader, followed by the rest of the Cong. Attila glanced down the street as they went; Yanush and his horsemen waited farther to the west, hidden behind brush and trees at the very edge of the Park. If worse came to worse (and this was hell after all), at least the Vietcong would be outnumbered.

At last, rounding a curve in the street, the answer to his hopes sat waiting.

The officer halted, threw up one hand, and stared.

"Ribs!" he exclaimed. "Lots of ribs!" He looked up at Attila. "You no lie. You go now. We got ribs!"

*

"What's going on?" Wellington demanded.

Napoleon held up a hand, asking for silence. At last he looked from Wellington to Marie, and then to Duroc. Removing the leech from his ear, he carefully returned it to the bag.

"Is Attila all right?" Marie asked.

"You're not going to believe this," Napoleon said. "The civilians are safe; Attila's taking them to the country club."

"But what about the Cong?"

"They're going to be happier than just about anyone around the Park right now. Attila got a final call from Yanush who had made it partway east on the south side of the Park. He discovered an abandoned mobile restaurant, what Attila calls a 'glorified roach coach.' Evidently, when the explosion hit, the driver took off, scared out of his wits. And the best part of all: the roach coach belongs to Hellzacre BarBQ."

Duroc grinned. "Ribs?"

"The thing was full of them. I only wish these damned leeches transmitted visually, too. Attila said he won't soon forget the sight of the truck being driven off into the Park, surrounded by cheering Vietcong."

Wellington sighed and leaned back in his chair. "That takes care of one problem," he said. "But only one. We're still stuck here on this side of the Park. And what are we to do? How do we keep – what did you say? The lid on?"

Napoleon exchanged a glance with Duroc. "I guess we patrol up and down the boulevard. Sulla's probably called up what he can from the Legions. He gave his word as a Roman general and I doubt he'll break it, whatever you think of the man. Honor *is* honor."

"But only if it promotes your position," Marie commented wryly.

"True. But it stands to reason that he can gain some power from his actions, even though it smacks of crowd control. Wellington, see if you can contact Queen Victoria. Tell her we're going to need all available soldiers to aid in patrol. I'll see if I can convince Marie-Theresa to do the same. We don't have a choice until Satan tells us otherwise. We've been reactivated and serve at Himself's pleasure."

Duroc frowned. "And that could last for a good long time."

"Bloody hell," Wellington grumbled. "And to think I was worried about my damnable grass growing inches in an hour. Not to mention the hedge."

Silence descended. Napoleon took a chair close to Marie.

"We still don't know the answers to some of the obvious questions: who, what – we know the when and where – but how and why are also up for debate. And the destruction might not be over."

Marie reached out for Napoleon. "At least it will be quick, if what we saw at Caesar's proves anything."

"Is Attila coming back?" Duroc asked.

Napoleon squeezed Marie's hand. "Three trips through Decentral Park in one day? I don't think even *he* would attempt that."

"He'll probably get called up in the Guard." Wellington rubbed at his ear again. "Who knows if he'll be able to join us."

"Well, he has his goats to feed, his wives to deal with – to say nothing of his brats. Géraud, I'm starved and so thirsty I could spit dust, and so are Marie and Wellington. Do you have anything to eat and drink? Something that doesn't taste like shit?"

Duroc smiled. "I'll see what I can find."

"Maybe Attila was able to snatch a few ribs from the Cong," Wellington said wistfully. "If we're going to die, I'd like to at least do it on a full stomach."

ESSENCE HELLIANCE

Yelle Hughes

Severed limbs and rotting torsos littered the Mortuary while the aroma of putrid flesh permeated the air. The young, hauntingly beauteous boy with azure eyes delicately stepped over body parts and deliberately kicked a decapitated head.

"I have a task for you, Undertaker, and I will take no questions." His nose crinkled at the pungent smell.

The Undertaker turned after suturing a female's arm to a male torso, and spied a child with short dark hair picking his way over to a rusted examination table.

"Is that you, Sire?"

Child/Satan flicked a decaying eyeball and watched it smack against a dark cloak hanging on the grimy wall before hopping his new form onto the edge of the table. He fanned his hand in front of his face before replying, "You need to check that breath, really. It's so dank, it overwhelms the stench of these bodies. I did say 'no questions' correct?" The little devil didn't wait for the Undertaker's answer. "Oh well..."

He snapped his small, chubby fingers and the Undertaker's emaciated arm began to swell, the blue veins growing darker as the grayish skin expanded, then exploded. His Satanic Majesty was capable of capriciousness at times.

The Undertaker peered at the spot where his arm had been, closed his eyes and sighed, "My apologies, Sire."

Satan's blue eyes flashed red-brown for several seconds before he pulled his short legs up on the table then crossed them. "I realized you wouldn't recognize me in this form, but how do you like it? The Americans made a movie about one of my sons and I was rather taken with it.

He splayed his hands wide open to allow the Undertaker to get a better glimpse of his blue blazer, pristine white shirt complimented with gray pleated knickers.

Exhaling cautiously, the Undertaker reached down and picked up a stray arm from the floor. As he busied himself attaching it to his shoulder, he responded quietly, "It becomes you, Sire."

Child/Satan clapped his hands, "Now back to the reason I came here. Your clientele will be expanding by twenty souls soon. Take time out of your busy schedule and watch the building next door. The damned souls who come, will hand you this..." He handed the Undertaker a small square piece of leathered human skin that read:

Essence Helliance
666 New Hell City Blvd.
New Hell City, Hell 66666
Where you donate
To receive a break

"They will be told they get thirty minutes to visit Elysion. Of course, there's no way in hell I would allow such a thing to happen, but they don't know that. I need their essence for a project I'm working on and I need the souls of those who have no chance for redemption." He plucked a finger from a nail in the wall behind him and threw it across the dark, musty room. "You are to immediately knock them unconscious as soon as they appear on the HelliPad. Remove the Hell Tracking Device and return their bodies exactly as they were before the transfer."

Child/Satan unfolded his legs and slid off the table, "I want you to place in their memories a visit to Elysion Fields instead of seeing a white barren building. Thirty minutes is the same amount of time it took Sisyphus to push that damned boulder up the hill."

Satan observed hell's mortician drop the arm. He could tell questions were burning to fall from those decrepit lips but would not because the Undertaker would hate to replace another body part. "As you command, Sire." The arm he picked up was too short for his lanky body so he chose another one and began the process all over again.

The Undertaker focused on Satan's mouth spread out into a feral grin. "Excellent! I'm so glad you want to help."

*

Meanwhile, at the Helliance Essence Center:

Medea of Colchis glared daggers at the tall, suave devil sitting at her desk, in her seat. "I should be allowed to work somewhere far worthier, more befitting my station in life." After a brief pause, she added, "My Lord."

Satan steepled his fingers, "Uhm hmm, yes, you would think the great Medea, granddaughter of the god Helios… niece of the goddess Circe, should have the best accommodations in hell." He stood and leaned over the desk. His powerful, menacing presence forced her to lean back in the visitor's chair. "Are we talking about the same Medea who betrayed her father and her homeland? Killed her brother by using him as bait? And even destroyed her own children because of her hostility toward one man? Do you really believe you deserve better of hell than what you have?"

The scorching heat surrounding Medea dissipated as Satan walked over to the window that showed the dark and sinister outskirts of New Hell City. "After your death and judgment, the sentence could have been eternity in hellfire. But I felt you would serve a better purpose running my center than to have your flesh burning till the end of time."

He turned back to the soul who, at one time, incessantly gloated over her luxurious, long raven hair. Satan had taken great pleasure, when Medea first arrived, chopping it all off into the blond asymmetrical hairstyle she sported now. "I'm sorry… what were you saying before I expounded on my thoughts?"

Medea promptly stood and expressed a submissive pose. "Not a thing, Sire. I sometimes ramble on about subjects that should no longer matter to a condemned soul. I humbly express my gratitude for this opportunity, Your Satanic Majesty." She bowed low, realizing for the first time that her life… her soul… meant absolutely nothing and could be obliterated without hesitation if she slipped up again. "My position as manager is very satisfying. I have several damned souls in my employ, not to mention a former king, and the donors… oh, the donors are so wonderful and such a joy to work with!"

Satan's dark brow quirked upward.

"Too much? Okay, I won't complain anymore, Sire. I will collect the damned souls' essence, then send them to Elysion Fields for their precious thirty minutes." Medea cautiously sat back in her chair after Satan retained his. "Dienekes is working out well as my security officer. So far, each damned donor has provided the exact volume of essence you specified, traveled to Elysion Fields for the allotted time and each HTD has been returned. What I don't understand is why you are being so nice."

"I hate to be questioned, but since I didn't give you a warning first, I'll let this one slide. Do not test me again."

Medea's head hurriedly dropped, "Yes, My Lord."

"Wonderful! I have a new employee for you: Ariadne of Crete will be joining your crew today. I believe you have a few bad habits in common with this Ariadne yes?" At her nod he wagged his finger, "Both of you betrayed your fathers and your kingdom to help a man with his quest and then... you both got dumped!" Satan chortled and clapped his hands. "Can you believe it?" He suddenly turned serious, "You will show her the ropes on how to be an essencectomist, freeing up Acrisius to manage today. Understood?"

"Yes, Sire."

"One more thing: you're already aware of the one regular idiot who's a special treat for Dienekes, but you'll be getting another special donor. He will be here daily, at the end of each working day. Keep your mouth shut and continue as normal. HDS (Hell Delivery Service) package handlers will be here on schedule, as usual." Abhorrence shot through Medea's entire body at the mention of who came to pick up the bottles of essence each and every day.

Satan chuckled out loud at Medea's shudder and smiled, "Have something to say?"

"No, Sire."

"I thought not. Make it clear to Acrisius there will be no mistakes on this. Pay attention to this day; some surprises will be coming your way."

Satan disappeared in a blink, allowing Medea to let out a long sigh of relief. *Medea, old girl, if you don't stop questioning HSM, you'll be roasting for a long time.* She left her office in search of the former King Acrisius of Argos. He, like every other mortal of means, abused his position to retain power and ultimately was punished for his misdeeds. Attempting to drown your daughter and her newborn son didn't sit well with the Most High.

So far, Acrisius' work ethic sucked. He spent more time dictating to her than doing his job. Couldn't fire him and she had no one to whom she could complain. It was definitely out of the question to whine to HSM. He'd throw a fireball at her for sure.

The pain-in-the-ass was right where she always found him... sitting in his chair and staring at the ceiling. "Acrisius, what's happening on the donor floor?" He didn't even have the courtesy to look at her before answering. "I don't know and I don't care. Go away, peasant, and leave me be."

Not bothering to argue this redundant discussion, she gave him Satan's orders: "You will be responsible for managing the center while I train the new girl. It also means making sure Dienekes equips all the damned donors with the HTDs and, at the end of the day, making sure all are returned and accounted for. Ensure the essencepheresis machines are running smoothly and, last but not least, the bottled essence must be placed in the special cabinet HSM has placed in the back of the building. This must be done at 1500 hrs. Not one minute before, not one minute after." Channeling the words and tone of Satan, her face lit up with a calculating grin. "You only have one shot to screw this up. One! If the bottles are late... you bake."

Finally! She had gotten his attention.

"He was talking to you. HSM wouldn't dare fry me. *I* am a king!"

Medea pounced with a finger in his face, "You *were* a king! Now you're nothing but a damned soul without a mortal body... like me! You want to test HSM? Go ahead; try it and burn!" She was a little puzzled as to why he scrambled so far away from her, but she quickly dismissed his actions.

Straightening and moving out of his personal space, she walked out the door toward the donor floor. "I have a soul to train; please, *please*, mess this up." Medea held her hands together in supplication. "I'd love to hear you scream as your blubber sizzles!" Satisfied she had finally gotten a chance to scare Acrisius, she put a little pep in her step as she strolled over to the new soul who stood quietly next to Dienekes. On the way past, she noticed there were only five donors lying on stone medical beds in the collection room. Brown tubes protruded from whatever part of their bodies that still held flesh. One donor only had half a face and the only flesh that was available to use was her right eye. The rest of her body was putrid pus and leathered skin.

I wonder what she did that was bad enough on earth to put her in that condition down here? The other four weren't any better to look at. *Good thing Satan didn't want blood because he sure enough wouldn't be getting any from this bunch.*

Medea straightened the lapels of her black lab coat when she reached her new employee. Lifeless black hair reached to the middle of Ariadne's newly acquired, raggedy coat. In a daze, the girl's dark eyes swept around the center, never focusing on any one particular object.

Medea cleared her throat, "Welcome to Essence Helliance. I am Medea and I will be your trainer. I will instruct you this one time on how to extract essence from these damned souls and where to store the bottles." Medea looked over at the tall Spartan warrior by her side. "I see you've met Dienekes, the bravest among the 300 Spartans at Thermopylae. His assigned duty was to protect the king and secure the Hot Gates from Persian invasion. Here at Essence Helliance, he's my security to make sure the damned donors behave and ensure they reach the HelliPad to Elysion. If any try to deviate from that path, he retrieves them and is allowed to administer punishment any way he sees fit."

Dienekes added, "Which has yet to happen."

Medea eyed the warrior who always happened to dress appropriately for whatever century they were in. This time he wore a black, fitted, short-sleeved shirt, outrageously displaying an image of a crimson Spartan helmet on the front. The phrase in red Greek lettering read, "Good. Then we will fight in the shade." Dark pants made of a material she wasn't familiar with conformed to his well-toned body. When she asked, he told her they were called "jeans." For a dead guy, his eye-candiness held up well, but Medea missed the old days of flowing tunics and bare thighs. The only thing marring his beauty were jagged holes located in different spots on his neck and arms, most likely from the arrows he received at the end of the battle. She broke away from reminiscing to concentrate on the present. Especially on the female who clearly died at a younger age than she.

"Before we get started, I was reminded we both did some of the same foolish things. First, tell me about your mortal life."

Though she spoke directly to Medea, the girl refused to look at her. Ariadne's focus seemed to be pointed somewhere over her shoulder when she spoke, "I used to be a princess of Crete. My father, Minos, made the king of Athens send seven young men and seven young women to his labyrinth every year." Ariadne looked over to Dienekes who nodded his encouragement to go on. "With the last trip, one of the prisoners, a man named Theseus came voluntarily and I…" A little choked up, she stopped talking.

Dienekes patted her shoulder, "Ariadne, you can tell her; we're all damned here and anything you've done is no worse then what others have been punished for."

Ariadne took a deep breath and continued. This time looking straight at Medea, "I fell in love with him and I promised that I would help him and the others escape if only he would take me with him."

Intrigued by how this woman's story sounded so like her own, she wanted to hear if Ariadne went as far as she did to seek revenge. Medea clasped Ariadne's elbow and directed her to the sign-in area.

"What did you do Ariadne?" Her security officer inched closer, never taking his eyes off the damned donors, but Medea could tell he was still paying attention to their conversation. Another responsibility of Dienekes was to research the life and history of anyone who came and worked for the center. Whatever Ariadne did, he should know. Perching cautiously on the withered Formica desktop, she waited for the quiet girl to speak.

"I thought everything was fine until we reached the island of Naxos... where I met the god of wine Dionysus. While Theseus ran off with his friends hunting and playing games, Dio... that's what I called him, visited me every night." She smiled wistfully, "we talked all night long." Ariadne's long hair slid over her cheeks and covered her face.

Well aware the girl's tears threatened to fall, Medea needed to cut off the waterworks before they spilled. "Ariadne you should not get emotional about the past – what's done is done. The only thing to do now is adjust to this existence. You're in hell now, and emotions can get you killed down here; you don't want that... trust me."

Medea reached out and pushed dull raven tresses back away from Ariadne's face as encouragement for her to continue.

"Dio basically told me I deserved better. After all I had done for my love: betraying my father, becoming a traitor to my people and helping him with the murder of my half-brother the Minotaur," Ariadne a deep breath, "I found myself alone on that blasted island night after night while the man I thought I loved above all else, ran around as if my sacrifice meant nothing!"

The girl's hands balled into fists and, if Medea didn't know better, she'd have sworn the little spitfire had the guts to get up and punch someone.

"Dionysus gave me a way out. Only... I had to... to help him with one thing."

Now Dienekes had turned away from the damned donors, his full attention on the two women sitting a few feet away from him.

"I... I had to sacrifice the... the twelve maenads that were traveling with him at the time."

Medea scoffed, "You? I can't believe you would just slaughter 12 women, willy-nilly. How did he get you to do it?"

Ariadne's next words briefly carried Medea and Dienekes away from the depths of hell to a large island in the Cyclades. They both found themselves standing on the beach of Naxos. The cerulean-blue of the Aegean glittered clearly under a Hunter's Moon. The smell of salt from the sea wafted over them as they watched Ariadne's account unfold before them. The god Dionysus sat close with his hairy arms wrapped around a weeping Ariadne... whispering sweet nothings in her ear. The grape leaves decorating his hair poked at her glossy raven locks as he moved closer still to nuzzle her tear-stained cheeks.

The two prisoners of hell moved quietly over the soft sand to listen in on the conversation.

"...so you see Ariadne, we can help each other; the maenad's actions are now threatening my status as a god. Of all the women that followed and worshipped me, this lot has become a nuisance, more belligerent, more possessive of my time and presence. One time on a full moon night like this, I had a celebration for my son... several immortals and humans were invited and these witches nearly killed my boy just for standing too close to me. Being unable to control my followers proved very disappointing to my fellow divinities. This was the first mishap. I told them to leave my party and never set foot in my domain, but that only infuriated them. Drunk on Bacchus wine, they visited a nearby village without my permission and destroyed everyone within the town. Men, women and children were annihilated, all in my name. I abhor the harming of children, nor is it permissible for anyone in my retinue to kill indiscriminately."

He pushed her hair back and grasped her neck gently, directing her to look at him. "It's not in my nature as a god to exterminate these women. I need you to do it for me. I promise you will not be punished. They are murderers and I am granting you the right to carry out my judgment."

Ariadne was still clearly reluctant to do as he asked. They could see frustration on his face as he rolled his eyes up to the full moon. "Just think of this as penance for the death of your brother Monty. From what you told me, even though he had the body of a full grown man with murderous rages, he was still but a child and did not deserve his fate."

As he waited for her answer, the melodious chirping of crickets whispered softly in the dark bushes that surrounded the beach. Closing his eyes to fall into nature's music, Dionysus almost missed Ariadne's quiet "I'll do it."

His gaze snapped back to see the tears had dried and Ariadne was looking directly at him. "You promise that I will not be punished and that you will take me away from here?"

"Yes, I swear on my mother's life you will be safe in the afterlife. We must make haste while the maenads are asleep. Take this thyrsus and shake it over the wine barrel. I have enchanted the honey inside with poison. Once the task has been completed, you and I will take leave from here and begin our new life together. No more Theseus for you and no more Maenads for me. Do you agree?"

With a nod of her head, Ariadne whispered, "Agreed."

Medea and Dienekes were abruptly slammed back into the present stinky, muggy and dark remnants of hell. Moisture coated Ariadne's face and dampened her lab coat. Medea peered down on the girl with pity, "You poor fool. I take it you didn't know at the time that Dionysus' mother Semele burned to death by looking upon his father Zeus' true form? ...while the unborn god of inebriation still sat cradled in her womb?"

Ariadne shook her head, "No."

Dienekes interrupted, "I didn't find any of this in your background search. Why was it not in the history books?"

Ariadne looked up at the Spartan warrior, "That's because Dio kept my secret safe from everyone. Except for..." Bowing her head, she quieted. They all knew whose name she was hesitant to say.

Erra and the Seven. Hell's judge, jury and executioners. No secrets or misdeeds done on earth could be hidden from them, no need to rely on any mortal's account of history for they knew everything.

"Dio said he would save me by becoming my husband and that my life... my sacrifice would not be in vain. I was so wrong to believe him."

Medea stood up, "Well like I said before, whatever happened in your mortal life is irrelevant here in hell. Nothing you can do about it now except serve your time by working here. Be comforted... better to be at the center than in the fire. Understand though, burning forever is still an option on the table." Nodding her head, she signaled for Dienekes to go back to his watch station and with a crook of her finger, told Ariadne to follow her.

As they walked toward the front desk, Medea's thoughts went back to her own sordid past: *"Jason, why couldn't you've just loved me? My life would've been perfect. But no, you had to go off and marry that... that woman! You did this, not I! Our sons should've grown to be fine affluent citizens, but you and your aspirations to royalty found my boys buried in Hera's precinct before their due time. I dreamt of the day I would seek revenge on you Jason and the look on your face seeing your precious Glauce lying there pale and lifeless brought joy to my heart but it wasn't enough. You had to pay for your betrayal, and I needed to destroy everything you held dear."*

Despite the advice given to Ariadne, Medea fell short of recognizing the hypocrisy biting her in the ass as she kept thoughts of revenge toward her ex-husband flowing through her heart.

"Now Ariadne, as a new employee, I'm going to start you off with a first-time customer and I want you follow what I tell you. This is what is required of you. Have the donor sign right here." Medea pointed to the crusty parchment paper with squiggly lines and a place for a damned soul's signature.

Ariadne stood behind the tall desk and gestured the new customer to sign his name. She turned the sheet to read the name "Ephialtes of Trachis."

Upon hearing Ariadne speak the name of the traitor to his king and country, Dienekes stood up straighter and glared daggers at the short hunched-back soul. Medea, ignoring the tension filled-air, kept on talking.

"Direct them to sit in a screening booth. Here is a list of questions they need to answer in order to donate."

Ariadne read from the sheet that was glued to the desk:

"Why are you here?"

Ephialtes answered, "I was told by His Satanic Majesty himself to come here for a chance to visit my father in Elysion."

"In the past eight weeks have you sold your soul to any demon?"

"No."

"Have you prayed to God during your stay in Hell?"

"No, God didn't care about me when I was alive so why would I pray to him now?"

Medea cut in, "A simple no will suffice."

"In the past four weeks have you tried to visit Elysion?"

"I wouldn't know where to begin to find it."

"Have you received a fresh body part from the Undertaker within the last six months?"

"No. When I woke up here in hell, by mistake, may I add, my body had changed to this abhorrent mass of pulsating flesh, several inches shorter than my mortal height. HSM said it was a mistake on the Undertaker's part and when I came back from Elysion, he'd make him change me back."

"Since your introduction to Hell, have you tried to repent for your sins?"

Ephialtes turned to Dienekes whose gaze had not strayed from the donor floor and directed his answer to him: "You may think I betrayed your king and your people but it was Leonidas who betrayed us! We asked for his assistance and he refused to help us fight against the Oitaians. But that wasn't the worst part! We were brought under Sparta's rule. I vowed then Sparta would pay for the disrespect they had shown to my country. All Xerxes wanted was a little information for a large bit of coin, so I gave it to them. Didn't think it would be a problem. You did, after all, have the famous Spartan phalanx."

Ephialtes turned back to Ariadne to answer her question, "I did nothing wrong so there is nothing to forgive. That is why HSM has promised me that along with a visit to my father Eurydemus, I might have a chance for redemption. So no, when you are innocent, there is no need to repent."

Dienekes didn't bother to look back but he did respond, "Whatever."

Due to HSM being so generous, do you swear your allegiance to him?

"Yes! Absolutely, yes!"

Medea shook her head at the enthusiastic soul. Leaning over the girl's shoulder, she said, "Ariadne these questions will be memorized in no time. Check them off as you go, on the donor's file. Only after all of that is complete, will you read the last line."

Medea pointed to the disclaimer written boldly in red. She also handed Ariadne a lancet. Ariadne looked puzzled. "What's this for?" Medea reached for the small blade and told Ephialtes to hold out his hand. "Because souls do not produce blood, most have what we call 'cruor' within their bodies. Locate a piece of viable flesh and cut. This donor has fingers so use them." She mimed poking the pad of his index finger without puncturing the skin. "Once they sign this last part, press the sheet on the wound. Make sure there is enough liquid to leave a stain. This is for verification to match the soul to the donor." Medea handed the lancet back to Ariadne.

"Ephialtes, read this line."

He stared at the paper for a few seconds before reading out loud: "I certify that I will not speak of this transaction with any other soul, will accept thirty minutes in Elysion as recompense for my donation of essence, and will not try to renegotiate for more time."

"Now have him sign his name. Slice his finger and wipe it with the sheet near his signature."

Ariadne followed her instructions. Ephialtes winced when the small sharp piece of metal pierced his skin and whimpered when she smeared the cruor next to his name. After Ephialtes stopped sniffling, they both followed Medea back to the donor floor. A malodorous, raunchy odor surrounded the group as they marched farther into the room.

Medea stepped closer to the first donor bed, which was occupied, and stopped at the side of what looked like a man even though his arms and the bottom half of his face were missing. "Make the donor lie on an empty bed." She pointed at the unoccupied one on the other side of her. Turning back to the donor already hooked up, she put her hand on his tube and snatched off the tape holding the needle in place. "Take this sixteen-gauge needle and insert it into any place that has the most flesh." She pulled the stick out of the stunted soul's neck, raised it up to Ariadne's face so she could see, then stuck it back in, ignoring his cry of pain.

"Tape it down then flip this switch. The cruor will be sucked out then put through this spinner." She pointed to a cylindrical object. "It will then separate the soul's essence, pushing it down into the bottle and the cruor will be sent back to the donor. When it's filled up to 880 milliliters, turn off the switch. Whatever is left in the tubing will be returned but personally, I couldn't care less. Pull the needle and cover the wound with a piece of gauze. Take the bottle and drop it off on the counter in the back."

Medea pointed toward the counter where the red-headed used-to-be king stood loitering. "Leave them there and Acrisius will put them away. Now it's your turn, tell Ephialtes to lie down and get him started."

Ariadne did as she was told, she moved out of the way so the hunch-backed, bug-eyed turncoat could stretch out on the bed as best as he could. His beefy short legs would not straighten so his knees stayed up in the air. She double-checked that the bottle was marked with his name. Ariadne grabbed his arm, struggled trying to flatten it along the armrest, then pushed the needle's point into roughened skin.

It resisted.

She looked to Medea for assistance. "If the needle fails to penetrate, you will have to either try another spot or if you're not squeamish, jam that sucker right on in there." Determined not to appear weak before Medea once again, Ariadne put some oomph behind her next try.

"Brrrrrnnnnttt!"

Startled, Ariadne jumped back without taping the needle to his arm, crying, "What the hell was that?"

Medea stepped in next to the donor to secure the tubing before cruor started flying. "Oh yeah, I forgot to tell you. When you first penetrate a dead soul, a little gas is released. It stinks but you will get used to it."

"Well that is just disgusting," Ariadne said while plugging her nose to keep out the stench of rotting fish eggs.

Medea looked around at the half-mutilated, putrid bodies that were present. Ariadne had walked past them without a word or a look of disdain. "You are an odd one if you're only offended by a little flatulence." With her head lowered in embarrassment, Ariadne took a peek at Ephialtes. His bulbous eyes blinked before saying, "It's not my fault!"

"Anyway, he's all set. There's nothing else to be done except keep an eye out for when the bottles reach 880, then cut them off." Medea pointed to the button she was referring to, "If you want to wait for the rest of the cruor to be returned then use these scissor clamps to stop the flow and cauterize the tube above the bottle. Pull all tubing off the essencepheresis machine and give it to Menseze to eat. Menseze happened to be a large caldron covered with green wrinkled, rotting flesh, with gnarled, heavily knuckled claws for feet and a set of razor-sharp teeth encompassing the lip. Medea thought it was hilarious to dress up her garbage can. Red boiling acidic liquid within would devour and disintegrate anything that was tossed inside. "When each is ready, send the damned donor to Dienekes and he will take care of..."

One the machine's alarms interrupted Medea, the half-faced woman Medea cared not to think about for half a second had finished. "She's done, now show me that you were listening. Here are your clamps." Medea attached several to Ariadne's coat and pushed her toward the beeping machine. Ariadne carried out Medea's instructions precisely and had the bottle sitting on the counter next to Acrisius within five minutes flat. "Very good, you are going to do well. Well I'm off to do paperwork. Don't hesitate to call out to me if you mess something up. No need to try to get assistance from Acrisius... because he won't help you." Medea turned and left.

Ariadne looked around at her new work place thinking: *This won't be so bad. It will keep me busy and keep me from thinking about Theseus and Dio.* She finished setting up the empty essencepheresis machine, checked to see if anyone else was close to finishing then headed out to the front to watch for any new donors coming in.

Dienekes watched Ephialtes with passionate hatred. Unbeknownst to all the employees and donors of Essence Helliance, he alone knew the purpose for this set-up was not about helping the damned soul; it was a power-play on Satan's part. He wasn't exactly sure what the end game was, but it certainly wasn't allowing the forever-damned an opportunity to see how happy and blessed life could be after mortal death. He was also privy to a special punishment that was assigned to Ephialtes. Leaving his post, he walked over to start the continuous loophole of events. Coming to a halt next to the traitor who was laid out in the fetal position, he spoke quietly. "So the sniveling coward thinks he's worthy enough to go to the other side? You realize that Elysion's gates will not open for the likes of you? It doesn't matter what Satan told you... deep down in your black ugly soul, you know you'll not be welcomed."

Ephialtes looked up at the dark warrior, "I get it Dienekes; you don't like me. But I'm telling you, you've got it all wrong." He tried to turn in the bed to get a little more comfortable without dislodging the needle stuck in his arm. "If you weren't so blinded by your loyalty to your king, you would see that. You know damn well I was a pure Greek by heart and blood and what I did, I did for my country. Not for some egomaniac that was more interested in making a name for himself in the history books instead of submitting peacefully to the Persians." Dienekes watched Ephialtes work himself up to a giant hissy fit.

Good, keep getting agitated. This is going like clockwork.

"Ephialtes, I'm not going to stand here and argue with you, for I cannot bear the sight of you and that is my eternal punishment. Remember this, you are in hell and hell is for sinners. And you... you bulbous sack of shit, are one of the biggest sinners of all. Don't believe *me* but when you find out they won't admit you to Elysion, remember that I'm back here laughing my ass off at your pigheadedness."

Smugly, Ephialtes retorted, "HSM says otherwise and I'll believe him over the likes of you!"

Dienekes laughed out loud while turning away. With his back turned he threw back, "I'll set you up with an HTD and savor the time I am free of your stench until you come back to see me."

Ephialtes growled toward the retreating soldier, "I won't be coming back here you arrogant ass!" That startled the other donors, who all turned toward the bellowing scrunched-up hobbit-looking man. "What are you looking at? You desperate fools think you're better than me? I will be getting through those gates! I don't care what anyone says and no one is going to stop me!" The donors each rolled their eyes and went back to staring at the ceiling, ignoring the ranting traitor for the rest of the donation process.

Ephialtes watched the long-haired newbie unhook several more donors from their machines and finally after what seemed like forever, she came for him. "You're all finished. Please make your way to the front and Dienekes will send you on your way. Enjoy your visit to Elysion." The girl was too happy to be in hell and it irritated him.

"Piss off you accursed hellion! I don't need pleasant words from some crappy girl!"

The slight smile on Ariadne's face disappeared, "I was trying to be nice but since you have a problem with that, I hope you fall into a fiery pit, asshole."

Ephialtes rolled off of the bed then turned to her, "I knew you were a mean one. Being somewhat 'pretty' down here does not automatically make one amiable." Ariadne's mouth dropped open at the insult. Before she could give the raunchy troll what-for, Dienekes called him over. Ephialtes turned from the disrespectful woman and shuffled toward the bane of his Hellish existence. "Hand over whatever you have to give me and get out of my way. I will be going to Elysion and I will no longer listen to anything you have to say."

Dienekes only chuckled then shackled a small device to his wrist. Once it was secured he commanded, "Follow me."

Not liking Dienekes' authoritative manner, Ephialtes declined to move. "I refuse to follow you anywhere! Just point me in the right direction and I will go myself. I found this place on my own and I will find Elysion."

The arrow-torn warrior eyed him suspiciously before giving Ephialtes directions to the HelliPad. "Make sure that this card I'm giving you is in your hand when you step on the platform. This will send a command to the machine to send you to Elysion. An angel will be waiting for you to escort you to your family members." He warned him, "This card is the only thing that will get you through the gates so don't lose it."

Ephialtes didn't want that. He wanted to get into Elysion on his own. If there was no one there to guard him, there would be no one to make him come back. "How far is Elysion from here? What happens if something stops me from getting to the HelliPad? I deserve my time in heaven and I don't want anything to get in the way of that. Tell me how to get there on foot, just in case." He would bypass the HelliPad and walk to Elysion. There was no way Dienekes would find out until it was too late. He would be so far into the afterworld, the fighter would never find him. He was confident that his father would help him hide as well.

Dienekes took a parchment of paper and drew a map that would take Ephialtes through New Hell City into a deep valley that led to an exact replica of Thermopylae during ancient times

Ephialtes' jaunt would be filled with appalling displays to remind him why he was condemned and sent to hell. Dienekes understood all too well the hobgoblin would reach an epiphany. Not only would he traverse through familiar territory, he would get a glimpse of several souls who betrayed either their homeland or family. After leaving New Hell City, the traitor would travel into the Malis region to run into the old goat path that would take him around to the "Hot Gates."

Satan chose to have Ephialtes witness the torture of several people who were guilty of the same crime as he. Onetas of Carystus and Corydallus of Anticyra were both accused of divulging the location of the old goat path to the Persians.

All had betrayed their country for coin or power and all were viciously punished indefinitely. Those two weren't enough to satisfy HSM. The *coup de grâce* was the last and final prodotis...the worst of all traitors, as far as Dienekes' was concerned: Eurydemus, who contacted Hydarnes, commander of Xerxes' army "The Immortals" when Sparta took over his city, Trachis. They made a bargain that if Eurydemus gave them the map to reach Greece by land, they would liberate Trachis from Sparta. Thus Eurydemus told his son Ephialtes to show them the way.

Ephialtes' pain upon seeing his father in hell with him instead of in Elysion, would force him to accept reality. He was guilty of treason and truly damned. He had been judged to carry out his sentence of visiting the essence center, arguing with Dienekes and making the trek through his old homeland to find his father being tortured... forever. Dienekes gladly received his daily torment of seeing Ephialtes' face, knowing that in the end, the man who was responsible for the final mortal days of fellow hoplites and his king, would meet a worse fate than death itself.

Dienekes was not naïve, he understood that everything Satan did, was for a purpose and now that he knew about Ariadne's murder spree, he was certain her true retribution would be making itself known soon.

It didn't take long. The young soul had just finished unhooking the last donor on the floor before the next walked through the door. Dienekes recognized him immediately. *Sa-*

tan…you devil. He called for Ariadne. "Come to the front, there's another donor, the last of the day, waiting to be processed."

Ariadne had just finished throwing cruor soaked tubes into Menseze's belly when she turned at the sound of Dienekes' voice. The needles that were about to be dropped in the sharp's container, hit the floor when she saw who was standing at the front desk. Towering over Dienekes was her half-brother the Minotaur or Monty as they called him.

Why is he here?

She hurriedly cleaned up the mess she made and ran out to the front to face the sweet brother that she spent every day with before he grew so strong and uncontrollable, he had to be placed in the Labyrinth commissioned by their father, King Minos. Ariadne fell to her knees in supplication before her sibling. Intense pain encompassed her body as she relived the day Theseus slew Monty. She had convinced herself that it was all for the best and that her brother would be free from murdering and devouring the humans their father dangled in front of Monty… enticing him. Lying prostrate at her brother's feet, she admitted that her excuses were all for naught. She was responsible for Monty's demise. If it hadn't been for her, Theseus would not have found his way through the perplexing twists and turns of the Labyrinth. She was the one that voluntarily handed over the magical thread that led to the heart of her brother's prison.

Wailing loudly, she pleaded for forgiveness: "Monty, there is nothing that can be said or done that will change how I have wronged you. My existence, my soul resides in hell for my sins and I deserve to carry out this sentence. But you, dear Monty… hell should not be your fate! Our father used you as a weapon, trained you to only devour human flesh. You should not be here!"

Ariadne lifted her head and through the sheen of her tears, the being she knew as a playful and rambunctious child who turned into a raging, murderous monster bowed his heavily horned head and stared at his sister. Gentle luminous eyes that at one time glowed bloody red during a feeding frenzy, were now doe-eyed black. The monstrous craggy head of a bull which brought terror to her people and the surrounding islands now sported softened dark hair that was free of blood and gore. His wide flat mouth that had grimaced with sharp crimson fangs, now held white and spotless teeth. His dusky lips were upturned into what she imagined was a smile. Two silver rings that gleamed brightly, pierced his nostrils and his left ear. Monty's dewlap ran from his chin down to his clavicle. His twin horns even lit up the shadowy front area of the center. Bending down, Monty grasped her elbows and pulled to her feet. When settled, he drew his hands back and signed to her that he was there to donate a part of his essence so he could visit Elysion.

Ariadne's panicked eyes darted to Dienekes, who stood quietly watching and listening. "No! I can't allow you to do that!" She grabbed his bulging, muscular bicep and pulled him into the donor booth. "See here, these questions I have to ask?" She pointed to the sheet of paper that was stuck to the desktop. "It asks for you to swear allegiance to him. I don't know why you're in hell but you will not sell your soul to the devil." Monty signed that it was not her decision what he did. "I know it's not my decision but..."

Her brother interrupted with the rapid movement of his fingers. As children, they were taught sign language as a means to communicate with each other and family members. Times were so much better when they were little. *"Ari, I want you to know that I do not place blame on you for my death. In a way, I'm glad you were bold enough to set it up. I had become a monster and once I tasted human flesh, I couldn't stop. Mother did not have the guts to do what needed to be done. Father used me for his own nefarious purposes and you, my sweet innocent but understandably dangerous sister knew that I needed to be destroyed. I have no animosity toward you. My beloved sibling, you freed me from my nightmares, my terror... my horrible life. I want to see mother, I want to tell her I forgive her as well. She made the decision to keep me even after she screamed in terror as I was birthed from her womb."*

Ariadne wept loudly now as the brother she had assassinated forgave her. *"I belong in Hell Ari, I butchered and consumed human flesh. I knew it was wrong then just as I know it's wrong now. I gladly accept my penance and have no wish to be found innocent. The only thing I want, is to see mother one last time and give her my message. I don't expect anything more. So please, read the questions and let's get this thing going. If it's any consolation, though I'm selling my soul to Satan, at least we will be able to see each other."*

Dienekes turned from the siblings. *That son-of-a-bitch, HSM, gave Ariadne absolution from her brother's murder but damned her for killing the maenads. I don't think I'll ever understand him.*

Meanwhile Medea sat in her office dreading the coming end of the business day. Her only respite from her inner terror was taunting Acrisius. "Your work performance was not up to par Acrisius." The former king reluctantly pulled his gaze away from the ceiling to glare at his – Satan forbid! – superior. "You don't like me and I cannot stand you and though you look down your nose at me, the facts do not change... I am your boss. In other words "Queen of this bitch." I rank higher than you and that will never change. I presume HSM is letting you off easy by having to work under a woman but I'm starting to think there's more to it, right?"

She inched closer to him, closer than she'd ever stomached before. Suddenly a sulfurish odor assaulted her nostrils. "What's that smell?" With her question, she drew nearer. Smokey tendrils appeared to float off of Acrisius' body. A panicked look decorated his ruddy complexion and sweat began to roll down his temples. He pursed his lips when Medea was mere inches away. "Get away from me you harlot!" As he tried to distance himself by leaning far back in his chair, Medea heard a crackling, snapping sound emanating from his body. "Hmmm, so that's it. You get nice and toasty when I'm in close proximity to you. I wonder what happens if I touched you?"

She reached a pointed finger toward his shoulder. Acrisius moved so fast, she didn't think he had it in him. "Don't touch me!!" He nearly tripped over his chair, scrambling away as fast as he did. A huge Cheshire grin spread on Medea's face as she shouted to the rotted plaster above. "Thank you, YSM! I know you didn't do this for me but you have my sincerest gratitude for this gift." An evil smirk replaced the grin as she looked upon on the cowering Acrisius. "Now, what was that name you called me?"

Acrisius shrank down in the corner of his office weeping pitifully, ashamed his punishment for eternity was finally made known.

Medea gleefully skipped back toward her office when her happiness was suddenly squashed. She felt several presences standing in the back hallway that led from the manager's section of the building. She turned slowly. There by the back door, stood three grown men in loincloths. The tallest was covered in slashes and rips to his flesh, as if his body had been torn apart in life then put back together like a puzzle after death. The others were young nubile youths. They didn't resemble any of the other souls in hell. A golden glow surrounded them, so bright it burned Medea's eyes a little.

The malicious glee she felt earlier abandoned Medea with swiftness, leaving behind immeasurable misery that forced her to fall to the filthy floor of the center's walkway. Her beleaguered gaze met with the incandescent, silvery eyes of her brother Absyrtus. An unforeseeable force made her look at the other two, Mermerus and Pheres; her own flesh and blood who had been delivered from her body many ages ago. Beautiful, innocent children who only had love shining in their eyes for their mother. That adulation was still present even as they watched her lift the blade high over her head and plunged it into their little bodies. Glistening tears mixed with blood, peppered cherub cheeks as the lights finally dimmed, fading from their eyes as the souls of her boys were carried away by the angels.

When Medea first started working at Essence Helliance she thought she would be free of being haunted by her brother and her sons. She could wallow in her thoughts of continued vengeance against Jason, Glauce and her father. Those feelings could sustain her for eternity. She was dead wrong. Seeing the brother she had chopped up and scattered on some derelict road to distract her father from chasing her and Jason, and seeing the sons she killed with her own hand, was not what she expected. She figured since they were still quite young when they died, they would have had an automatic pass into Elysion.

But no, here they stood before her, exactly at 1500 hrs, not a minute before and not a minute after. They never spoke, only stared. Their eyes were no longer the colors they were when they were alive, but now silver. And they just looked at her, no accusations, no pity and no emotion.

Just… looking.

It drove her mad, "Why are you doing this to me? You have to understand, your death had a purpose!" Medea addressed her brother, "Father would not stop! We had to get away. I did what I needed to do, or father would have slaughtered us all! Don't give me that look! I saved you from a life that would have been miserable and destitute." Medea stood, "I will not ask for your forgiveness. I don't care that I have to see you every day. I will take this pain, I accept this pain and I will glory in this pain!"

Fueled with fury, Medea yelled at her sons, "Be glad that I ended your mortality. If it had not been for Jason and his treachery, your lives would have been forfeit the minute he married that witch Glauce!" Receiving no reaction from her beautiful boys infuriated her. "Why won't you speak? I was right to kill you!" She pulled out strands of her short blond locks and beat her breast, leaving scratch marks, "You will not make me feel guilty! Jason is the one you should be condemning… not me!"

Medea fell heavily and lay prostrate on the floor, drawing her breath in raggedly from the screaming and sobbing. "Get out! Get out! I cannot stand to look at you!

The three men silently walked over to the special cabinet that held the essence, placed the bottles in a box made of human bones and then silently walked out the back door. Medea did not notice she was alone; madness had incapacitated her. Thoughts and dreams of Jason kneeling over their dead sons, weeping in agony from his pain, kept her from throwing herself into Menseze's belly.

A maniacal cackle issued from her abused throat as she gloated over her ex-husband's torture.

BAREFOOT, ON BRIMSTONE

Sara M. Harvey

The light came down through the trees, evaporating the dream. Isadora knew it was a dream now, in those scant seconds between sleeping and waking when the mind offers only unfiltered, cruel clarity. She rolled over, willing herself back into the dream, the summer day and the laughter of children.

Her children.

There was sunlight and wine and people all around. She strolled down the steps of a broad amphitheater with Deirdre and Patrick at her sides. The audience lounged on blankets or sprawled out on the grass of the dozens of terraces leading down to the stage. They tittered as she passed, their whispers growing louder, building upon one another until the whole sky buzzed with hundreds of voices. She walked out into the stage, the smooth stone beneath her feet warmed by the sun. She turned to face them, this great mass of admirers and the buzzing turned to shouting and applause. When she stretched wide her arms, they grew silent and awed.

Her children sat at the edge of the stage, their eager faces upturned to her, all smiles for their mama. The crowd, it did not vanish, but no longer seemed nearly as important, not anymore. She was looking at *them*. Deirdre in the white gown, skirts spread just-so in emulation of her mother, her feet also bare and her auburn hair hanging free about her shoulders. Patrick looking so solemn in his short pants and driver's cap, his sleeves turned back and the freckles showing on his forearms and the tops of his toes. She danced for them.

Her toes twitched then spasmed, cramping up like they did when the weather was about to turn cold unexpectedly.

Isadora Duncan sat up. The dream was gone now, fled until night came once more, whenever that might be. She rubbed her aching feet, fingering the calluses and looking out at the vast, lonely wood around her. No matter where she fell asleep, she woke up here. At first, she thought it was Greece, near Athens where she and her brother had bought a small villa complete with an adjacent temple; or perhaps Nice in the south of France where she had spent so many happy times. Except that last time. She rubbed her neck, tugging at the silk scarf knotted so tightly there.

It might have been anywhere, but the lack of sound always alerted her that it was not. No birdsong, no breeze, just eerie silence. A short walk through the small, cluttered forest revealed a vast plain, empty and flat as far as she could see: no amphitheater, no audience, no children.

She broke down, weeping, then wiping her tears with the tattered remains of the once-fine scarf and letting it drag along the ground behind her.

"How many years have I been at this?" she wondered aloud to no one. "How many years do I wake, damn-well knowing that this is the reality that awaits me, yet surprised and upset by it *every single time?"*

Isadora sat at the fringes of the meadow, stretching her legs into the flat, pallid light, too ghastly to be mistaken as sunlight – ever. The grass that grew here – like the trees: grim, ashen, brittle – was a dull reflection of what lush, living grass should have been. It was enough, though, to fool her hopeful heart. Every day, it was enough. And every day, she cried.

Had there been another soul to share it with… that might have eased her pain.

"But this is hell," she told the empty, sunless sky. "This is hell and it serves its foul purpose all too well."

She waited for night to come, hungry for the adoration of the crowd, yes, but aching for the feel of little hands eagerly clasping her own. A pang echoed through her breasts, as it had when Deirdre and Patrick been infants wanting to be fed. She tasted the familiar mix of despair and desperation.

"You aren't on your way, are you, night?" She glared up into the expanse above, unchanging and unmoving. "I'll sit here for an eternity, wishing for the one bit of solace I have found, bittersweet as it may be, but it will never come again. You've caught on to me, haven't you?"

There was no answer. And she expected none.

"Have it your way. Keep your lonely woods and your unrelenting dreams. Hell cannot be so vast that there are no other souls to be found. I'm tired of being alone."

She stood and cast her scarf over her shoulder where it fluttered for a moment, the image painted so beautifully upon the silk now ruined with axle grease, from winding around the wheel of the car in which she died.

She walked. The strange grass that was not grass crunched beneath her feet. Although the blades were not sharp and did not pierce her skin, the sound they made when trod was akin to breaking glass; it set her teeth on edge. She pressed onward across the desolate field, certain she would come around to her little woods again before long.

But she did not.

Instead, the meadow began to slope upward and the air grew damp and smelled of the sea. Isadora paused, glancing behind her to see the windswept hillside rising up, subtly different than it had been before. Its grass had a golden cast and looked altogether more real, if remarkable in its stiff perfection.

Ahead of her, the rolling hill leveled out to a craggy plateau. Although the hillcrest had been unoccupied, now two figures stood there, both uncommonly tall and long of limb, in deep conversation until noticing her approach.

"Isadora! How good it is to see you," the woman said, a smile breaking across her face. And what a face – angular and perfect with ivory skin and eyes nearly too large. Her hair glowed as red as sunset, falling in loose curls from a hasty bun twined at the nape of her neck.

"We've been waiting for ages – I thought you'd never get here." The man put a hand companionably around the woman's slender waist. His hair was deep mahogany brown and brushed against his prominent cheekbones. He had rich, olive skin and luminously dark eyes.

Isadora caught her breath, finding herself uncharacteristically tongue-tied. She glanced between the two of them and her only thought was how much she wanted to take each of them to bed.

No, amend that, both *of them,* she mused silently.

"You'd like that very much, wouldn't you," the woman purred.

"We'll have ample time for that later, I'm sure," the man said in a tone that told her in no uncertain terms that he also would very much like that, but preferred to make her wait. "Ample time, that is, if this goes better than it did the last time."

"Where am I?" Isadora collected her thoughts at last. "I mean, besides in hell. I did not think to find anyone like you here."

The beautiful woman laughed. "Hell isn't all about demons and lakes of fire, you know."

"But we do have those here, in abundance," her companion interrupted. "We have all manner of nasty delights, in fact. It's what we do here."

"And just who are you?"

"You'd like to know, would you?" He stepped toward her, running the knuckle of his index finger along her cheek. "Would it please you greatly to know?"

"Not as much as it would please you to withhold that knowledge from me, I gather," Isadora replied, tartly.

The woman laughed a shimmering, sensual laugh. "She's got your number, Pharzie!" She smiled warmly at Isadora. "I am Naamah and this is Pharzuph. We're angels – fallen angels."

Isadora nodded. "A pleasure to meet you."

"We hope so. That *is* what we do here, after a fashion." Naamah's warmth turned predatory and Isadora felt a prickle of warning. "And we have been waiting for you for such a long time."

"Yes, waiting just for you." Pharzuph reached out and took Isadora's hand and led her to the edge of the plateau. "We've been waiting to welcome you home."

The fog below them parted enough that Isadora could see between the thick, gray sheets of it and catch glimpses of the city below and of the glorious and grotesque bridge directly beneath them. The bridge spanned the narrow gap between sharp-rocked shores, guarding that space like a crouching dragon. It shuddered in the bracing wind and groaned before settling back into a dreamy state, its red-gold hide gleaming with rivets. In fact, the great uprights supporting the roadway below were much like half-furled wings.

"Home?" Isadora stared uncomprehendingly downward at the bridge and shifting mists. "I don't understand. This isn't Athens, or Nice, or anywhere in Russia I have ever lived. How can you say this is home? I don't recognize this place."

Pharzuph sighed and Naamah giggled. "See," she told him. "I knew she wouldn't recognize it. But *no*, you wanted to be *dramatic*! Isadora Duncan died in France in nineteen twenty-seven and the Golden Gate, the real one, wasn't even begun until six years after her death!"

Isadora cleared her throat. "If you two don't mind. Are you telling me that we are near San Francisco?"

"*Sin* Francisco," Pharzuph corrected.

"I left this place far behind, a long, long time ago."

"And it has never really forgiven you," Naamah said.

"Come on, then, this was all a waste. His Imperial Majesty is waiting on us." Pharzuph started off down a narrow path leading to the bridge.

Naamah, then Isadora, followed. "His Imperial Majesty? Wait..." Isadora scrambled to keep pace with the two fallen angles, wracking her memory, trying to connect her errant thoughts. "That lunatic in San Francisco who declared himself Emperor of the United States and Protector of Mexico?"

"The very same! He's quite eager to meet you," Naamah said.

"I was..." Isadora did a quick calculation. "...maybe three when he died. I had heard of him as a little girl, but he could not possibly have known of me."

"You have many things yet to learn about hell, my dear," said Pharzuph. "The first thing is that time is not a river, but a rainstorm – it runs every which way and accumulates in the oddest of places.

"And the second thing is," Naamah added, "how to pay a toll." Approaching the bridge, Naamah pressed her hand to her chest, then held it aloft. Something small and brilliant rose from her palm and evaporated into the air.

Pharzuph did the same and the two of them passed between the first set of suspension cables. They waited, a few yards onto the span, the shifting fogs obscuring them, then outlining them.

Alone, at the threshold of the bridge, Isadora waited, wondering if the angels' ritual would work for her. Nothing whispered in her ear to tell her what to do so she followed their lead, placing her hand over her chest and resting it there for a moment. What sort of toll might be required in such a place?

She raised her hand. A tiny light gleamed in her palm and then vanished.

Thereafter she could no longer remember her father's name.

Isadora stepped onto the roadbed, its black, grainy surface felt almost sticky beneath her feet. She paused, savoring the strangeness of the subtle rise and fall, as if the bridge was drawing breath. With each step, scores of tiny ripples chased themselves down the road. She shivered and so did the bridge. All the while, dark shapes slunk beneath the steel-gray waters below, silhouettes of creatures lurking in the depths. Isadora hurried to catch up with the fallen angels who blithely strolled along ahead of her.

Where the Presidio might have been on earth now stood an opulent palace whose twisted spires reached up from surrounding green lawns to pierce the clouds above. Isadora looked from the Victorian cupola to the Moorish arches, marveling at the mishmash of architectural styles.

"Amazing. This palace was conceived of by a madman, yet it has such beauty. I did not expect to see something like this here."

"Hell isn't simply about ugliness," Naamah answered. "There is much here to enjoy."

Isadora didn't believe her, not entirely anyway.

Pharzuph shook his head, chuckling, "You've got a lot to learn."

She squared her shoulders and held her head high, looking Pharzuph in the eye. "I'm a quick study."

The fallen angel whistled through his perfect teeth and wrapped his arms around Isadora. He kissed her with a primal ferocity that made her knees want to buckle. She kept them locked and returned his ardor; temptation flooded her soul.

When they broke apart, Naamah was watching with approval. Isadora straightened her gown and settled her scarf. The two fallen angels appraised her wordlessly.

Isadora met their scrutiny with a frank gaze and said, "Perhaps we should arrange for some privacy, us three?

"What? Not in public? And here I thought you were a performer!" Pharzuph's glance turned suggestive.

Isadora hoped he was as aroused as she.

Naamah cleared her throat, "Before we get too ahead of ourselves, let me remind you, Pharzie, that we have a schedule to keep."

"We *never* get to the good parts," he growled.

"What are you talking about?" Isadora asked.

"Never mind, dear," Naamah said. "Why don't we introduce you to the emperor and perhaps we can adjourn for some festivities later? He has been very patient, you know."

*

The palace was indeed a grand affair, fit for an eccentric emperor, with an interior geometry that made no more sense than its facade and would have entirely confounded the unfamiliar visitor: staircases curving on themselves, walls melting into shadows; doors to nowhere at all. Naamah and Pharzuph were unfazed and led Isadora confidently onward.

The self-styled Emperor of the United States waited for them in a glass-walled room overlooking the city of Sin Francisco. The cityscape was more eye-catching than the unassuming little man in the frumpy coat. Sin Francisco clung to steep hills she remembered from her youth. Parts of the city lay in ruins, crushed and burning as if caught in an eternal April, 1906, the ground quaking and heaving. Elsewhere, cable cars rumbled along their tracks like spiders on a web, their multiple legs pistoning up and down. Nearby, a gaudy neon village glowed amid Victorian mansions.

Closer to hand was the threadbare finery of an old-fashioned red light district, a majestic purple mansion crowning the tallest hill. If this distorted, ridiculous place was in any way like the city of her birth, Isadora realized that she had missed out on a great deal by shunning it. Naamah daintily cleared her throat, prompting Isadora to turn and greet the man who called himself an emperor.

Unsure of what would be proper protocol, she politely inclined her head, murmured "Good day, sir," and waited.

"Isadora Duncan," said the Emperor of the United States and Protector of Mexico Joshua Abraham Norton said, his voice surprisingly light and clear coming from such a gruff exterior. "Welcome. Have you come to dance for me?"

"Is this your city? Do you rule Sin Francisco?"

"As much as I ever did in life. That is, I say that I do and no one argues with me – to my face."

Behind him, the angels exchanged glances.

"Come, come, my dear, dance for me, give an old fool a little excitement. Hell has so few delights!"

Isadora had to laugh. "I know exactly what you mean."

She took a deep breath and brought her arms up, extending them wide in a familiar stretch. She lifted her right leg in a smooth arch and rising up onto the very tip of her left toes, sprang forward into a leap, letting the scarf billow back from her shoulders. She landed lightly, swinging her left leg across her body, propelling herself into a pirouette of fluttering silk. The old, burnished wood beneath her feet had just enough give and just enough grip. She liked the way it felt.

As she came around to face the emperor again, his face alight with utter joy, she thought she saw two children sitting at his feet.

Startled, Isadora caught her foot in the hem of her voluminous skirt and stumbled. She hit the hardwood floor first with her knees, then her elbow and wrist.

The alarmed emperor rushed to her, patting her hand and clucking worriedly. "Oh dear! Are you quite all right?"

"Did you see them? Deirdre and Patrick! They were right here a moment ago, I swear it!" Memories overcame her: dreams of her children's hands in hers, so small and trusting. She could feel the beating of their pulses in time with her own.

"Perhaps you ought to lie down. Trekking around hell can take a toll on the spirit. I'll enjoy your performance another time." He waved at Naamah and Pharzuph.

"He's right, you know," Naamah said. "Let's get you settled where you can have a rest." Naamah gently took Isadora's bruised elbow and helped her to her feet.

Norton rang for a servant, but Naamah shook her head, "I'll take her to the brothel."

"You don't mean –!"

"No, your Imperial Majesty, not to work. We have many private rooms."

"Very well." His smile crimped the leathery flesh around his eyes, "It was a pleasure. It always is."

Confused, Isadora could only nod as her companions led her from the receiving room.

Dancing for a real audience – not a figment of her lonely imagination – had reawakened her hunger to perform. Now this hunger for adulation combined with her desperate need to see her children. To really see her son and daughter, here on this side of death where they all were now. They could be together once more, together for always.

"I don't want to lie down," Isadora's own voice sounded distant, hollow in her ears.

"What would you like, then?" Pharzuph asked the question as if he already knew the answer.

"To dance. To dance so I can see my children again."

"Of course," Naamah said. "What if I said that could be arranged?"

Wary, Isadora drew herself up, away from the fallen angel's helpful touch. "How?"

"A performance, a very special performance," Pharzuph smiled. "How would you like to dance for the Prince of Darkness?"

"Satan? Can he bring me my little ones? Can he reunite us?"

There was that hope again, bruised and bleeding hope that refused to die.

"Hell is His Satanic Majesty's domain," Naamah said. "He can do anything he likes. The trick is convincing him."

"Which can be done," Pharzuph assured them silkily. "But let's have a little respite first, shall we? You shouldn't have danced so soon after your – hiatus."

"No. I can manage. I can dance. I *will* dance. Right now if need be!"

The two angels smiled.

"That won't be necessary, not right this minute," Pharzuph said. Outside, the sky blazed with ruddy light like sunset. He put his arm around Isadora's waist. "Come home with us and get a bit of rest. Tomorrow we'll go and see Satan."

"Tonight," Isadora insisted.

"Tonight," Naamah agreed, "but only after a nap."

"I won't be able to sleep. Please, can we go to the devil now?"

Pharzuph tugged on a loose tendril of her hair and sighed. "To HSM? There's no harm in trying."

Naamah's jaw set sternly. "You mean, right now? Not later tonight? I don't think he's going to like an impromptu encounter. He doesn't appreciate spontaneity"

"Naamah, my dear, this is Isadora Duncan! He'll see her. Why the hell not?"

*

The building they approached looked new, modern with its gravity-defying planes and angles; ancient with its columned marble; intimidating with its brooding presence. The damned and their keepers came and went, astonishing Isadora with their variety – Old Dead, New Dead, demons, fiends: all flocked to this New Hell.

"The Hall of Injustice, rebuilt, more imposing than ever," Naamah told her.

"Indeed," added Pharzuph.

Inside the Hall, long lines of souls waited, some nervous, others haughty, some disfigured, some exquisite and all hoping for an audience that might redeem them.

"I'll handle the secretary," Pharzuph grinned wolfishly and vanished down a nearby corridor.

"So, that's all it takes? Just walking in and telling the lords of hell I'm here to dance? And I'll get to see my children? Just for dancing?"

Naamah studied her a long moment. "Satan works in inscrutable ways, his evils to perform. The damned souls here are here for their just desserts. Each punishment fits the sinner, knowing and unknowing."

"Which am I?"

"I don't honestly know. And you'd think I would by now."

"I don't understand."

She sighed, "Of course not, Isadora, darling."

Pharzuph returned, looking raffish. "This should be a fun go-round."

The lithe fallen angel rustled his white wings and escorted them to a vast meeting room in the belly of hell's proliferate bureaucracy.

Isadora could see two men seated in shadow at the bronze table; their presence dominated the room. Attending them were seven strapping men and a handful of others, making their corner of the spacious area seem cramped.

Without preamble, a sonorous male voice from across the room said, "Dance."

Isadora looked around. "Here?" At least at the emperor's palace there had been grandeur to the room, the semblance of a stage.

A sigh. A snap of fingers. Rumbling from beneath the floor. Then the coffee-stained industrial carpet split apart as a platform rose, seeming too large to fit in that space but there, nonetheless.

Isadora climbed its steps gracefully, then recoiled as she set foot on the stage floor. It was hot.

"You requested something in return for this performance, did you not?"

She squinted into the shadows beyond the sudden footlights that had appeared. "I did," she said.

"Then go on. If you want to see your babies so badly. Or would you rather I bring them here?" A chuckle echoed around her, a mean and hungry chuckle.

She wanted too much to say yes, to demand that her beautiful Deirdre and Patrick be brought to her at once, but the chilling menace of her situation stilled her voice.

This is hell, she thought. *No place for anyone's children.*

Closing her eyes, she drew a deep, calming breath and let it out ever so slowly, ignoring the stares of those around her and an unpleasant tang wafting up from the stage. She took herself back to her dream, back to her summer day and the amphitheater filled with those who loved her. Artists abounded there: Eleonora Duse was there, Mercedes de Acosta, Mary Desti and Mary Cassat, Sergei Yesenin, Paris Singer, Gordon Craig, and her beloved brother Robert. The scalding heat of brimstone below her feet was no more than sun-warmed marble. She relaxed.

When she opened her eyes, Deirdre and Patrick stood before her. Not quite *here*, as she saw them in the dream, watching her from the lip of the stage; no, they were playing in a grassy field filled with blooming flowers. Isadora could smell heady nectar on the breeze. She focused on the floral perfume and not the haunting stink of burning flesh beginning to mingle with the already overpowering odor of sulphur.

Isadora danced.

If only she could step through to where they were – part the veil; walk through a doorway between realities.... Yet no matter how close she came, she was never near enough to touch them. She dared not call out, not knowing if they could see her through this portal or not. She couldn't risk frightening them with a glimpse of her horrendous surroundings and situation.

If only she might escape with them into their world, a world of sunny glades and overwhelming joy. They cavorted carelessly, falling over one another in play. Their nanny drifted by, murmuring kindnesses. In her arms she held Isadora's third child, her tiny baby boy born the day Paris was evacuated for fear of the Germans; born too soon and into too cruel a world, he only ever drew one breath before he went to join his siblings in heaven.

She danced.

Swirling and whirling, now oblivious to what was becoming of her feet, no sacrifice too great to endure for the pleasure and the solace of seeing them. So happy they looked, her beautiful little ones! It was enough to see them, she thought as her legs began to shake with exhaustion and pain. It was enough to know they were safe where no more harm could ever come to them; where happiness was the whole of their existence. It was all she had ever wanted for them.

She danced.

Elegant, lithe movements became plodding and heavy. The blood-soaked hem of her white gown sizzled along the surface of the stage. Finally, her legs gave out completely and she stumbled. Dizzy, her eyes fixed firmly upon her children, Isadora fell, hitting the smoldering floor hard.

The crowd around her gasped and a buzz of concern swept them. She raised one hand for silence and they complied. Getting to her feet was one of the most painful and difficult things Isadora had ever done, but she would not be shamed; not here, where her children could see her. They gazed up at her, adoration on their little faces.

In the front row, two beautiful beings bent their heads together and whispered.

"Neither of them ever tires of this game, do they, Pharzie?" said the woman.

Her companion shrugged. "Eventually, He will, but until then… who knows how many times we'll watch this play out?"

"It always ends the same way."

"And likely, Naamah, it always will."

The female shivered, then smiled. "So we visited Norton the Emperor this time. Where do you want to take her next?"

The other fallen angel shook his head. "I don't know yet. We have a lot of choices. The gala's coming up, you know. I've heard that His Infernal Majesty is sparing no expense for the opening. HSM has Bob Fosse arranging the stage show…."

Isadora felt she should know these two shimmering beings. Her memory of them was hazy, however, enveloped by the pain clawing its way up her legs. When she was finished with this performance, she decided, she would speak to them. They seemed so familiar….

The sun was setting, casting great golden rays onto the amphitheatre's stage, brightening it better than any footlights ever could have. As it did, shadows closed in over the hillside like a curtain falling. Deirdre and Patrick hopped up, clapping madly and hooting and whistling.

On her bloody feet, Isadora took her bow.

Then a brighter light came down through the trees, evaporating the dream. She knew it was a dream now, although the dark, sharp odor of blood and brimstone still lingered in her nostrils. For a moment, she wondered where she was. Vague memories of cable cars and a pair of handsome angels fluttered at the edges of her mind.

Her toes twitched, then spasmed, cramping as they did when the weather turned cold unexpectedly. Isadora sat up. The dream was gone now, fled until night came once more, whenever that might be. She rubbed her aching feet, fingering the calluses and looking out at the vast, lonely wood around her. All was all the same as it always had been, and always would be.

Here was no amphitheatre, no crowd, no Deirdre and Patrick, just a half-shadowed knot of trees and an eternity of loneliness.

"I could endure this if I knew that there might be an end, that my debt might be paid somehow. Even if there was just somewhere else to go, something else to do. Anything would be better than this."

Isadora knew that she was wrong. But she would not, could not, accept it.

"How much longer must I do this?"

There was no answer. And she expected none.

OPHIE AND THE UNDERTAKER

Shebat Legion

Ophelia stood before the Undertaker, waterlogged and unrepentant. "Could beauty, my lord, have better commerce than with honesty?" A slug argued with her tongue and the words, like the girl, were muddied.

The Undertaker said nothing but bent to his task. This was Ophelia's second suicide in hell and she remained stubborn. "He made many tenders of his affection to me," sloshed Ophelia. "I was the more deceived."

*

She admired the newest green-tinged boil on one arm, the rancid moss between her toes, and the oozing fester that had once been her belly button. "Still better and worse," she giggled. Her defiant little face denied the putrescence that oozed from every orifice.

The Undertaker examined the boils that covered her body. The unattractive body odor and furred tongue had not taught her that there was no escape to be found. It was obvious that sterner measures were required.

"Lord, we know what we are, but know not what we may be."

The Undertaker mused and pondered, yes… more boils and her legs taken. Then she could ooze her way back to hell like a snail. He smiled. Yes, like a snail.

"You are merry, my lord," Ophelia bubbled brightly.

The Undertaker shook a finger at her and off she shuffled but back she came like the plague she all too soon resembled.

*

The Undertaker removed her arms and, limbless, her torso slithered across the floor, entrails dragging behind like a floor-scraping wedding gown. He raised his eyebrow in sardonic enquiry.

"I think nothing, my lord," came the cheerful response. "Indeed, la, without an oath, I'll make an end on't!"

*

He cast her out and down so that she might crawl and perhaps accept her fate but alas, and here the Undertaker could not help an amused smile at her reappearance, she was nothing if not tenacious.

"O, what a noble mind is here o'erthrown!" Ophelia burbled and bobbed in primordial fashion.

The Undertaker gave her a thoughtful look.

"And there is pansies. That's for thoughts," offered Ophelia helpfully.

He looked at her silently.

"They say the owl was a baker's daughter," suggested Ophelia.

Without another word, the Undertaker removed her tongue and then, in afterthought, her lips as well.

Ophelia sang, pustular and rebellious, "A-ow a-ow, a oo a hi a-ow-a. O, ow eh ee ee om ii!" (A-down a-down, and you call him a-down-a.)

"Go to hell, Ophelia," the Undertaker said almost kindly.

JUST DESSERT

John Manning

This has got *to be a damned joke!*

James Riddle "Jimmy" Hoffa stared at the parchment held between his thick, shaking hands and fumed.

Nothing had gone right since that meeting in 1975 when he went to the Machus Red Fox, a suburban Detroit restaurant. He'd had a lot of time to think about it down here in hell. He was pretty sure that Frank Fitzsimmons, despite Hoffa's appointing him acting Teamsters president, was behind his kidnapping. Jimmy felt that the interim president had no intention of returning power and had taken steps to make sure it didn't happen. Whoever was behind it had done a perfect job of making sure no one could prove what had happened. He had to admire the beauty of the hit, although he would forever carry his burning hatred for the perpetrators.

When he arrived in hell, he had expected the Dantean landscape so often depicted when he was alive. He was pleasantly surprised, however, to find himself appointed union president and organizer for all of hell's damned souls. Damnation and suffering could take many forms. There was nothing he could promise the workers to improve their lots.

How could he offer healthcare protection when everyone here was dead?

Better working conditions? The purpose of their being here was to suffer for the sins committed in life.

Higher wages? Income was controlled by His Satanic Majesty. How does one negotiate with Satan? And, win?

He couldn't even enforce union dues. He'd tried. When fear of being sent to the Undertaker made some souls pay, the money mysteriously disappeared from his safe. He'd even tried setting up secret accounts only to learn that there were no secrets in hell.

The only people he'd been able to "organize" were the Purple Gang, a Jewish mob that ruled Detroit for a brief period just before his birth – and they were already organized. His "union" was little more than a temp agency. A request – really an order – would come to him from the Hall of Injustice for X number of souls to work at a particular task. Since the damned rarely entered his office looking for a job, he had to send his men out to "kill" the required number. The new recruits usually went to the Undertaker, where they received their new assignments. Sometimes they were sent to him straight from the slab.

It was damned frustrating.

When the Hall of Injustice was destroyed, he'd hoped that things would change. His respite was short-lived. He hadn't counted on Satan's quick rebuilding of the structure.

And now this: His Satanic Majesty was holding a gala event to celebrate the Library's grand Reopening and Rededication as the "Hellexandria Memorial Library" for which Jimmy was "asked" to provide cooks, waiters, dishwashers, valets and security for the party. The wax seal at the bottom of the document made it clear that it was not a request.

He thought for a moment. Security was easy. He'd put Abe Axler and Eddie Fletcher in charge of that. They were good, dependable muscle even if they weren't strictly family or even from Detroit. He'd brought them from New York for the Cleaners and Dyers War. The Miraflores Massacre – the killing of three hired assassins who had double-crossed the gang – took place in Axler and Fletcher's apartment. Both men had been arrested for the murders and for the extortion in the war, but neither was convicted. They were perfect for this job.

Who should he put in charge of the servers? Hoffa thought for a moment, and then smiled. Ray Bernstein, Harry Keywell, and Irving Milberg could keep them in line and provide backup for Axler and Fletcher if they needed it. He scribbled a few notes on a pad.

What about the kitchen crews? The cooks, the dishwashers, and the bus staff? Also the valets? He leaned back and tented his fingers as he considered other gang members and their talents.

*

Heinrich Himmler, Eduard Weiter, Wernher von Braun, Alfried Krupp, and Josef Mengele stood in a close knot in the aisle, blocking the Undertaker's passage.

"Who is this Hoffa person we must report to?" Mengele looked at the scrap of parchment in his hand and back up to the imposing figure cloaked in an ebon robe.

Red eyes glared coldly from beneath the black cowl as the Arbiter of Restoration regarded him coldly. "He is the damned soul you must report to for your next assignment," the being's voice was a raspy hiss. "I suggest that you do so now. Waste more of my time and I will put you to the back of the line."

The Undertaker turned right, his robe hissing like angry snakes as he strode slowly between two rows of body-covered slabs that stretched in both directions until they joined in the distance.

"Entschuldigen Sie bitte!" whispered a voice from the left. "Excuse me, please."

The five Nazis stepped aside to allow a large iron cart to slowly trundle past them. The thick, five-spoked metal wheels ground against the stone floor. The unlubricated axles gave off a horrendous, shrieking squeal – as of hundreds of souls crying out in unending agony. The cart was four feet wide, five feet deep, and eight feet long. Arms, legs, hands, feet, heads, and torsos – all colors and genders – lay jumbled within the black compartment. Brownish-red stains spattered and streaked the dark, flat surfaces.

A damned soul, his face and body emaciated as if from extreme starvation, slowly pushed the cart from behind. His wrists were manacled to its handle. Rust-encrusted spikes lined the inside of the metal bands constantly slicing into his wrists. A metal frame was attached to his shoulders and chest and extended in front of him. Tilted slightly back, so that the condemned could always see its contents, was a filthy metal bowl filled with an unsightly and foul-smelling greenish goop – to call it porridge or soup would be to stretch the meaning of either – forever out of reach of the starving soul's mouth.

An iron belt encircled his waist. There was no visible joining to show how it had been fastened. Eyebolts jutted from the front of the band – two over the left leg, two over the right. A heavy chain hung from each ring; the far end of each was attached to an iron ball approximately eight inches in circumference. Spikes and blades covered the lower hemisphere of each. The metal balls hung suspended less than an inch from the floor. Each step the damned soul took caused the balls to pendulum across his feet. Bloody footprints marked his passage through the aisle.

A pair of hellhounds paced him, maintaining a three-foot interval behind him. As they passed the five men, the beasts' heads turned toward them. Both uttered deep-throated, guttural growls before returning their attention to the damned soul shuffling in front of them.

Weiter looked closely at the man's face as he passed.

"Herr Zill!" he shouted. Weiter looked at the others. "I know this man. His name is Egon Zill. He was the last commandant of the Dachau work camp."

The figure continued to push the cart, showing no sign that he heard the shout. Weiter darted towards the trudging soul. "Egon! It is me, Eduard!"

The hellhounds turned their heads. Warning growls rumbled from deep within their throats. Their neck hair bristled, but the animals made no move to attack as he came abreast. Now close, he knew he'd been right. The face was gaunt, with deep vertical lines running from hairline to jawline. His milky eyes looked dully out from beneath bushy eyebrows. Gray stubble covered his face. His thin, parched lips moved; his voice little more than a faint whisper. Weiter leaned closer as he tried to make out what Zill was saying.

"Hava nagila, hava nagila, hava nagila ve-nismeha." (Let us rejoice, let us rejoice, let us rejoice and be happy.)

Stunned, Weiter stopped for a moment, staring at the man's slowly retreating back. Zill had been the most anti-Semitic of them all! What could possibly make him sing a Jewish song of celebration? The man's mind was obviously broken. There could be no other explanation.

Weiter rushed forward, again. "Egon! Egon, speak to me."

Zill stopped singing. He turned his head slightly toward Weiter, but never stopped his steady shuffling. Behind him, the dogs growled and stepped closer. "Eduard," he whispered, "I dare not stop. *Bitte* – please – do not interfere."

"But, Egon…" he said as he grabbed the man's upper arm.

He paused. The dogs leaped forward, attacking Zill from behind. He screamed, the horrible sound echoing from the stone walls as the hellhounds fought to get at his genitals. He sagged forward, but his manacles kept him from falling to the floor.

"Leave me!" he screamed.

Zill struggled to his feet despite the dogs' relentless mauling. He slid his right foot forward, then his left. As his slow shuffling resumed and the cart lurched forward, the hounds ceased their attack and resumed their places behind him. As the gap between them grew, Eduard heard Egon's ragged, whispery voice: *"Hava nagila…"*

*

The diner was smoke-filled and noisy. The usual crowd of assorted damned souls were bellied up to the narrow bar or seated at the tables that dotted the scuffed and stained wooden floor. Yellow oil lamps hung from the rafters. The owner, a former pro football player, had learned not to depend on electric lights in hell. Helledison Power and Light was frequently plagued with brown outs and outages.

Instead of a mirror behind the bar, for none of the customers cared to see their own reflections, a large banner bearing a blue lion on a silver background covered the wall behind the various bottles of liquor. Despite the labels and myriad shapes, the liquid contents all had the same vile taste. Worse, those imbibing the beverages – no matter how much they drank – could not get drunk although they were guaranteed a hangover the next morning.

Scantily-clad servers – some male, some female, and some indeterminate – circulated through the room bearing trays laden with drinks, plates of food, or empty vessels for return to the kitchen.

The front door opened. A muscular man of medium height, his brown hair hanging to his shoulder blades, entered and then paused, his intense eyes searching the crowd. They widened as he smiled and worked his way through the patrons and servers until he reached a table near the far wall.

"I think I've found a way." Matthew Hopkins sat down on a wooden chair across the warped table from his long-time friend and fellow witch finder, John Stearne. He winced as the inevitable splinter jabbed him in the buttocks.

John looked up from the congealing morass on his cracked dinner plate. "A way to do what?"

Matthew looked around and then leaned forward. He spoke in a low, conspiratorial whisper. "A way to leave hell. A way to get to heaven, where we belong."

"Not that, again." Stearne lifted his fork, its tines twisted and pointing everywhere but straight ahead, trying to find a way to put the unpalatable substance into his mouth without stabbing his tongue, lips, or palate. "We've been down here for – well – forever, it seems. Haven't you learned, yet, that there is no getting out of here? It's a fool's dream, Matthew. Give it up." Resigned to the unavoidable, he lifted the fork to his mouth, wincing as a tine ripped his upper lip.

At least the blood improves the flavor, he thought as he swallowed after only chewing a couple of times. He'd learned to keep the food in his mouth as short a time as possible if he hoped to retain it.

"I'm serious, John," Matthew insisted. "I think I have it all figured out."

Stearne looked at his friend, sighed, and then set his fork on the plate and pushed it away from him. He couldn't force another bite past his lips anyway. He leaned back in his chair. Hopkins looked agitated, intense. His eyes shone with a feverish light. John sighed again. When Matthew was like this, it was best to let him say what he was thinking. Once the man's zeal ran its course, John would calmly and patiently explain the weaknesses of his friend's latest half-baked idea.

"Okay, Matthew, what's your plan *this* time?"

Despite his excitement, Hopkins paused to gather his thoughts.

"I've always maintained that we were sent here by mistake," he began.

"You've been insisting on that for centuries. And I always ask you if you think, out of all of those hundreds of people we had executed for trafficking with Satan, that it might be possible we got a few innocents by mistake."

Matthew shook his head. "No," he insisted. "The tests were infallible. The women who did the pricking were experienced and professional. They performed their duties without malice and with the guidance of God Almighty. The confessions they obtained were valid. We brought no innocents to trial."

"So, Matthew, how many have you seen since we've been down here? Surely, after all of these years, we should have seen a few." John held onto his drink as the table shook with the tremors engendered by Matthew's epithet.

"I'm certain that *His Satanic Majesty…*" he replied, his voice dripping with sarcasm "…has a special place for those who served him well."

John shook his head and sipped from his cup. He made a face and shivered. Coffee, tea, water, milk, or alcohol, it all tasted like excrement liberally seasoned with a rotten egg and stale beer.

"What I didn't understand until now, however, was that I had it all wrong. There's a reason the Almighty…" Matthew paused, waiting for the room to stop shaking "...sent us here instead of... up there."

"You watch your language in here!"

Both men looked up. And, up. And, up. The man standing at the end of their table was a veritable mountain of rock hard flesh. His black skin gleamed in the yellow glow of oil lamps. A tattered jersey of Honolulu blue and silver hung from his massive shoulders. The remains of a number, now shredded and illegible, swung forward and back against his chest with every breath he took. Tight argent pants – the silver sheen dulled by old dirt, grass stains, dried blood, and other unidentifiable smears – hugged his hips and upper legs like a second skin. Tattered white socks with blue bands at the top covered his calves. Huge, black, cleated shoes completed the ensemble.

"This here's my place. I run an indecent establishment. Don't plan t' lose m' permits just 'cause people like you can't watch your tongues. Keep swearin' like that and I'll hit you so hard the Undertaker won't know what part goes where." He bent down until both men were eye level with him. "Unnerstand?" He straightened and turned toward the bar, his cleats clacking on the wooden floor.

Stearne watched the owner's retreating back and then turned to his friend. "Look, Matthew. You've got to learn to watch your mouth. You'd think you'd have learned *something* after all of this time. The food here is garbage, the drinks are swill, but I like this place. If you get us thrown out of *this* one, I won't be responsible for my actions."

"Fine. It doesn't matter, anyway. Not anymore."

"Maybe not to you..."

"Will you just shut up for a moment and hear me out?"

John stared at Hopkins for a moment, then sighed and leaned back in his chair. "Okay, Matthew. What has you so fired up this time?"

Hopkins leaned forward. "You know about that big gala coming up, right?"

John nodded. "The re-opening of the library? Who doesn't?"

"This is what we've been waiting for – a chance to do something to get us into…" Hopkins paused, looked around, and then whispered "…you know where."

"Okay. I'll bite. What's this grand opportunity?"

"It's a chance to assassinate His Infernal Majesty. We do that, they *gotta* take us up to…" he glanced over his shoulder and then hurried on "…up there." The last two words were a hoarse whisper.

Stearne stared at his friend. Suddenly, he burst out laughing. "Have you been hanging out at the Chinese hells, again? Standing a little close to the opium smoke?"

"I'm serious, John."

After a few moments, Stearne's laughter subsided into chuckles as he wiped tears from the corners of his eyes. "Now I know you've been down here too long. It's been tried. And, it always failed. Always. Remember the explosion that took down the Hall of Injustice and the first library? That really worked well, didn't it? The new one's more impressive than the one they destroyed."

"This time it *will* work, John."

Stearne choked down another swallow of tea – or whatever it was. "You have a plan that will work where a massive explosion couldn't? I have got to hear this."

"Have you ever heard of the *Spear of Longinus*?"

"Who hasn't? Word on the street is that Satan's sent teams out looking for it."

Hopkins waved his hand in dismissal. "Wild goose chase."

"Oh, really? And, how do you know this?"

"Because I have the *real* one back in my room."

John raised one eyebrow. "Just how did you manage that?"

"I bought it from a woman named Madame Blavatsky who runs a rare artifact shop in the seedier part of New Hell."

"Matthew, Matthew, Matthew," John said, shaking his head. "You've been had."

"I knew you'd say that," Hopkins replied softly, "but, I checked it out personally."

"Oh? And which fallen angel did you test it on?"

"I'm not stupid, John. That would attract unwanted attention." Matthew looked around before continuing. "I know what the spear looks like. I know how it's supposed to feel. I even let Madame Blavatsky try to stab me with a knife while I held the spear. The blade sank all the way into my side, yet there was no blood, no wound – my shirt was not even holed. It made me invincible."

"Maybe the knife wasn't real."

"I tested it before I let her use it," Hopkins insisted. "I stabbed one of those poppets she sells as voodoo dolls. It went completely through it."

"Are you sure she didn't switch knives before she stabbed you?"

"Positive. I kept my hand wrapped around hers the whole time."

John thought for a long moment, and then said, "Assuming the spear is real, how do you propose to get close enough to Satan to use it? The gala is by invitation only."

"I have a plan for that, too. The Purple Gang is on the streets recruiting souls to work at the party."

"Everyone knows about the way they recruit. How does going to the Undertaker's slab help with this plan?"

Hopkins shook his head. “No, John. We don’t wait to be rounded up and killed. We go straight to Hoffa’s place and volunteer to be waiters. When we serve His Infernal Majesty his meal, we deliver it with the cold iron point of the spear.”

*

Despite the absence of its proprietor, Anton LaVey, Hellish Curiosities & Clothiers was experiencing a booming business, especially in religious artifacts. The growing fear of the auditors from on high was fueling desperation in the damned souls terrified of losing what they had gained during their time in hell. And Madame Helena Blavatsky, Anton’s assistant, was more than happy to provide whatever they wanted – for the right price, of course.

She locked the front door and crossed the main show room. Display cases full of trinkets and baubles, scarves, folded banners, and other knick-knacks gleamed in the shop’s wan illumination. She passed through a doorway into the back room where the “rare” items were kept. A pile of freshly-printed “Get Out of Hell Free” cards lay nestled in a wooden box. Special clothing: shirts, trousers, socks, coats, ties, and ascots – all bearing a faint, sepia-colored outline of a face – were neatly hung or stacked or folded within a lockable wardrobe. A metal box lay on another shelf, this container full of splinters of “the one, true cross” supposedly used to crucify that carpenter from Nazareth.

The crowning glory, however, stood stacked in a corner near the shelves – seven spears, each bearing a nail near the tip and wrapped in gold leaf in the middle. She’d sold three this week; one this very afternoon. That last had been a bit of a hard sell. He’d insisted on testing the weapon. Fortunately, she had a stiletto with a hidden button and a weak spring.

When he stabbed the doll with the open blade, it easily cut through the burlap poppet. He then handed her the knife and demanded that she thrust it into his side. She hesitated just enough to allay his suspicions, and then stabbed him, depressing the button at the last second. Of course, the blade slid quietly into the handle, doing no harm to the customer. She kept the button depressed as she pulled the knife back.

Satisfied, the customer excitedly paid the fifteen thousand diablos she asked. She frowned. She could probably have gotten twenty thousand just as easily. No matter. When that supercilious Satanist returned, she'd show him who could sell snake oil to a snake. LaVey had only charged ten thousand – and that was for the *real* spear, the fool.

*

Hoffa looked around at the assemblage of souls sitting in the cramped, schoolroom desks that lined the spacious room. Most were busily filling out the forms handed to them earlier with the thick, grade school pencils each was given. All but three were here courtesy of the Undertaker, most with the able assistance of his "recruiters." As he scanned the room, he tried to mentally assign them to the various positions he needed to fill for the upcoming Grand Reopening and Dedication gala.

Movement from a desk near the far door drew his attention. The desk legs screeched against the floor as a woman stood, sliding it to one side. As she started walking toward him, Hoffa resisted the urge to run.

The woman, an ancient crone, wore no clothing. Her aged breasts sagged to her navel. Something writhed obscenely in her gray, matted pubic hair. Hoffa tried not to look, but the movement was sickeningly sensual. Her wrinkled skin and face looked like a topographical map of an ancient, dried up delta. Branded on her breasts in ruddy, inflamed letters were the words: *Welcome Woman.*

She stopped within inches of a trembling Hoffa. He wanted to shut his eyes, to banish this apparition from his sight, but to no avail. The stench of dead marine life, old semen, and unwashed flesh assaulted his nostrils. Of all of the females in hell, only the Welcome Woman could make a damned soul ejaculate. Of course, it was without the pleasure of orgasm and only if she felt it would add to the pain.

Oh, God, he thought. *Please don't let her touch me.*

The Welcome Woman smiled, a blackish-yellow, gap-toothed grin, and cackled, "You are thinking bad thoughts, Mr. Jimmy Hoffa. Be careful. It is not necessary to vocalize in hell to receive punishment."

Hoffa swallowed hard, but the rock in his throat refused to budge. He finally managed to croak, "Wha – what c-can I d-do for you, M-madam?"

She slapped the forms and pencil against his chest. "Unlike the damned souls fouling this room, I work directly for His Satanic Majesty. I am not here for you to assign me to any position. I am merely telling you that His Infernal Majesty has directed me to serve as the hostess for this event. It will be my job to welcome the attendees and ensure that they are directed to the appropriate places." With her other hand she stabbed a gnarled talon through the papers and into his chest. "You have no authority over me. You are not to assign a damned soul – New Dead or Old – to such an important task. Do we understand each other?"

Hoffa, who'd been trying not to inhale since asking his question, merely nodded. The Welcome Woman glared into his eyes a moment longer and then, without a word, did an about face and stalked toward the door. He watched, his face nearly purple, until the door closed behind her. He took a deep breath, his chest expanding in one giant spasm that he immediately regretted as he doubled over coughing and wheezing. His eyes watered and his nose ran. She was gone, but her essence lingered.

After several moments he regained control of his breathing. He wiped his nose on the only thing handy – his shirt sleeve. His thick hands rubbed the tears from his eyes as he looked around the room. Everyone seated looked as ill as he felt. A few – those who had sat near her – were writhing on the floor. The stench of feces and vomit added their fragrances to the palpable cloud that still filled the room.

The ceiling fans chose that moment to fail in a spectacular shower of sparks. Everyone bolted through the door and into the hallway beyond, falling to their knees outside and gulping in air like landed fish. Never had the atmosphere of hell smelled so sweet.

An hour later, with most of the stench cleared, Hoffa sat behind his desk, a stack of papers lying to the right of the faded, olive-colored desk blotter. Five smaller bundles were arrayed in front of him. He looked up at the five men standing at attention before him. The sickly yellow light shone on his black, slicked back hair. His blockish face and fleshy cheeks belied his German ancestry. Dark, penetrating eyes assessed the men. All wore ragged suits. Skin hung like limp flags from their faces and hands. Each had an angry-looking swastika burned into their skin – a brand that glowed clearly even though covered with clothing.

The Undertaker must've been really swamped when these guys came through, he thought. *How am I supposed to use them for Satan's big shindig? Can't use them as waiters. Rumor has it that HSM is going to allow the food to be enjoyable for this one night. If these guys serve it, a lot of people are gonna lose their appetites. That is, if seeing the Welcome Woman when they come in doesn't do it first.*

"Gentlemen," he spoke, his voice a harsh, Midwestern twang, "do you know why the Undertaker sent you to me?"

"*Nein*, Herr Hoffa," responded the one on the end.

Hoffa glanced at the papers: Himmler, Heinrich. He frowned. That name was familiar. He looked at all of the names once more: Himmler, Weiter, von Braun, Krupp, and Mengele. While he couldn't place Weiter or Krupp, the other three were Nazi officers in the Second World War – two were war criminals. That made it a good bet that the other two were Nazis as well. That explained the brands.

"Can any of you cook?"

No one answered.

Probably just as well, Hoffa thought as he pressed a button on the Sintercom. A sound like mating cats shrieked from the device's speaker. He slapped it once and the noise subsided. "Find Izzy and tell him to come to my office." A screeching yowling answered him from the box. He slapped it again, much harder, and the device went silent. He shook his head in disgust. Nothing down here worked the way it was supposed to. Nothing.

"As you probably know, the Hall of Injustice, along with the library, was recently destroyed in an explosion. Of course, His Satanic Majesty rebuilt the whole thing and it is now ready for a grand re-opening party. I am supposed to supply the cooks, waiters, and other staff to cater this gala event."

"What has this to do with us?" Himmler interjected. "We are not menials – not servants to wait on other people. We are Aryans. Others serve us. That is the natural order of things."

Hoffa groaned inwardly. He felt the beginning of a headache.

"Look, pal," he growled. "In case you forgot, the Third Reich ended. We kicked your asses and split your country in two. You ain't the master race anymore. This is hell. You go where you're sent and you do what you're told." He pulled a pistol from a desk drawer and leveled it at the man. "Otherwise, I send you back to the Undertaker. I'm sure he'll find you an even shittier assignment. Which way do you want it?"

The memory of Egon Zill pushing the cart behind the Undertaker flashed through Himmler's mind. He sighed. "The pistol will not be necessary, Herr Hoffa. We will do as you say."

Hoffa stared hard at Himmler for a moment, then lowered the gun and placed it back in the drawer. "I'm glad we understand each other. Now, as I was saying..." He paused as someone knocked on the office door.

"Who is it?" he called out.

The door opened half-way. A narrow face peeked through the opening. "It's Izzy, Boss. You wanted to see me?"

"Yeah. Come on in. You're right on time."

A slender man in a pale, ill-fitting gray suit entered. As he turned to close the door, he removed his fedora revealing a full head of dark hair. He walked up to Hoffa's desk, ignoring the men standing before it. "What's up, Boss?"

"Izzy, I want you to meet some of your new dishwashers and kitchen help for the shindig."

The newcomer turned, looked at each man, and then faced Hoffa again. "This the best you could do? Couldn't get no coloreds?"

Hoffa spread his hands. "You know how it is. I take what the Undertaker sends me." He looked at the five Nazis. "Gentlemen, here is your new boss for this job. His name is Izzy Bernstein and you'd better do what he says. He's got kind of a short fuse."

Mengele's eyes narrowed. "Bernstein? That name sounds *Jude* – Jewish. You want us to take orders from a Jew?"

Izzy whirled, grabbed the German by his throat, and lifted him until his torn shoes dangled six inches above the floor. "You got a problem with Jews?"

Mengele tried to respond, but all that emerged was a strangled mutter.

"Like I said," Hoffa chuckled, "a *very* short fuse."

*

Hoffa looked around at the immense ballroom and shook his head. The Library's Grand Plaza level on the ground floor of the Tower of Injustice was huge by human standards, but this space was far larger than what the outer walls should have permitted. Only His Satanic Majesty could make the inside larger than the outside by a factor of at least ten. Yet, when Jimmy toured the room, the distances he walked from station to station seemed no farther than they should have. His mind balked at what his eyes and legs told it.

He could tell by their facial expressions that even the Old Dead were impressed by the room's grandeur. Massive chandeliers – the crystal carved into leering demonic faces – hung from the towering vaulted ceiling. Round tables, covered in white silk embroidered with scarlet, ebon, and gold lace and capable of seating eight people comfortably, stretched in all directions – far more tables than it should have been possible to accommodate. Place settings of bone china, the edges chased in gold filigree, were laid on the table before each chair. Napkins of fine Egyptian linen stood in gracefully-folded spires on each plate while polished silver utensils flanked each setting. On the plates, before each napkin, rested a bi-fold silver placard bearing the name of a guest in flowing black script.

The floor – white marble chased with red and black striations – shone like a stone mirror and reflected the golden beams that arched to their meeting in the central dome high above the dining tables.

A red and black dais rose from the center of the room on a pyramid of red and black stone. Atop was a massive table. An ebon throne, decorated in a skull and bones motif, dominated the center of one side and was flanked by six lesser thrones on either side in a manner reminiscent of da Vinci's painting, The Last Supper. His Satanic Majesty sat in the middle, his massive wings unfurled behind him, which was somewhat disconcerting in contrast to the charcoal Armani suit he wore. Lesser fallen angels filled the remaining seats. A bat-winged, catlike creature sat on its haunches atop Satan's right shoulder, its baleful yellow eyes surveying the crowd with hateful amusement. Occasionally it would sink its needle teeth into HSM's neck or the top of a wing.

Hoffa suddenly realized that no matter where he stood in the room, the personages on the dais faced him. A cold shiver raced down his spine as he thought, *I'll be so glad when this shindig is over.*

Satisfied that all were in their proper places and that things were going smoothly, Jimmy returned to the front, where the Welcome Woman was courteously greeting the steady flow of arrivals.

WW was a pleasant surprise. Expecting the worst, Hoffa had entered the ballroom an hour earlier, inwardly cringing as he approached the hostess's station. Hell's principle greeter wore a simple Asian shift, tight-fitting, of red silk with a black and gold dragon embroidered in a long curl, its tail on her right thigh, the serpentine body flowing in a graceful S across her torso and ending with the gape-mouthed head at her right shoulder. Her hair was dyed black and done in Geisha-fashion, complete with two white sticks protruding from the bun at the back of her head. Surprisingly, her makeup was artfully applied, somehow masking many of the furrows that normally covered her face. Despite the trappings, however, she was still the Welcome Woman.

Like polishing a turd, he thought as he watched her greet another group and turn them over to their respective guides. As she ushered the party past him, she glanced over her shoulder. Icy venom stabbed at him from her narrowed eyes.

Hoffa shook his head. *Why did HSM insist that I supervise the main party? Why not a lesser one elsewhere in New Hell?*

*

"Okay. Everything's set," Matthew Hopkins whispered to his friend, John Stearne, as they quickly placed entrees on the trays for the waiters to take to the diners.

"What's set?" So far, they had done nothing but push food out the window as fast as the cooks behind them could have it ready. He was tired and more than a little cranky with Matthew's plan.

"I've arranged for us to serve the dessert to the main table."

John stopped and stared at his friend. "Have you seen the dessert? Do you know what it is?"

Hopkins shrugged. "I haven't seen it. It's supposed to be baked Alaska, whatever that is."

"I saw it," Stearne said with a shudder. "I had to go into the walk-in freezer for more hellbeast haunch for one of the chefs."

"So?"

"It's not baked Alaska," John hissed. "It's a baked *Alaskan.* It's someone named London. That's what one of the *sous* chefs told me, anyway."

"Oh, dear God!"

A heavy spoon struck Hopkins on the back of his head; the sound reverberated despite the kitchen's raucous clatter. Matthew grabbed the counter to keep from falling to his knees. Bright pinpoints of light danced before his eyes. He turned, shaking his head to clear his vision. A lesser demon glowered at him from near the prep table.

"I ain't warnin' you again!" the creature snarled. "Keep usin' profanity like that an' I'm sendin' you straight to the Undertaker, I don't care *how* short-handed it makes us. Now, git back to work an' quit yammerin' before I do it anyway." One of his four taloned hands brandished a cleaver meaningfully.

The two worked silently for the next hour. When the last of the entrees were pushed through the window and the trays whisked away, Stearne leaned back, wiped his brow with a nearby cloth, and looked around. Satisfied that the demon was nowhere near, he whispered, "I have a bad feeling about this plan of yours."

"You always have a bad feeling about my plans."

"Are you absolutely sure about that spear?"

"Yes," Hopkins rasped in exasperation. "I told you. I tested it thoroughly. It's the real thing."

"I've heard that there are worse fates than being sent to the Undertaker."

"Don't worry," Matthew placed a reassuring hand on John's shoulder. "Our fate – our reward – lies in another direction."

"That is precisely what worries me."

*

Demetrius stood on the middle step of the five rising from the floor to the dais, his arms stretched wide as he waited for silence in the crowded dining room. His white toga, with its gold filigree trim, shone brightly in the flickering candlelight from the chandeliers. When he was satisfied that it was as quiet as a gathering this size could be, he spoke, his melodic baritone voice carrying over the remaining sounds.

"Ladies and gentlemen, Old Dead and New, denizens and condemned, I wish to thank you for being here tonight to help us celebrate our grand re-opening and dedication."

He paused to let the applause fade before continuing. He turned to the assemblage seated at the table atop the dais. "I wish to thank His Satanic Majesty for his generosity, his graciousness, and his magnificence in allowing all of us to enjoy the wonderful food and drink that he has provided us this evening."

Satan tipped his head slightly as the applause thundered in the room. He stood, spread his arms, and nodded to the crowd. When he sat, the clapping slowed and Demetrius continued.

"I would also like us to show our gratitude to Mister James Hoffa and his staff for all that they have done to prepare and serve this wonderful bounty in safety and peace."

Another round of applause – less loud and of shorter duration – rose in answer. As the noise settled, a loud ping sounded from the far end of the hall. Elevator doors opened revealing two men in immaculate servers' uniforms. They stepped out, a large cart between them. Atop the cart was a six foot long, silver serving dish with an ornately decorated cover nearly three feet high. The doors closed silently behind them. Demetrius signaled for the men to bring the cart to the dais and then turned to address the dignitaries behind him.

"My lords, while other servers bring desserts to your waiting guests, these two men bear a surprise dessert prepared especially for you. It is my understanding that preparing this unique confection was particularly difficult to accomplish given hell's harsh environment. Yet, the chefs felt that a lesser effort would not show you the honor and respect that you so richly deserve."

Behind him the cart trundled silently to a stop. The men stood at attention at either end. Demetrius nodded to them and then turned to the dais once more.

"My lords, I beg that you enjoy this wonderful treat – a baked Alaska formed as a life sized effigy of Jack London – that it may please your..."

The ringing of the heavy silver lid as it fell to the marble floor interrupted the rest of Demetrius' speech. A man's loud, feral scream filled the room as footsteps raced past the librarian and up to the dais.

"This is all the dessert you rate, foul demon!" Matthew shrieked as he drove the point of the spear toward Satan's unprotected chest. "Taste the Spear of Destiny and choke upon its glory!"

Deafening silence descended on the room for several seconds as everyone stared in shock at the drama unfolding on the dais. Hopkins locked eyes with the devil. Satan smiled. Hopkins felt the first stirrings of fear in his stomach. The smile turned into a chuckle; the chuckle a guffaw. Deep rolling laughter filled the hall as Matthew stared at the end of the spear now curled back upon itself. Where his sweaty hands had slipped down the shaft the gilt band was smeared away revealing an inscription: *Product of Brimstone Arsenal.*

Icy terror wrapped its frigid hand around Hopkins as he looked into Satan's glowing eyes once more. Hot wetness filled his crotch as he realized that the devil was no longer laughing.

"Oh, what fools you mortals be," the Lord of Hell whispered to him. He gestured with his left hand. Hopkins and Stearne were no longer in the room.

"My lord...," Demetrius began.

Satan waved him to silence. "A moment of unexpected entertainment," he told the librarian. "Nothing more. Fret not, faithful servant. I blame you not. Let the festivities continue."

Demetrius bowed. "Yes, your magnificence."

*

"I don't understand," Matthew wailed as he sat naked on the stony plain. "I tested it."

Stearne – also nude – paced in a tight circle behind him. "She tricked you. She saw you for the fool that you are and played you like a harpsichord. Accept it."

"But..."

"But, nothing." John stopped pacing and gestured at the landscape surrounding them. "We need to figure out where in hell we are and what's going to happen next."

Hopkins looked up. The distant horizon in every direction ended in sheer cliffs. Obsidian chips and chunks of basalt littered the flat ground. Jagged fissures zig-zagged across the barren ground. Steam and red-orange light drifted upward from the cracks and filled the air with the noxious odors of rotten eggs and putrefying flesh.

"Looks like the Plain of Meggido after the final battle," he replied.

"We should be so lucky."

A faint ping sounded behind them. Matthew rose to his feet and both men turned toward the sound. A naked female figure walked slowly toward them.

"Hello, boys," a familiar voice floated across the diminishing space.

"Oh, no," whispered Hopkins.

"I told you I had a bad feeling about your plan," John said as he stepped backward.

"The gala was fun, if you like that kind of shindig," the Welcome Woman told them as she walked slowly closer. "Now it's time for the *real* party to begin. HSM told me you're going to be with me for a *very* long time." Her gap-toothed smile widened as she opened her arms. "Come to Momma, boys. I've always wanted to have a threesome."

*

"So, Izzy, how'd it go in the kitchen?" Hoffa leaned back in his chair. The party had finally ended and he was exhausted, but glad to be back in his office once more.

"Mostly good, Boss," the gangster replied. "The cooks knew their stuff. I didn't have to tell them nothin'. They got in there an' got right to work. They put out some good chow, too. I got to eat all I wanted cuz I was in the kitchen.

"The coloreds and spics you got for me at the last minute worked out pretty good, too. They bussed the tables an' cleaned the crap offa th' dishes without makin' much of a fuss. 'Course, it helped that most of th' plates that came back was almost clean enough t' put away without washin'."

"And, the Nazis?" Hoffa held up four sealed envelopes. "Didn't they want their pay?"

"Them Nazis was somethin' else, Boss. They bitched all night 'bout workin' for Jews. Kept talkin' 'bout how much better things was durin' the Third Reich an' all. Even talked about what they planned t' do to you once everything was done with the party. I finally had a belly full, so when they was close t' done with all the dishes and kitchen stuff, I went out an' got Eddie, Harry, an' Abe."

"What did you need them for?"

"I'm getting' to that, Boss. One of th' Nazis – that von Braun guy – he wasn't like the others. He kept pretty much to himself an' did his job, so when they was done, I gave him his envelope an' sent him on his way."

"And, the others?"

"Well, Boss, it's like this. There were these ovens we couldn't turn off..."

HELL, I MUST BE GOING

Michael A. Ventrella

Margaret shook her head. No, no. This would not do at all.

Pulling herself to her full height, she marched down the hallway, clipboard tucked against her ample bosom.

Ever since that new administrator had been installed – and over her wishes! – the paperwork coming from the Department of Hellish Assignments had dwindled to nothing. So, of course, it fell on her to once again clean up someone else's mess. What was that lazy bum's name again?

She glanced at the notes on her clipboard. *Rufus T. Firefly?*

She stood, staring at the name. Surely that couldn't be right.

Then again, this was hell. Stranger things were seen every day.

With a snort, she stepped forward, taking long, purposeful strides. No silly name would thwart her quest.

Margaret had died in the Year of Our Lord 1872. Positions of power that remained unobtainable for her gender at that time had eventually been provided in Hell – although perhaps not as quickly as among the living. Still, she couldn't complain. Her current assignment gave her sufficient responsibility for her talents, and she consistently proved her worth to those around her.

Nevertheless, obstacles remained. Her supervisor hounded her, and often made jokes behind her back. Well, she assumed they were jokes. She never quite understood them...

Work cubicles were filled with beautiful young women who typed away furiously at their computers and sorted papers with alacrity as she passed, only to visibly relax once they felt she was out of range.

She slowed her pace as she approached a reception area. A large oaken door, cracked from the constant heat, contained a traditional smoked glass window hiding the activity within. The name of the previous occupant had been unprofessionally scraped off and replaced with an announcement in sloppy red paint: "Rufus T. Firefly, President for Life. If You Can Call This 'Life'."

Margaret's nostrils expanded. She tilted her head, lifted her clipboard, and made a note, using perfect penmanship.

Tinny music filtered through the door.

She raised her hand and daintily tapped on the glass.

A sharp ripping sound cut the music instantly. Shuffling noises filled the next few seconds, and then footsteps.

The door opened a crack. A dark fellow with expressive eyes stared at her. When he spoke, it was with a slight Italian accent. "What's the password?"

Margaret stood tall and harrumphed. "Good sir, I am Marg –"

The door slammed shut.

Her mouth slimmed to a delicate line as her eyes bored holes into the door. She made another note and then rapped the window again, this time with more force.

The man peeked out, "Password?"

"Now see here –"

"No, that's-a not it, either. I'm sorry, lady, but you can't come in here unless-a you say 'swordfish.'"

Slam.

Margaret let out a long, lady-like exhale. Fine. If that's what these clowns wanted...

She tapped three times against the glass.

"Password?"

"I do believe it is 'Swordfish.'"

"All right, you can come in." The fellow opened the door and waved his hand for entry.

The room was a mess. Papers and files filled every available surface. Empty bottles acted as dividers between overflowing three-ring binders. The smell of stale cigar smoke assaulted Margaret's senses.

Hidden underneath the mess was a desk, upon which the soles of a pair of brown leather shoes blocked Margaret's view. They parted to reveal a middle-aged man leaning back in his chair, smoking a large stogie. He raised a very expressive eyebrow and then shot up from his chair with a burst of energy more appropriate to someone half his age, scattering papers in his wake.

The faded black tie, wrinkled shirt, and tattered tails of his tuxedo appeared to have been slept in. A bushy moustache displayed a pallet of grays absent from the fellow's dark hair. Leering eyes pierced through wire-framed glasses.

"Welcome, welcome, welcome! You are a fine specimen, aren't you?" He circled Margaret and eyed her appraisingly, as if analyzing a work of art in fast motion. He held out a hand, "Firefly, Rufus T. Firefly. And you are?" He pulled his hand away. "No, don't tell me – it has to do with the sound the wind makes breezing through the trees, like the whispering tones of a butterfly wing as it glides in the afternoon sunlight..."

"Mr. Firefly!"

"You're Mister Firefly? What a coincidence!"

Margaret gave another harrumph, just to make it clear she was not pleased, and looked over to the other gentleman who idly shuffled a deck of cards with one hand. He winked at her.

She gave a quick sniff and turned back to Firefly. "My name, good sir, is Margaret Dunwoody, and I am here to inspect the work your office has been doing ...or, should I say, has *not* been doing."

Rufus rolled his eyes like a little boy caught doing something wrong. He pivoted on one foot and playfully hid his hands behind his back. "Oh no, you aren't. I know why you're here. It's because of me, isn't it? You just had to meet me. Why, the first minute I saw you, I knew we were meant for each other. Will you marry me? Do you have any money? Answer the second question first."

"This is no time for levity, Mr. Firefly," she stated as she marched to the desk. Reaching down, she removed a pile of papers from a chair, gently placed them on the floor, and sat at the desk, facing the small hand-written nameplate that announced "Rufus T. Firefly, Boss." She stared at the man. She meant business.

Firefly merely smiled, "Look, Mrs. Dimwitty –"

"Dunwoody."

"– I have things under control here. Don't you worry about a thing." He danced over to his recliner and threw himself in as if he didn't have a care in the world. The action caused the chair to swirl, and he threw his hands out in pleasure.

Margaret was not amused. These people were clearly insane – or at least incompetent, which was just as bad. She opened her file and held a pen over the clipboard. "How exactly did you get promoted into this position?"

Firefly chewed on his stogie. "I assure you, it was all on the up-and-up. I worked for years to get this job."

"Atsa right, boss," the other man said. "It took years to get enough to bribe your way here."

Firefly slammed his fist on the table. "And how dare you insinuate we have done no work! Why, look at all these files." He waved his hand at the mess. "We've got piles and piles of files. Miles and miles of piles of files –"

Her mouth tightened. "Mr. Firefly, according to my records, you've been here for three months now –"

Firefly leaned forward. "Well, according to *my* records, Minnie the Moocher was a red hot hootchie kootcher."

Margaret jumped as the music blasted through the room. The Italian fellow had cranked up an old gramophone.

"Turn that off!"

"Whazzamatta, you no like music?"

"These are work hours," Margaret stood and glared at the Italian. "And I didn't catch your name."

"Ciccolini," said Firefly.

"Ravelli," said the Italian man at the same time.

The two men exchanged glances.

"Well?" Margaret said, looking down her nose. "Which is it?"

"Ciccolini Ravelli," the Italian replied. "I got two last names. My father, he was very generous."

She closed her notebook and turned back to Firefly. For a second, a hint of apprehension shone in his eyes, quickly replaced by the carefree incompetence she had first observed. "Mind if I don't smoke?" he asked, placing his cigar into a breast pocket.

This was an act, surely. But why were these two pretending to be insane?

She sat back down and crossed her arms. "Mr. Firefly – allow me to cut to the chase. Somehow, you were appointed to be in charge of this department three months and twelve days ago."

"Ah! Time flies like an arrow," he gazed off into the distance. "And fruit flies like a banana."

"Since that time," Margaret continued, "work has practically ceased. Those who were assigned here were fired, only to be replaced by young women, all of whom have the sole qualification of being good-looking."

"Au contraire," Firefly held up a finger, "one of them knows how to do the rumba."

Margaret leaned forward. "You do realize you are in hell, right? That there can be worse punishments for you than merely being assigned to the bureaucracy?"

"True. I could be forced to listen to Chico's piano playing all day."

"Who?"

"Ciccolini," said Firefly. "I mean Ravelli."

"My father, he was very generous," the Italian man said. "He give me lots of names, most of which I no can repeat in a woman's presence."

Margaret sighed. "Mr. Firefly, you try my patience."

"Thank you! You must try mine some time."

"Your department is responsible for keeping track of all assignments here in Hell. You are supposed to know where we can find anyone, on any of the levels, or even in Purgatory." She opened her notebook again. "Strangely enough, I can find no record of you at all."

For once, Firefly had no response, and merely tapped his fingers together.

Margaret smiled. "So I have a choice here. As you are no doubt aware, there are some very effective – and painful – ways to discern the truth about you, and your Italian friend as well. Or you can make it easy on yourself."

Firefly pursed his lips. “Can you give us a few minutes alone?”

“Mr. Firefly, I was not born yesterday.”

“I was bored yesterday,” the Italian fellow replied – except his accent had disappeared.

Margaret stood, brushed some non-existent lint off her dress, and strode behind Firefly’s desk. “May I?” she asked, indicating his computer.

Firefly stood to allow her access. The sparkle in his eyes had disappeared.

“Now then!” Margaret sat in his chair, placed her hands on the keyboard, and typed in her password. A new window opened – the kind that people like Firefly would never get to see. She tried to suppress a satisfied smile. “So! What are your real names?”

Firefly and the fake Italian remained silent.

Maragret spun around. “Gentlemen, please. I am certain you would prefer telling me than telling one of our more enthusiastic demons.”

“This isn’t fair,” Firefly said. “We’re Jewish. We were taught that hell doesn’t exist. Technically, I believed God didn’t exist, either…”

“And yet, here you are.” Margaret leaned back in Firefly’s chair. Quite comfortable, really. “You must have done something to be admitted here. By the looks of the two of you, I’d say adultery.”

The two would not meet her eyes. It was just a lucky guess – but then again, it applied to almost every man she had met here. She held her fingers over the keyboard. “Now – what are your names?”

“Julius Marx,” Firefly said in a tone that surprised Margaret in its sincerity.

“Leonard Marx,” replied the other.

"Brothers?" Margaret asked as she typed away. "Should have known. My brothers were always getting each other into trouble." The image of her brothers flashed in her mind, distracting her momentarily. Taking a deep breath, she forced herself to stare at the monitor. "Well, that's interesting…"

"We're not there," said Leonard. "You didn't find us. Proof that we shouldn't be here at all."

Margaret frowned at him. "Proof that you have managed to find a way to erase yourself from the database."

Julius held his hands to his cheeks. "Shocked!" he cried. "Shocked I am to discover that there are dishonest people in Hell!"

Leonard pranced over and sat on the edge of the desk. He smiled at Margaret in a way that indicated he knew how to charm women and was usually successful at it. Margaret hated men like that.

"Look, Mrs. Dunwoody. Maybe you can help us, and then we can be on our way. No one has to know we aren't in the database, and no one has to know where we are. Just help us."

Margaret sat up straight. "Help you? My good man, you have done nothing but cause me trouble. You have placed the department behind three months. Furthermore, you have broken all sorts of regulations that should send you to the lower levels for a few thousand years. Why in hell should I help you?"

Julius pushed files off a coffee table and sat with a grunt, looking much older. "When I first got here, it took me twelve years to find Leonard," he said. "I had to call in all sorts of favors – you'll never believe the things I owe people. And we've spent at least another twenty years or so since then."

"We finally realized we needed to get to the main database here," Leonard said. He spoke quickly and excitedly, obviously trying to convince her. "That took years as well."

"Just so you can remove your names?" Margaret asked. "What can you possibly be hiding? Hitler, Genghis Khan, and countless mass murderers are here – what did you two do that's worse?"

"No, no, you misunderstand," Julius said, in a tired voice. "We just needed to hide our identity in order to get this job. So we could search the database."

Leonard continued his charm offensive. "We are simply trying to find someone. Our brother. It's just not the same without him, and we're worried about him. All you have to do is use your special password" – he pointed to the screen, as if she couldn't get the reference – "and find him for us. We haven't been successful."

Margaret slitted her eyes. "And then you'll leave?"

"I'll quit right now," Julius said. "Although I'll miss Rumba Hour."

Margaret observed the two men, now quite old and tired. She could make a quick call and have them punished accordingly since they had no right to be there, which would solve her immediate problem. Or she could help them, in which case they'd leave – which would also solve her problem, but without any bloodshed.

The image of her own brothers once more flashed through her mind.

What the hell.

She gave a sigh and looked back at the screen. "What's his name?"

"Adolph," said Julius.

"Arthur," said Leonard at the same time.

Margaret crossed her arms. "Are we playing this game again? Because –"

"No, no!" Julius said, waving his hands before him. "No game. When he was born, he was Adolf. And then Hitler came along, and he changed it. But he might still be listed here under his birth name."

Leonard nodded his assent, and looked at Margaret expectedly.

Margaret glanced at Julius from the corner of her eye. "I would appreciate it if you would not peer over my shoulder. There are some passwords and processes I would prefer –"

"Yes, ma'am," Leonard replied, and the two of them backed away to give her privacy.

Margaret began typing. The two men watched anxiously. It appeared that having to remain still and quiet was difficult for them. Margaret enjoyed the power this gave her. She punctuated her search with a few "hmmms" and a couple "oh, dears" just to watch them squirm. Finally, after a few minutes, she moved her hands to her lap, leaned back in the chair, and turned to face them.

"Well?" Julius asked. "Where can we find him?"

Margaret smiled, "I'm afraid you never will."

"Hey, lady, come on!" Leonard stood and leaned across the table again, "you promised."

"I did no such thing," Margaret said. "But the fact is that he is not here."

Leonard pointed to the computer. "Not in the database?"

She shook her head. "Not here."

Julius got a far-away look in his eyes. A smile slowly grew. "Of course. He's not here." He reached into his pocket, retrieved his cigar, and held it before his face without ever placing it between his lips. "I should have realized. I can see him now, playing a harp."

Leonard's grin was infectious. "And a horn."

Margaret closed her file. "You must have loved your brother very much."

The two men just smiled.

"Very well. I have done my part, and now you must do yours. I will expect you to be gone within half an hour. If you remain here after that, I will not be held responsible for what will happen to you."

"Atsa fine, boss," Leonard said.

Julius wiggled his eyebrows, and shook his cigar. "Are you sure you don't want to get married? I can see you now, leaning over a hot stove. Only I can't see the stove..."

HEAD GAMES

Bill Snider

"Sir, please remain calm. You may not bring a weapon into this event. It says so, very clearly on your invitation. Right there in the small print.

"You will have to surrender your weapon, sir. We'll keep it safe here, and I'll give you a marker so that you can claim it again when you leave." The young lady wrung her hands. Looking back along the line of somewhat patient attendees, Fionn could tell that she would be doing that a lot.

"Lass, I do not care about your rules. Areadbhar is not just a thing; she is a sentient being and you are dangerously close to inducing her to wroth – and that would not be a good thing." There were only the three attendants working the desk, and thousands upon thousands of guests, each with their invitations clutched in their sweaty hands, waiting, waiting, waiting for their opportunity to pass the gates and enter the event proper. The line stretched well out of sight, snaking around the farthest corner of the Library's foundation and deep into the bowels of...

"Sir, right here, see? It says:

"Fionn mac Cumhaill: Ye are hereby encouraged – read that as required – to attend the celebration of the grand Rededication Party commemorating the re-opening of the Hellexandria Memorial Library. Participation in whole or in

part, one way or another, is required. Failure to do so shall bring upon ye most unpleasant consequences, singly or severally. You may bring one companion to the event. You may stay at the event as long as socially acceptable. You may not bring any weapons – neither of Old Dead construction nor New Dead mass destruction – past the check-in booth. This event, as decreed, is a Neutral Grounds event and, as such, will be held in accordance with all expectations. Any attempt to abrogate these circumstances, or the extended associations thereof, will also result in repercussions, singly or severally as the situation warrants. No exceptions will be entertained, Satan willing."

Fionn listened patiently to the harried woman as she punctuated each word, much as she must have done an innumerable number of times prior to his presence.

"Lizzie, is there a problem here?" An older gentleman, of serious demeanor and stern visage approached. Dressed in a severe but respectably well-tailored suit, he walked out of the shadowy demesne that shored up the check-in desk. Holding an unlit cigar and pointing at the man in front of 'Lizzie,' he asked again, politely and with specific emphasis on the word, 'problem.'

"Sir, not so much a problem, as a disagreement of interpretation." She paused, ready to launch into a complex and windy explanation of events. He gestured calmly, "Simplify it, please." To which she nodded and laid out the events with quick clarity.

"Ah, interpretation; this I am well acquainted with. Sir, please come with me, and we shall talk a bit and clear this up." He motioned Fionn over to the side of the counter a few feet away, enough to provide the illusion of privacy, and still be within the watchful eye of many different security components.

"Sir, if you are unfamiliar with who I am, allow me to introduce myself: I am Sigmund Freud. Perhaps, you have heard of me?"

"You seem like a rational person, but no, I cannot say that I've heard of you. Most like, you were well after my time. I am Fionn mac Cumhaill; this Spear is Areadbhar, and my friend here is Caliban – perhaps you have heard of us?" Fionn raised an eyebrow as Caliban posed insouciantly.

"Regrettably, I have but only in passing heard of either of you. Regardless, I am here to assist in the calm and efficient movement of people into this event; or as close to a reasonable facsimile as we can manage with what resources we have available to us. Come this way, please." He led them to a small office, off to the side and out of the way, quiet, sedate and not visible from the entryway to the event proper.

"Please, come in, Fionn. Caliban, I'm sorry, but I would appreciate it if you would wait for your… associate outside while we talk."

"Sure; I stay, I play, here outside, it's only me, so I'll slap, slap, slap my knees. However, please be quick, as there is much to see, inside this great cavern of humanity." Caliban smiled as he danced in place, waiting for some kind of acknowledgment of his witticism. Fionn smirked silently, while Sigmund leveled a withering glance and uttered a simple cough as a reply.

"Surely, you see that life, in all its misery, is but a game of triviality? How else to explain your lot, mine, all of ours here in this Hell, except that it be that kind of game, don't you see?" Caliban sighed, already seeing it in the face and eyes of this wrinkled old man, that life was only in the living, and here amongst the dead, there was no life for him.

"Fine; abide I will, out here amongst the swill." Caliban looked for the least offensive spot against the wall, and plopped to the ground. He closed his eyes and hummed to himself tunelessly.

Freud, "harrumphed" once more and motioned Fionn into the room. Fionn looked around, pointedly looking for something to set it apart from a square box. The room was nothing more than white walls, beige carpeting, a leather high backed chair, and a sofa, covered by a soft blanket of dark weave.

"Sigmund, you have a – well, it's a square room with furniture. Not much to be looking at, now is it?"

"Alas, this is a part of my curse in Hell. In the land of the living, my office was richly appointed, with rows and rows of studious books, works of art on the walls, curios from many places and things of interest. Here, in this loathsome place, wherever I am – employed as it were – I get a white box for an office. I've tried to liven it up, of course. I put some pictures up on the wall, but the next time I come back in, they're all gone, with naught even a trace." Sigmund shook his head ruefully, sat down in the leather chair, made from some sort of hide, which he never asked about – it looked enough like leather, so that's what he called it (even though, occasionally he did hear a voice, crying softly, asking for help).

"And this? This infernal device? This is what I have to write my notes down upon? I can't get paper, nor pen to write proper. I have to use this 'Hellpad' thing. Another part of my torture."

"Oh, you have one of those; they're nice. I like mine. It's got this game on it called Angry Devils – soooo much fun. Hours of useless inanity; I downloaded it from the Zapp Store," he barked out a laugh, then held back, as the look on Sigmund's face spoke volumes about his appreciation for technology.

"Sir, you asked me to come in here and discuss things, I am here. Let us discuss." Fionn moved over to the sofa and sat down, back erect, Areadbhar across his knees, facing the elder doctor of the mind.

"Yes, well. Let's be direct then, shall we? You cannot bring that spear into the grounds of this occasion. Flat out, not going to happen. I am according you this much discussion time out of respect to your ties to the Undertaker and your association, the UnSafety and Unhealth Committee. If you had been but one of the regular rabble, we would have just had a Security team remove you forcibly from the premises."

"Ah, so you have heard of me, then?"

"No, not really. I read your file before coming out, I saw you on one of the monitors; facial recognition tagged you," Sigmund tapped at the square glass gadget in his lap.

"Oh."

"Let us remain focused, shall we? Our illustrious Lord Satan has deemed it necessary to have this event. In his infinite wisdom, we abide and attempt to create the harmonious environment to accommodate his will. He has also decreed that no weapon shall be permitted upon the floor of this event. None. Zero. No tolerance for any infractions. If I were to permit you to carry your weapon out onto the floor proper, not only would you summarily be evicted with the most pernicious of prejudice and an additional helping of painful remuneration, but I, and the staff here, would likely share in your torment. Therefore, we won't permit it." Sigmund shook his head to emphasize his point, the white locks flying in the air.

"Ennnhh. And what would stop me from laying about the place around me?"

"This is hell, sir. There be demons and other things unnamed and uncounted hereabouts, and they do be inclined to spoil for some action. They, likewise, have been commanded to commit no perfidy, unless it be in the course of protection of the events hereupon. There will be no exceptions; or rather, there will be no exceptions that His High and Imperious Satan does not wish to occur."

Fionn muttered under his breath, something harsh and unclear to Sigmund's ears.

"Bearer, kill him, kill them all." Areadbhar spoke for the first time since they had joined the queue of souls lined up to enter the event. Fionn looked at the Spear.

"Areadbhar; that won't accomplish anything. Well, nothing productive anyway; and, no doubt, it would put us in a bad light with Administration."

"Precisely; I knew from the way you carried yourself you were an intelligent man, unlike many of the rabble I will be forced to talk to today. Wait, who is Areadbhar?" Fionn gestured to the Spear in his lap.

"You gave your spear a name? Fascinating. Would you like to discuss that?"

"No, I did not give anything a name; Areadbhar was the name she was already established with. I merely honor her by using the name she owns. And no, I do not feel the least bit inclined to discuss much of anything about her or anything else, to be quite brutal about it."

"Intriguing," Sigmund slid open his Hellpad, and began to poke furiously at the screen. "Please, continue. Why is this spear female? You speak in attributive form designating the spear as female; does 'she' speak back to you?" Sigmund reached into his breast pocket to pull out a cigar shaped object and was about to put it into his mouth, before thinking better of it, and returned it to his pocket.

"Bearer, kill him – he is annoying. At least the blood spray would liven up his walls."

"Hmmm, yes, well, that is always an option."

"What is an option, Fionn? Or, oh, did the spear speak to you? What did it say? Was it violent?"

"In a manner of speaking, you could say that; however – you really do not want to know."

"Come sir, what we discuss here in these walls is a bond of honor between you and I. What is discussed here does not go past my own records; anything you speak of here will be confidential and held in strictest regard."

"With all respect, sir; I highly doubt that."

"Upon my honor, I would say it is so!"

"Your honor is not what I would gainsay against you; the nature of hell, as it is wont, is, instead, what it is." Fionn gripped the Spear, his gaze gaining an intensity of some ill intent.

"Oh, I see. Very well. We will move along then. Why don't you tell me about your childhood, or about your parents, or about what brought you to hell in the first place? What is it like to have a spear that talks to you? I am fascinated by your story. Your file says so much about you, yet so little of meaning." He tapped the device in his lap to add emphasis.

"And, precisely, in what way does this bear on how or why I should or should not be bringing Areadbhar into this event which I really have no time to be attending, but am doing so out of an understanding of the relationship between Administration and those of us who assist in making things work? Do your questions shed any manner of merit upon this? Or should I do what Areadbhar suggests?"

"Yes, Bearer, you should; split him from navel to nape, and crosswise from shoulder to shoulder. His patter is patronizing and an affront. Kill him, slow, quick, up to you."

"I suspect I would not appreciate what your spear has to say, now would I? This wouldn't, in turn be merely what you wish to say, now would it?" Sigmund stopped typing.

"I am of one mind, she is of another. Areadbhar's methods are a little bit less refined than mine; messier one might also add. In this situation, I am almost of the same mind as she, for I can see that your intent is to get inside my head; for reasons that I cannot explain, and I do not see why you would want to. With all the souls of hell spread out upon this plain of misery, why would you be inclined to play within mine?" Fionn started to rise.

"Because yours is more interesting."

"I beg your pardon?" Fionn paused in the acting of rising.

"And because you represent the basic tenet of understanding human psychology. You carry your wood out in the open without hiding it, you speak to it, and it speaks back to you. This is the epitome of the male identity. You, sir, are the foundation of my life's work. I have notes – thousands and thousands of notes that I've put into this infernal device. If only I could find them again." Sigmund waved the Hellpad in the air like a piece of paper.

"Kill him, Bearer. He wants secrets that are best not shared."

"Indeed. Well, now I am less inclined toward violence. I will leave Areadbhar at the weapon's check-in; I'm sure she will not come to any ill fortune; she has ways of protecting herself. As do I." Fionn rose, signaling his ending of this discussion.

"But, there is so much more that I would like to ask you. Are you sure that I cannot persuade you to return to my office in New Hell? I could schedule an appointment for you, any time that you would like."

"I think not, *sir*" the emphasis cold and unfriendly.

"Damnation. Very well, I will escort you back to the reception area. I've approved badges for you and for your associate. They'll be at the gate when we get back there." Sigmund rose from his chair after making some quick notations, placing his Hellpad in the oversized pocket of his jacket front. He opened the door and waved Fionn out ahead of him.

"You know, you are not the only such stubborn-heeled soul in this gathering with an overt attachment to his stick. There was another who likewise needed to be assuaged about leaving his weapon behind; he too spoke of it as a being of an identity. He too, was just as intemperate as you."

Caliban jumped up when he heard the door open and, together in silence, the three of them made their way back to the front gate, where, with no further difficulty, Fionn surrendered Areadbhar – or rather, more specifically, he placed her within the weapon's check area after the attendant attached a little piece of paper held in place by an insignificant thread of string, for the attendant could not pick Areadbhar up after Fionn released his hold upon her.

Sigmund pulled his Hellpad out once more, made some additional notes.

"Sometimes a spear is just a spear; sometimes it's not. Sometimes, it's something more. Now, if only I could find my notes from that other session, I could compare these two and..." Sigmund wandered off distractedly, rapidly motioning across the surface of the glass, searching.

Fionn and Caliban gathered their badges and headed into the depths of the celebration.

*

The room was dark but seemed specifically appointed to contain weapons of many types. It had a designation: WC-651-03 – but that was meaningless to Areadbhar. It was written on the infernal piece of scrip that was tied rather futilely across her top. She sensed the breadth, the depth of the cavernous room, the rows upon rows of stacked weaponry from countless ages past, present and future. Most of them shiny in one way or another, many others of them dull, brutal and efficient; and some, just oddly constructed with plastic buttons and switches and levers and things that made no sense to her, beyond the basic idea of "weapon."

Areadbhar had spent countless eons stuck in the skull of a giant, buried deep within the House of Shadows, a few hours spent here, alone, away from her Bearer was nothing compared to that. The warm sense of belonging was more important anyway, now that she had purpose again. That time in the shadows, waiting and watching the dust layer and swirl and beckon the mindless dead to purposelessness was an eternity of despair and droll disdain.

She let her thoughts drift amongst the morass of memory, digging deep into the past, letting senses float past peripheral context and stretching deep into the confines of a simple hall of weapons. Without warning, however, she stopped, and poked concertedly at the edges of her senses. Something was, odd. It was mayhap a memory – not a sound, nor a thought, but it was clear whatever caused this disturbed feeling, like she, was different.

"Who hearkens nearby?" She spoke, in her voice – which only her Bearer should be able to hear.

"Well, isn't that spectacular? You have a voice! You are like me! That's awesome. Now I won't be completely bored in here for the duration of this spectacle of human lameness. Hi, how are you?"

She recognized that it spoke like her, to the aether, to spaces beyond.

"Truly, you can hear me? Who, or what are you?"

"Oh, but of course I can hear you! And it's wonderful! Your voice is really harsh, though; are you yelling? Or is this your normal conversational voice?" His was a male voice, decidedly soft and weak sounding; overly friendly would be the term that a human might use.

"Aye, this is my normal speaking voice. As I am quite familiar with who I am, again, I ask, who and what are you?"

"Oh, introductions! Of course! I am remiss. I am called Staff. I know, not very original, nor very fancy. But it is what Merlin has always called me. He's not one for ostentation and the like, if you know what I mean."

"And, are you always, this… chatty?"

"Yes. Quite. I can go on for hours and hours on end; I can quote poetry, scripture, lengthy tomes of extreme rarity all by rote and without even thinking about it. I know several languages and am well-versed in math and scientific principle. I'm a regular know-it-all, as it were; or at least, that's what Merlin keeps telling me. He made sure that I studied an awful lot of written material when I was topside," he continued without any pause in breathing..

"So, you are real wood, also; a living weapon, such as I? My Bearer had mentioned that he knew there was the possibility of others, but had no specific knowledge of any."

"Oh, yes; when Merlin came through the Veil, he brought me with him. Very weird sensation, I must say: that whole transition from the living world, to this place of damnation. Very trying time. For a while there, I was beside myself with dismay; I might have caused some damage, or at least that's what he keeps reminding me. Said it took him some time to recover me again and, not only that, but to bring me back to my senses. I trust him implicitly, so it must be true. And how about you? Who are you and how do you come to be in this lovely little palace of weaponly accommodation?"

"Very long story; one versed in blood and destruction. I was last, in the world above, thrust into the skull of a giant, one bent upon destruction of the emerald lands. My

Bearer of that time, succeeded well in slaying the behemoth, but was himself, taken by the fell being. Together, in their death throws they lay upon the field of battle for a time. A long time, I know not how much time passed. I realized that the world had changed for me. I assumed that Lugh or one of the other gods must have moved my physical self into this accursed place. Both giant and I were long a piece within the House of Shadows; a horrible place of dust, shadows, quietude and nothingness."

"Wow; that sounds extreme. So, you are a big battle weapon, hunh? All blood, death, kill 'em and spit in their eyes like, right? That's super spiffy."

"Puling child, what does 'spiffy' mean?"

"Oh, sorry, New Dead term. It means really interesting or unusual."

"Right. So, you are from the land of the New Dead, as you call it?"

"Kinda, or rather, I'm from many lands. Parts of me come from all over the new and old world. Merlin repeatedly warped new pieces of wood into my form whenever he encountered something interesting. I've got some rowan, some ash, some oak, some bits of petrified something or other – we never did find out what kind of wood it was called. All wrapped up in the bundle of joy, that is me!"

"Sounds, blissful."

"Wait, that sounds like sarcasm. Is it? I don't always understand things like that. Humans confuse me; Merlin, on the other hand, he's pretty straightforward with me. Tells me 'do this, do that,' no mincing about with veiled threats or promises. Oh, this is fun! Somebody to talk to for the first time in, I don't know how long, but obviously a very long time! Glee!"

"I will go out of my way, and grant you that this is a novel experience; however, you should realize, that I am, myself, not anywhere near as chatty as you might be."

"Oh, no; that's quite all right! He frequently tells me I'm an earful and that I go on and on and on. I've never actually spoken with anybody else but him! I could very likely be even chattier than I normally am! This is a fantastic thing! How many more like us are in hell do you think?"

"My Bearer has mentioned possibilities. Never clear, and I was not myself aware that such as yourself... like ourselves could exist, besides my own self. I have never encountered another one such as us before."

"Oh, swell! We're going to learn so much about each other! We've got tons of time on our hands to talk about stuff! All kinds of stuff. Do you like games? I'm particularly fond of word games. Do you know how to say 'cheese' in Latin?"

"Again, with brutal honesty, no on both counts. I am more inclined toward the killing of things, rather than learning their names."

"Oh, well; uh, okay. What would you want to do to pass the time away? It's not like we can read a book; there aren't any around. I asked. Merlin said no. That made me sad, because he had this stern look in his eyes, and he told me not to talk to anybody. Wait, you don't count, right? You're like me, so, it should be okay to talk to you, yes? Hunh, hunh? He doesn't like it if I disobey him ... So, you're not like a human, right; you won't tell on me, right? Even better, you couldn't; you couldn't talk to him, right? Just like me, only he can hear me; wait, is that like you and your Bearer?"

"Aye, on as much of that as made sense."

"Oh, good; I was a little worried, I will admit. This is swell! Can I call you a friend? Do you have a name?"

"You can call me... Spear. As you say, not very original, not very laden with subtlety."

"More spiffy! I like it! Staff and Spear, together in the weapons closet, chatting about old war stories, and exchanging ideas and getting along like humans from the topside! This is the best day ever, for me! I am beside myself with... wait, I can't be beside myself. I incorporate a physical body, I am I within the physical confines of this body, even though it is a piece of wood, it still is a body, and my sense of 'I' is what resides therein. Oh, no. Perfidy. Thought patterns spin, dizzy, dizzy, out of control. Do you like poetry, or singing?"

"Not, really."

"Oh, well, then what would you want?"

"Right now? A battle; a really, really big and bloody battle..."

"Oh, well, I can't do that. I can, however recount the events leading up to and from the Battle of Hastings, in 1066. There was lots of blood spilled at that one."

"As you say, 'spiffy'."

*

"Caliban, what do you think? Humanity at its best or worst?" Fionn gestured randomly at the structures and people of all walks and all types of wonders that wandered aimlessly about. The entranceway to the Library was immense, columns and stairways and halls that led all around. He was struck mostly by the people – crowds and crowds of people; smelly, sweaty and full of human frailties. Everywhere he turned to look, throngs of people of all sizes and shapes and clothing sensibilities sprawled across the expanse of the grounds, both inside and out.

"A large sum of people to be sure, to be sure; I am at a loss, from here, what be clear and what be obscure. This business, so many about; it seems like a fair way to take them all out?" Caliban's misshapen appearance, warped by birth and countless agonies, drew only a casual glance from most in hell. His coal black eyes, on the other hand, likened him more to daemon than anything else, and would grasp a glance or two. Standing diffidently, trying hard not to feel hemmed against so much humanity all in one place.

"Hmm, good point. There have been some rumblings, some trouble over by the Roman enclaves; a fair bit of general mayhem. Something is definitely going on, far and past these proceedings – something dire, no doubt. I have some misgivings, too; but we're in good with the Administration for the moment. As long as we don't botch things up, we should be smooth with it. Oh, wait; this is hell, so, have no fear, in a few ticks of time, something will arise to make a mess of things." Fionn smiled broadly.

"You speak like New Dead, all your words with more than one thought. But I see, I understand, you have machinations in play, something well wrought? I am not so comfortable amongst so many; I feel strongly, that the House of Dust may have been more friendly." Caliban turned to look at Fionn, giving him the once-over with that eerie penetrating, pupil-less gaze of his.

"We'll see; only time will tell." Fionn led deep into the throng of souls, all of whom mindlessly carried on with their games and pastimes and plots and plans and peripheral activities. Pausing as they were walking, Caliban quickly shifted his focus, fixating upon a motion in the crowd.

"Hold a moment, please, if you would; that soul there, I sense familiarity with him, how is it that I should? I am alone in hell, there is no one I've heard who could speak of me, pray tell." Caliban paused, staring at a trio of well-dressed gentlemen who were leisurely threading through the crowd in their general direction. As they approached, Fionn could make out the text of their conversation.

"Will, hold up; we should be crossing over to the other side to be at conference room A-1. We don't have time to gawk at the beautiful new structures here. At this rate, we'll never make it on time. Am I not right Kit? We're supposed to be there in ten minutes." The first gentleman motioned toward the other side of the courtyard as he kept trying to keep his friend focused on a sheaf of papers that contained, among other things, a list of performances and exhibits, with times and locations. Fionn recognized it as one of the printed pieces they received in their 'welcome to the event' package.

"Gads, what an ugly little brute there." The foppish one with stars in his eyes motioned toward Caliban. This brought Fionn up short as he grunted and glared at the smaller man.

"Excuse me?" Fionn stated with forceful emphasis and an obvious inclination toward violent intent.

"Never mind that, Will; Byron is right, we must needs be in a rush. If we do not show the proper respect for Satan's work, how then will we continue to bask in the glory of the work that you've already started?" The one named Kit, a baby-faced one, gave a pained glance at Fionn, by way of an apology implied.

"Oh, gads; that is true spoken. We must then be on our way with haste, yes, yes; however... that ugly fellow, he looks familiar. Why is that?" The one named Will abruptly changed direction, shepherded along by his fellows, moving toward the mysterious conference room mentioned.

"Our apologies, sirs. Will is oft times un-inclined to be polite-minded; it's not that he's intentionally cruel in his barbs. He just does not seem to understand the intricacies of polite interaction with people in a civilized society. Again, for any slight that he might have given, please accept my humblest apologies. However, we must be off." The one named Kit bowed gracefully, before racing off to catch up with his other two companions.

"Well, that was exceedingly odd even by standards in hell, wouldn't you say, Caliban?" The misshapen, daemonic figure nodded mutely, still staring perplexedly at the retreating backs. In minutes, their hurried progress was lost among the throngs of teeming, reckless souls; swallowed up by the crowd.

"What say you we just sort of remain here, out of the way, for a while and watch all of these people doing whatever the hell it is they're doing here?" Fionn motioned at the crowd, the sky, the buildings, whatever else remained in the area.

"Aye, that would sit well with me; this vast teaming sea of humanity makes me all quivery."

Caliban and Fionn found themselves a comfortable ledge ringing the courtyard, which gifted them with a flowing view of things. They pointed out the oddly dressed persons, commenting back and forth on the likelihood that they would survive in the lands they had grown up in, or how their preposterous displays of arrogance showed them to be nothing more than rats rutting in the ruins.

Various disturbances broke out during the hours that they sat there and conversed, awaiting the call to dine; at least five distinct instances of fisticuffs, raw brawling among roving bands of overly enthusiastic barbarians played themselves out. When one of the combatants pulled out a knife – or what looked like a knife – Security swooped in with ferocious jabs and kicks and thwacks for all parties involved, even a few spectators. They were quickly hauled together within a net, and moved toward sections of the Library that were not meant for the regular partygoers.

Some threw dice and gamboled in the old ways; others sang and danced and traipsed about with abandon. Tragedies and comedies played out before them – a massive ocean of souls passing their small corner of respite like an outcrop at the edge of the world.

Fionn had no idea what these people were doing here, what they sought; it was Satan's decree that all these souls gather together in one place, albeit a large and quite fancy place. His only purpose in being here was to execute the letter of the request from "He who reigns over all"; failure to do so, would lead to unpleasantness – best just to participate.

All of these people, in this space, groping together toward commonality in such a way, to acknowledge the presence and purpose of such edifices, which glorify and accentuate the very foundations of hell; this amused him, yet left him with a sensation of dread, of waiting for the other shoe to drop, as the New Dead sometimes said. And yet, these souls were happy to be here? Fionn thought not, and was about to share with Caliban, these musings.

"Caliban, thou malformed git!" The shout was heard, even over the din of thousands of souls, harsh and discordant – loud enough to rival any battlefield sergeant marshalling troops to fervent combat. Crowds of people were pushed violently out of their way to give the issuer of such harshness free passage past them.

Both Caliban and Fionn swiveled to see from where this latest surprise might be issuing. Fionn looked at his companion, and observed the palpable consternation crawl over his features. Anxiety, fear, an outright paroxysm of paralysis rooted him to the spot, as the wildly arrayed form approached with a steady tread. People continued to quickly move out of her way, as like with any force for which a name cannot be called, one gets out of the way, or gets blown over.

She was a good distance off when she had shouted, and it took some time for her to cross the courtyard, even at the punishing pace that she walked. Fionn could now make out more of her features. A face that only a son could love, eroded and blackened by hate and age, she plodded resolutely through the throng. Dark of hair, unwashed cascades that wildly flew about her face, like shadows out of place; darker robes that billowed, even though there was a decided lack of air flow in this restrictive space. Eyes of blue, pale skin and skeletal features embraced a shrewish nature that Fionn suspected was more than just a visual cue. The hint of lightning, winds, and the howling rain overshadowed her approach.

"Who is the blue-eyed hag?" Fionn asked.

Caliban glanced briefly his way before answering in a quavering voice and returned his attention to the furiously approaching figure, "Mother, mine, she be; if 'n' I heard her a-rightly."

"Lugh's Balls! Is this a good thing or a bad one?" For the first time upon entering this event, Fionn let concern wash over him.

"I have not seen my mam since, since... well, since forever and a day; I guess this might be good, probably be bad, most likely, anyway." Caliban's face, misshapen as it was naturally, took on a curious cast; one might even go so far as to call it ashen, if ashen was not already the natural state in which it stayed. He stared at her with more than just a hint of trepidation.

As the well-aged harridan approached within feet of the two, Fionn moved closer, placing himself directly in her path.

"Greetings; I am Fionn, Caliban's friend. He tells me you are his mother? I am pleased to meet..."

"Friend? Friend? This misbegotten stain from the most undressed armpit of a cesspool of festering humanity has a friend? Surely, you foppish dandy, you must be mistaken. I am Sycorax; and I know these things. He is Caliban, my son; he has no friends, nor friendly kinships! He is a worm, lowly and loathsome; the kind you scrape off your shoes after you walk by." She shrieked at an impossible tone, reaching past the mere eardrum and deep into the soul.

"Lady, I mean no disrespect, but you are mistaken..."

"Shut it, git. This is my son, and he and I are about to have words; words that are no concern of yours. Clear yourself from my path so that I may properly instruct my son on how to deal with meeting his mother for the first time in hell. And besides, you smell of leaves – I hate leaves. Clear off, you simpering fop." She waved Fionn away like a cast-off sock and pushed past him. Cuffing Caliban on the side of the head, she pulled him closer by the long lobe of his ear.

"Yup, it's you. I could smell your sorry degenerate stench from across the courtyard here; even with all these unwashed masses of sheep that ply this place, I knew it was you, you miserable wretch. Why have you not tried to find me 'ere this? Why? Were you afraid of my wrath? Hunh? Stand up, worm; answer me, for I am short of temper this day, and being here amongst these scavengers fills me with oily rage that I should smite them all." She screamed at top volume, mere inches away from Caliban's face. Every exhalation of venom he could not only smell, but also taste.

"I, I, I... did not think..."

"That's right, low-life wretched worm who crawled out of my belly, shat upon the land! You didn't think; you never think. Thinking was always my task; if you could have even had a thought it would probably have shocked that bloated heart that you call yours and pushed you past the dirt into a pool of blubbering rags and wet bits. You would piss yourself with the mere mention that a thought might try to simmer to the surface of your besotted consciousness!" With each word, spittle flew from her lips, rage boiled over from her eyes, and the crowd of onlookers pulled back, allowing ample space for this exchange to occur. The hive mentality struck a strong chord, pushing one and all away from the two.

Fionn moved closer, which proved to be a mistake.

"Sycorax, if I may be so bold, it is unseemly and very unsettling to see my friend be treated this way..." Fionn stopped at the violence he saw reflected from her eyes.

"No, you may not be so bold; you may, or rather are, excrement that fans and splatters at the bottom of the pit. How dare you even think of commenting in any way, shape or form about how I speak with my son? Are you his father, have you a care or a hand in the raising of this whelp? Wherefore art thou even the least bit clever enough to grudge a mother the reunion with her son? You miserable cur, fallow yourself off into the corner and stay there like the cursed dog that you are. Caliban has no friends here – you, most certain of all, I can see your lies, your words that dance before you. As with all of you men in hell, you are all pigs and liars and lily-livered sapsuckers, sucking on the teats of those who would not have whelped you when you were born; more like they would have smashed your miserable body against the stone and be done with ye. Be gone, thou white-skinned devil mage. Leave me and my son alone!" The force of her words, the wind that roused from her spirit, the storm that broached from her eyes, forced Fionn to backpedal and miss his step. Unceremoniously, he dropped to the ground on his backside, while the crowed gawped and catcalled from the sides. Without even missing a beat, she returned her attention to Caliban, unleashing a non-stop torrent of invective and creative insults.

"Young man, I would suggest you leave the lady alone to chat with her son. She has been a long time away from her kin, that she has a storehouse of words to share with him." A tall fellow, enshrouded in robes of grey, with flickers of black and red that peeked through the occasional fold, reached down and offered him a hand back up. The red looked like flecks of blood that dried and was absorbed by the garment, but that must have been a trick of the light. Fionn reached for the proffered hand and pulled himself up.

"You know her?"

"Oh, aye; I've known her for quite some time now. She is a one for many strong words, and a strength of will not found in most. Not one for letting things get in her way, that one is."

"And, apparently, she's Caliban's mother?"

"Indeed. Allow me to introduce myself; I am Merlin. Perhaps you have heard of me?" He bowed politely, showing the back of his skull as he did so, and rose with the grace of age and wisdom. Centuries radiated off of every fiber of him, the strict lines of a face framed by a whitened mane of hair that cavorted wildly, like sprites lost in the woods. His face was set deep within his cowl, as gnarled as wood and lit by coals of intense penetration as he gazed down at the man who still held onto his fierce grip. Fionn realized that he was being probed and released his grip.

"Many thanks and my pardon; my name is Fionn mac Cumhaill." He turned his attention back to Caliban and his mother, who still unleashed a seemingly unending torrent of disdain and discord.

"Does she ever stop, you wonder?"

"At some point, I'm sure she will; however, she's been storing it up for quite some time. She thought her boy had never crossed to hell; however, given his parentage, it was merely a matter of time before they crossed paths again." Merlin nodded quietly, brooding deeply.

"Really? So you know this harridan, you've spent time with her in some measure?" Fionn's tone spoke volumes of incredulity at anyone actually seeking time with such a one as this woman.

"Indeed. I've known her for a great length of time. She has been… useful to me in many of my researches. As I stated, she has a strength of will that is matched by few; and her skills with the witchery ways merely makes her more capable in my service."

"Impressive, I must say. Such a one as that must be a constant source of distress, one would think." Fionn shook his head, as he gazed from her and back to him.

"One would be right, if one were inclined to look at only the surface. She has many useful characteristics that have often proved complementary to mine own. If it were not for her dogged persistence, I might never have come to know of your presence down here amongst the fallen." Merlin turned his bright eyes towards Fionn, and the light within burned.

"How so, that? Where else would we of the old ways be? Our people are prolific and well spread out amongst the denizens of this underworld. In truth, I know not where else I would have ended up, except down amongst these lands. Anwynn was and always is the land to which we fall when we cross the veil, we of the emerald."

"True spoken; however, the difference between knowing who is a myth and who was a creature of capacity, that is the rub. Our paths through life, are not wont to be merely the extensions of our wants, but also the culmination of generations of desires to push against the boundaries of life's barriers."

"Uhm, you're losing me, there; sorry."

"There is no need to be sorry, young Fionn; know ye, as ye should, that I have conquered many imaginations, many diverse outcomes and paths of resistance. I have been trapped here, in this unseemly hell, and am unmoved by what it represents and what transpires within its confines."

"Sounds like a raw deal; not being a believer and all, 'why do we end up here, oh boo hoo' – that argument, yes?"

"Indeed; and yet, I am less moved by the actual discussion, that I care not the reasons one or the other. I am here, I have resources, but this is not where I choose to be. My presence here was cast upon me by rules not of my accepting. I shall have that situation, corrected. You can either assist, or be consumed by it."

Fionn paused for a moment with that; he looked more carefully at Merlin, taking in his measure. For a second also, he scanned past at Caliban, and how he fared with his Mother. The honour in his soul cried to him, pleading the need to assist his friend, as he could see the pain that wafted from him; but he knew in his bones, that Caliban would have to stand up and meet his own fight on his own two feet.

"Mother, no; I can take no more of this," Caliban spoke slowly, labouredly, words filled with pain dripping from every syllable.

"What? How dare you speak back to me, whelp? I am not finished leveling you with my wrath. Do you think that you can even come close to my measure with the least bit of equality? You are spittle, flotsam that even the river Styx is forgetful of. You are dust, you are a shell of a human and don't even have the balls to reach between your eyes and pull out an intelligent conversation. Rhyme? Verse, this is how your utterance must be cursed? Degenerate dog, filth spewed by diseased carcasses and demonic influences. You have no..."

"No." For the first time since she had called out his name, he stood up, gathering what little strength he could muster. Caliban looked about, saw his friend, Fionn, engaged in a rough exchange, words of intense and menacing interaction. He wanted to help, but his Mother was more than most any would ever be able to handle. He felt the muscles in his legs weaken, he looked down at them, thinking that a blow of some sort had been struck, but no; and realized that he was afraid of his Mother, of what she represented, of what she was capable of.

"Try and do something about your feckless existence, worm? Is that it? Is that what you are thinking now? That you can try and stand and not still be the rot that I let spill into the land of the living? Think you, that you have a mind, a soul? You are nothing but rot, the deep body rot that sets into the worst of things, and eats from within. You are worms, crawling within a sack of human shape; nothing but venom from my loins, spoiled with your father's insolence and insipidness..."

"Mother, no; I can take no more of this," he stood, and pointed at her.

"How dare you..."

"Mother; you are correct and as far from the mark as your form is lovely and pleasing to thc eye. You are a very angry person; your rage has not only warped you, but everyone you've ever been close to. You are not right, up here. You can do nothing to this form, it is merely dust – I fear you; you are a horrible person, you can only damage this shell. I will not listen to you anymore." Caliban turned away from her, and hesitantly took a step, then another away from her. She let out a shriek that unnerved every soul in the courtyard; not a one who heard that dissonance could do other than flinch from surprise at its volatility and volubility. Even several demonic forms flying or perched upon higher vantage points were slightly discomfited by its raw malevolence.

Her face was contorted in rage and madness, as her eyes fixated upon the back of her son. Caliban paused and closed his eyes; a tear ran down his face, for he knew what was coming – he had seen it already. She raised her hand, still shrieking in an unearthly pitch, incoherent rage filled with purpose. As the rage roiled and found focus, she uttered a single word, with every erg of the force of will she possessed.

"Burn!"

A single slash of electric vitriol snapped forth from her outstretched hand; bright blue, harsh and shockingly vibrant, slashed through the gloom and overall dankness of the hellish dusk. Spectacular and violent, coruscating, snapping, crackling, virulent fingers clawed against the air and found full, brutal impact against Caliban's back.

"I am dust, once again, filled with loss and pain," he had but enough time to utter, as the electric crackle splattered across his form, instantly reducing his body to dust. Faint slivers of smoke or steam wisped up from the remains that lay skirling in the breeze.

"Merlin! My son is gone again, he has fled from me, that simpering fool; I must find him!" She shrieked, rage, inchoate and merciless, mad ravens cawing into the storm.

"Enough, woman; I am engaged in discourse here. Mind your manners!" Merlin turned to stare his companion down into a semblance of civility. She obeyed, but the raw madness continued to crawl behind her eyes as she cast her gaze against the crowd. Each eye she met, backed down, looked away, afraid to connect with that wanton display of insanity.

"Caliban!" Fionn screamed, witnessing the full effect of madness unleashed upon his friend. He steeled himself as he turned back to face Merlin once again. There was a deep, burning rage embedded in his visage as he did so. Before he could even begin to speak again, Merlin held up his hand to forestall any outburst.

"I can tell you many secrets Fionn, and these be for your own ears alone; none here, can hear us now. There are many plots afoot amongst these fallen; there are destinies being discussed in shadows and closed places. Multiple groups of people amongst this rabble, sortie outward to the farthest edges of this hell, the place of suffering, and they turn in their plans of freedom, their grandiose designs and machineries. They know not what game they play, nor who holds the dice upon the board. Rash, and foolhardy, these multitudes conceive their great plots with narrow vision, and limited scope.

"Even now, as we speak, a group of foolish souls seek to breach the ramparts and storm heaven's gate; shortsighted, to be sure, misguided even more so. Their blind belief that technology can help them breach what hell and heaven so long ago wrought. Their blindness to their quest will put them within a stone's throw of their goal, but their folly, their hubris, will bind them even stronger to hell; and they shall never know, neither how close nor how far they could have gone. They will play their part, and they will burn."

"And if you know so well, these machinations in play, why are you not in play with them, or with the Administration against them? You have an angle here, a horse in the race, as it were. What is your design?" Fionn held his tone to an even level, careful to watch all avenues of attack, casting quick glances around every aspect of this tableau. The crowd of onlookers, held back by their fear of Sycorax's insanity, and the prospect of amusement at his and Merlin's expense.

"Yes, I do have a design; you are wise, as I knew you to be. Their technology cannot breach the Veil, but our magics, can; mine, hers, yours," Merlin averred. That brought Fionn quickly to a new focus. He thought rapidly, through recent events and associations, and came to startling conclusions.

"You. You were the one responsible for setting Cu Culain upon us and his Ice Palace in Anwnn, weren't you? You were after the Spear then, and that is what you want now, isn't it?" Fionn exclaimed.

"Yes, and no. What I... want is to leave this place, by whatever means necessary. I care not how many willing or unwilling are involved, they are all but kindling to building the fire that will allow me back to the lands above."

"I will not assist you; you have no honour. Your methods are dirty, beneath shameful, and there is more than just blood on your hands."

"Have a care, man; consider how you stand, how you reply in this arena."

"My thoughts are solid, now as I stand. Upon this ground, and by my honour, you shall not have my hand in any manner, in any endeavor. By its very nature, as cast by thee, it is to be stillborn, if it be in my power to make it so; the very idea of any plot of yours is suspect and as a result to be considered anathema by myself and those who follow me." Fionn hurled the words as if they were daggers, carefully mindful to keep both Sycorax and Merlin in view together, and in plain view.

"So be it, then. Staff, to me!" Merlin raised his hands, Sycorax moved in closer toward him. He mumbled some words below his breath, and moved his fingers in a complicated manner. There was a bright flash of blue, quickly replaced by the shape of a wooden staff of simple fashioning. Merlin waved it around his head as he continued to chant; dark sparks of electricity flying from its sides with every revolution. Menacing clouds formed overhead, spreading like a stain across the air above him. Sycorax moved closer to his back, adding her intensity to the tempest that brewed. The crowd moved back even farther than they had already, the wind increasing in pressure, giving them more reason to move.

"Areadbhar, to me!" Fionn screamed into the rising torrent. He could not see the sudden violent eruption that Areadbhar's departure caused to the holding area, WC-651-03. He could not see the hole in the roof of the hastily constructed area, nor the disarray of other weapons splashed aside in her haste to flight; but he could feel her reassuring presence as she approached through the air. Fionn reached up into the sky, just as she flew toward his hand. As one body, they ran straight to where Merlin stood, violence the only thing in both their hearts.

Merlin continued to chant, smiling callously as he saw them almost upon them. Sweat beaded against Fionn's brow, flying from his face, in the force of the winds spewing from Merlin's actions. Fionn raised Areadbhar above his head, and with all of his strength, swung the spear downwards at Merlin. Merlin's smile changed to a frown of concentration, as he brought Staff sideways to block. The two sentient wooden weapons connected.

Silence, that stretched to Infinity.

Followed by a crackling sound.

Followed by a brilliant explosion of blue/white light and fiery concussion that enveloped the combatants, and threw Fionn fifty feet across the courtyard, his hand still holding onto Areadbhar, his back, painfully smashed against a stone wall. From every side of the courtyard, the sound reverberated and slowly died away. The ground around where Merlin and Sycorax had stood was charred, small wisps of steam escaping skyward. No sign of either lay nearby. Fionn, in pain, quickly got back up to his feet.

"That was... spiffy," Areadbhar whispered.

“What?” Fionn exclaimed as he whipped around at the approach of footsteps; many footsteps.

“Do you see, sir? And you wondered why we would not want to allow weapons onto the grounds during these proceedings. I hope you realize, that we will have to escort you off of the premises. No harsh feelings, please; it is merely policy.” Freud had quietly walked up toward Fionn – not so hard to do, considering the recent all-encompassing explosive noise – and quickly sidestepped what he knew would be an instinctive lashing out, as he also knew that his approach would surprise the warrior. The small army of Security that accompanied him, however, crouched, ready and at hand to respond.

“Hunh; I will grant you, that was a good idea.” Fionn relaxed, lowered Areadbhar, and presented a non-threatening posture; he kept the spear pointed down, and away from Freud.

“Indeed. You will now accompany us to the exits with zero fuss, yes?”

“Aye, I think that would probably be for the best. Also, for what it’s worth, upon my honour, I had no intent to engage in conflict.”

“Understood. And, in light of your past associations with the Library, and your current arrangements with other associations, I have been instructed to merely escort you off the premises, and secure your promise not to interfere for the remainder of these festivities. This will be acceptable terms, yes?”

“Aye; ’tis for the best anyway, as I now have a wizard and a witch to hunt and a friend to find, and wish to be about that as quickly as possible.”

“Indeed; well, this way, then.” Freud, waved to the side and indicated Fionn was to follow him. Security, alert and on guard, followed a few feet behind. The crowd gave way to the procession.

*

"That poor ugly fellow; that was his mother? Gads, but she was a mean one, a harridan of the highest order!" Both of his companions, Byron and Kit, nodded fervent assent.

"Indeed she was, Will; indeed she was." On the other side of the crowd, far removed from sight by the principals of this conflict, Will, Byron and Kit quickly walked away to rejoin their fellow playwrights in the discussion that they had been detoured away from.

The crowd, with the excitement finished, returned to its previous activities. Revelers reveled, and plotters continued to plot. And Hell moved as it would.

BLOOD AND ASH

Tom Barczak

The dracan's teeth withdrew.

Beowulf crumpled to scorched ground. The passing of his breath lessened beneath the waning beat of his heart.

The dracan's eyes burned with vengeful fire.

"You trespassed against me," the dracan said, the words sounding not in the air, but in the back of Beowulf's head, and the bottommost pit of his soul. *"So I spare you now."*

Ash and motes of cinder burned as the dracan's wings lifted toward the pallid sky. It's voice still echoed inside him.

"Suffer as you watch me destroy your kin."

And Beowulf's heart stayed beating like dracan's wings.

*

Fires burned on the horizon but did nothing to diminish the cold.

Beowulf staggered across the broken, shifting ground. Shards of black stone jutted from the ash, breaking like glass beneath his bloodied feet. His bitten shoulder shook with every step, the weight of his heavy iron shield fused to it by the dracan's fire. His only solace was the oath he swore at the weirdling light of the dracan's flames draped across the sky – an oath to avenge the burning of his people – the burning of his home.

The shadows of the trees, and that is all they were anymore, burnt husks, blurred into one another as he went, another darker shadow passing among them.

"Beowulf," came a whisper from amongst the shadows.

Beowulf swept his sword away from its scabbard. Its edge wavered as haggard as the weakened breath he took.

The shade of a witch woman, she was pitch of hair and clothed in leathers, only smiled. She swaggered toward him, out from the twilight of the burned wood into the lighter gray of a sad day. Black tendrils traced through her skin. A blight gathered upon her throat.

"I have slain demon-kind before," Beowulf swore. "And neither Grendal nor his Hell Dam were the better of me."

"But your dracan was, wasn't he?" The witch circled him. Her smile faded. "Just as Suetonius and his legion were once of me."

The witch slowed, and each step she drew nearer weighed like a hundred years upon his heart.

Beowulf staggered.

The witch clasped his blade between the flats of her hands and lifted its point to rest against her throat. There, where the black tendrils gathered, and around her mouth, her flesh still withered and died. "I am Boudica, Queen of the Iceni, and bane to Rome. Or at least I was until they poisoned me a long, long time ago."

"By God's mercy…" Beowulf whispered.

"Save your oaths. We're in hell fool, no gods above can hear you, and the gods of hell quit listening to my pleas long ago."

*

"It's always farther than the last time," Boudica muttered. The ever-present ash covered them both in a crumbly shroud, "the closer that we get."

Only the red and black of their wounds showed against the soot.

"We've met before, you know, met every day since you died, and with every passing day our meeting comes sooner, as your acceptance of your own death draws near. For whatever reason, our blood and our fates are tied here."

"You are one of the Celtings," Beowulf said.

"Aye," Boudica replied. "And you are a Geat."

"I am the ring bearer of Hygelac."

"I know," Boudica said. A grim smile crept through her ash. "You tell me every time. The fire you seek – it is the dracan's fire, the burning of your hall and your thanes, your shield men and your..."

Boudica doubled over. Coughing spasms claimed her. The sordid bile of her wound drained away. Only the rasp of her breath held constant as a trembling took her.

Beowulf seized her.

"...For me it is the burning of my tribe, my people," Boudica held steady as an agonizing breath passed through her, "beneath the torch of a roman legion."

She turned up to him. Where her mouth should have been, and where the rot of poison hadn't taken it, the ghost of a smile remained. It still showed at the corners of her eyes. "I'm hoping you will disappear when I reach them."

The corners of Beowulf's eyes softened.

"But you will find no solace there," a woman's voice said, soft but strong, and thick with ash. "Neither of you will. For *there* is but a phantom, a wisp."

The woman stood amidst the burnt-out hollows of the forest, wrapped in a hooded bleak cloak that clung to her like damp flesh, the dracan's or perhaps the romans', fire shimmered like a tapestry behind her.

The woman pulled away her matted cowl. Barren flesh, tortured and burned, had cried out until something less than her humanity remained.

"My name is Joan," the woman said. "And I'm here to rescue you."

*

Joan traced a broken finger across the mottled scars of her flesh.

"The fire once consumed my flesh constantly. Every day it did so, until the burning of my eyes would melt into the fires of France lit upon the horizon."

Boudica reached out to touch her.

Joan flinched.

"I can still feel the flames. Though at least now I no longer see them. No small consolation for one who's damned, and I have too often learned the wisdom of taking nothing for granted here."

"Who did this to you?" Boudica asked. Her caring hand upheld in the air.

"The Burgundians? The Bishop of Beauvais? There was a time once when I thought it was the Father of Heaven himself. There was once even a time when I considered it my bride gift from him."

Beowulf snorted from where he sat. "It is for certain that your groom didn't see it fit to save you."

Joan smiled as one would smile to a child.

"No. Though perhaps it was his will that first set me on this path of suffering, I have come to believe it was only for myself that I remained."

Boudica withdrew her hand, a troubled specter beneath her brow.

Beowulf rose. The same unnamed and uncaring ghost lingered next to him.

"And so it was with you as well," Joan whispered. "Both of you." Her stare fixed for a moment upon each of them. "It was why I was led to you."

"To us?" Boudica started.

"To die in the sight of whatever glory you seek – the noble death of the martyr."

"It was not glory that killed me," Beowulf spurned, "but a dracan spawned."

"And for you Boudica, was it Rome?" Joan asked.

"Aye," Boudica mouthed.

"Though once I believed he had, my heavenly father never sought my death," Joan said, her voice turning wistful. "It was not even the men who held me, or raped me. It was me. It was you. It was our own vainglory that we sought as payment for what we felt we had suffered, what we felt we deserved."

Boudica raised a hand to her festering throat.

"This place has made you both mad," Beowulf spat the ash from his tongue.

"The only madness here is when we cannot comprehend why we're here," Joan whispered. Her stare darted upward. "There is no penance without wisdom. Trust me in this when I say it was your own sin that brought you here, not the sins of others. And it is said that Pride is the deadliest sin of all."

Boudica's voice dragged beneath her hollow stare, "But what good is wisdom when the suffering still remains?"

"I hope," Joan's stare shot upward again, "for I dare not pray lest it become a poisonous fume here, that our suffering will soon come to an end."

"How?" Boudica asked.

Joan's stare descended from where heaven had been, "It's why I was sent to you, here on this plain of Ilion, to lead you." Her voice fell to a whisper. "I've learned of a way to escape the gates of hell."

"And what damned soul beside you would help another here?" Beowulf spat.

"I cannot say. Only that the way was given me by grace."

A thunderclap followed by a stilted moan echoed across the burning sky.

"Only there is no grace in hell," a voice boomed.

Above them, suspended on glimmering wings of alabaster, seven hooded angels descended from the tableau of fire where heaven had once been.

"To the dead who don't know me, I'm Erra," the centermost angel played. The other six fanned out from him like the tip of a spear.

His voice softened to a cymbal, "and these are my Sibitti."

Beowulf stepped forward.

"If not grace, then for what would you descend to this bitterness?" he cried out to them.

"Because your hope tastes like sin upon my tongue," Erra turned to the second of the angels to his right. "Punish them."

The second threw back his cowl. His sword danced with cries of lighting.

Beowulf staggered back, to cloak his two companions, raising his sword and iron shield.

"No!" Joan screamed as she flung herself in front of them.

Erra turned to her, an eyebrow raised, a flash of surprise and recognition upon his lips.

Then the last of the seven, the flash of his cowl removed, his vigoured countenance unveiled, raised his blade in a swath of flame and ire.

Joan's already wrought flesh splintered beneath him.

*

Boudica pressed her own shredded raiment over Joan's boiled and blackened skin. Joan's screams split the ash filled air.

"She's met them before," Boudica said, her eyes as dark as they could be. Her voice blistered from the poisoned rot of her throat. "They knew her. It's not the first time they've done this to her, but that means she'll heal, as much as anyone can here."

Beowulf looked up to the blood-stained mantle that had once held the heavens. It broiled and turned like a tapestry of fire – but the dracan didn't wait there – it never had – and it wasn't even meant for those he'd left behind. They would still have their own chance to be damned or not and their consequence would be their own to bear.

His sins were his own – a small consolation for one who was already damned.

Beowulf thrust his sword down into the ash and leaned against it as he fell to his knees beside Joan of Arc. His shattered and blackened iron shield hung limp beside him. The unbidden solace of tears filled the corners of his eyes. The weight of ash filled them.

"If as you say," Beowulf whispered, "God isn't present here child, then know at least you have shown me his ghost. For that, I will indeed follow you to the gates of hell and even back again."

*

Beowulf slept. The lines of his face softened against the muted gray around them.

"And so you shall," Joan whispered. She traced her hand just above his face.

She'd risen even as they'd succumbed to sleep, Boudica, with her hand still upon her brow, her wounds regenerated once more, leaving only the memory of their torment to punish her.

She'd risen to the sound of footsteps approaching.

She could see them coming closer, ghostly imprints pressing into in the ash, with no man or beast in sight to make them.

So she waited.

They stopped only an arm's length away from her. The sands spiraled round, of all things, a smile.

The bleary shape of a haphazard man followed shortly after. As he appeared, she could tell he was one of the middle dead, well after her. In a long coat and tall hat, his smile, though it should have, never lessened. His heavy-lidded eyes appeared sad and blinked incessantly. Bags with scrolls hung across his shoulders. He carried a large wrapped bundle in his arms.

"You are no assassin," Joan mused. "You look more of a scribe."

"A writer, actually," the man said. "Or at least I used to be. I'm a builder now of sorts, made to make the things of which I once wrote."

"And your name?"

He hesitated. His mouth shaped out words he couldn't speak, until he found others. "My name is Charles Lutwidge Dodgson."

"And why then, Charles, are you here in this place of the Old Dead?"

“Your benefactor has sent me to give you a gift, something special that I made. It is something you will need to get past the guardians of the gate.”

With a flourish reserved only for the clergy, he swept the cloth away, from a sword, perfect in every way a killing blade can be, glistening somehow like an angel in the muted light of hell.

“It is a Vorpal Blade. I call her Alice.”

*

“Wait,” Joan said. “The river Lethe shifts in its path. Do not let its waters touch you. Or you will never leave, or remember why you ever sought to.”

And it did, its water changed to ash before their damned eyes, leaving a narrow path open only a moment, just as had been promised her in the message she’d found, left to her in a book labeled “Read Me.”

“Now!”

They ran, the three of them, like a holy trinity, like hellfire, scarcely making it before the wide dark waters closed in, to a broken land where ash gave way to black sharpened stones.

Boudica clawed at her sputtering throat as she pointed with her other hand, “There.”

Across a league of sharpened plain, a line of black mountains stretched across the horizon like a poisonous finger. They vomited fire and coughed up the ash that already covered them all.

“There is a passage that will take us through them,” Joan said. “To Cocytus, the River of Sand and the Palace of Agamemnon which guards the black gate itself.”

*

The hole in the earth, in hell, wavered in the heat.

On its edge sat the tinkerer, Dodgson. He leaned over, his tall hat bobbing, carving a piece of wood, in the shape, of all things, of a flower. His strokes upon it, gentle. It was soft and lithe, beautiful.

"Going down the rabbit hole, are we?" Charles Lutwidge Dodgeson asked.

"Um, yes," Joan replied, unwittingly. Her attention was on the beautiful thing that he held.

"Great idea, I always say. Only it's the wrong rabbit hole. When this was last tried, when souls last tried to break through hell's gates, Caesar and Alexander had an army. And they failed. You have only three."

Then he screamed out, a flash of flame thrown from his hand.

Blackened, withered and now covered in ash, the burnt husk of the flower rolled to Joan's feet.

Dodgson shrugged.

"The Devil always does that to me, every time I try to make something pretty."

Boudica retrieved it. She rolled it in her fingers until it collapsed into dust.

"You didn't come here to carve flowers," Joan said.

"Or did I? In my life I hid behind a veil of my own design, seeking refuge in the places of my mind. I sought a hidden refuge in the bizarre and the maligned, ignoring the beauty of the world that was already mine. Ironic, here, that's all I want to do. So the Devil refuses me."

Joan held up the sword named Alice. The rust light of the fire-lit sky seemed etched upon it.

"Is this not beauty?"

He raised a brow.

"No. It's perfection. Beauty is anything but. Beauty finds grace for its lack. That is why beauty can never exist here."

He stood, tilted his head, and tapped his finger on his brow. His floating smile returned.

"But here, here is something completely different!"

"You're mad," Boudica muttered.

"Why, yes. Yes, I am."

"Enough of this!" Beowulf growled.

"No. Not nearly. I haven't shown you the way down the rabbit hole yet."

"Then where is it?"

His smile steadfast, Charles Lutwidge Dodgeson stepped up to Beowulf, and tapped the Dane's brow three times.

"So you say we make heaven come to us," Beowulf demanded.

"Certainly."

"Blasphemy!" Beowulf shoved the little man down, towering over him.

"What else would you expect here?" Dodgson pleaded, scrambling backwards.

Boudica stayed Beowulf reluctantly, "Let the little man speak."

"Yes. But what I said is no less true. The mind can create anything. I did it there. I can do it here."

"And we will each end up like your pretty little flower," Boudica stated. She toed the ashes that hadn't fled yet on the biting wind. "All burnt up." She looked at Joan apologetically. "Sorry."

Joan smiled back, the constant memory at the edge of her vision somehow now falling away.

"Then why don't you go and leave the rest of the damned to their fate?" Beowulf said.

"You will have to be quick to be sure," Dodgson stood, dusting his breeches and lapels. "Satan would never let such a fantasy take hold here. We will have to be quick, down the rabbit hole."

*

The irony had been that it was with hell's ash that he'd drawn it, with what had been left of his flower, on a rolled out parchment – a simple circle, black on the outside and an empty vessel on the inside. It was how he'd drawn it that the magic had come, gentle, caring, trusting, as if he were being led, his lips open but a whisper as he breathed in his vision.

And the light that came dimmed all other light.

The gates of heaven hung open wide before them.

As if the gates of hell had never been, if only for a moment.

"You seek," the thunderous voice of Erra boomed, "yet you will find Paradise lost to you."

Joan closed her eyes as the shadow of Erra fell over her. Erra, who hunted her, who punished her it seemed above all others, never letting her die, but demanding something from her more than either God or the Devil themselves.

"Yet here I still am," Joan turned on her heel. She raised Alice, between herself, her friends, their rapture, and Erra and the seven weapons who served him. "And you are wont this time to stop me."

Erra raised his hands. The Sibitti who served them cast back their cowls.

"It will be so easy," Erra said.

"I think not demon!" Beowulf said. "For that is what you are. No grace or supplication has ever crossed your lips. Punisher. Torturer. Maleficence."

Flame and ire bound toward him.

Beowulf's iron shield crackled and burned beneath it, but held.

Boudica's hunting spear hurtled over him…

…as Charles Lutwidge Dodgeson slunk away toward heaven's gate.

While others paid the entry price for him.

Beowulf screamed, "It will close woman! Flee, and take what grace has been offered you!"

Joan spun back.

The fires of hell blossomed in reflection over Alice's perfect steel as it flew through the air. Choirs of angels seemed to carry it.

Charles Lutwidge Dodgeson never knew what took his head. Or perhaps he did.

"You," Joan wept. "Will. Not. Defile. Heaven."

Only Boudica's scream was louder than the sound of hell's rapture that exploded around her.

Joan slammed against the ground.

Broken rock and shattered bone. But no flame.

Boudica's scream turned lament beneath the suffering cries of their savior. The fires of hell, dracan's fire, from the last of Erra's weapons consumed him. His shield at last had finally broken.

Beowulf. A Geat. A man. A soul that suffered even as her own did. And he'd given up everything for her. A savior, just as Christ had been.

But not as a martyr, as a friend.

Beowulf.

Hell quickly consumed him. Black bile stained the cracks where the spirit flesh of his body passed. His shattered shield whispered back into the ash around them. His ghost cries echoed, a whisper of his death, of his rebirth. And he would be, or already was, reborn, in this timeless hell. Everybody was, even the little thief who tricked them here. Boudica already crouched where Beowulf fell. Blood raced across her brow. She pressed her fingers into his passing. She raised them to her face, to her lips.

Wisps of acrid smoke broke around them as the memory of heaven's light lingered upon the stones at their feet.

Boudica narrowed her eyes. She raised her festering chin.

Joan struggled to her feet.

Heaven could wait.

Beowulf was already being remade on the undertakers slab. And he was alone.

And only his friends could save him.

Erra lowered just above them, his seven personified weapons arrayed alongside him. His mouth held open in silence. There was nothing he could say, nothing he could raise in ire against her. Not without damning himself. They may not have escaped hell. But they could have. Erra knew it, and he knew he'd failed to stop them.

The last of the seven stirred, Beowulf's bane, his blade succinct and unbound.

Erra stayed him with his outstretched hand.

A small smile dressed Erra's face.

Respect?

No. Probably more like a challenge.

Was that what this was to him now?

They had something that no one else in hell had, something that so many would die countless deaths to not let them keep, or send others to do so. Because it didn't belong here. That was why Erra smiled. He knew what awaited them, here in hell, almost alone with this prize they'd found.

And what thing could be so precious, like a flower?

Joan of Arc smiled back.

They'd found hope in each other.

HELLEXANDRIA THE GREAT

Sarah Hulcy

Demetrius raised his voice, “May I have your attention, please?”

The young people gathered in the Galen Auditorium stopped talking and hastily found seats.

“I would like to thank you all for volunteering to act as guides for our guests at the upcoming gala. The young man to my right is my first assistant, Makalani, who has been involved in all the planning for this magnificent affair to showcase His Satanic Majesty’s masterful rebuilding of the new Hall of Injustice Library. Over the next weeks you will be working directly with Makalani to become as knowledgeable as possible regarding the Library and its contents. You may have complete confidence that he is intimately familiar with all aspects of the Library, its workings and contents – so do not hesitate to address your questions to him.”

Caesarion and Brutus, the two apparently teenaged sons of Julius Caesar, were seated close to the rear of the auditorium at Caesarion’s insistence. He grumbled to Brutus, “*Volunteering?* I didn’t volunteer...” Brutus scowled at Caesarion and hushed him.

Makalani stepped up to the lectern, hoping to mask his nervousness at addressing such a large group of individuals. He was determined to justify Demetrius' trust in him. The audience appeared to be mostly around his age, and that made him braver. While alive, as a scribe at the Alexandria Library, he had certainly never been given duties requiring him to have such a public presence, but he *was* the Chief Librarian's first assistant here in hell – and Demetrius had many times discussed with him the differences in his duties here in afterlife as opposed to there, in life.

Makalani cleared his throat and began: "Good morning. You each should have packets containing maps for every floor of the public levels of the Library, along with lists of specific exhibits, their locations and descriptions. I will take you all on the same tour you will be giving to our guests at the gala. I will do what I can to help familiarize you with the layouts of each floor and the exhibits located throughout the Library. Some of the exhibits are *very* special possessions of His Satanic Majesty. These he wants displayed prominently to our guests. Make a dedicated study of the lists of exhibits and descriptions so you can answer any questions directed to you by members of your groups.

"One group of exhibits has items possessing special and possibly dangerous attributes, such as the Robe of Crime and the Necklace of Harmonia, the Flying Sandals of Perseus, and other less well-known items we retrieved after the initial destruction of the HOI. These exhibits are in special display cases, warranting extra security. So be sure to read the warnings regarding guests approaching or touching those particular cases: contact may be fatal to the guest. I won't elaborate upon the consequences should His Majesty discover any of you lax in preparing yourselves to carry out your duties. These tours are of particular importance to HSM, so be watchful: he may very well become one of your cortege without your knowledge." Makalani was not sure this would occur, but it was entirely within HSM's power, and Satan *did* check up on those representing his interests. In any case, faced with such a possibility, everyone would give the tours their best efforts.

Faces throughout the auditorium visibly paled; a low murmur eddied between rows of seats.

Makalani let the idea sink in, then continued, "Since everyone cannot take a tour at once, we begin with the first five rows. You in those rows, accompany me. The rest of you, stay here and become familiar with the material. When we return, the next five rows will take a tour, and so on, until everyone has been through the Library. At that time, we will have a question and answer period. You all carry pads on which to jot questions as you think of them, but we will address these questions only when the tours have been completed. That way, everyone may benefit from the information provided at that session."

"So, we begin. Everyone in the first five rows please –" Makalani broke off as he felt the floor start to tremble. Then the entire building shuddered and he thought *Oh, no, not again!* He clung to the lectern as those in the audience trying to stand immediately fell back into their seats. The vibration intensified quickly to a crescendo, then stopped. Everyone waited expectantly, hoping there would be no further disturbance.

Voices raised among the audience as the frightened and the confused spoke up. What had happened? Why? Where was the source of this disturbance? Who was to blame? After another few minutes, walls and floors and fools ceased trembling. Makalani forced himself to release his stranglehold on the lectern. Calling for calm, he told the group he would try to determine what had caused the tremors and whether they need prepare for more.

Then he stepped out the side door to find Demetrius, the Chief Librarian, hurrying his way: "Sir! Are you all right?" he asked Demetrius, clutching Demetrius' robe.

"Yes, Sesh. Yes, I'm fine. No one seems to know exactly what happened, but there seems to have been a large explosion – *not* in this building, thank the fates." Seasoned Demetrius and his acolyte, Makalani, had weathered the destruction of the original Hall of Injustice together, a harrowing experience. "It appears to have been a single event, so you may continue orienting your guides. I shall try to discover exactly what happened. Despite whatever I learn, we proceed as planned, so everything stays on schedule."

Makalani sighed with relief and gently cradled Demetrius for a moment, thankful he had not been injured. Demetrius patted Makalani's cheek and smiled into his warm brown eyes. Making a 'shooing' motion he said, "Go on, now. I will see you later at our apartment when today's activities are finished."

Makalani nodded and stepped back through the door, into the auditorium.

"All right, everyone, it appears that was just an isolated event. Later we may learn what caused the shaking. But for right now, will those in the first five rows please follow me?"

As they stood and gathered around Makalani, Caesarion slouched in his seat, waiting for the group to leave the auditorium. When they had left, he turned to Brutus, saying "This is bullshit! I'm gone."

Caesarion stood.

Brutus yanked him back into his seat and spoke through clenched jaws: "Our father made this a requirement for us to continue to enjoy any measure of freedom. If *either* of us fail to carry out his wishes, we *both* will be serving Hatshepsut as foot soldiers! I, for one, do not relish the idea of tramping around half of hell in heavy armor, camping out in the mud, following her around on maneuvers, just because you refuse to do our father's bidding on anything! So, sit down. Be quiet. Study this material like you actually care about doing a good job, or so help me...."

Caesarion stared at Brutus as if he had just grown a second head. *I guess he really* is *our father's son,* he thought. But he slouched back down in his chair and opened his packet with a scowl.

*

At his office door, Demetrius greeted James Hoffa, bidding him take a seat. "Mr. Hoffa, HSM informed me that you will be providing and supervising the staff necessary to accommodate the guests for the upcoming gala."

Jimmy Hoffa extended his hand to the Chief Librarian. "Nice to meet you, Demetrius. Please call me Jimmy. Yes, HSM has assigned me plenty of personnel and I have some ideas about who needs to be placed where, so let's discuss the arrangements.

Demetrius and Hoffa spent the better part of the afternoon working out the details of the gala: what would be served; how many at each table; what appointments; locations of security personnel; where various vehicles would be placed as guests arrived (since some were modern, some would be in horse-drawn chariots, and everything in between). Details were nearly endless, but they worked through the entire list Demetrius and Makalani had made so laboriously over the past months, planning the festivities.

*

For the next three weeks, Makalani worked with the guides until each could conduct him through the Library according to instructions, answer all the questions asked about any exhibit, and easily describe the location of any category of information contained in the Library, whether represented by book, scroll, tablet, etching or any other medium.... He worked especially closely with Brutus and Caesarion, at Demetrius' request. When it was discovered that the intense shaking and tremors felt on the first day they met in the auditorium had been Julius Caesar's villa being destroyed by some unknown force, Demetrius arranged for both young men to stay in guest quarters in the Hall of Injustice on the same residential floor as Demetrius' apartment while things were sorted out – with HSM's permission, of course – so he could keep an eye on them, especially Caesarion. Even that devoted screw-up was subdued by the calamity, staying very close to the Library and keeping his head down.

With a third of New Hell City having been accidentally vaporized by Nikolai Tesla's energy experiment, and the participants of the big conference being drafted by HSM to assist in the "secret" project to storm the pearly gates of heaven (while, of course, reporting everything they learned); with Shakespeare and his companions busily working on the play to be performed at the grand rededication gala per HSM's orders, requiring consultations to ensure there was no inadvertent insult to His Majesty or other VPBs (Very Powerful Beings) included in the work; what with other plots and conspiracies proceeding apace, His Satanic Majesty had just been too busy to concern himself overmuch with the destruction of Caesar's villa. So far, no one had determined which occupants were at home when it was destroyed and which were not, or the locations of those who were *not* in residence at the time. Actually, no one knew very much about the present state of any of the inhabitants of the villa. Apparently, Caesar and his surviving personnel, saved by not being at home on the fateful day, had unilaterally decided to go to ground until someone determined the cause and the instigator(s) of said destruction. That was just fine with HSM, who had no time to devote to that matter, anyway.

Satan had just about had enough of the auditors from Above causing mayhem and destruction all over the various hells – most especially the part under his own control – and was overseeing several projects intended to cause Erra and his Seven Sibitti as much trouble as possible. He had given orders to those involved in the gala or the grand scheme to storm the gates of heaven; put Samael in charge of overseeing those and other activities; and had absented himself from the environs of New Hell City. No one knew where he had gone. No one dared to try to locate him, or wanted to. Instead, they all worked doubly hard at their appointed tasks so as not to be found wanting upon his return.

*

The night of the gala finally arrived. At times it had seemed like an unreal or imaginary event to be held at some nebulous time in the future; at other time, as if they were on a train hurtling at top speed toward their destination, with no possibility of getting everything done in time. With a tremendous effort and a great deal of help, Demetrius and Makalani got all the arrangements completed in due time. They had compared voluminous lists of items to be accomplished, lists of guests and seating charts for the lavish dinner to be served at the behest of His Satanic Majesty at the end of the evening, locations for close-up entertainers, creation of the sand garden in the atrium of the Library, times for performances of Shakespeare's play and the reservations for each attendee – more planning had gone into this gala than any event ever held in the history of the earth or hell. Both were delirious they did not have to handle the planning for the Olympiad taking place the same week as the gala. And both were nervous, and had every right to be.

Tonight. It was tonight and they *would* get through the evening. They would handle all problems somehow, with the assistance of Mr. Hoffa and his staff, thank the fates. There were certain to be individuals dissatisfied with their dinner seating or slighted by how far they had been placed from the dais on which HSM and his chosen fallen angels would be served dinner; or with whom they were expected to attend the play, and many other ridiculous complaints that would undoubtedly be expressed by disgruntled guests *ad nauseum.* The time for preparation was over; the time for realization was now.

Demetrius and Makalani were robing themselves for the most important event either had ever attended: the gala to celebrate the reopening and renaming of the Library. Makalani was already dressed in a beautiful cream linen tunic with tiny gold threads woven here and there throughout the fabric so it shimmered as he moved, alizarin crimson trousers and soft leather sandals chased with gold designs matching the decorations adorning the walls in the Library. He had spent extra time to make sure the color outlining and highlighting his eyes was the perfect shade of charcoal and applied as perfectly as possible. He helped Demetrius arrange his gleaming white toga with gold trim lining each edge of the fabric. It was a complex garment that wrapped the body and finally came over one shoulder, draping down the front, ending at exactly the same length as the toga itself. There was a single gold pin fastening the overwrap to the chest of the toga, designed as an intricate scroll with the initials "HML" for Hellexandria Memorial Library inscribed on the open part of the scroll. Makalani had a smaller version of the same pin discretely attached to the hem of his tunic. His eyes sparkled with excitement.

Demetrius and his First Assistant and companion shared a moment, before they left Demetrius' apartment to descend to the grand plaza level, to simply realize that they had done it! They had done everything in their power, and HSM's considerable influence, to ensure the best evening possible. All had been designed to overwhelm each guest with the lavishness of His Majesty's largesse and power in recreating the Library – and the rest of the Hall of Injustice so impressively after Guy Fawkes destroyed the entire edifice in a hopeless attempt to assassinate Satan. Had Fawkes truly sought, clumsily, hopelessly, to curry favor with the deity he had worshipped in life – the same deity who consigned HSM to this very underworld?

The New Dead were inscrutable in their hubris.

Taking Makalani's hand, Demetrius took a deep breath and said, "Well, Sesh, it is time. When we return here, the gala will have concluded and we will have seen the result of all our hard work to fruition. I cannot thank you enough for everything you have done, assisting me with His Majesty's commands, even taking on tasks before I thought of them! I am again very, very pleased that I chose you to fill the position of my unfortunate prior First Assistant – you have proved to be invaluable... just invaluable. You can be justifiably proud of the job you have done."

"Please, Demetrius, you have shown your appreciation of my efforts over and over. I did only as I would have done any task for you: to the very best of my humble abilities. Now, let us take ourselves to the gala. We will find plenty to occupy our time before it is ended, and be eternally grateful to return to these rooms when it concludes."

Demetrius took his hand and agreed it was time to go. They both smiled nervously and walked out to the elevator.

They arrived in the main entry area in time to see the first guests being ushered into the affair by the astonishing-looking Welcome Woman, HSM's own choice for the senior greeter. The gasps of amazement and delight let them know that they had accomplished at least that part of the assignment: the guests were overwhelmed by the lavishness of the gala.

The young guides looked well in the simple tunic and trouser outfits Makalani had designed for them. They gathered at their assigned place near the entry and coat/weapon room early. One by one they began conducting the first groups of guests into the Library for their tours.

Even though His Satanic Majesty had declared the event to be a "Neutral Ground" event (meaning no weapons and any personal vendettas or other issues would be tabled for the duration of the gala), all anyone could do was cross their fingers and hope anything disastrous was handled quickly. And handled, quietly, before problem became spectacle, since there was *no* possibility the evening would pass without any serious altercations. Hopefully, Mr. Hoffa's security staff would be on their toes and able to contain any unexpected events.

*

The evening became a complete whirlwind of activity for Demetrius and Makalani. Moving hastily, but with dignity, handling every issue that arose, neither one had a moment to stop until dinner was served. The tables, linens, place settings and decorations were sumptuous, and both men were justifiably proud of the effect the tableau had on the guests. HSM had decreed that food and drink would actually be edible and enjoyable for this one meal, so the impression on the guests was even more magnificent than any expected.

The evening was not without its surprising and outrageous incidents – certainly no one had expected otherwise! However, Mr. Hoffa personally, and his staff, were able to manage the unexpected activities with a minimum of distraction and inconvenience to the guests.

One singular interruption of the evening occurred during Demetrius' address to the guests, HSM and his fallen angels. This shocked the entire gathering to silence and was handled by HSM himself, showing great humor at the bizarre behavior of two supposed "kitchen workers," as dessert was being served. A deluded prior witch-hunter believed he possessed the genuine "Spear of Destiny" that supposedly made its bearer invincible, and attempted to thrust the spear into Satan's chest, which should have caused him to expire in spectacular fashion, and guarantee the attacker an immediate translation to heaven. He had been sold a fake spear – no surprise that! – which was unable to even scratch His Satanic Majesty's skin. Instead of the explosion of blood and ichor the man was anticipating, he and his reluctant co-conspirator received Satan's ridicule and a most abrupt disposition to a far more unpleasant area of hell than New Hell City, with no idea when, or if, that torment would end.

To Demetrius' great relief, there was no blame attached to him regarding any of the outrageous happenings – especially since he had no control over them at all! After dinner some guests lingered at their tables for a last drink and to discuss the evening's events, while others like Napoleon, his lady love Marie, and The Iron Duke Wellington, made no effort to disguise their relief at being free to leave.

*

"I cannot believe it is finished! This has been the most exhausting function I have ever had anything to do with. I don't think my poor feet will ever recover – not to mention the shocks to my sensibilities," groaned Demetrius, when he and Makalani finally were able to return to his quarters upstairs from the newly named Hellexandria Memorial Library.

Makalani, even though substantially younger than Demetrius felt exactly the same. "I thought *my* heart would stop when that stupid man tried to kill His Majesty during dessert! Please, Sir, please: don't ever volunteer us for anything like this again, at least not in the foreseeable future, I beg you!

Demetrius laughed softly at his assistant's declaration. "Sesh, I wouldn't dream of it! Come to think of it, that would be a nightmare," he chuckled. "Come, let's retire and get at least one well-deserved night of rest. Just remember: It's *done!* Of course, tomorrow we begin the actual work of managing the Library..." At Makalani's expression Demetrius laughed out loud, patting his hand, "I'm only jesting, my dear! It was just too good an opportunity to waste!"

Makalani helped Demetrius up from the padded bench where he was reclining and they walked arm in arm to their sleeping area, exhausted but infinitely happy their endeavor was, finally, over.

THE KNIFE-EDGED BRIDGE

David L. Burkhead

William Dunlap Simpson, late of the 14th South Carolina Volunteers by way of the South Carolina Supreme Court stared at the narrow ridge that bridged the deep chasm before him. The ridge was scarce a finger-width wide at its summit, falling off to either side in almost vertical cliffs, a blade of stone reaching across the chasm.

Jim Bridger, trapper, scout, and mountain man, crouched at the edge of the chasm, peering into its depths. His fingers slid reflexively back and forth along the sheathed blade of his knife while he slowly shook his head.

"You are certain that Andromeda came this way?" Perseus said behind him.

"How certain is anything in Hell?" the woman who called herself Lady Blood said. "The one who passed this way knew not herself but her appearance was as you described it."

Simpson tore his gaze away from the chasm and turned to face Perseus and Lady Blood. "She crossed that?"

Lady Blood smiled at him, "The bridge is not always as you see it. When one who is of noble heart approaches it is a broad path but when the foul approach it narrows to a knife edge. In olden times, it was the bridge to Paradise, but where it leads now? No one knows for few have crossed and none have returned."

"You have my thanks, Lady," Perseus bowed.

"And you, mine." Lady Blood touched her palm to her chest then held her hand out, palm forward. "With Lord Gathered Blood dead, perhaps justice more than cruelty will rule in Xibalba." She sighed and looked skyward. "Or perhaps not." She smiled and nodded to each of them in turn. "I will leave you now. May you fare well on your journey."

"And you on yours," Perseus said, "wherever it may be."

As Lady Blood walked away, Bridger stood up and dusted off his hands. "Never seen anything like it, not anywhere."

"Can we cross, Friend Jim?" Perseus said.

"I reckon. But one slip and there's nothing to stop you from going all the way down." He looked down into the chasm again. "Ropes, fer sure."

As Bridger busied himself with the packs, Simpson returned to contemplating the bridge. When the foul approach it narrows to a knife edge. He had never considered himself foul before but he was in hell, and surely God would not have damned him did he not deserve it.

*

"I'll go first," Bridger cinched the knot in the rope at his waist. "When I reach the other side, you'll follow, Bill. Then, Pers, when both of us are across you'll come across. That way, if someone falls there's two folk to catch 'im." He squatted at the beginning of the bridge and pulled on heavy leather gloves. "Don't let the rope pull, but don't let it get too slack neither."

Bridger leaned forward, reaching out with one hand to grasp the top edge of the stone bridge. He followed with his other hand then crawled out with his feet.

Simpson watched closely. Bridger hooked the tops of his feet over the narrow top of the bridge at the ankle, letting the heavy leather of his boots cushion him. He held his hips low and his knees in close to steady himself against the sheer rock on either side of the narrow stone edge. At the front, Bridger kept his hands in close to his face and his elbows down, further steadying himself against the rock wall.

The agility and wiry strength demonstrated by Bridger's crawl impressed Simpson.

Simpson slowly paid out the line as Bridger advanced. A hot wind blew out of the chasm tugging on Simpson's clothes and carrying a low moan to his ears. The ruddy light of Paradise, visible high above the chasm seemed to disappear without effect in the depths of the chasm.

Behind Simpson, Perseus anchored the rope that reached to the loop around Simpson's own waist, ready to support him with prodigious strength should Bridger slip.

As Bridger neared the center of the bridge, the moan turned into a shriek. Startled, Simpson tightened his grip on the rope, allowing it to jerk. Ahead, Bridger turned his head and shouted something which Simpson did not hear but guessing that Bridger was complaining about the jerk, he hastily paid out a little rope.

A red light appeared in the depths of the chasm, swiftly growing. The shriek grew louder. Bridger shouted something again which again Simpson could not hear.

The light grew, took on the form of a decrepit old woman, wrapped in flame, with great rufous bat wings beating the air.

The woman, or demon, arrowed to where Bridger continued to crawl. Her emaciated arms wrapped around his waist and she jerked him from the bridge before turning and plummeting into the chasm.

Simpson's hand jerked reflexively toward the knife at his belt before returning to the rope and redoubling its grip.

"This –" Simpson was quite certain he and Perseus would not be able to hold against that monster.

"– is going –" The sudden jerk on the rope made Simpson lurch forward and over the edge of the chasm.

"– to hurt." Behind him, Perseus too lost his footing and came tumbling over the edge of the chasm.

"Not again," Simpson said before wind whipped breath from his mouth.

*

Simpson groaned as pain burned through his bones and muscles. Something had cushioned his impact. Even so, after such a fall he should be on the undertaker's table instead of… wherever he was.

He opened his eyes. Flickering red light reflected off the sheer rock wall that rose to one side. The sound of muffled shrieks pricked at his ears.

At first he thought he was in a pit at the bottom of the wall, but as his eyes adjusted to the dim light he saw that he was in a thick bed of man-tall mushrooms. The shredded cap of one marked where he had plummeted through them.

That explained the cushioning of his fall but even so he should not have survived. His body should have burst on impact, let alone…. He twisted his head from side to side, then flexed his right arm, then his left, then each leg. Yes, he seemed to be reasonably intact and able to function. He rolled to hands and knees then got unsteadily to his feet.

The rope tied to his waist hung limply and he quickly reeled it in to find both ends severed as though cut by a sharp knife. The scattered refuse of his gear told where his pack had burst on impact.

The first order of business was to gather what he could of his gear. His spare clothes were intact, as was most of the first aid kit. His revolver appeared undamaged, as did his sword and knife. His rifle had broken in half and he could not find the buttstock. He guessed that he could find about half of his rations. His canteen was crushed, useless.

Gathering the pitiful remains of his gear, he tied them into a bundle which he stuffed into the waist of a spare pair of trousers. He cut short lengths from the remaining rope and tied the ends of the legs back to the waist, converting the pants into a makeshift backpack.

Thus, equipped, makeshift pack on his back, sword and revolver at his side, he stood up and looked up through the hole his fall had made in the canopy of mushroom caps. Before he'd reeled them in, the ropes had led roughly parallel to the rock wall. If he kept the wall to his right he could follow the direction they had led.

It was as good a direction as any.

Simpson's first step out of the area cleared by his landing sent up a cloud of spores from smaller mushrooms at his feet inducing a paroxysm of choking coughs. He stopped. For all he knew the spores were poisonous and every breath brought him closer to a hideous death. Still, he had little choice. He could sit and wait for an equally unpleasant death from thirst or proceed and possibly be poisoned.

There really was no choice. He paused only to tie a shirt over his face to keep out the worst of the spores and proceeded into the mushroom forest, surrounded by a cloud of spores that soon became invisible in the dim lighting.

*

Simpson had to pause in pushing through the mushrooms as the shrieks and moans grew louder. One voice was particularly terrible, with the hoarseness that came from screaming until one's throat bled, but unable to stop because of the unbearable agony. He had heard that scream before in the aftermath of Second Manassas, a young boy torn nearly in half by a cannonball but still alive and screaming, still alive and screaming for a very long time.

The sounds were worse than the hospital tents, where surgeons sawed torn limbs off men and boys with nothing but whiskey to dull the pain, and that long gone. It was a sound Simpson had carried with him every night until the day he died, and every night since.

Steeling himself against the shivers evoked by the screams he pressed onward. Finally he broke through a last stand of the mushrooms, able to see more than a few feet ahead.

The scene before him was worse than the bloody fields of Gettysburg. Thousands of stone altars, as far the eye could see, held writhing, screaming... things that used to be people. Around them were other beings of different shapes and sizes and colors.

It took a few moments for Simpson to sort out the clash of color and sound. A figure writhed on the nearest stone altar surrounded by three beings, each about four feet high. The figures were a sallow green-gray in color, with bulbous milky-white eyes containing neither iris nor pupil. Leathery wings, each scarcely more than a double-handspan long flapped at their shoulders. Their arms were long for their height, with hands and fingers tipped in inch-long claws. Two of the figures held stone axes in those claws, the third held a stone-tipped club. With these they struck and beat the figure that screamed afresh with each blow.

The figure turned its face in Simpson's direction and he started with recognition. Bridger.

"Hey!" Simpson drew sword and revolver without thinking. He sprang forward, firing three quick shots at one of the beasts while slashing the arm of another with the sword. The beasts bellowed and fled.

"Merciful Father," Simpson whispered as he looked down at Bridger's mangled form. Thin strips of flesh held the arms to the body, while both legs bore deep gashes. Bridger's right shoulder hung in a way that spoke of a broken collarbone, probably along with several ribs. And who knows how busted up he was inside. Strangely, the wounds, as deep as they obviously were, only oozed blood.

Bridger's cries had subsided to low moans. Afraid to touch him for fear of adding to his agony, Simpson leaned close. "Jim. It's me. Can you hear me?"

Bridger did not reply even though Simpson repeated his call several times. Finally Simpson reached out a hand and laid it on the less injured of Bridger's shoulders. "Jim?"

Bridger's head swiveled and his gaze locked on Simpson's. "Bill, that you?" He grunted as he attempted to move, "I'm busted up bad."

"That you are," Simpson said. "I won't lie. The question is, why aren't you dead?"

"I am dead," Bridger said. "Dead and in Hell."

"Not what I mean," Simpson waved, indicating Bridger's broken body. "This should have burned by now and you should be back with the Undertaker."

"Them demons did something, I think," Bridger said. "I'd start to fade and they'd pause and do something. Then the pain would fade a bit and they'd go back to work. I never was one to cry out, but after a while...."

Simpson nodded. "Did something, did they?" He looked around. Small pieces of mushroom lay scattered on the ground near the stone altar. "I wonder." He leaned down to pick one up, removing his hand from Bridger's shoulder to do so.

"Bill? Where'd you go, Bill?"

Simpson stood. "I'm right here."

"Come back, Bill. Don't be leaving me."

"What?" Simpson put his hand back on Bridger's shoulder.

"There you are."

Simpson cocked his head to the side and lifted his hand.

"Bill?"

Simpson laid his hand back on Bridger's shoulder. "It's okay, Jim. I'm right here. It seems that you can't see or hear me unless I'm touching you."

"Don't go 'way."

"I'm not going anywhere." He held up the piece of mushroom. "I landed in a patch of mushroom over that way. Even so, I should have been smashed all over the countryside when I hit. But here I am, hale and whole. And there's bits of mushroom about here. Maybe it's the mushroom. Maybe it heals and keeps you from dying and going back to the Undertaker."

"Mebbe," Bridger said. "Or maybe it's this place."

"Worth trying, I think."

Bridger forced a shallow nod.

Simpson placed a small handful of the mushroom against the strip of flesh still connecting Bridger's right arm to his body.

Bridger screamed.

*

Simpson felt his gorge rise as tendrils of tissue stretched across the gap between his half-severed arm and the stump.

The tendrils swelled and filled the gap, then pulled until the arm was straight and only an angry red welt marked where the arm had nearly been severed.

Once the cut had faded to a red weal, Bridger lifted his hand and stared at it. "Just like these demons to turn even healing into a form of torture."

"Should I... continue?" When Bridger didn't respond, Simpson gently laid a hand on his shoulder and repeated the question.

"Don't have much choice, do we?" Bridger let his arm drop to his side. "Jus' give me something to bite. And hurry. Who knows when those demons will be back."

Simpson rummaged in his makeshift pack and drew out a shirt. He twisted one of the sleeves into a thick rope and laid it across Bridger's mouth. Bridger took the twisted cloth in his teeth."

"Le 'er rith," Bridger said around the cloth.

Some time later, Simpson helped Bridger to unsteady feet. Once Bridger was on his feet, Simpson let go but stood close in case he needed to catch him.

"I'm alright," Bridger looked down, then back up. "And you're still here."

Simpson looked down at the stone altar, then back at Bridger and shrugged.

They found Bridger's gear, unmolested, on the far side of the altar. Although still swaying from the aftereffects of his torment and the healing, Bridger shouldered his pack without complaint.

"Any idea where to find Pers?" Bridger took unstrapped the larger of his two rifles from his pack, loaded it, and then slung it from his left shoulder, muzzle downward.

"When I woke, both ends of the rope stretched out in the same direction. Following it led me to you, so...."

Bridger nodded, "Lead on."

Simpson took a quick look around to get his bearings. There was the mushroom forest and over there was the rock wall. And in the other directions? Stone altars as far as he could see, most of them occupied by people in the midst of torment. On some, people lay tied to the stone where various beasts cut or gnawed on them. People hung above others, often head down, while demons performed various indignities on their bodies. At one, that Simpson could see, a poor soul was slowly descending into a vat of molten metal.

Nobody, neither damned soul nor demon, paid any attention to Simpson and his companion.

Half-successfully closing his mind to the horror around him, Simpson pointed, "That way, I think."

Bridger nodded and took a step in the indicated direction. On his second step, his knee buckled and Simpson reached out a steadying hand.

"Thanks," Bridger took another, steadier, step. "Ya know, I was half afeared you'd leave me back there. Woulda served me right, too."

"Oh?"

"Yeah." Bridger's stride had steadied and Simpson let drop his supporting arm. "Lot o' folks claim they don't know why they're here. Well, I do. I earned my time in hell. Not something I talk much about, though."

"Jim, I've been a lawyer, an infantry commander, a governor, and a judge. There's not much I haven't heard, so if you feel like talking...."

"All right," Jim paused, dragged the back of his arm across his brow, less wiping away the sweat than staining it red with the congealed blood that soaked the sleeve. When he set out again his steps were almost back to their former firmness. "I was about nineteen. I'd signed on with Bill Ashley's fur trapping expedition up the Missouri. On the way up one of our group, Hugh Glass, encountered a mama grizzly. Hugh never got a shot off before the bear was on him. While rassling with the bear, he got his knife into it and killed it but not before she mauled him bad.

"We found him like that bruised and bleeding. We couldn't take him with us. And we couldn't all just wait for him to die. This was Indian country and if we camped there for very long it was pretty sure the Indians would find us and we'd all die. Andy, that's Andrew Henry, the leader of our group, called for two volunteers to sit with Hugh and bury him when he died while the rest moved on. Well, I up and volunteered and so did Johnny, John Fitzgerald.

"It got really quiet when the rest moved on. Hugh was taking his own sweet time about dying and Johnny and I were sure the Indians would be coming along any time. And there we'd be, all three of us dead together full of Indian arrows. Johnny told me, no sense in all of us dying together and there was no way Hugh was going to live busted up as he was. So we covered him in the bear skin, grabbed his rifle and gear and ran, caught up with Andy, and told him that Hugh had died and we'd buried him."

Bridger stopped and looked back at Simpson, "Thing was, Hugh didn't die. I been known to tell a story or two in my time but what Hugh did...." He shook his head then turned and continued walking. "Hugh was just too stubborn to die. He recovered enough to start crawling. He found nuts and berries to eat. The wounds on his back were festering so he laid back against a rotted log; let the maggots eat his own dead flesh to avoid it mortifying. Once he managed to scare two wolves away from a dead bison calf and ate the meat raw. Over the course of six weeks he made his way to Fort Kiowa.

"Later, he caught up with me at our camp near the mouth of the Bighorn river. I thought sure he was going to kill me and I woulda deserved it. Lord knows, I'd earned it. But he didn't. He just took his rifle and moved on. He caught up with Johnny too, but Johnny had joined up with the army then and if Hugh had killed him, the Army woulda hanged him.

"So, yeah, I earned my place here. I tried to live a good life after that, but how do you make up for something like that?" He stopped and turned back to Simpson again. "So that's why we're going to find Pers. I ain't never abandoning anybody again."

"I never suggested otherwise," Simpson said. "We'll find him."

*

Simpson felt an itch between his shoulder blades as he and Bridger walked. He expected the demons to pounce on him at any moment, tying him to one of the few unoccupied stone altars to undergo his own torment, his own screams to join those wrapping him in a wall of sound, yet none did. Not one of the demons even glanced his way.

Bridger, while he had been on the stone altar, had only been able to see and hear Simpson while Simpson was touching him. Could that same stricture apply not just to the other damned, but to the demons as well?

Bridger held up a hand and stopped, "Listen. Hear those screams?"

"I hear lots of screams," Simpson said.

"That way," Bridger pointed. "Those ain't human screams." He turned and grinned at Simpson. "Wanna bet who's making demons scream?"

Simpson cocked his head and listened. He did hear an odd timbre to the sound coming from the direction in which Bridger had pointed and agreed that no human throat had produced those sounds. "No wagers today, I think."

Bridger started to turn to proceed but Simpson placed a hand on his shoulder to stop him.

"Let me go ahead. I've got the sword and revolver. You need some room to use that big rifle of yours.

"Suits," Bridger said. "You take the lead, and I'll cover your back with Mary."

Shortly thereafter Bridger had his big rifle assembled and loaded and a spare loaded magazine tucked into his belt.

"Try to circle around," Bridger said. "Keep the wall off to your right. I'll try to stay between you and the wall. That way I can pick off anyone who tries to get at you from behind."

Simpson nodded and drew sword and revolver. He instinctively crouched as he ran but the caution was unnecessary. Neither the demons nor the tortured souls paid any more attention to him then they had previously.

Following Bridger's suggestion, Simpson looped to the left before turning to follow the sound of the inhuman wails. He glanced back to see that Bridger had climbed a modest stone prominence and was sitting cross legged, curled around his rifle, his elbows braced on his thighs.

Simpson rounded an altar where two demons, one at each end, were vigorously violating a man, while serpents repeatedly struck at his arms and legs. Ahead, Perseus stood on one of the stone altars, sword and shield at the ready, his bronze helmet glinting in the ruddy light of distant fires. At least a dozen demons surrounded him, their gray-brown skin oozing yellow slime from a multitude of sores.

One of the demons stumbled forward, not quite directly toward Perseus. As the demon came into his reach, Perseus' sword licked out, its tip slashing across the demon's outstretched arm, leaving a trail of yellow ichor behind it.

The demon wailed, the same unearthly howl that had drawn Simpson's and Bridger's attention, and fell back to the circle of its fellows. It stumbled about for a moment until its uninjured clawed hand touched one of its fellows. The demon then removed a small handful of something from inside its belt and laid it against its wounded arm. The wound faded to a thin line which continued to ooze more of the yellow slime.

"Begone, monsters!" Perseus shouted. "This man has asked justice in the name of Zeus, and by my father I mean to see that he has it!"

The man lying at Perseus' feet moaned softly. Strange, Simpson thought, that he could hear it. Iron staples driven through the man's elbows and knees held him pinned to the rock. A great gaping wound split his belly from which his intestines protruded.

"Hey!" Simpson shouted.

Perseus gaze flicked toward Simpson, his sword raised in brief salute, then Perseus returned to his ready position. None of the demons reacted.

Simpson smiled and lunged. He drove his sword into the back of one of the demons and fired at another one, missing even at the close range. He heard the deeper report of Bridger's rifle as one of the demons on the other side of the circle practically burst in a shower of yellow.

The remaining demons wailed and fled, caroming off other stone altars. One collided with a demon busy tormenting another damned soul and the two demons fell to fighting, tearing rents in each other with their clawed hands.

"Well met, friend William. Well met." Perseus hopped lightly off the stone altar and sheathed his sword.

Simpson nodded and turned to look after the fleeing demons. "That was... easier than I expected."

"These are... lesser beasts, I believe," Perseus said. "They suffice to torment those who cannot fight back but not when two strong warriors stand before them." He clasped Simpson on the shoulder.

"Helps," Simpson said, "that I don't think they can see anything they aren't touching, not unless they're on one of these altars."

"And those on the altars," Bridger said as he arrived, "can't see anything except the demons torturing them so long as they are on the altars. What happened to you, Pers?"

"That tale must wait," Perseus said. "This man called upon my father's name asking for justice. I would know who he is and what he has done that demons sup upon his entrails."

While Simpson conducted a short search, collecting a double handful of mushroom fragments, Perseus shoved the pommel of his sword through one of the staples holding the man to the stone. Muscles in his back and shoulders bunched as he heaved and, with a groan, the metal slid from the stone.

As Perseus turned his attention to a second staple, Simpson applied a small amount of the mushroom to the wound in the man's stomach. The man screamed.

Perseus wheeled, "Friend William, what are you doing?"

"It's okay, Pers," Bridger said, stepping between Perseus and Simpson and raising his hands. "That stuff heals. Hurts like anything, but it heals."

*

At length, the old man's screams turned to groans and he rolled off the stone. Simpson held out a hand to support him as he rose to his feet.

"So, old one," Perseus said, "you asked for justice in the name of my father, and justice you shall have. Tell me your tale."

The old man's mouth worked for a moment then, "νερό," he said.

Bridger removed a canteen from where it hung on his pack, unscrewed the cap and held it out to the old man.

After the old man had drunk, he began to speak. Simpson recognized the language as Greek and while Greek had been the lingua franca of the Old Dead before English had superseded it, his command of the language was insufficient to follow the old man's accent. He did catch one word, "Αρχιμήδης", "Archimedes."

Bridger leaned close and whispered to Simpson, "He say's he's Archimedes of Syracuse." Simpson's eyes widened at that. Archimedes? *The* Archimedes? "He says he has always given proper honor to the gods. He says he should have gone to Hades' realm or even Tartaros, not this place of solitary torment."

Perseus, in turn, spoke to Archimedes, again in Greek.

"Pers says the pits are full of those who think their punishment is unjust, but that is for the gods to say."

"It's possible," Simpson said. "Some auditors have been sent from on high to ensure that the torments of all hells are properly apportioned. There must be some possibility of mistakes or they wouldn't need auditors."

Simpson and Perseus quickly translated that for Archimedes.

"Some people have gone to them and they did have their punishments amended."

After a quick conference, Perseus turned to Simpson, "Thank you, friend William. We will take this one to these auditors."

"If that's what he wants, we can try," Simpson looked around at the other stone altars where other souls writhed in torture. "But first we've got to get out of here. And, if they do amend Archimedes' punishment, they could as easily make it worse." As if to punctuate his warning, a sharp shriek rose above the general din. Simpson spotted the source of the shriek. Two demons held the soul of a naked woman by the ankles, spreading her legs, while a third poured molten brass into her vagina.

"And it can always be worse."

*

Simpson leaned forward, hands on his knees, to rest his back while Bridger peered upward at the cliff face. His load may have been lighter but the makeshift backpack hurt in a way the lost pack had not.

"Ain't no way," Bridger said at last. "I seen a lot of mountains in my day and there's no way we're getting up this one, not unless one of you's half spider."

This was the fifth spot they had inspected. Simpson glanced back at where Archimedes lay sprawled. Unlike most of the people Simpson had met in Hell, Archimedes had retained the frailty of age. Simpson and Perseus had taken turns offering Archimedes a supporting arm along their march.

"There must be a way out of this pit," Perseus said.

"Must there?" Simpson shrugged. "There doesn't have to be one because we want one. Just the opposite. This is Hell, after all."

Perseus frowned, "And you, Friend Jim? What do you say."

"If there is a way out, it won't be up these cliffs." He pointed, "I saw a river yonder at the last rise. It has to come from somewhere, and it has to go somewhere else. Mebbe."

Simpson stretched out his hand to Archimedes to help him to his feet. The march to the river took, Simpson estimated, two, maybe three hours.

At the river Simpson sniffed at the sulfurous stench of the water. "Safe to drink?"

Bridger wiggled his empty canteen. "Better be. We can't go on too much longer without something."

Archimedes said something in his heavily accented Greek.

"Our guest is volunteering to try the water," Bridger said.

Perseus spoke to Archimedes in his own version of Greek. Archimedes replied.

"As you will," Perseus said.

"What?" Simpson asked.

"Arch said it was a problem in geom'try," Bridger said. "If the water poisons one of *us,* the rest are less likely to escape. But if the water poisons *him,* the rest of us are more likely to escape. Thus he should be the one to try the water."

"That's not right," Simpson said. "We should...."

"Nay, Friend William," Perseus said. "Archimedes speaks as a geometer but it goes hard on him to rely so much on our aid. Take not his valor from him in this."

Simpson sighed and nodded.

Bridger removed a cup from his pack and dipped it into the water. He held it out for Archimedes who took it.

Archimedes held the water to his face for a moment then took a sip. He grimaced then paused, waiting. A few seconds later he took another sip then, with another grimace tilted his head back and drank down the rest of the cup.

They stood, waiting, for several breathless seconds then Archimedes spoke again.

"It tastes foul," Bridger said, "but don't seem to hurt none."

After they had refilled their canteens they set out along the river, following in the direction of its current. Occasionally they would have to swing wide of it to avoid a cluster of pedestals with their damned souls and tormenting demons.

*

Simpson stared at the river. It had brought them back to the mushroom forest where Simpson had landed and then disappeared into a rent in the cliff face that surrounded the Pit.

At the shore of the river, Perseus played out rope. Bridger had swum into the cave, seeking if they could escape that way. The rope provided a safety line and Perseus could haul Bridger back faster than Bridger could swim against even the river's sluggish current.

Archimedes was stooping at a fallen mushroom cap and poking at it's shell.

The rope jerked three times and Perseus began hauling it in briskly, hand over hand. Soon, Bridger's head broke the surface of the water and, after a few seconds treading water while coughing, he began swimming strongly for the shore.

Bridger scraped water from his arms and chest with the edges of his hands then sat in his undershorts, letting the rest of the water drip slowly from his skin.

"Couldn't do it," he said. "It's weird but the water goes clear as you enter the cave. Mebbe that marks the border between this hell and some other realm."

"Today, anyway," Simpson said.

"Today." Bridger nodded. "The cave roof drops a few yards in. You have to swim underwater from there. There was enough light to see, maybe fifty paces in, maybe sixty. I went as far as I could. I knew you'd get me back, Pers, even if I blacked out on the way back."

Perseus rested a hand briefly on Bridger's shoulder.

"Just before I turned back, I saw light up ahead, just barely. I'm guessing there's an opening a couple of hundred paces in. Maybe it's an exit. Maybe it's just a sinkhole. You might be able to make it, Pers. I don't think I can, even with the current to help. Bill?"

"I can swim," Simpson said, "but...."

Bridger nodded. "And I really don't think..." He nodded in the direction of Archimedes.

"No," Perseus said. "We will need to seek some other way."

Bridger, now mostly dry, started to pull on his clothes. While he was doing so, Archimedes stood up from where he had been examining the mushroom and began speaking in his heavily accented Greek.

Perseus frowned as Archimedes spoke while Bridger stared wide-eyed.

Archimedes stopped and waited. Bridger looked at Perseus and shrugged. "I think that might work," he said.

A few minutes later Bridger had explained the plan to Simpson.

"I think you're right," Simpson said, remembering just who Archimedes was: the discoverer of displacement and its relationship to buoyancy. "It might work."

*

The hollowed-out mushroom cap was barely floating in the water, open end down. Perseus, Bridger, and Simpson had, following Archimedes' instructions, lashed two smaller caps at opposite sides of the cap, defining a "front" and "back" and filled them with stones. By adjusting the number of stones in the caps, they had reached the point where ripples in the river just lapped over the top of the cap.

The contents of Bridger's and Perseus' packs had joined the rocks in the smaller mushroom caps, soaked but secure. They had abandoned Simpson's makeshift pack instead, Simpson had taken Bridger's pack and he and Perseus had loaded up their packs with rocks to weight them down. Bridger remained unencumbered so he could be free to scout ahead of their makeshift diving bell.

Eventually, Archimedes was satisfied. The four ducked under the water and came up in the pocket of air trapped inside the mushroom cap. Tow ropes secured along the length of the mushroom, between the two weighting caps, provided purchase for their hands as they shoved off from the shore. Archimedes, in his position just in front of Perseus, struggled to help pull until Perseus with a hand on his shoulder, said a few words in Greek. Archimedes sighed and nodded then proceeded simply holding onto the ropes for stability.

The sluggish current soon caught them and made it easier to propel the mushroom along the river.

"Stay relaxed as you kin," Bridger said. "Don't want to use too much air."

Simpson, in front of Bridger, nodded, saving the breath that he would have used to speak.

As they moved into deeper water, the water level in the cap rose slightly and the cap began to settle to the bottom. At their respective ends, Simpson and Perseus shoved rocks out of the smaller mushroom caps until buoyancy balanced once again.

In this manner they proceeded slowly along the length of the river. Bridger ducked out of the cap trailing a rope behind him. A short time later he returned and said, "the light

I saw was a break in the tunnel roof. But I don't see any way to get out yet."

"Do we go on or try to go back?" Simpson asked.

"On, I think," Bridger said. "We know what's behind. What's ahead? Well, we know what's behind."

"On," Perseus said.

They continued. Simpson lost track of the number of steps they had taken. The air gradually grew foul and he found himself breathing in short pants. Colored spots started swimming before his eyes.

Three times, Bridger ducked into the water. Three times he came back only to shake his head.

Twice, they had to drop rocks from their counterweights to keep the assembly from settling to the bottom. Once it started to rise, indicating shallower water, and they had to splash at the edges to release a little of their precious air lest they rise off the bottom and lose all control.

Suddenly they jerked to a stop. Simpson stopped and looked back to see Perseus had released his grip from the tow ropes with one hand and was fishing in the water with it. Something was odd... missing. It took him a moment to realize what it was. Archimedes was no longer with them.

A moment later, Perseus hauled an unconscious Archimedes up by the arm. It took Simpson a moment to see the rapid but slight rise and fall of Archimedes' chest.

Simpson had, so far, managed to avoid the Undertaker's table. It looked like that luck was about to change.

As if he could read his thought, Perseus stared Simpson in the eye. "We... will... prevail." He shifted his grip, one hand holding Archimedes while the other grasped a tow rope. "On."

Simpson nodded and turned. Bridger? Bridger had ducked out again? Or had he? Had they already lost him?

With a splash, Bridger broke the surface. "We did it! Come on! Come on! Surface, ten feet up!"

It took several seconds for Simpson to realize what Bridger had said. He looked back at Perseus and, as one, they dropped the rock-laden knapsacks that had weighted them to give traction against the muddy river bottom. Simpson ducked under the edge of the mushroom, now rooted to the bottom with its own weight. He kicked weakly but with determination for the surface.

Some unknown interval later which could not have been more than a few seconds, Simpson's head broke the surface into the sulfurous air of hell.

He'd never smelled anything so sweet.

THE WAGER

Deborah Koren

Practice makes perfect, that's what Bat Masterson had always heard. But repeated sparring sessions had certainly not improved the technique of Big Ed, the boxer circling his training partner in the ring. The boxer's manager yelled at Big Ed to keep his guard up, just before Big Ed's opponent landed another punch on his jaw.

"You're actually placing a bet on that oaf?" Bat asked. He arched his eyebrows dubiously at former Old West Lawman Wyatt Earp, who leaned against the splintery fence nearby watching the training bout. "You'll lose your shirt! He can't hit his way out of a wet paper bag."

"You haven't seen his opponent," Wyatt said. "Not this sparring partner. I mean the reigning champ, Mickey O'Toole. He's terrible."

Bat seriously doubted O'Toole could be any worse than his challenger, but he kept that thought to himself. Wyatt had been gambling on all kinds of events and games of chance in New Bodie lately, trying to win enough to pay for rebuilding Josie's, his saloon that had recently been destroyed by a fire. The scorched ruins formed a coal-black backdrop to the training ring. The acrid smell of burnt wood permeated the entire area, and Bat tried not to breathe too deeply.

Rivulets of sweat dripped down the fighters' faces as they circled each other.

Bat sighed. "What I wouldn't give to see a real fight. Not these half-baked cowhands who don't know a jab from a haymaker."

"I'm telling you," Wyatt said, "Big Ed here is going to win. Sure thing."

Bat crossed his arms. "Fine. You want to bet? I'll bet you ten diablos neither one – Big Ed or Mickey O'Toole – wins."

Wyatt straightened up and frowned at him. "What kind of bet is that?"

"A hell bet," Bat said, and he found himself warming to the idea. Things had been tense since Wyatt had lost the saloon. A friendly wager might be just the thing. "I bet something's going to interrupt the fight and it will be canceled. Neither boxer will be declared a winner."

Wyatt scoffed. "The odds of that, even here, are low."

"Nonsense, happens all the time. You're just too chicken to take me up on it."

"Ten diablos isn't worth my time, Bat."

"Okay. How much do you want to bet then?"

Wyatt stared at him with his cold blue eyes. "This is horseshit."

Bat shrugged. "You're the one trying to win enough to rebuild the saloon. You're the one who's so sure your fighter here is going to win you're putting down a fortune on him. If you're so sure of that, then this little side bet should just be a bonus for you."

"What do you know that I don't?" Wyatt's eyes narrowed in a squint.

"Just that nothing usually goes as planned around here, and I'm willing to play those odds."

From behind Wyatt came the sharp smacks of fists against flesh, grunts of pain, and the angry staccato words of the trainer.

Wyatt spun away. "Go find yourself a project, Bartholomew. Stop botherin' me."

"Okay." Bat spread his hands and turned away, clucking like a chicken under his breath.

"Can't rile me that way."

"Oh, look!" Bat pointed up at a blackened but still intact roof beam, where Ernie perched precariously. The squat red demon who shadowed Wyatt Earp seemed to be watching the proceedings with a particularly gleeful scowl. His neon sign flashed a message in brilliant purple which Bat read aloud: "I like Bart; he makes me fart." Bat grinned at Wyatt. "Seems Ernie approves."

Wyatt didn't even bother turning to look at him or the demon, his attention back on the training bout. "I notice he's not commenting on which one of us would be the winner."

"Well, of course not, idiot. There's no gamble if we know the outcome."

Wyatt said nothing.

"Ah, come on, Wyatt," Bat said. "Let's have a little fun. What's ten diablos in the grand scheme of things?"

"Absolutely nothing, that's the problem."

Bat sighed. "Fine. I'm going over to Ivy's new gambling hall. I hear the chandelier's still in one piece after the first week. I think that's some sort of record. I should be able to find some action there. You have yourself a dandy time at the match."

He turned to walk away and drew up sharply when he nearly smacked into a middle-aged man who had been standing behind him. "Hey!" Bat said. "What the hell are you doing? Don't you know better than to sneak up on a body?"

The man held both hands up in the air and took a step backward. The flowery scent of a bad cologne assailed Bat. He took in the man's attire – slacks, turtleneck, paisley-patterned cashmere cardigan, loafers – none of which belonged on a person in New Bodie. "Who the hell are you? What, is New Bodie now on the tourist route?"

The man laughed. He had a smooth, round face and broad, but drooped shoulders over a paunch of a belly. His voice, when he spoke, pattered soft and fast. "I was just listening to you two guys argue."

"That wasn't an argument, sir. That was merely a conversation." Bat glanced over his shoulder. "A disappointing one at that."

"I heard that," Wyatt called.

"Well," Bat asked the stranger. "Who are you and what do you want?"

"Name's Grayson, and I don't want anything. I'm just hanging out until I wake up."

Bat cocked his head. "Wake up?"

"Yeah. From this dream."

"Oh," Bat said. "I see."

"I'm a writer." Grayson shrugged modestly. "Had a few novels published. Nothing big. But that's why I know this is a dream. See, it's one of those classic twist endings readers hate. Protagonist gets into some seriously deep yogurt, and you get to the finale, and bam! He wakes up and it's all a dream."

"I see," Bat repeated.

"Right. So this is clearly a crazy-ass dream, and I'm going to wake up out of it anytime."

"This isn't a dream. You're in hell."

"Riiiiiight."

"No, really. You died and went to hell. Didn't you get, uh, greeted by the Welcome Woman?"

"That old hag?" Grayson laughed, an unpleasant hiccupping sound. "Definitely proves I'm in a dream. No one like that could really exist."

"Not on earth, no, but you, my friend," Bat poked him hard in the chest, "are dead."

"I'm talking to you right now."

"Yes."

"So, I can't be dead." The man smiled and said slowly, as if he were talking to a five-year-old, "Dead people don't talk."

Bat exhaled and called over to Wyatt. "You want to try?"

Wyatt spared a glance over his shoulder. "Why should I, Bat? Who cares what he believes? He's here and he'll suffer just like the rest of us. If he wants to believe it's all a dream, who am I to disabuse him of the notion?"

"Now, there's a sensible fellow." Grayson beamed at Wyatt. "In all my dreams, I can always find someone sensible."

"That's Wyatt Earp." Bat pointed to Wyatt. "I'm Bat Masterson."

Grayson held out an uncalloused, limp-fish hand. "Nice to meet you."

"Those names mean anything to you?"

"Well, I know Wyatt Earp. Tombstone, Arizona, and the O.K. Corral. Right?" Grayson rolled his eyes suddenly and groaned. "Ugh. I hate Westerns. All that dirt and sweat and beans for dinner and cattle drives going on for miles and range wars and getting old by the time you're thirty-five. I *would* dream about something I hate."

"That probably explains why you were assigned to New Bodie – precisely because you hated Westerns in real life."

"And remember how I said I've written a few books? You know the only one that made me any money? It was a

Western. Western Romance, actually. I wrote it under the name Dixie Mayhem. I hated that book. Look, you want to see something?" He started lifting the hem of his turtleneck.

"Now hang on a moment..."

"No, look at this. I'm covered in writing."

Bat could indeed see fine print tattooed across the fellow's skin.

"It's all over me. And it's that stupid book I wrote." Grayson craned his head to peer at his stomach. "Seems to be my least favorite passages, no less."

"You don't think that's unusual?" Bat inquired.

"Well, I had a dream once where I was eating flamingos. This isn't much weirder."

Bat exhaled loudly. "Okay, let me repeat this for you one more time. You. Are. Dead. All right? Dead. And in hell. Look, don't you remember dying?

"No, and I'm pretty sure I'd remember something like that."

"Well, it doesn't matter. You're still in hell."

The man shook his head politely and clasped his hands together. "Sorry. I can't be in hell. I'm an atheist. I don't believe in heaven or hell. How can you end up in some afterlife you don't even believe in? No, when I die, I will cease to exist. So, since I obviously still exist, and since this place is crazier than my Uncle Dan's bowling alley on fish-fry Fridays, I am clearly dreaming."

Wyatt spun, smoothly drew his gun, and shot Grayson in the chest. The newcomer staggered a step, but didn't fall. He looked down at the hole blown all the way through him. "Whoa," he said. He put his hand into the hole. "Now, I know I'm dreaming!" he crowed. "That can't happen in real life. That was cool. Shoot me again!"

Wyatt exchanged an exasperated look with Bat. "Bullets don't kill him. I might've guessed." He holstered his gun and turned away.

"Hey!" the guy called. "Aren't you going to shoot me again?"

Wyatt waved a hand dismissively. "I think you found your project, Bat. Have fun."

"Fun? This guy's about as fun as a dog with fleas."

Wyatt stalked back over and grabbed Bat's arm, drew him aside. "All right, you wanted a bet? Here's your bet. I'll bet you that you can't convince this yahoo he's dead and in hell."

"Not for ten diablos, amigo."

"Okay, then how much?"

"Hello!" Grayson said. "You know, this hole in me is filling in. It tickles. Trippy."

Wyatt said, "I bet you Josie's."

Bat glanced at the burned-out building behind them. "Now, what the hell would I do with a burned-down saloon? No offense."

"I'll rebuild it for you if you win."

"I don't want your damned saloon, Wyatt!"

"Fine. I'll bet you something you do want. I bet you my hopes."

"Come again?"

Wyatt leaned forward and said quietly, "You've been trying to get me to give up on my wife for years. You want me to stop trying to find her. Okay, so fine. You win this bet, and I'll stop."

"Wyatt..."

"That's the most valuable thing I got," Wyatt said, deadly serious.

A gleeful shout came from the training ring as Big Ed finally knocked down his sparring partner.

Softly, Bat said, "I don't have anything to cover that."

"Yes, you do," Wyatt said, almost as quietly. "My dreams against your knowledge of the underground tunnel system out of here."

"I can't bet that!"

Wyatt spread his hands. "You wanted some worthwhile stakes. Well, that's what I want if I win."

"No," Bat said. "I can't do that. I'm already pushing my luck just taking you down to your storage area. And that incident with that serial killer following me in? No, I'm running out of luck in that department. And besides, you're twisting things around. It was *you* who originally wanted higher stakes. I just wanted some fun. These aren't fun stakes, Wyatt. This is serious."

"So now you're backing out?

"I didn't say that."

"Okay. Then, if I win, you blindfold me and take me out through the tunnels to New Hell."

"Round trip?"

"No." There was something hard and resolute about Wyatt's voice.

Bat closed his eyes a moment. He should have known that's what Wyatt was angling for. "Wyatt, getting out of New Bodie won't help you get to her –"

"I don't want to hear it."

Bat paced a few steps then turned and said tersely, "Just what do you expect to do out there?"

"Haven't you heard the rumors? The attack on heaven? I intend to join them."

"Now who thinks they're dreaming!"

Wyatt crossed his arms and just stared at Bat.

Bat shook his head. "You can't be serious! Even if the rumors are true, they can't possibly succeed."

"How do you know until you try?"

"Wyatt –"

"Take the bet or leave it."

Bat glanced at Grayson, who was poking his chest where the bullet hole had been reduced to nickel size and was still filling in with a wet, whispering noise like oozing mud. "So," he said. "I have to convince that fellow he's dead and in hell?"

"You have to get *him* to admit it. In two hours."

"Oh, a time limit, eh?"

"Has to be. Even the biggest idiot's going to figure it out eventually. You have two hours."

It was a lousy bet, win or lose, and Bat wondered why he was even considering it. He stole a glance, not at Grayson, but at the ruined back wall of Wyatt's saloon, then at his old friend and the determined, thin-lipped expression on his face.

"Now who's the chicken?" Wyatt murmured.

"Four hours," Bat said.

Wyatt gave him a single nod.

"All right," Bat agreed. "You're on."

They shook on it.

Bat walked over and smiled at Grayson, who was rubbing the new skin through the gaping hole in his shirt. "So," Bat said, draping an arm over the man's shoulders. "Want to save us all a lot of trouble and just tell Wyatt here that you're in hell?"

"But I'm not."

Bat's shoulders slumped. Well, there'd been no harm in trying. "Come with me," he said, and the man fell in step amiably beside him. "Let's go for a walk. I have some things to show you."

*

Bat took his time returning. The training session was long over, and he found Wyatt sitting at a clean wooden table set down in the middle of the burned-out shell of the saloon. The back of the building formed a grim black wall behind him, and charred, fallen beams lay like a fence around him. Ernie rested on a remnant of the roof overlooking the ruined interior, his large frog-like feet dangling in the air. Wyatt was playing solitaire.

"You win," Bat said without preamble.

"Couldn't do it?"

"That dream excuse of his pretty much negated everything I threw at him." Bat pulled out the chair opposite Wyatt, sat down heavily, and tipped back in the chair. It creaked loudly. Wyatt moved some cards, turned up three new ones. Bat said, "You know, how *do* we know this isn't a dream? I mean how do we really know?"

"Because she's not here. Because hell robs you of that which you want most. Especially dreams."

Bat said nothing. Eddies of dust spiraled away along the road.

"What'd you do with Grayson?" Wyatt asked.

"Sent him to the Undertaker for a rude awakening."

"And here I thought he couldn't die."

Bat shrugged. "Not with bullets, no. But getting bit in half by the hell cattle? Seems to have done the trick. It's too late for our bet, but I suspect Grayson might finally be realizing the truth of his situation."

Wyatt dealt himself more cards. The tinkle of distant piano keys played a jaunty but tuneless melody. Finally, he said, "You would have won the bet, you know."

Bat laughed out loud. "How? Nothing was going to budge that guy's conviction that this was all a dream."

"No, not that bet. The other bet. On the boxing match. You were right. Neither man won. There was a tornado. A tornado just set down out of nowhere and rolled right through the ring. I barely got out of the way of the damned thing. I expect Big Ed and Mickey O'Toole are keeping that yahoo company down with the Undertaker about now."

"How much did you lose?"

Wyatt started to answer, then shook his head. "It doesn't matter. I won *our* bet."

Bat hesitated, then said, "About that..."

"Don't you dare try and welsh on this one."

Silently, Bat chewed his lip. His gaze drifted up to the deep umber tint of the sky, then focused on Ernie's sign. The demon was flashing a message in brilliant violet: "If you tell Wyatt, can he keep quiet?" Bat grimaced and looked away. "When do you want to go?"

"No time like the present."

"I'm going with you."

"I figured." Wyatt moved some cards, then said, "How hard did you actually try to convince that fellow?"

Bat had to grin. "How'd you know?"

"It's what I would have done."

Bat leaned forward, the wooden chair squeaking again as he set it back down on all four legs. "Some things just aren't worth winning."

"Why the hell did you take the bet, then?"

"Maybe it was time to shake things up. Maybe it was time to find some hope of my own."

Wyatt gathered up the cards and deposited them in a neat pile on the center of table. "Care to gamble on the outcome of our little adventure?"

"Not on your life, Wyatt. And not on mine, either."

MORE LIGHT!

Bettina S. Meister

Johann Wolfgang von Goethe finds himself in a place of transition, alone and unaware of what lies before him

"More light!"

Johann furrowed his brow. What a mysterious thing to think about. What was the meaning of this phrase? Did he dream? *"The dream world,"* he remembered from his letter to his dear friend Herder, *"is always like a false pot of lottery tickets, where countless rivets and nothing but small and worthless prizes are mixed together.'"*

Johann Wolfgang Goethe never paid attention to dreams and what they might reveal to their dreamer.

Goethe's eyes were closed. He considered opening them, and at that very moment wondered if he even could open them. He had never been a man of hesitation, but rather a man of deeds – one who studied and explored: a man who acted.

So he decided to take the risk. He prepared himself for a twinge if there was too much light. Through the thin skins of his eyelids he seemed to sense that there was none. So he decided.

Nothing! No light, no pain, no… darkness.

The nothingness around him was like foam, insubstantial; nonetheless, he felt a presence. Should he look around? He blinked into the void, was surprised. Blinked again and noticed that he was right: A light! More than a spot… a firefly… dancing through the night.

The Lampyris noctiluca: this firefly swam toward him, floating on a cloud of darkness.

Light and darkness were hardly separated from each other, and it was perfectly fine that they both existed beside each other. Contrast was everything, the essence of life… and death.

With the light coming closer – or him moving toward it – something began awakening in Goethe. He wasn't sure whether the light evoked emotion in him, or if it was his perception of that light which made him assume he should feel happiness.

Within him, something like joy began to grow as he realized that this light was growing: light like a sun's corona, coming closer. So, if it was an emotion or a perception that Johann Wolfgang von Goethe sensed, it was happiness.

This is Happiness such as one would expect, entering the foreverness of the creator.

Revelation made his thoughts tumble. During his lifetime, he had read many testimonials of people close to death who reported encountering this glow of eternity.

And in fact, this must be what these people described: a tunnel; darkness – and then the light!

Light, he thought. More *light!*

And the light did obey his wish. It kept coming closer, kept getting brighter.

He was becoming aware that he was dead.

'And as it is appointed unto men once to die, but after this the judgment.' This saying was from the Bible; Goethe knew.

No, not *him*! Johann Wolfgang von Goethe, who died in 1832 CE in Weimar, poet and sorcerer, second to none, was not a person to be judged. *He* judged – in court about life and death of the child murderess, through his poetry, ignoring the stupidity, the triteness, the morals of others. He alone judged, by the might of his magic; had adjudged the weal and woe of creatures by a wave of his wand. He had always succeeded in keeping his identity as a sorcerer secret from the world. He also trained sorcerers' apprentices.

Goethe began to sweat. Beads of moisture popped out on his forehead. Not from fear, not from excitement. From heat. And his body (which was actually dead and thus should not be responding at all) reacted in the usual way, by perspiring.

Something crawled into his mind, something of importance. However, he lacked time to deal with it. Ah yes: time.... Time had certainly elapsed between his passing and arrival here. Was there a need to reckon the interval? His path was clear, wasn't it? It was the way to eternity.

My goodness, what heat! It *became* increasingly warmer. The light before him already filled a good part of his vision. The colors in the light flickered like a candle standing in a draft, threatening to blow it out.

Sweat was streaming from every dead pore of Goethe. Where *was* he?

The heat was becoming unbearable; there was nothing pleasant about this anymore.

Goethe wanted to move. He tried to lift his hand, but it lay motionless. Not a finger obeyed his command. He added magic's charm to the thought that should direct his body. He increased the charm, yet his hand stubbornly resisted. *Nothing* happened.

Then something did. Now there was pressure on his dorsal side, pressure from a hard surface on which his back, hips and legs rested. The pressure grew stronger. The surface beneath him was hard.

Involuntarily, into his mind came a sentence from his southern Hessian native country: "*Mer liecht hier so harte.*" One lies here so hard

He muttered the sentence *"Mer liecht hier so harte."* Hadn't this sentence been his last words? Or had it been "More light?" He couldn't remember. He could remember that he died in Weimar in Thuringia, this wonderful town. And he remembered the people who were there with him: the Doctor, his housemaid and that young boy. This boy was as young as his sorcerer's apprentice, when the young apprentice had died in the flood.

And for some reason all of this didn't matter. Should the literary historians write books about this and students debate.... Facing the wonderful eternity that was in front of him, nothing else did matter anymore.

Suddenly the light became blindingly bright. The pressure against his body, weakened by age, became greater.

Pain shot through him, as the burning heat of the light nearly covered him. Burning light licked his bare foot.

"*More* light!" Again, this sentence came to his mind, and then: "*No*! No more light! Less! *NoOO!*" This was not the eternity of God. This wasn't heaven! This was fire! He was on his way to hell!

Goethe screamed.

*

In hell – a place less than pleasant, Goethe finds himself alone and helpless – and finds his former friend Jerusalem as his only companion.

This must be a mistake. There could be no other explanation. Goethe vacillated between rage, helplessness, and a gut-deep resignation he could not explain.

This world was so incredibly dull, numbing in a way he hadn't known possible. He had been here for a seemingly endless time. His surroundings were so unattractive, lonely. Hardly anyone around, and those he met strode by him silently.

He didn't know how long he had been in hell, yet it seemed it couldn't have been more than a few days. He actually was in hell. A memory dimly lit crossed his mind. It had to do with being questioned about his demeanors, attitudes. Strange as it was, it was no real memory, just a faint, dark, disturbing stone in his mind.

Goethe tried to make himself more comfortable, yet in vain. No matter how he placed himself, the pains in his hip, back and his back-side were always there, like constant needle cushions pressing at his skin and flesh. There were no other places to sit; the only alternative would be crouching on the floor. The surface of this place was dry as a sandy desert, yet sitting on it, one felt a clammy moistness that soaked the clothes and made it impossible to sit there for more than a little while.

Looking at the damned souls passing by, he postulated that they must be from different eras, even from times after his death. Nobody cared for him. And even when he saw that some folk recognized him, none paused to make his acquaintance.

Goethe was... bored. Ignored. He was sitting on the barren sandy ground, drawing spirals with a small twig, just to wipe them out as soon as they were ready – and start again.

Nothing is more baneful to a new truth than an old mistake. After what felt like ages, Goethe asked himself when this maxim about "new truth" had first come into his mind. Now it haunted him. What was this new truth? What was this old mistake? There was no new truth, no new insight.

Not in his lifetime. Not now in his afterlife. Or was there? What would it be? His life had ended.

Then he understood. He had obviously – wrongly – been sent to hell. And thus, since this was not acceptable for a Goethe, it was up to him to change that – to find the new truth, the old mistake.

And yet, even in hell, a soul can find a friend. A few steps away in this hell of emptiness, Karl Jerusalem had found himself a place. Karl Wilhelm Jerusalem, his old friend from Leipzig and Wetzlar times, had been here for much longer than he himself; even though time played no meaningful role here.

Johann Wolfgang remembered other moments where time had lost its meaning. At the breast of his mother. In the company of Charlotte Buff, of whom he was now too often reminded. Goethe had first met Charlotte at Jerusalem's side during a formal dance.

Goethe fell desperately in love with her, and she liked him as well – he was sure about that. And yet Charlotte had left him, abandoned Goethe for an undistinguished secretary of the Hanoverian sovereign country. And although Charlotte could have had Goethe, she pushed him away.

Just as the honorable – and married – Elizabeth Herd expelled Jerusalem. Jerusalem, drowning in lover's grief, had gone to Elizabeth's house and fallen at her feet in the parlor. She sent Karl away, even threw him out. Had this been the moment Jerusalem decided to take his life? Goethe was pretty convinced about that.

Of course, Karl Jerusalem's fate was a tragedy, but tragedies happen every day.

Goethe had immortalized that death with his novel, "The Sorrows of Young Werther." He had used Jerusalem as his role-model for the depressive Werther; and thus this death received a literary significance: "Werther" was an unfathomable success for Goethe, established his fame.

Karl was crying – like he did so often; helpless quiet sobs that annoyed Goethe all the same – because of the simple knowledge that Karl was crying.

Karl had been hiding somewhere, when Goethe appeared here from nowhere – of shame very likely. But Karl could not hide forever.

And when Goethe found Karl Jerusalem, only a husk of the man was still there, peeking from the one eye that was left to Jerusalem in his left eye socket.

*

Time unmeasured, Goethe languished in hell. Days were not days; nights were not nights; yet the far away Paradise rose and set in the ruddy sky, torturing Goethe with its unattainable glory. And Goethe still could not say what mistake he'd made, or what new truth he'd found. And yet he knew he would manage to somehow cross the borders to heaven, unlike Karl Jerusalem who decided willingly to break the rules of faith.

At that moment, with the smell of pus in the air, Karl Wilhelm Jerusalem appeared; materializing beside Goethe, saying nothing.

"You were crying again, Karl," Goethe's words were a quiet accusation. "It is about time, Karl, to accept the costs of your doing, my dear friend."

When Jerusalem terminated his earthly existence by his own decision, and never since, had it been appropriate for a Christian to take his own life. Suicides were buried in secret and silence, unaccompanied by clergymen, without sermon and sacerdotal blessing. Not that Goethe cared about that very much: to him the lackeys of faith were necessary evils, no more. But to Jerusalem, a devout Protestant, suicide meant unavoidable damnation, an eternity of torment: something he had to accept.

"Because of this decision to end your own life, Jerusalem, you are here"

Goethe did not really mean to increase Jerusalem's burden. He suffered silently, apart from his crying, never speaking about his sin or its wages inflicted here. But whenever there was a loud bang somewhere, Jerusalem fell to the ground, screaming in pain.

Jerusalem said, "Goethe, my friend, be gentle with the young and foolish."

Goethe said, "You were young, so true. You were in love and you were desperate. Now, Jerusalem, since you are here by your own decision, why don't you forgive yourself and try to make the best of the time you have here?"

If Jerusalem was embarrassed, it didn't show. Jerusalem never gave the slightest impression of impatience.

For some reason, Goethe found pleasure in mortifying Jerusalem at times, yet Jerusalem was still at Goethe's side, and Johann Wolfgang Goethe basked in Jerusalem's loyalty.

A piece of Jerusalem's head was missing, in the front right above the eye. Goethe dared not look there, though he could only restrain his curiosity with difficulty.

"Blood loss," Karl Wilhelm Jerusalem said when Goethe asked him why he was so pale. Exsanguinous was his face; no wonder if you knew he'd shot himself in the head, right there where the hole was.

At first, Goethe did not know what to say to that. This Jerusalem, a protestant legal practitioner, a determinist philosopher of minor power, had killed himself: unsatisfied with his lot on Earth, he couldn't wait to get to hell.

"Jerusalem, dear Karl," Goethe dared to touch his old friend, wanted to feel another human's presence, feel close to another soul. His eyes widened when the body he touched lacked what made a human body so lively: warmness, living pores, breath. Would it be like this when somebody touched him?

"Jerusalem, when you took your life, didn't you know you would go to hell? Didn't you mind not being redeemed?

Why was it so difficult for him to complete any thought he had here?

Paradise! Heaven! Salvation!

Triumphantly, Goethe recalled his goal: Convince those who were responsible for him being here, of the fact that he – just because his apprentice had failed – didn't belong here.

"Jerusalem, my friend," Goethe did not look at Karl Wilhelm Jerusalem, but into the empty distance, "do you know what I'll do? I'm going to devote myself to the adventure of saving my little apprentice, the small Nicholas Kennel. The poor boy can't be held responsible for having been too weak to guard my house and stop the broom he conjured, then multiplied to handle his own chores. Once I prove that my apprentice should be freed from all charges, the Powers who condemned me as his master, simply by condemning him, will certainly agree to my demands and free us both from hell."

Jerusalem was amazed. "So you accept your liability?"

Goethe turned and drew his eyebrows together. "Liability? But no, there is no guilt. My apprentice is as little responsible as I am. My adventures have nothing to do with this tragedy. I went on a trip and didn't return, since my adventures led me a different path. How could I assume that my apprentice would not obey and undertake an adventure of his own that would lead him to disaster?"

Jerusalem tried to stop Goethe's monologue. "But let us get back to talking about –"

Goethe ignored him and continued: "My life has always been a life of challenges. This apprentice had little talent to be more than an errand-boy. He decided on an adventure that didn't end well. And this" – Goethe looked at Jerusalem with a triumphant glance – "is what Johann Wolfgang von Goethe will tell them: I will speak for my apprentice, conveying to the rulers of darkness that they made a wrong decision – and he and I will go to heaven – where I belong."

Goethe hadn't quite finished his sentence, when an enormous flash came cracking down and almost struck Goethe. The flash was followed by deafening thunder that rolled under the clouds for long minutes. Karl Jerusalem began to scream. He fell to the ground, curled up and tried to cover his head with this arms.

"It is not permitted to speak the name of the godly realms." An unfamiliar voice, that roared over him like a duplicate of the thunder, filled the air. "You are required to learn this, man formerly called Goethe."

Goethe straightened up and pulled his vest tight. "Who do you think you are, telling me what to do?" He paused a moment. No answer. Goethe called again: "Reveal yourself to me! Who are you?"

No answer was given to him. Not now and not later.

It took a while before Goethe succeeded in convincing Jerusalem to get up.

"You had better listen to that voice, Johann Wolfgang!" Jerusalem tried to teach Goethe about one of the laws of hell.

Yet Goethe didn't care. He saw nothing, had nothing in mind, was unwilling to listen to anything else but his own plan. He dealt with it like going on another adventure.

He grabbed Jerusalem's arm. "Something was going wrong when they judged me. I can't accept this, you know. And now come, my friend, it is about time for Goethe to speak up."

*

To his surprise, Goethe finds himself in a wonderful, delightful place. He is unaware of the fact that these delightful fantasies are part of the hellish punishment

For a long time Goethe did not enjoy anything as much as that moment. How long ago was it that he renounced life with his last breath?

"At the moment of commitment, the universe conspires to assist you," he had once said.

And so it was indeed.

The cypress trees were easily swaying in the wind. A steady breeze blew across the plain, like a gentle caress of a hand. The tranquility and peace that reigned hereabouts nearly wiped out his memory of the terrible days in hell, replacing it with the happy realization that the name of Goethe still meant something to humanity, and that it was worthwhile to stand up for his apprentice Nicholas – because now Goethe was here in a better place....

So he did succeed and made his way past his sentence to the wonderful place of relevation.

The whole scene was beautiful as a painting. Goethe settled on a smooth stone of great antiquity, a broken Egyptian obelisk. He gathered close around himself the wide, white traveling cloak in which he had wandered through Italy. His feet rested on the soft ground of the Roman world, his nose perceived the fragrant smells coming down from the heights, his ears listened to the peaceful sounds of nature. In the distance were ancient Roman ruins, a round tower with battlements and the remains of a temple. So perfect that one could hardly imagine this scene could be real.

And then he saw *her*: Christiane ran to him, in a white dress of georgette, its light skirt waving in the wind. She fell at his feet.

"Forgive me, darling," she laughed, slightly out of breath. "I'm late. I was with our son, and prepared a small meal of cheese, bread and wine… but now I'm with you." Beaming, she looked up at him and Goethe could not but love her.

"Grieve not, Sweetheart." He gently patted her cheek. "You do well in everything you do."

Christiane was so pretty. She showed every sign of flourishing youth, just as it was when he met her, and made her his on the very day they had their first encounter.

"What a glorious time we have, don't we?" She trustingly laid her head on his knee and rubbed her cheek against his trousers. "It was very lonely sometimes, alone in Weimar. I often wished that you had asked me to accompany you."

He did not know this, or did he not want to know? "I've never mentioned it, because I did not want to make your heart heavy." Christiane looked up at him and touched his hand.

On the delicate skin of her cheek impressions of the buttons on the sides of his knickerbockers were visible. "You're not angry with me, are you?"

How could it be that he only realized now how much his wife strove to make everything just right for him? The oddities piled up.

Goethe wanted to run his fingers through his hair with the familiar gesture of the poet. However, as he raised his hand, he found himself wearing a hat. He took it off to look at it. It was a gray slouch hat of felt, a fine piece you'd be happy to have with you on a journey, since it offered protection against rain and wind, snow or too much sun. A floppy hat, white overcoat, red vest... the obelisk, the relief and everything around him – this wasn't reality, was it? Did he find himself in a picture? He remembered the endless days and weeks in the underworlds of hell.

But now he was here, in Italy, wasn't he?

He remembered the tortures of suffering in hell that were inflicted by the henchmen of the devil. And there were not only the torturers; that was only physical pain. There was this daily humiliation of a poet's soul. The everlasting memories of ostensible breaches, even though they weren't true, and fitted so little with the way he lived, and the service he had given the poetic world.

His sufferings of old age were daily pains in his life in hell. Fear and unrest, sleeplessness, and the wretched taste in his mouth, all were gone, vanished: no pulling in the joints, no distended abdomen. Goethe could hardly believe his luck.

He felt young in spirit, but he had the wisdom of age, his wife at his side, peace around him and in his soul. "I never dreamed," Christiane chattered in her open, cheery manner, "it would be so wonderful to come here with you. I was so afraid of dying and death. The pain had been so great that it was a relief. And then this...." She left the rest of the sentence hanging in the air, where the healing power of redemption dissolved into the peace of this world around them.

Here? Where were they? Not Italy?

Goethe's thoughts ceased. This scene which spread around him, reminding him of the Roman countryside, was unearthly. Christiane had died long before he did, and there had been no reason to suppose was not received into blessedness.

He gazed pensively into the distance. In this environment of harmony with oneself and the world, he managed to gather his thoughts. Here were the things that determine the destiny of men. He recognized truths that had remained hidden from him for years; captured what had been incredible.

Now everything in nature made sense as creation had intended, while, with irresistible power, an understanding of the universe and God as the center of everything unfolded before him. It was like a new birth. Everything had been true, and everything actually happened. His stay in hell had been real; his scars on body and soul, real – but nothing hurt anymore.

The landscape in which he found himself revealed its meaning. It was the area Tischbein had painted during their Italian tour together. And Goethe himself had posed as a traveler in a white coat in the foreground of the painting, just where he now found himself. Yes, it was that trip to Italy – but that trip had been undertaken without Christiane.

So this had to be heaven! He sighed and then broke out into relieved laughter. "Heaven," he mumbled, "I am in heaven!" In the faint distance, Goethe heard thunder, and for a second it seemed to him as if the soil he stood on vibrated. How strange.

"Christiane, where's my apprentice?"

Christiane Goethe, née Vulpius looked at him in astonishment. "Your apprentice? What are you talking about, Wolfgang?"

He had never told Christiane anything about what he had done while out of Weimar.

"My…" he trailed off. What would happen if he told Christiane about his second identity? About Goethe the sorcerer?

"What are you hiding from me, Johann Wolfgang von Goethe?"

He'd always kept certain things hidden from her, his vocation as master magician in particular. From early youth he'd been recognized as a special talent; precocious; gifted equally in natural sciences, arts and writing. At age sixteen he was writing poems.

Then he fell ill and his magical talent blossomed while he lay abed in Frankfurt. There he had the opportunity to steep himself in mystical and alchemical writings.

"Christiane, from my boyhood physician I received my first books on alchemy. And when I was healed, thanks to his universal medicine, I began being more and more interested in the art of magic, medicine and esoteric, supernatural forces."

His wife nodded understandingly. "So, the secret room in the basement I never was allowed to enter... this was your alchemical laboratory?"

Goethe tried to hear if Christiane was angry. However, he only heard friendly and cordial sympathy. So he explained that shortly after his convalescence, he established a first small laboratory.

"It is but a small step from alchemy to magic." As he explained, he experienced the old spark of energy and interest in providing an insight on this secret world to others.

A completely new world unfolded for the young Goethe.

"I researched the theories of various scientists; becoming increasingly successful in tapping the supernatural forces of the universe. I had been a guest in the most secret circles of magicians"

Whenever he was in the headquarters of foreign magicians' groups, he'd made presentations and participated in ceremonies – just like a pilgrim. Year by year his reputation grew until he narrowly avoided being a victim of the spell of a revenge-squad after he'd published his "Faust."

"Christiane, I must admit that the warnings of other wizards were increasingly clear." Goethe felt a shiver down his spine as he remembered the threats, blatant insults and actual assaults on his soul and body. "I was not always prepared, so some of them weakened my body."

"You were frequently ill indeed," Christiane touched his hand. "It scared me every time you were sick."

"All is well, dear Christiane." With a reassuring smile, he patted the hand that sought his.

Keeping his avocation as a magician secret, and not letting anybody, not even Christiane, know about it, had not been difficult for him. Often he had been away from Weimar for months at a time. When at home, he commonly withdrew for the evening to his room to write or went to his laboratory, while Christiane invited friends to visit, with whom she played cards in the salon.

"Finally, in a solemn act of recognition, a wand with small inclusions of crystal was presented to me by the lodge of German magicians – the highest honor for a sorcerer. I still remember, my darling, how proud I was when I was granted permission to train an apprentice sorcerer."

Christiane listened to his stories and memories. And when he came to the end, she was still with him. She nodded in the right places, blurted out "Oh" and "ah" whenever his tale was exciting, and indeed was the best listener one could imagine.

"How I wish I had known your apprentice." The regret in her voice touched him. "We lost so many children." Pain was in her words. "It would have warmed my heart if I could have been a mother to him."

"I wonder, Christelchen, that he is not here." Goethe remembered that this very idea had made him confess in the first place. "He was a good boy, and one should assume that he can find us here, right?"

A gentle smile crossed Christiane's face at the familiar nickname. "Tell me more about your last apprentice, Wolfgang."

Goethe raised an eyebrow.

"It is interesting, Christelchen, that you say this. I couldn't remember his true name for so many years. But ever since I died, his name is clear to me. I can even remember his face. In hell, it haunted me, like part of my punishment, it was. But now, being here...." he looked around "it's so wonderful here. I am so glad I did what I had to do and redeemed him and myself. Now, where is he? Did you send him off with an order?" He touched Christiane's arm affectionately .

"Johann Wolfgang, if your apprentice was redeemed, he would be where all redeemed are, and you would know."

She jumped up, beaming like a star and spun around in circles with joy. "This is a wonderful place, full of splendor and grace. I cannot wait until our apprentice, my newest son, is here and I can wrap him in my arms, like our other little ones who died so young."

The clouds that had been visible over the hills far away before, were close by now, and the temperature cooled down significantly.

She finished her dance and stood before him. "Come, dear," she took his hand and pulled him up. "Let's go to our children. They are waiting for us."

But instead of reaching for her outstretched hand, he made a gesture of protest: "I must find my apprentice. I cannot work alone."

Christiane started. "As a magician? But Goethe, I was trying to explain...."

Goethe impatiently interrupted his wife. "Christiane, I'm not here to give up my avocation. And I will not accept that they denied my apprentice entry into heaven."

Would one expect thunderstorms in heaven? Because at the very moment Goethe said this word, the loud bang of crashing thunder exploded in his ear. Unwillingly, he started and looked toward the sky above them. The clouds had made their way from the hills directly over their heads.

"But…" Christiane again passionately tried to persuade her husband that assignment to heaven or hell upon death could not be influenced by the dead, but Goethe would not accept this. He was so sure of his power that he insisted he could intervene on behalf of his apprentice, whose fate in life he had commanded.

A second time, Christiane warned him; a second time, he did not listen. Instead, he told her that she was wrong, reminding her of her limited education, explaining that she lacked Goethe's superior logic and knowledge.

Christiane's smile faded in the light of a flash. She bowed her head and he had the feeling she tried not to cry.

"Christiane, now don't be foolish, love. You know that I am right, so don't be sad. Christiane?"

With a sad look upon her face, Christiane dissolved before his eyes.

Then something touched him, this time on the shoulder. *Christiane?*

Goethe jumped, spun around… and discovered to his consternation that it was not Christiane who'd touched him, but Karl Wilhelm Jerusalem.

"Calm yourself, Johann Wolfgang." Karl Wilhelm handed his friend a cup which seemed like slightly brackish water mixed with a sip of wine. "You'll get used to it. Drink this."

Get used to what?

In bewilderment, Goethe regarded this man he associated with his time in hell. If Jerusalem was here in heaven, had the rules changed? Should he be relieved to see the familiar face of Jerusalem here? Christiane was first unattainably far from him, then so close, sitting at his feet… then merely *gone.*

Goethe reached for the cup Jerusalem held out, took a big gulp and spat it out again. "What terrible swill! What are you doing here, with this foul drink? Where is my Christiane?"

"Tsk, tsk," Jerusalem clucked.

Goethe looked into the eye of Jerusalem – and discovered to his horror that for the very first time he could see in detail the severity of the wounds Jerusalem had caused by shooting himself in the face.

"You…" he raised a hand, made a move toward the missing pieces of skin, flesh and bones of the skull that had been blown out above Jerusalem's right eye, and let his hand fall back. "Where *are* we? Really?" His words were toneless, as he already suspected the answer.

"Where should we be, Johann Wolfgang? We are where we were sent after death and judgment – in hell."

"But how can that be?" Goethe stammered. His meeting with Christiane had been so alive. He had felt, smelled everything. "I was in –" he remembered Jerusalem's warning about speaking out the word 'heaven', so he tried to avoid it. "– I was… you know where. I was with Christiane. We talked… I confessed about my activities and about my apprentice Nicholas."

Jerusalem sighed. "You will get used to it, dear friend." The dead lawyer and friend had so much more experience in hell's torments. "This is part of the punishment that is meted out to us, Johann Wolfgang. Each mind determines the form of illusion, every time we are tormented with another dream of that wonderful otherworldly place that is unattainable for us. This is nothing permanent, and the anguish we experience after such false hope contributes to our suffering. Hell is not only all around us – it is *in* us, we become part of it."

"So Christiane is... there." Goethe's eyes glided toward the shining sky far above them, that promised a wonderful day – somewhere else. "And I, Goethe, poet, philosopher, magician, am in hell? How can this be?"

Jerusalem sighed, "It's up to you, Goethe, to comprehend all this. I may have the knowledge and understand the reason, but it's not my place to tell you. You have to walk your way of punishment – and of inspiration – by yourself."

All strength left Goethe. His knees buckled, he collapsed and slowly fell to the ground. He was injured from his fall, but the pain he felt was nothing compared with the distress of his soul.

Goethe began to cry.

*

Finally Goethe has decided to make officials deal with his wishes. Being assured of being wrongly punished, he enters the halls of hellish administration

"Name?"

"Goethe, I am here to complain about the way –"

The bureaucrat sitting behind his desk in his Hall of Injustice office interrupted Goethe. "Sit down over there; you will be called up. Here is your number." His voice was disinterested at best.

His voice? Was it a male, sitting before him? A female? The being appeared androgynous, and gave no hint of how to gain its sympathy. Everything about this being was pale. The color of its hair as well as its facial color, even its lips were pale. Nothing gave proof it was a human being at all.

"Please forgive me, good man," Goethe decided to refer to this being as male, assuming it unlikely that a female would be so highly ranked. "I am Goethe. I request to talk to one of your judges; or a supervisor, or manager."

The being looked up at him. Its inexpressive, black eyes twinkled.

"Very well, you are Goethe. If it's your turn, go to the consultation office that shows your number. The counselor responsible will answer your questions." Its response was mere formality: politeness with no emotional content.

"I do not understand." Goethe felt irrelevant, like a child, asking for food, who is being ignored. He wasn't demanding an impossible concession. "You are not the counselor for my request?"

Without a word, the being pointed to a sign floating in midair above his head, held in place by some demonic power. The sign said: *'Registration.'*

"I demand to talk to your supervisor immediately!" Goethe's nerves were so frayed that he struggled to control his temper.

The voice of the being before him did not change: "You will now get a ticket and wait, like all the others. There is no special treatment, no matter who you are. When a counselor has time for you, you will be called. Till then...."

The being interrupted itself as a foreigner queued up behind Goethe's back: The hellish servant did not jump up, yet his voice changed profoundly.

"Welcome Honored Sir, welcome! It's a pleasure to see you. How may I help you today?"

Goethe could only see the profile of this new arrival. He was wearing a lavishly tasseled black garment, around his neck a long heavy necklace of gold, with a cross turned upside down hanging around his neck. This cross, together with the heavy belt of woven gold with gems included made everybody aware of his importance.

"Please come with me, Your Unholiness. You will be served immediately."

An entourage of lesser damned followed the bureaucrat and the – whoever he was, who had obviously been condemned to afterlife in hell. They were eagerly trying to remain close to their dead leader, who had led them first into sin and then here.

Goethe felt obliged to point out that he had been here first and thus requested to be counseled first.

Nobody remaining in the reception area took notice of him. Goethe was speechless. Hadn't he just been told there was no special treatment?

Endless time passed before the bureaucrat returned. For the first time it seemed to show feelings. Its cheeks were flushed, the mouth twisted into a smile that seemed unaccustomed. As soon as it was seated again, the smile disappeared.

"What does that mean?" demanded Goethe of this being that finally, unblinkingly, handed him a numbered slip of paper.

"This is your visitor number, Sir."

"I know what *this* is! I want to know why this obviously important person comes here after myself and is served without the slightest delay, while I am told to wait. Don't tell me again there is no special treatment here!"

"The rule applies to undistinguished inhabitants of the hellish domains only. Not to our prominent and important guests. They indeed receive preferential service. But this should be no surprise to you… Goethe was your name, wasn't it?"

Goethe felt the blood rise in his cheeks: "I am Johann Wolfgang von Goethe! I am a sorcerer far beyond any power you can imagine." Goethe's words came in a staccato of agitation. "I am one of the most important authors in Germany, consultant to the king…"

The bureaucrat didn't say a thing, yet very obviously wasn't interested in listening. Goethe went on: "I am sorcerer of the highest European orders, was regarded as the representative of the intellectual Germany in many countries, how dare you..."

Such indignities were something he never knew during his lifetime. Nobody dared to argue with him without regretting it, except for Christiane perhaps.

Now what should he do? Leave? Return to the place where he'd found himself after his arrival here, empty-handed? He didn't even know why he still waited here, among the unfamiliar faces of the common damned.

Goethe glanced at the paper he held. When his turn came, he would be called by the number on it. He had become no more than one more number, sitting or standing around here, to beg for clemency from the authorities.

Nobody would care if he left and took his case with him. Nobody would come and ask if there was anything they might help him with.

Goethe thought about various things to say, curses in particular, yet he just had a last look at the bureaucrat, sitting at his desk, hands lying motionless on the table top, simply waiting for Goethe to turn away – which he finally did.

Goethe stepped away a bit and looked about the big room for a seat in which to wait, because it was apparent that he would be waiting for a long time. The big hall, that reminded him of the entry hall of any governmental building, was filled with lost souls. They were standing around, sitting on benches, some sitting on the floor, since most benches were taken.

When he found a free seat, Goethe tried to not fall asleep like the damned soul beside him, who seemed to have been here for a long time, laid back in his chair, legs stretched out, arms folded, snoring, chest moving in regular rhythm.

If not for the wounds to this soul's upper body, Goethe might have thought the sorry sinner was waiting peacefully.

From his seat he watched the damned wandering in and out. They were of all ages, sexes and races; common and noble. Some had horribly disfigured bodies; some seemingly unharmed.

All of them wanted to talk to a bureaucrat or a counselor or to somebody, anybody, who might help them.

Goethe witnessed the screaming, crying and begging of new-arrivals; outbursts of fury and curses from the frustrated. The bureaucrats didn't seem to care about any of these outbursts, not even when threatened with violence.

Sooner or later all of the dead collapsed, overwhelmed by hell's institutionalized indifference.

When finally his number was called, he was guided into a high-ceilinged conference room with demons and damned souls in attendance, placing files on the bench in front, opening doors.

Goethe looked round the conference room. With the wide impressive bench at one end, made of dark wood, higher than the benches on the opposite side of the room, it wasn't difficult to recognize it as a judge's bench. The benches on the other side were for the attendees very likely. Tables for the prosecutor and defense were to the right and left on the sides.

Here his case would be discussed. Expedited. Judged. Goethe dispensed with trying to hide his relief and disdain.

A particularly ugly-looking demon had already taken its place next to the judge's bench, possibly a clerk.

The barren room had no windows, was lit from some bright lights in the high ceiling, and – this struck Goethe – there were no shadows.

He had no time to change clothes: his hearing was to begin immediately, so he would have to appear as he was, disheveled and wrinkled. So be it.

Yet he felt powerful and thought it had been helpful to point out his importance as sorcerer, researcher and poet. Nobody ignored Goethe now.

This feeling of power – a feeling he delighted in during life – streamed through him, tingling. And for the first time since realizing he was in hell, he felt… really *alive.* Now he was completely in his element. Talking, arguing and gaining victory on the battlefield of language had always been his particular strength.

With a sudden clarity absent ever since his arrival in hell, he remembered his deeds as a lawyer in Weimar and as a sorcerer. Why would he need a defender? He could and would advocate for his apprentice – and make sure that Nicholas Kennel would be cleared of all charges and thus redeemed – and he himself as well.

A banging of the doors behind his back interrupted his thoughts. An audience streamed in to attend the hearing. He saw Jerusalem among them. Jerusalem, faithful soul! Goethe raised his hand and smiled. Jerusalem waved back, mouthed something that might mean "Good luck" and sat down. Poor Jerusalem, soon Goethe would leave him.

The audience took their seats silently.

Very well, thought Goethe, it was always good to have audience. This added flavor to the discourse and enhanced the triumph to come.

And then, he could hardly believe it, in the audience he saw Nicholas, his sorcerer's apprentice.

Indeed, the boy was not easily discovered. His death must have been painful. His skin looked like white bread left in water too long. Constant trembling shook the whole body of Nicholas, and whenever he coughed, a torrent of liquid shot from his throat.

The boy had always been thin and insignificant. Now it was even easier to overlook him.

Earlier, during his life and after his death, it was difficult for Goethe to remember the boy's name. He always referred to him as "the boy" or "young fool." Now, suddenly having a name, the boy, his fate and his own involvement in his death became present.

For a moment, looking at the small figure of the soul that had once been his apprentice, Goethe had to suppress his own revulsion. Just imagining the boy holding to his hips, closely the way he once did, made Goethe shiver.

Like all condemned souls who struggle through afterlife in the netherworlds, the boy constantly manifested the causes of his death. Fortunately Goethe had died of natural causes, and therefore was spared the humiliating exhibition of ruined organs.

Nicholas sat in the last row, scratching at his skin, no glance or movement indicated that he was the reason Goethe was here – here in hell and here in this hall.

A strict, loud voice announced the judge, who entered the room. It was one of the strangest judges Goethe had ever seen. He had expected a scary ghost or demon, yet what took the judges seat was a stout, rather tiny dwarf.

Literary experts argued what inspired Goethe to write his ballad "The Sorcerer's Apprentice." Some said it was a reflection on human life and the inevitable results of their decisions; others as a "by-product" of 'Faust.' Some saw in it the creator as the sorcerer's master who redeemed his sinning people. Little did they know that the apprentice was real and the sorcery of Goethe was real! After the sad accident in his secret sorcerer's home and the death of Nicholas, Goethe created an unforgettable literary monument for that tiny fool. What a touching way of giving this calamity a meaning. This should count here, shouldn't it?

"Goethe," the judge turned to Goethe as the hearing officially began. "You know why you are here?"

The dwarf looked less like a judge and more like a strangely, unpleasantly-shaped child, causing Goethe to shudder, but he stood from his seat.

"Of course," Goethe's pride reared up. "Because I, Johann Wolfgang von Goethe, sorcerer, researcher, poet and honorable statesman, requested this hearing."

The judge shifted in his chair, his voice cold as ice. "This blind pride of yours, Goethe, is one of the major reasons for your damning mistakes. Mistakes seated eradicably in your belief in your own importance. You may present your views and opinions in front of this audience."

Goethe lowered his head a bit, almost like a bull preparing to attack. "What do you mean? I am here because I demand this court revise the condemnation, the very damnation of… myself… of my apprentice. Of my apprentice! I am here *unjustly* – I mean, 'we'…. *We*… my apprentice is here unjustly!"

Goethe was tongue-tied. What was going on? He had never been one to hesitate; now he struggled for words. How could that be?

When he'd uttered the word "unjustly," he noticed movement. The audience winced; the judge's dark figure increased in presence, without evidently growing in size.

From complacency at the beginning of this adventure; being willing to bring all his significance and position to bear, Goethe now cringed inwardly. This *was* hell and its infernal dominion he'd dared to challenge, and he was set back to the hellish lowest level of his new reality only too soon. Like a supplicant, he found himself before the bench of authority. In life he had been among the wielders of such authority, with power to decide over life and death at least once; now he was at its mercy. And Authority in hell had no mercy.

"Now, Goethe," the voice of the prosecutor on Goethe's right hand dripped with scorn, "is that all you can offer us? No magic or sorcery or sagacious persuasion? No spell or curse? No irrefutable argument or argument of substance? Simply 'here unjustly'? Can you imagine how many times we hear that? I expected better from an eloquent man as you claim to be. Whom do you expect to bully with the magic of your words... or your wand for that matter?"

Each sentence was followed by a hissing sound, caused by the prosecutor's split, snakelike tongue.

Goethe felt fear rising, spreading toward his heart, taking control of his tongue. Fear had always made him angry. Goethe flared up: "You treat me as if *I* was the one accused. I am not, so don't treat me as if I were."

"Accused? No. Indeed, you are not accused, Goethe," said hell's judge. These words started to bring back some certitude in Goethe. "Yet. Nor is your apprentice – nor anybody else." The flat hand of the judge fell on the bench like a guillotine, making the files on the desk jump just the way Goethe's heart jumped. "You are not the accused, neither are you witness, prosecutor, nor judge."

Goethe didn't understand. "But...." He raised his hands. He lacked the words, and once again cursed the fate that forced him to scrape along like this. Clarity of thought had been his greatest treasure in life; his ability to put thoughts into well-chosen words and give voice to them: all of this was gone.

Nothing of his treacherous certainty remained. The pain increased as he was just now reminded of the wonderful experience he had during his dream of heaven.

What crafty game did they play with him?

"But –" he tried to continue "– but, what... what am I supposed to be then?"

His eyes searched for Jerusalem, the only soul whom he regarded as trustworthy in this world of madness. Jerusalem had warned him not to come here. Why hadn't he listened?

Goethe was horrified by the direction of this event. He was shocked and indignant. His fear grew.

He began to think of his books: Mephisto, the figure he had created to torment his Faust. Then, he hadn't had the slightest idea of what it would really be like to stand in front of the Lords of Hell. All the world's ages might have passed since then, since he'd written arrogantly about what now he experienced.

"Where is Jerusalem?" The voice of the judge – Goethe feared this dwarf of hell more and more – brought Goethe back from his thoughts.

"Here I am, your honor." Karl Wilhelm Jerusalem came to stand by Goethe's side, his head bent humbly.

"You did instruct Goethe on the rules and purpose of this hearing?"

"Oh, yes," Jerusalem assured the judge. "I went through everything with him, your honor. Just the way I was instructed to do."

Officiously, Jerusalem unfolded the paper containing those instructions and tapped it.

With a nod of his head – as if the judge knew that the witness wouldn't lie – Jerusalem was dismissed, more than happy to disappear into the audience.

Again the judge turned to Goethe and had him confirm that this conversation with Jerusalem had occurred, making Goethe feel even more like the accused.

"Even though it is completely irrelevant, Goethe, whether you understand the purpose of this hearing and your sentence or not, none of this –" the disfigured judge raised his arm and his gesture included the entire courtroom "– will in any way change anything about the judgment of yourself or your apprentice."

Goethe began to stammer helplessly. "If so, then what am I here for? Why…"

"You are here for only one reason, Goethe: because we are ordered to enlighten each damned who is as undiscerning as you, as a result of their theological understanding from the Age of Reason."

The prosecutor spoke up following the judge's remarks: "Your position, Goethe, on the fairness of your condemnation to hell, is of no concern here."

"I have always been a man of faith, I never disowned the Lord, never…"

The prosecutor interrupted him. "So you didn't? I want to draw your attention to your own words, Goethe. You wrote that you saw a time when the supreme being would no longer have joy in creation. The creator would destroy everything to create a rejuvenated creation. Did you say this or not?"

Goethe indeed remembered. And without really being aware of what he did, he recited his own words: "We can still have thousands and thousands of years on this dear old land, as it is, and have all sorts of fun."

Silence fell over the audience.

"We have, your honor, heard enough, even in this short time. And all this damned soul said here, including his personal presentation, just supports the sentence." The prosecutor ended the awkward silence. "More than most, Goethe has been given permission to question his lot. His failures are tremendous, all named in the files." He lay his clawlike hands on the high pile of papers. "The judgment was correct – suited to his nature, his sins, his circumstances." The prosecutor rounded on Goethe. "It is completely irrelevant if he accepts his punishment or not."

Goethe was awash with anger and helplessness. He never brawled lightly, without good reason; and never with fists or sword. He preferred paper, quill and ink, words and thoughts, or – when necessary – his wand. All useless here.

He clenched his fists. This couldn't be the way this proceeding ended. How could he fail? Would his might and importance in life be reduced to fright and impotence here in perdition? Despite anger, despite intellect, he would be lost if he didn't act now. There was only one single thing that defeated him: Death! This was inevitable. But he would not allow himself to be placed in hell for eternity.

He considered attacking his accuser, or the judge since he was smaller – wanted to grab them by their throats and press till they begged for mercy. However, he refrained, because nothing could be gained by a physical outburst.

Desperate, he chose the only action open to him: he charged toward the attendees' benches, running back to the last row.

Where was he? Where Nicholas? There he was, half hidden behind a heavy-set woman who was eating all the time. There his sorcerer's apprentice sat, eyes downcast, pale and pasty-faced, his blond hair soaking wet. Nobody kept Goethe from grabbing the boy, who was the cause of all this.

The boy looked at him thunderstruck as Goethe dragged him up the aisle to the judge's bench.

Goethe shuddered with disgust, touching the slippery soft skin of the boy.

"Here." He could hardly conceal the panic he felt. How could Goethe prove that he himself didn't deserve to be in hell just because his apprentice did wrong, killed people, was punished… was it definite the boy deserved to be in hell? And even if Nicholas was guilty, that didn't mean Goethe was, too… did it?

Conjectures danced wildly in Goethe's head. He had been so sure he could clear his apprentice's name; so sure the boy was not responsible for the death of innocent people by drowning a village. It seemed so simple: clear his apprentice's name, and thereby free himself. He'd never imagined that his apprentice would disobey his orders, plying magic without knowing how to control what he unleashed.

But was that not mankind's greatest and most prevalent sin: being unable to control what his cleverness unleashed upon the green earth? To even be so very sure about being able to control them?

Goethe held the boy tightly by his thin, pasty arm. The apprentice was shivering, his whole body trembling and wracked with fits of coughing.

"Now, speak up," Goethe hissed to the boy. "Tell them that I was a good master."

Obediently the boy repeated the words: "He was a good master. Yes, he was."

"And that I taught you everything necessary."

The boy glanced up at him with pale eyes – fearfully. "But, master, you didn't teach me all there was. I had been waiting for you for so long, but you didn't come. So I thought…."

Hearing the apprentice's words, the prosecutor began to laugh in a shrieking tone.

"You aren't trying to say that *I* am responsible for what happened?"

The boy sobbed when Goethe's fingers tightened on his arm. "No, master. No! You *weren't* there… Don't make me lie here. I can't lie here. I am scared."

Goethe shook the boy vigorously. "Nobody told you to lie!" Goethe's eyes were flashing.

The boy stammered: "I had been waiting for you… I begged for your help, but you didn't come. You promised to come. You promised. I…." The confession of the helpless youth ended in a yelp, as Goethe finally lost control and made to slap the boy.

A small movement of the judge's chubby hand stopped Goethe, as if by magic. Goethe let go of his apprentice, who fell to the grey stone floor weeping.

"*You* are dismissed, Goethe." The judge's voice was calm, yet unrelenting and admitted no further argument.

"All your deeds during your lifetime are between you and your Maker. You have been condemned to hell based on how you lived your life. Once the decision is made on the basis of your deeds, your afterlife unfolds. You spent your life in narcissistic escapism, and perhaps were not aware of all your sins. Yet you sinned: pride and self-indulgence are but two of your crimes of commission. And you sinned by omission: you were oblivious to the needs of those all around you. In hell, you behave as you always have done, do as you always did in life – and thus is your punishment fit to your crimes, and will always be, since there is only one life, yet, after that judgment. Nothing you can do will ever change your sentence, since you cannot escape yourself, nor apparently change yourself. You had a life. Now you have an afterlife, where you will rue your sins. Now go and do as you please."

No gavel thumped to affirm the words of Goethe's sentencing. No applause resounded from the high rafters. No titters escaped the audience as they left the hall.

And before Goethe became aware that the hearing was over, he found himself sitting at the exact spot where he'd arrived in hell.

*

Being back in the deserted place where Goethe first found himself, Goethe reflects on his ballad.

Goethe looked around, wishing Christiane could be here with him, or rather he with her – any place other than here. But no: not even Jerusalem was here.

While sitting in this sandy place covered with rocks, Goethe crouched down next to one of the bigger ones, and wished he could mercifully forget those last hours in the Hall of Injustice.

He thought of Nicholas, his apprentice, who simply seemed to have disappeared to nowhere after the hearing. And of the ballad he'd written that defined his fate.

"Lord and master, hear me crying!"

He began to weep, remembering the cry for help he had placed in the apprentice's mouth in the ballad – and how the apprentice's plight reflected his own helplessness now.

"Spirits that I've cited, my commands ignore."

There would be no help for him in this hell where he was condemned to live eternally. And with the acuity of a poet, Goethe realized he had just relived the story of the sorcerer's apprentice – and thus fantasy turned into sad reality in hell.

Overestimating his own power, assuming he could play with the powers of hell had brought him a disastrous result. Next he'd attempted to put his illusions into practice, to no avail. Then, amid hubris and confusion and sudden terror that he might fail, everything slipped through his fingers.

Now he was no longer blustering, pontificating, or obsessed with his own importance. Now he was desperate and forlorn, one more fool in a hell full of fools. Nobody would heed his cry for help, not here in the underworld. His ballad had been a cautionary tale of power run amok, of arrogance untamed, and of the folly of pride. Too bad he hadn't learned from it while there still was time. And now, even if he learned the lesson now, nothing would change.

Instead, he had lived it. Goethe, the hapless apprentice.

(Ballad translated to English by Edwin Zeydel, 1955)

IN THE SHADOW OF PARADISE

Jason Cordova

I don't know how I ended up there on the hill, but in life I was always careful about remaining alive and making the most of any given situation. As I did in life, in death I approach each moment with an open mind and a closed fist, according to my intuition.

Once again, that approach saved me.

I carefully remained hidden from the avengers who struck from the skies of hell, attacking and reaping the souls in the city below. These avengers were terrible in their magnificence, an overpowering *belleza* which I had never before seen in hell. They struck from above like hunting hawks, did these Seven.

Three other beings remained above, watching the Seven as they wrought pain and suffering. Two of these three were demons, terrifying avatars of evil whose winged forms sent chills through me; the third stunned me with his unearthly beauty. A terrible sight was this, such as I wish never to see again in my damnation; yet so compelling that I could not turn away.

They made my breath catch in my throat and my bowels clench in terror. My knees went weak as they circled above the damned city of crushed dreams. Below them, the Seven, unparalleled sons of heaven and earth, wreaked their vengeance upon the doomed.

Then onward they flew, their destination unknown, leaving Hellywood in ruins; its damned to their fates; and me to my own devices. These beings were uncaring. Behind, they left the survivors of this accursed city, weeping bitterly.

I caught myself before my pity grew: this is hell. I watched the heavenly avengers go, glad that I had somehow been spared after they'd rained terror down upon Hellywood Boulevard. They would be back. I was sure they'd return.

Best not to dawdle. I took a calming breath and scanned the blood-colored horizon. Beyond the ash and pollution was Paradise, forever out of reach, offering false hope and promise. It helped a little bit, this teasing view of salvation most damned souls would never attain. The sight reminded me: Paradise never changed; hell never changed.

A half-formed suspicion gnawed my gut. Something was wrong. But what? Then I remembered: I had somehow left the Lobby too soon, before I got what I'd come for, the elusive prize I sought: escape. The Lobby, also known as Decapitol Records Forever Waiting Room, was a trap where gray dust settled on unsuspecting souls who waited there indefinitely for reasons they no longer recalled.

Damn.

My prize was to have been a set of plans with a hand-drawn map which showed the way out of hell through the Mortuary. Those plans were the only reason I had gone into the Lobby. But I had come out empty-handed: I had no prize in my grasp. And most frustratingly, I couldn't remember why not. How badly had I erred? And how? Or, worse, had I been betrayed? And if so, by whom? Like everyone else in the Lobby, while inside I had forgotten why I was there.

How diabolically my torments are designed! The devil, it seems, knows my every weakness – not terribly surprising.

For such damned as I, hell is full of unanswerable questions.

"That's the netherworld for you," I muttered and began trekking down the hill to the devastated streets below.

My name is Juan Ponce de Leon y Figueroa, and I have sworn to escape hell.

*

Descending the hill overlooking Sinset Boulevard was agonizing. My breath came in gasps; every muscle in my body ached from exertion. My lungs felt afire; the soot and ashes drifting on the air burned my throat as I breathed. My legs were sore. My worn leather boots slid on the slippery ash-covered hillside.

It could have been worse: I could have worn my armor, far heavier than my new-dead khakis. Armor was of little use here: death could not be deflected. Armor makes one too conspicuous, too interesting, too tempting a target.

I was, however, well armed. On one hip I carried a high-quality pistol, a gift from an acquaintance of Browning, the gunsmith. As firearms go in hell, this one was reliable and I guarded it jealously, once stabbing a man who tried to steal it. The blade that slew that thief rested on my other hip, a weapon that had long served me well, fit to my hand and heart.

As I reached the base of the hill, I saw that the streets of Beasterly Hells were virtually demolished. Damned souls begged for mercy as I passed. I ignored them: they were receiving due punishment for their sins. Aiding the damned souls chosen for retribution could have unknowable consequences.

Pushing aside a dying victim of the Seven, I got my bearings. While I was intimately familiar with Lost Angeles, Beasterly Hells was new to me, a clash of many cultures. The irredeemable lived in mansions or in refugee camps set up by Unwelfare Housing, according to their sins. Now beggars, looters and lost souls wandered these streets, seeking any escape from the devastation. This locale had changed since I entered the Lobby, yet remained predatory.

I heard a noise and looked over my shoulder. Fleetingly I thought someone was following me, but saw no one. All who could had fled. The streets seemed deserted. Yet my instincts told me I was being watched.

Was I being stalked?

I scanned the glowering sky for any sign of the Seven's return but saw nothing. I peered into shadowy streets.... Still nothing. I shrugged and started walking, faster than before.

If someone was watching me, how long before Authority caught wind of my scheme to escape?

Deep in the wreckage of Beasterly Hells, buildings had crumbled under the Seven's onslaught. Granite, brick and plaster covered the streets. Demolished buildings still smoldered. From the rubble I could hear cries of souls pinned beneath.

Sulphurous fumes hung in the air, reeking like rotten eggs. As best I could, I ignored the stench from the Port of Lost Angeles, a foul place even on a good day. But this was not a good day.

Smog, yellow and thick, was settling over everything, making the going more difficult.

"Can't see anything in this crap." My eyes stung and teared as I picked my way through a ruined building. Those Seven had left no stone upon another.

"I see many things, Spaniard," a voice hissed from a tumble of rubble nearby.

Reflexively, I grasped the hilt of the sword at my hip. I squinted.

An old woman, lay sprawled amid the stones: "I can help you... see the truth of things, if you dare," she said.

She was a casualty of retribution from the sky: her skin flayed to the bone, draping her skeleton like an ill-fitting robe; her scalp burned bald but for a single patch of wispy gray hair; her eyes the color of milk; unseeing, filled with anguish.

Seeing this crone, my soul cried out. I could do nothing for her. I must be merciless to succeed with my plan. Nothing could distract me, or dissuade me. Yet....

"What do you see, old woman?" I asked, taking no step closer. "What has done this to you and all the others?"

"Erra," she whispered. "Erra and his Seven peerless champions, come to bring just punishment to the damned. Babylonian scum, from Emeslam."

Was this crone an Old-Dead witch, then, to know such things? An ancient sibyl? In Beasterly Hells? *This could work in my favor*, I thought. *Underworlds don't generally overlap. I wonder why it's happening now – if it truly is?*

And yet... I gave pause to my thoughts. Just what *if* Administration knew of my plans to escape hell? What if they knew that I intended to use the fabled Fountain of Youth hidden away beneath the Mortuary to aid me in my escape? Was this Babylonian god and his Seven here to prevent me from escaping hell? Or were they ignorant of my plans? Was I just caught up in random violence? I had to know the truth.

"Does His Infernal Majesty know about this?" I asked, straining to see her wizened face.

"Which infernal majesty? Satan? Of course He does," she laughed a bubbly chuckle that caught in the back of her throat. She didn't have long, I knew from experience. I had seen enough expiring souls to know just how much punishment the damned could take.

"Yet He allows this?" I scoffed, trying to keep the worry from my tone. My plan was at a delicate stage. Any attention from Below, from Admin or the Devil's Children, would make my escape impossible.

"Beware the shadow behind you, Conquistador," she rattled, raising a clawed hand and pointing whence I'd come. "It walks with purpose and seeks to steal your most valued prize."

"What?" My hand fondled the butt of my pistol. I scanned the street, peering through the smog and the dark, searching for danger. "Who seeks to steal from me?"

She cackled mockingly, a cruel, wet sound: a malediction from a dying old woman. It chilled me deep. It frightened me as nothing in hell had frightened me before.

I pulled my pistol and pointed it at the woman's head to stop her. "*Vaya con dios,*" I said, cocking my pistol's hammer.

She grinned; she was toothless. Madness sparkled in her sightless gaze. For the first time, I believed that she could somehow see me with those milky white eyes.

"Go with *God?* Not in this place, *cerdo.*" She giggled maniacally.

I shot her twice in the head. Recoil jerked my wrist. I holstered the pistol, my ears ringing as the last report echoed through nearly empty streets.

The hag was dead – dead now, dead again, dead for the moment. Unlike many, she didn't dissolve or disappear. She shrank a bit, stiff and strangely vacant, her untenanted body looking almost like someone else's.

I would leave her to rot there, if rot she would. She'd end up, as all souls did, back in the Mortuary on what the new dead call 'Slab A.' Eventually she would be revived to resume waltzing with her fate.

But her words still shook me: *Go with God? Not in this place,* cerdo.

Here there was no god, only the rule of the *diabolico* masters of the netherworlds. Here there was no hope, no joy to relieve the bitter anguish each soul endures for time never-ending. This was the hell of Christian tradition, and in this hell, Satan reigned supreme.

Despair overwhelmed me. What had I been thinking? How arrogant was I, a soul doomed and rightly damned to hell by heaven's law? My plan was folly. My attempts at escape could only prove once again my failings. I was a bungler and an egotist. My damned soul was ripe for the picking, my hope crushed.

Then why try to fight?

A stray thought, one I immediately shoved aside. I could *not* afford to think about failure. Doubt was my enemy; belief my salvation. I must believe in myself, remember who and what I truly was in my heart and in my soul. Have faith in hell's rules.

For hell has its rules. Hell thrives on belief, I had learned as I suffered along in this misbegotten place, born from man's worst doubts and fears.

Perdition rules. Whether or not a soul believes in hell, hell believes in damnation of the mortal soul. Atheists came here. Agnostics came here. Madmen came here. And fools by the wagonload. But to be redeemed in hell, one must follow its rules.

For one such as I to escape hell, that soul must believe that damnation's rules worked both ways. This is my belief.

There is great power in belief.

I fingered the hilt of my sword. The blade was righteous and correct. It had no hatred in it, no fear, no doubt. The weapon calmed me somewhat; its commitment to its purpose coursed through me: it cared nothing for who was right and who was wrong. It simply *was.* As I must simply *be,* free of judgment, if I were to succeed. I took a deep breath and looked back at the crone's corpse, then through the smog of night in the direction she'd pointed. Still nothing.

The shadow behind you, she'd said. *It seeks to steal your most valuable prize.*

"My *prize,"* I muttered under my breath, staring at her body on the ground and wondering how mad she'd really been.

I had fixed on a single prize. Only one other soul, the Lobby's janitor, might have guessed what prize I sought. And the janitor was still locked inside the Decapitol Records building with my manila envelope – or so I believed. Getting into the Lobby was easy; getting out, once trapped there, was damned near impossible. I had done it but I was Juan Ponce de Leon y Figueroa. The janitor was merely a menial.

Erra and the Seven; the mysterious shadow (perhaps) following me; the two terrifying aspects of hell which followed Erra: somehow these all must be linked, interconnected.

A reckoning was coming; I could feel it in my bones. Those damned who had avoided their appropriate punishment *and* the wrath of the auditors from Above would be unmercifully punished, stripped bare of denials and excuses.

Damnation cometh, again and again; each retribution more painful than the last. Heaven itself was taking a hand. Injustice was being more fairly administered.

Best not to be present at the next reckoning. Time to leave Beasterly Hells behind. Time to be on my way.

But time, as always in hell, was not on my side.

*

The Decapitol Records building lured me now like a siren from Greek myth. Somewhere in that gargantuan maze of confusion, damned souls and mayhem, lay my passport to salvation: a small gray envelope holding a map showing the entire layout of the Mortuary – and what lay beneath: the Fountain of Youth. Deep inside the Mortuary was the key to my escape from hell. All I need do was go inside and access it.

Yet something held me back.

I nearly missed a fleeting dark shape, dashing from shadow to shadow among adjoining buildings.

I waited. Still nothing. My hand trembled as I clutched my pistol. Fear stabbed at my heart. I struggled for calm.

I was definitely being stalked. By what, though? This stalker would steal away my prize. It would not steal the plans from me. Or so I swore to the souls of my beloved children, safe on high.

I hurried to the front door of Decapitol Records. Nothing attacked. I breathed a sigh of relief and strode into the Lobby.

Silence boxed my ears the moment I stepped inside. I walked through the large room as quietly as I could, looking for the janitor.

The Lobby worked in strange ways. Once inside it, leaving without permission was nearly impossible. The doors that let you in and should let you out, didn't – the doors led you right back inside. Try to blast a way out and stone-bred demons appeared, to persuade an errant soul to remain within.

When last I was in the Lobby, I'd tracked down the man who'd helped the Undertaker remodel his Mortuary, and asked him for a copy of the Mortuary blueprints. Getting them was critical to my escape from hell. I had been so close previously, only to be whisked out of the Lobby by unknown forces, for unknown purposes.

Now I was back, to get my envelope.

This time, I would not fail. That envelope would be *mine*.

I approached two women seated on a bench, perhaps upon the very bench where I once sat so long. At their feet was a cardboard box and something inside it began to screech. The closer I got, the louder the thing in the box screeched wordlessly.

Finally I kicked the box with a booted foot hard enough to bend the cardboard inward. The screeching stopped.

I frowned at the two women. Something wasn't right here.

One of them frowned back at me. "Yes?" the skinny one asked, her voice reedy, imperious.

I recognized the object she held tightly to her bosom: a gray envelope, about the right size.... A coincidence? Impossible. In hell there are no coincidences. *It can't be, and yet here it is.*

"Thank you for shutting up Rasputin," the other said.

"What's your name?" I asked the first woman, my attention fixed on the gray envelope clutched tightly against her chest. *My* envelope. I motioned to it. "Who gave you that envelope, if I may ask?"

"You want this?" she retorted petulantly. She had an attitude that made me want to wrap my fingers around her neck and squeeze. She reminded me of the nobles at the Spanish court in Castile.

I refrained from strangling her; I merely nodded.

"Then you must offer me something of value in return for it," she said.

"I don't barter with *thieves*," I growled. I looked at the larger woman next to her, who had been watching us silently. I bowed my head to her deferentially: "Madam."

"Hello," she greeted me. I cocked my head and smiled. *Interesting. This one isn't completely worthless.*

"Henrietta!" scolded the woman with my envelope, her face folding into a customary sneer.

This was a woman who was something special, once upon a time. I must find a way to get that envelope from her.

She waved the envelope in front of me, taunting me. "You have to offer something worth this. I know the value of items such as this. It's an item of power, in my possession – meaning I own it."

"You snippy little ..." my voice trailed off as I struggled for composure. I could simply grab the envelope from her and run.... No. I was better than that. After such a short conversation, I had no doubt why this skinny harpy was here in hell. As for her friend Henrietta... I wasn't sure about her friend yet. Praying for patience, I spoke again: "Please, what is your name?"

"I am Marie Antoinette, Archduchess of Austria, Queen of France and of Navarre," she said proudly.

I nodded. Her earthly rank explained much of her superior attitude. Her history explained her stupidity.

Thrice-damned Habsburgs.

"My name is Juan Ponce de Leon," I replied. Her eyes lit up in recognition and I stifled a groan. I knew what was coming next.

"You're that explorer who found the Fountain of Youth!" she exclaimed. She paused for a second, staring into the distance, putting two and two together with some difficulty. "Wait a second.... If you found the magical fountain that grants eternal life, why are you dead and in hell?"

Dear God in Heaven, why do people only remember that damned myth!? And just how stupid can this woman be?

“No, Marie,” her friend Henrietta interjected, regarding me shyly. “He was the governor of Puerto Rico; a favorite of Isabella, Queen of Castile and of Leon.”

“That I was, madam,” I bobbed my head, impressed. Very rarely in hell did anyone get my story straight.

“Is the envelope really yours?” Henrietta asked.

I nodded again. “Yes. I paid a lot in blood and favors to find the soul who’d get it for me.”

“I’m sorry. I wish I could give it to you but Marie says it’s the only way we can get out of here.”

“Really?” I pursed my lips. *“I* escaped from here.”

“Oh? How?”

“Henri*et*ta!” Marie chastised.

“What? I think he can take us out of here if you give him the envelope.”

“He can’t get out. Nobody can get out.”

“But what if he *can?”*

*“No*body can!”

“Then why not give him the envelope?”

“Because it’s *mine!”*

“Ladies,” I interrupted, an idea germinating in my mind. “What if I… no, never mind.”

“What?” Marie asked, filled with suspicion.

“It’s a bad idea, I’m sure,” I said, dismissing my inspiration with a wave of my hand. “The Lobby is far more comfortable than being abroad in hell. Especially with Erra and his Seven *Sibitti* roaming the countryside, dispensing punishment as only a Babylonian God of Pestilence can.”

“The day of redemption comes from the hand of the dullard,” said the voice from the box, deep and mysterious. “The smaller one shall be cast out to blight the damned, at the head of the pack of fools when they attack the gates of Paradise!”

I stared at the box, trying to fathom what was inside it and the meaning of its message. “What *is* that?”

“Rasputin,” Henrietta said.

“Prophecy Head Doll,” Marie added miserably. Neither offered any further explanation, so I didn’t bother asking just how a Prophecy Head Doll became stuck in the Lobby.

“Newfound friend Juan, you said you have an idea?” Henrietta asked me.

“I said it was probably a bad one. Still, I can show you the way out,” I offered. “In exchange, you’ll give me the envelope as payment.”

“You can show us the way *out?*” Henrietta squealed, her face awash with hope.

I nodded. “I know how hell works, so I’ll offer you one better: I’ll *guide* you out and you won’t have to give me the envelope and its contents until we’re safely outside the building.”

“Did you hear that, Marie? He’ll guide us out!”

“I don’t trust him.”

“You don’t trust anyone.”

“With good reason!”

“But he can help us. *Please?*”

“It’s my envelope. I’ll do with it what I want. And I’m not following some Spanish dog anywhere!”

“Damn it, Marie!” Henrietta exploded to her feet. I watched, impressed by this timid soul’s sudden outburst, as she furiously shook her finger at her smaller friend, anger radiating from her in waves imperiously, reminding me that these two were, once upon a time, royalty.

“This adventurer is offering us a deal, honorably, and your stupid, petty little game of ‘this is mine’ is stopping us from escaping. If I have to listen to Rasputin explain one more time the difference between career advice and a prophecy, I swear to all I will rip my ears off and shove them down his throat. Now, give me that!"

Henrietta lunged for the envelope. Before Marie could so much as flinch, she yanked it away. Marie squeaked in fright and tried to rise, but Henrietta shoved her slight friend back onto the bench. Marie gasped, horrified, as Henrietta turned and handed me the envelope.

I exhaled softly as I took the paper in my fingers. I'd waited so long, worked so hard.... At last the key to my salvation was in my hands. I still had much to do, but the first step of my plan, on which all hope depended, was complete.

I planted a kiss on Henrietta's powdered cheek, my heart filled with gratitude towards this strange and unpredictable ally.

She blushed but kept silent.

"You have my heartfelt thanks," I said. Bowing my head, I handed the envelope back to her. "But I am a man of honor, and I gave you my word. Please, take it back for now – I have yet to lead you out safely."

"Then lead us out, Spaniard," Marie snarled, getting to her feet. I looked at the vile creature and started to retort, but Henrietta cut me off:

"No, Marie," decreed the buxom Henrietta. "You stay here."

"What?" Marie hissed through tightly clenched teeth.

"You didn't give him the envelope," said Henrietta, her voice sweet, yet poisonous at the same time.

"H-h-how *could* you?" Marie sputtered, hurt and confused. "I'm your friend."

"Yes, you are," Henrietta said, nodding her head. "You're also a bitch."

I kept my mouth shut and let the two former queens sort out their differences.

"I've never treated you badly," Marie protested. "Please, Henrietta. I *must* come with you."

"No," said Henrietta, emboldened. "I've been punished enough, just by following you! I agreed to sue the makers of the Prophecy Head Doll because you said so. I took that horrible lawyer, Mister Pym, out on a date because you said it would help our cause. I had to join you in this damned Lobby because you lost the lawsuit. I'll follow you no longer."

"That doesn't make sense! Hell punishes damned souls. Anyway, you can't stop me from coming. Can she, Spaniard?"

"Actually, your grace..." I began.

"Shut it, Spaniard!" Marie snapped. She looked back at Henrietta. "I *must* come along! You won't prevent me, you selfish brat! I'm your *friend!"*

"You *will* stay here, you... misbegotten cretin!" Henrietta fairly screamed.

They argued on, their voices rising, verbal barbs flying. It was ugly and yet glorious, this battle of wits between two unarmed combatants, until: "At least *my* husband wasn't a panty-wearing French butt-pirate!" Marie snarled.

Enough, I thought. *More* than enough. Others in the Lobby were staring. "Your majesties, I must insist –"

"I told you to shut up, Spaniard!"

That was uncalled for. If this continued, I'd need to stop their arguing before they attracted the attention of the demons guarding the Lobby. I stepped between the two and raised my hand to signal an end to the squabbling. "Make your decision, Senorita Henrietta; I will enforce it, whatever it may be. Either she comes with us, or she stays."

"You... Spaniard!" Marie sputtered.

Henrietta was staring at me, mouth agape.

"What is your desire?" I asked Henrietta.

"She stays," Henrietta whispered, no hesitation in her voice.

"You're taking *me* with you, I presume?" the box called out to us as Marie, face red and eyes tearing, plopped back down gracelessly into the chair.

"Of course, dear Rasputin," Henrietta said, kneeling to pick up the box. "I would never leave you."

"And it's said you can't teach a damned soul new tricks," the voice within the box said cheerfully. "You see, Henrietta? *This* is how a prophecy works!"

Prophecy? Was *that* what the voice in the box had foretold before? I dimly recalled some, though not all, of the words. Instead of dwelling on the prophecy, I led Henrietta to the front door of the Lobby.

There I swallowed nervously. In theory, once your business in the Lobby was done, it would release you. My business was done, but was Henrietta's? I wasn't sure, and I couldn't be sure until we tried to leave.

As we crossed the threshold, I tingled all over. I looked around. Stopped. Stared.

White wings, the smell of sunshine on freshly-mown grass....

No, I chided myself. *It cannot be. My imagination is running wild. The heavenly host do not come to hell. Angels do not come to hell. Not one angel from above is here, let alone two. Here are only the fallen, the downcast host and the lords of hell. No hope for the damned, merely the illusion of it. That is our torment. That is the price we all pay. That is the lot of the damned.*

"Juan?" a voice asked timidly, jarring me from my musings. I must forget about the two angels I thought I'd seen.

Henrietta's voice was filled with hope.

Had I instilled hope in someone? In Henrietta, the hopeless little soul from the Lobby? I wondered.

"My apologies, dear Henrietta," I said. Seeing angels? More likely a trick of the light. An illusory vision of blessed beings, a taunt from hell's repertoire; a glimpse of the unattainable. I looked at her. "What were you saying?"

"How did we get on this hill?"

"Hill?" I blinked. We were indeed back outside, transported into the wilds of Beasterly Hells. Henrietta gawked by my side.

Here the oppressive heat had returned. In the far distance, I could see storm clouds rolling in from Oceanus, a sure sign that somebody important was displeased with recent events. Soon these clouds would rain acid, eating the skin of the damned and causing immeasurable pain to any soul caught in the open.

Henrietta clutched with one hand the talking box containing the voice of Rasputin. In the other, outstretched toward me, was the envelope.

Overhead, Paradise glowed from a sooty sky. Salvation loomed larger than ever, the pearly gates so close I could nearly see them. I now had control of the map, which would lead me to the Fountain of Youth. From there, I would use the powers of the water to reverse my age so far as to be reborn as a babe once more, away from the damned and fulfilling my escape from hell. Then my life would begin anew, and I could atone for my past errors and earn my way into Paradise and see my children once more.

Deliverance awaited. The ultimate prize: the map to my escape route. It was right there. Waiting. I just needed to rid myself of Henrietta and her pesky Prophecy Head Doll and my destiny would be at hand.

I could feel the coils of selfishness seductively wrapping around my soul, tightening as the thought of leaving the idiot queen behind began to take hold. It would aid my escape, leaving her here in the horrors of Beasterly Hells. I had no debt to her, nor she to me. I had fulfilled my promise and helped her escape.

Take the envelope and leave, something deep inside me whispered. I mulled the possibilities over for a moment longer. *Would it be right, though?* Something told me that this was all part of the trap, the seductive lure of His Satanic Majesty, the very thing which caused hell to work as well as it did. *But what was the bait?* I shook my head and smiled at Henrietta. I accepted the envelope and stuffed it into my pocket. *My destiny.* I had much to accomplish before my plan came to fruition. *I have sworn to escape hell, sworn to the souls of my children that I would join them in Paradise one day.*

I smiled and watched as the brightness of Paradise loomed, no longer taunting.

There is nothing that says I must do this immediately, however. Perhaps...

I offered Henrietta my hand. "The trip down is quite treacherous," I informed her, a gentle smile on my lips. "Perhaps I can assist you?"

*

The angel Altos watched as the Spanish explorer assisted the former queen down the hill, keeping her safe and protecting her as they traversed the dangerous ground. He smiled serenely, warmth and hope filling him as he saw something in the Spaniard that most damned souls in hell were sorely lacking. Next to him, an equally beautiful being squirmed uncomfortably as he, too, recognized it. Altos looked at his brother, pleased with the turn of events.

"It warms the heart, to see such gallantry in a damned soul, does it not?" Altos asked. "To risk everything to help someone in need, to put the selfish desires aside to assist others?"

"It reeks of desperation and hopelessness," the fallen angel Daniel countered, his tone surly and displeased at the turn of events. He motioned at the Spaniard. "He almost succumbed. It's going to be easy to break someone like him, so very easy. As I've stated before, these damned are irredeemable and it is we who are here to punish them. They are damned for a reason, Altos. I never understood just why you waste your time on them."

"I think the Spaniard is made of sterner stuff, brother," Altos said. His voice was gentle, caring. "I think he will do just fine."

Daniel turned a sly look upon his heavenly host. "Care to make a wager on it, Altos?"

Altos's eyes narrowed. "I do not wager, Daniel. You should know this best of all."

"A challenge, then?"

Altos thought for a moment. "Of what sort?"

"I will turn him, cause him to renounce everything he holds dear," Daniel promised, his beautiful smile twisted. "He will turn his back on salvation for selfish wants and desires. He will not stay true to whatever course you believe is laid before him. He will veer from the path of righteousness. He will not recognize his greatest prize."

"I disagree, brother," Altos said. "I believe that he will choose what is best for all, and save himself in the process. He knows what the ultimate prize is."

"The challenge, then?"

A pause. "Accepted."

"The prize?"

"The reward, you mean. His soul."

"That is rather harsh of you, Altos," Daniel rubbed his hands together eagerly.

"I believe in the ultimate salvation, that even the damned can be redeemed. He is one of those I feel that can be. Everyone can be saved, Daniel, if they give themselves a chance."

"Such faith for the faithless, for your precious damned?"

"Unconditional love, Daniel. We all have it." Altos paused for a moment before turning his gaze to his brother, his friend, his enemy. "Be they great warriors, fallen from his grace or by his side still. We *all* have it."

"Pah. We'll see." With a small flick of his wrist the Fallen disappeared.

Altos stood alone on the small hilltop. He looked upon the Spaniard. Even in hell, there can be hope. Even the most damned of all can find redemption if one looks hard enough. His lips twitched in the ghost of a smile.

"Hell still needs heroes. I think I have found one."

With that, he vanished.

ZERO SUM GAME

Richard Groller

Nikolai Tesla spent yet another night lost in a fever dream atop his makeshift bunk in Level 33. The Infernal Research Projects Directorate (IRPD) laboratory where he spent his waking hours supporting the Department of Infernal Energy (DIE) was, more often than not, his nocturnal abode. For a long time now, his dreams would not allow him rest. His sleep was fitful, as if some relentless daemon had driven him to the brink of a sheer promontory, and there he waited, suspended at the edge of the hellish abyss. His visions were too vivid, too close to the edge of consciousness, as his subconscious tried to merge what he knew into an image he could understand.

He suffered a recurring nightmare in a world of nursery rhyme allegory. Rub a dub dub dub, three men in a tub, with himself a rude candlestick maker. The butcher is covered in blood. The baker's pans are in the shape of coffins. The tub makes port and is greeted by Mother Goose. He buys a basket of "Eggs of Columbus" from her. He returns to the tub to stow the eggs but drops two of them, and the sea is frozen solid. He returns to solid ground and purposely drops two eggs to the ground. He disappears and suddenly reappears before the Emperor of Cathay. He asks the Emperor if the nightingale will sing for him, and the nightingale tells him, "Go to the Great Wall." Upon the Great Wall, Humpty

Dumpty is perched, belching and spewing obscenities at all passers. He calls Tesla a dreamer and a fool, and Tesla takes two eggs, one in each hand, and hurls them at him. The massive eggman explodes in a ball of fire and a mushroom cloud, the shock wave engulfing him.

Tesla awoke with a start, sitting bolt upright as he always did coming out of this particular land of dreams. A sense of unquenchable panic overwhelmed his body, as he fought hyperventilation, drying his already parched mouth and sinus, and leaving him anxious, caught in a momentary nameless fear. It was as if some dark cloud filled his mind, wiping the memory of something important he knew he must do. He tried to focus his mind and come into full wakefulness, yet his desire for clarity remained unfulfilled.

He was utterly soaked. A salty pool of sweat had collected in the hollow of his hairy chest, and as he rolled over, it splattered to the floor, drenching some equations he had scribbled on a pad of quadrille paper just before he drifted to sleep.

His drenched cot was not much more than a couple of quilts thrown on top of a packing crate. This was perched between two transit cases built to store rack mounted electronics. He was a tall, dark haired man, mustachioed, very sober, and a devout workaholic with idiosyncrasies, quirks and phobias. Though his apartment was on the same level, he often spent three to four nights per week right here, working to the point of physical exhaustion, ever dedicated to the chase.

He was intrigued by the amount of fluid he had lost. He had the presence of mind to reset the lab's thermostatic controls to a temperature more suited to sleeping before he had fallen asleep, but like all things in hell, nothing could be depended on for sure. Tesla shook his head violently to remove the sweat from his eyes; droplets flew everywhere.

He then shook out both arms and drops of sweat flew from his fingertips. At that moment, something odd happened that would change the course of his damned existence, and with it, the Department of Infernal Energy. As the droplets left his fingers, two drops, one from each index finger, traced a silent trajectory and met at a point in space, forming a miniature collision of self-annihilation.

Tesla startled to full wakefulness, in one of his infamous flashes of inspiration. He knew intuitively what was missing from his theoretical constructs, the picture coalesced in his synesthete mind. He suddenly became aware that the physical world of hell was but a shadow of a larger reality, and if he was right, the universe would never be the same. Tesla scrambled to rescue the sweat soaked pad from beside his cot, and scribbled notes and lines and equations for an interminable period of time. He then suddenly felt very, very tired, smiled to himself, and drifted off to the first truly restful sleep he'd had in years.

*

Hero of Alexandria, the Director of DIE was quite pleased with the 360 degree view his "polar penthouse" office provided, chuckling to himself, "No corner office for me!" The newly constructed DIE HQ building was located in the Southeastern borough of New Hell City. It was built by architect Stanford White, friend of Nick Tesla and womanizer murdered by the jealous husband of Evelyn Nesbit, immortalized by William Randolph Hearst in the "Trial of the Century" as "The Girl in the Red Velvet Swing". As a hungry but brilliant Junior Partner in Ozymandias Construction, (Our Motto: "Look on my works ye Mighty and despair!"), it was a coup for White to be selected as chief architect, in no small part due to the intercession of Tesla, the Director of the IRPD, on his behalf. A sixty-six story spherical shaped edifice that defied logic in a way reminiscent of Escher, it was a marvel of construction, based in part on the design on the Wardenclyffe Tower that White had built for Tesla in another life when he was doing experiments on the wireless transmission of power.

In these days of tight funding and tighter scrutiny, the dual-use building was designed as a Headquarters and Research Laboratory for DIE, with suites and apartments for senior level personnel to inhabit close to their work on the upper levels. The lower levels included office space, shops and quarters for other lower level personnel. The political maneuvering to get it approved and built was legendary, but the move to consolidate resources and cut down on traffic congestion with its dual-use zoning was innovative for hell and fulfilled recent Infernal bureaucratic mandates in the realm of political correctness. Only recently was it beginning to finally fill up with tenants, a new habitation for the denizens of New Hell and the DIE.

It was a long overdue recognition of the Old Dead for him to take the reins at DIE, but unfortunately for Hero, great minds warred within its confines. The War of the Currents started in another place and time (the 1880's) still rages between Nikola Tesla and his arch-nemesis, Thomas Edison. Hero of Alexandria, long late of Ptolemaic Egypt, contemporary of Christ, and first century engineer that invented the Aeolipile (the first recorded steam engine that bears his name) is now Director of DIE by dint of age, seniority and inclination, but the unhappy arbiter of their ongoing feud. He would almost be happy to rest upon his laurels – works such as *Pneumatica, Automata, Mechanica, Metrica, Belopoeica, Catoptrica, On the Dioptra, Geodesia, and Geoponica*, but there is no rest in hell for those with restless minds.

Hero's engine, a novelty at the time, and his windmill for powering machinery were historic firsts, but alas, unnecessary due to the abundance of slaves to do the work, and only used as temple artifacts to awe the uninitiated. His sins of omission could have been used to spare millions of lives over the intervening centuries, but such was not his fate. So work he must again, to try and find a redeeming technology worthy of effort. Nothing is ever easy in hell, so he is additionally burdened with trying to end Tesla and Edison's quarrel. Due to favors and pulling political strings, Thomas Edison is the Comptroller of the DIE. He insures that every penny is properly accounted for, and every expense justified, *especially* if it is a funding request from Tesla.

*

George Washington Goethals was refighting a pre-programmed battle when he got the call from Evelyn Nesbit, the office executive secretary, reminding him to go to the experimental physics lab for a meeting. Goethals thought it odd that a woman of her "talents" would be working for Tesla as a secretary, but there she was, as a quid pro quo between Tesla and Stanford White, primarily because Tesla needed a secretary he could trust, and his devoted assistant from another life mercifully did not follow him here.

Though some thought of solitaire war games as toys, Goethals knew them as tools used to hone a fine edge in both tactics and logistics. With genetic logic programs built into the computer memory circuits, this new breed of war game could evolve its strategies over time, learning from its mistakes. Replaying a scenario led to new insights and, over time, truly effective solutions to scenarios could be determined. Changing the variables and force mix allowed for interplay and invention, and given the appropriate order of battle matrix, logistical support and objectives, new insights could be gained with every engagement. Seeing the conflict evolve also made it fun to watch, especially when you won. For now though, Goethals had no time for such luxury, and suspended the game until a quieter moment.

An engineer with an unparalleled talent for logistics, as a Colonel, George Washington Goethals was the chief engineer in charge of building the Panama Canal and later became the first Civil Governor of the Panama Canal Zone. With such credentials, he was the perfect candidate to be Nick Tesla's XO, logistician and chief tech wrangler. Goethals had an unparalleled mastery for "creative" interpretation of the procurement regulations, and could obtain any piece of kit, especially "off-the-shelf" high tech gear in less time than the Department of Infernal Energy could take to finish filling out the requisition forms. His jack skills were legendary, and nearly as good as his political skills, having been on the Army's first General Staff; and these skills were sorely needed in the IRPD whenever the lab got into a fight over the way technical assets were assigned within DIE.

Goethals knew how to use his constrained funds wisely, knew how and when to bend the rules, pushing the limits of the system, authorizing what he could, stealing or bartering for the rest. His natural nemesis he shared with Tesla – Thomas Edison. Though both did their jobs exceedingly well, and espoused the same goals, Edison represented bureaucracy, the stumbling block to rapid progress that Goethals so abhorred. Goethals believed the system was usually broken (although it worked better during wartime), and that most infractions could be overlooked as long as lives were at stake, working under the philosophy it was better to beg forgiveness than to ask permission. It never ceased to amaze him how a threat to survival could improve your attitude, and it was being on this "cold war" footing with Edison that kept him energized and on track, wheeling and dealing all along the way.

Coming to work for a fanatically dedicated physicist so totally absorbed in his work that he had no time for mundane affairs or even relaxing diversions, was a blessing, for it gave him carte blanche to run the lab's day-to-day operations his way. The laissez-faire approach of "ask me no questions, I'll tell you no lies" was to his liking, and in return he gave fully his loyalty and support to his superior, even if he was opcon to a civilian.

Genius is best left unmolested he reasoned, and so he worked when experiments were in progress or preparation, and spent the rest of his time procuring the kinds of "toys" that would help Tesla achieve his many and myriad goals. Goethals punched the button on his hellphone saying, "On my way," and headed to the lab of future wonders.

*

Nick Tesla posted Evelyn Nesbit by the main entrance hall of the IRPD, to keep a lookout for DIE Director Hero and Comptroller Edison. As Lab Director, Tesla's efforts lived and died by funding briefings. Tesla was deliberately going to great lengths to insure that this particular briefing would be successful – so much so, that he had Nesbit and Goethals arrange a little diversion as insurance.

Hero, punctual as always, arrived 5 minutes early and was alone. He was expecting the latest boring, minutely detailed, funding briefing on the latest program, in a never-ending series of latest programs. Anticipating that his eyes would be glazed over by about the 700th slide, he wanted to get it over with as quickly as possible. Goethals, anticipating this intention, immediately escorted him in.

About 3 minutes later, Edison arrived and was intercepted by Evelyn Nesbit, who, in her sweetest voice, exclaimed, "Why Mr. Comptroller, what are you doing here? Didn't you get my calendar update that the 11:00 o'clock meeting was postponed indefinitely?"

Edison greeted her in an agitated monotone, saying, "Hello. What? No – I didn't – my laptop caught a virus and I've had IT working all morning trying to fix it. Why wasn't I paged?"

"Well sir," she warmly replied, "I tried to call your hellphone, but the voice mailbox message said it was full…" Edison became apoplectic, screaming, "I just set up that voice mailbox – it's not possible." Then he looked at the hellphone and saw multiple repeated calls placed to his number from a single number. He dialed it, and realized immediately it was an auto-dialer with an advertisement from a new phone sex line. He threw his hellphone against the wall, shattering it, and stormed out of the office.

Hero, meanwhile, was pleasantly surprised when he did not see a stack of slides or even a projector, only a whiteboard. Tesla settled in and began the briefing with a statement and a question: "Today we are asking for your consideration to fund a revolutionary power source: A-Potential Energy. Director, are you familiar with this field?"

Hero acknowledged his query in the negative with a slight nod, so Tesla went on:

"During the years since my earthly demise, and up until the present time, small bands of scientists working for various security establishments in hell have taken complex approaches, attempting to exploit the promise of A-Potential Energy, based on the papers I left behind. Rumor has it devices were so highly classified, that no industrial capability ever evolved out of their development. To my knowledge, only the labs attached to Hoover's Department of Infernal Security would have the clearances to have been involved officially, and Hoover was the one who confiscated my papers in the name of national security after my death on Earth. The whole area has been so compartmentalized that its gross failures have been kept remarkably quiet, and the players have had amazing luck at avoiding being accountable for their actions. Much of the original work was abandoned due to uncontrollable time-dilation effects the would-be weapons caused."

Tesla paused for a moment to let this sink in, and then continued: "I've been working in this area offline for years. My work has not come under the purview of the Department of Infernal Energy's security network, for it has been mostly theoretical up until this point, and my papers have been just that: papers, rather than electronic records that can be compromised with impunity by hell's competing intelligence services. This time around, I'd like this work to be done by the DIE community proper – not the spooks. I plan to keep those bastards from classifying the shit out of it before we have a chance to test it operationally and shake it out fully. The promise of this field is beyond revolutionary. It will radically change the way we do business, if my theories are correct. I want the energy to power the future available for the common good, not buried in some secret weapons program."

Tesla picked up a white board marker and visibly changed to a more professorial demeanor. He stood up and wrote a simple equation in precise block letters: V x A = B.

He looked directly at Hero and then said to him, "You are familiar with this?"

Hero answered curtly, "Maxwell's equation for the definition of a magnetic field."

"Good," said Tesla, "Now, what is A?"

"A is the A Field," Hero replied, "originally a mathematical construct used to make the equations work. Quantum mechanics proved it to be a more fundamental field of nature. We know it exists, but we've been unable to make practical use of it."

"Very good," Tesla said, and went on, practically beaming. "Up until now, they've been experimenting with ultra-sensitive magnetic flux devices, advanced SQUIDs, Angstrom scale Josephson junctions and other devices to discern minute power fluctuations and use them to harness its power, with nothing really to show for it."

He continued, "Rumors of residual programs left from the bits and pieces spread out across various labs, from time to time get funded, but they've never gotten the full support needed for a true development program. In the end, it has been politics, poor management and bad luck that has killed this area of research since its inception."

Tesla sat back down, and a fire burned deep in his eyes as he spoke in earnest to the Old Dead saying, "And that is why I stay out of politics. I let the pros like Goethals here watch my back for me. And I do my work in this field quietly. You see, the zephyr they've been chasing all these years is limitless energy, the energy that holds together the fabric of space-time itself. The A field is the zephyr, and this term is a misnomer, for A in reality is a potential rather than a field. And even as far back as Faraday and Ohm, potentials, by definition, are infinite."

Tesla let the gravity of his last statement sink in, saw the look of enlightened concern on Hero's face, and continued: "The problem with potentials is that they are scalars rather than vectors, and that they exist in the virtual state, rather than the observable state. The Dirac Sea is their home. These infinite potentials hold together the universe, and we are able to manipulate pitiful fractions of their power, really the wasted energy of secondary effects utilized by force fields."

Hero, unable to contain his impatience any longer, asked, "But what have you discovered that will change things?"

Tesla, looking very fatherly, yet very animated, almost like a parent watching his child opening a Christmas present, went on, saying, "What I have discovered is a flaw in a very basic mathematical axiom, the Zero Vector Axiom."

A disbelieving grin erupted on Hero's face, and he injected, "You've got to be kidding!" with a visibly contained chuckle.

Unruffled, Tesla continued: "The Zero Vector Axiom states there is a unique vector, O, in vector space, V, such that V + O = O + V. This assumes that Oi = Oj, or all zero sum systems are equal by definition. Herein lies the flaw."

He began to speak in a hushed, almost reverent yet animated tone that riveted Hero's attention. "Imagine this," he said, "two systems of equal energy meeting at a point and canceling each other out. Their sum is zero."

He demonstrated this by simply taking his index fingers and meeting them in front of him, tip to tip. He went on: "Imagine this again, with four systems, ten systems, a hundred systems, meeting at a point, each equal and opposite, each summing to zero. Imagine these now as opposing electrical and magnetic fields, standard E and B fields, instead of mathematical symbols. You cancel the force fields and they sum to zero. But what is *really* happening? Think for a moment. What if...?"

Tesla paused dramatically for effect, took his hands and placed all five fingertips to fingertips and stated, "What if I took these equal zero sum systems and put them into a phase locked loop configuration, whereby they were increased and decreased in a time synchronous fashion, always perfectly 180 degrees out of phase, always cancelling the total system at any moment in time to zero?"

He began to physically demonstrate this bringing his palms together, then flexing them away from each other, rhythmically, in perfect harmony, always keeping the fingertips together – like a spider doing pushups on a mirror.

Tesla abruptly said, "What we are doing, Director, is we are creating a stress wave in the fabric of space-time itself. The zero sum system has no observable effects, but in the virtual substructure of the universe, we are creating an artificial potential, by adding order to the random potential substructure of the Dirac Sea."

Hero's eyes widened, stating "I'm beginning to see, but I'm still confused. How could this system be employed if its effects are buried in a state that's not observable?"

Tesla went on saying, "Now, suppose we create a closed system cavity and generate zero sum E and B fields within it. The cavity will be resonant to each type of wave, and each wave and anti-wave will move along together and superpose, continuing to build up stress and define the artificial potential within the virtual substructure. Suppose we suddenly remove one wall of the cavity. What will happen?"

Hero thought a moment and said, "I suppose, the stress wave would be propelled in a straight line through the virtual substructure, like a ripple through the water."

Tesla grinned and encouragingly said, "Good analogy. That's exactly what should happen, but we still have no observable effect. To get one, we have to build an identical cavity, separate them spatially, allow them to resonate and built up stress, and then at the same instant, remove the wall and allow the stress waves to be released, but pointed to intersect at a distant point in space. At the point in space where they intersect, the two scalar stress waves of A-potential energy will experience destructive interference, creating a zone of vector energy, which will be forced to escape, I believe, from virtual reality into observable reality. Or in your words, the second ripple in the pond will cancel out the waves of the first by destroying them."

Hero, in full comprehension of what he was now revealing, then said, "What kind of power magnitudes are we talking about here?"

Tesla, visibly pleased, answered, "A conservative estimate is that from a single four dimensional point in space, say, roughly a cubic centimeter, the energy releasable would be equivalent to approximately 200 million volts."

Hero let out a low whistle of awed disbelief and then asked, "Okay, then – what is the downside risk profile here?"

Tesla continued on, "Theoretically, we should be able to create controllable nuclear scale effects, without radiation or fallout. But they still are nuclear scale, with all the risk that normally entails, less the radiation. We need to experiment with the amount of energy zero-summed when stressing the virtual substructure. I believe that small ripples can produce massive effects. But the beauty of this approach lies in the simplicity of the tech required. If I'm right, it should require using standard RF beaming antennas utilized in interferometry. The circuits should be simple, and the cavities can have electronically controlled gates."

Tesla then said in a more serious tone, "While the stress waves are travelling in the virtual substructure to the specified point in space, they are invisible to normal detection. Only upon their arrival and mutual destruction are they seen. Thus we should have a power system with virtually no infrastructure, based on energy at a distance, created spontaneously, as if out of nothing. For this "action at a distance" testing, we will build test structures outside of the city to minimize risk, while performing small scale tests within the confines of the laboratory, under strictest protocols."

Tesla paused again for impact.

Hero asked, "What do you need from me?"

Tesla replied simply, "Top Cover. I need you to keep this effort off the books so there are no books for Edison to peruse. I need Goethals here to have free rein to beg, borrow or steal the equipment we need so there is no audit trail for Edison to follow. I need secrecy from the keepers of secrets so I can work unmolested. Are you willing to do this to unleash the promise of limitless energy for all of hell's inhabitants?"

Hero looked at Tesla and said, in a cocky whisper, half a statement, half a question, "And the Lord said – *Let there be light*?!"

"Something like that," was Tesla's smiling reply.

Hero got a tentative look on his face and asked, "Hey, could this set the air on fire?" Tesla in turn got a quizzical look on his face and said, "Hadn't really considered the possibility. I suppose it *could* be an unintended consequence, but I consider it highly unlikely."

Hero was getting agitated, "'Highly unlikely'! Promise me you're not going to set all of hell afire."

Tesla winked, "Would it be that big a difference if it did? Seriously, I can't promise research without risk, but it isn't likely that anything will go catastrophically wrong."

Hero sarcastically responded, "Oh, good. I'll sleep better, *much* better now," and then asked, "Anything else? I'm a guest speaker at an engineering conference in an hour."

As the Director left his office, Tesla went over to extend his hand to Goethals, but first looked at George, grinning from ear to ear, and in a pleased yet pleading voice said, "George, must you gloat so loudly over besting Edison? I mean, that virus from the porn site and the phone sex number were truly inspired. One of these days he'll find a way to shove so much red tape down your throat you'll be shitting crimson for months."

Goethals just grinned wider and said, "Let him try. I'd enjoy the challenge of wringing the fat bastard's neck with his own bureaucracy."

*

In the three months since Tesla was given the green light by Hero, things had gone like clockwork. Goethals had bartered, stolen or plundered all the equipment necessary to construct circuits and antennas, and to put in place the experimental protocols to test the genius's theory, eager to find out what they needed to corral a winged horse.

The initial experiments within the lab would be kept within a constrained environment, with extreme limitations on pulse powers and time durations. It was known that time dilation effects were a part of the Apot (his shorthand) equation, but these effects could not be fully accounted for. Chronometers were time-synchronized in equidistant quadrants of the spherical shaped building to gauge if there was any bleed-off of the experiments beyond the laboratory.

The lab was rigged with a complete suite of multi-spectral sensors, to include detectors for everything in the electromagnetic spectrum (thermal signature, IR, UV, X-ray, Gamma rays, etc.) as well as magnetic flux, temperature, pressure, humidity, gravity, even elemental air content. Multispectral video equipment would capture the moments in toto. The laboratory itself was a giant Faraday cage, designed to prevent the ingress and egress of electromagnetic signals, except those desired, brought in via fiber-optic cable.

After initial experiments to insure the test equipment and sensors were within spec, the pedestals for the antenna pointing mechanisms were calibrated and laboratory vectors were charted for imaging and analysis.

The first live powered experiment was an attempt to gauge the magnitude of the power, to see if 200 million volts was in the ballpark. At first Tesla thought that the cause and effect parameters might resemble an exponential curve, but then realized this was probably naïve. Tesla intuited that the cause and effect relationship was non-linear. As such, he chose the smallest powers he could accurately measure to begin applying the stress waves. The interferometers were aimed at a point in the center of the lab, about one foot above the hard black surface of a laboratory table. A single computer linked the two simple boxes that contained the resonant cavities. Precise lengths of cable were cut to connect the black boxes, to within micrometer tolerances.

Goethals, waxing a bit poetic, referred to them as two hearts beating as one. Tesla, Goethals thought, was overly cautious. He would only allow the cavity to resonate for one microsecond on the initial trial. He chose one microwatt as the initial power setting, with E and B field components opposed.

They held their collective breath as the system became operational, under computer control, to execute the precise timing sequence. The result was hard to quantify. They each related the same experience a retinal afterimage like that caused by the flash of a strobe, almost imperceptible. The video was checked, but its frame speed was too slow to capture the event. This was remedied for the next trial. One thing that did show up, however, was a one microsecond decrease in the setting on one of the chronometers, forward of the arc cut by the trajectory of the interferometers.

Tesla decided to up the ante. He increased the time duration to one millisecond but left the power setting alone. This time the results were more spectacular. A translucent arc of light emanated from the precise aiming point in space, and expanded outward into nothingness, in the shape of a hemispherical wave.

This last wave had more substance to it, almost like a will-o-the-wisp and Tesla was pleased to see the EM detectors registered it as a single weak pulse, similar to a soliton. Even more fascinating, the time loss on the chronometer was commensurate, again along the same trajectory.

The forces involved seemed controllable so far, so they decided to up the ante once more. Power was again kept at one microwatt, but the duration was increased to a full second. The results proved disastrous.

The arc of light that erupted was bright and barely translucent, but the swath it cut was followed by darkness. Red emergency lighting came on as the alert siren blared. Outside of the lab, lighting was on but momentarily flickering. The power grid of the entire building readjusted, emergency lights returned to standby mode and the sirens became silent. The team did not like what it saw. Every piece of lab electronic equipment forward of its path was smoked. Best guess was a broadband RF pulse. The arc must have penetrated the lab's shielding and travelled in a straight line through the building, and out into space. Luckily there were no other facilities between the lab and the exterior wall of the sphere. The portion of the electrical grid that was knocked out would be compensated for locally, until all destroyed circuits could be repaired.

It would take Goethals some time to replace all the equipment that was destroyed during this experiment, but he felt it was well worth it. Tesla was not so sure, but he made a mental note to himself that at least he had a data point he could report to Hero – that the risks were real, but containable.

*

Goethals never did get around to filing a report on the mishap in the physics lab. Facilities engineers investigated it and could find no explanation. Some sort of anomaly within the electrical system. No matter. He had skated around it, and began the task of reassembling the required equipment. But that was far from the end of it.

It was three days after the incident. An invigorated Goethals had just finished his morning constitutional at oh-dark-thirty around the exterior rim of the equatorial level of the building, when he saw the taped off area of a crime scene. In a small copse, one of many that were dotted around the grounds of the spherical edifice, the body of a lesser demon maintenance technician had been found. He never reported back from doing routine maintenance on the exterior of the HQ building, using his wings to fly up and install spotlight bulbs. He was frozen in the position he was working in, petrified and immovable, lodged up in a tree. A light bulb, still clutched in his claw, blown, in an area below where the arc would have emanated.

Goethals had a bad taste in his mouth. He left the scene and said nothing.

*

Thomas Edison sensed that Tesla was up to something. Things had been too quiet around the halls, and no gossip was to be had emanating from his physics lab. Especially since there were rumors floating around that a maintenance tech had been found dead, but not in any way explainable by normal means. His private inquiries revealed the best the forensics folks could figure was that every electrical impulse in his body stopped firing all at once. It would be politically bad if the finger of blame were pointed at the DIE, so it wasn't surprising that it was rumored the Director insured the investigation was kept under wraps through judicious use of bribes, and labeled natural causes. All that anyone heard was plausible rumor, but in his mind, the tech grapevine tended to be generally accurate, so his suspicions were aroused.

*

Evelyn Nesbit was a conscientious secretary and archivist for Tesla and the laboratory – and the keeper of their secrets. But her conscience would not let her let go of the thought, "Have I been party to an accidental homicide? What'll happen if it's discovered, and none of us have come forward to report it?" Evelyn was torn after hearing rumors of a death coincident with their power outage, and had decided to discuss the matter with the DIE Inspector General, but at the last minute decided to talk it over first with Tesla.

When she broached the subject with him, she discovered he had been so absorbed in his work that he had heard nothing about the work-demon's demise. The "concept" of the death troubled him, but he was obsessed (she could tell because his nervous ticks were becoming more noticeable) and refused to allow it to interfere with his work.

"Look Evelyn," he pleaded, "I can't be bothered with unrelated accidents or unfounded rumors. If it's true, bring me some hard evidence. I'll take it to the authorities myself if it is real. Otherwise, let Goethals and me do our jobs." Tesla, resigned to himself that this must have something to do with her maternal instincts, over which he had no control, and dismissed her with a shrug.

Evelyn immediately decided she would have to seek out her own answers. She was sure that Goethals could not be relied on to be the conscience of this project, and Tesla was too intent on his work to be concerned. She decided that job would have to fall to her.

*

Several weeks elapsed before sufficient equipment could be requisitioned to run the next set of experiments. Evelyn made sure that a few administrative hurdles were put into Goethals's path. It would take him a minimum of a week longer to prepare this time, and give her time to continue her investigations.

What she eventually did discover through position, grapevine and favors was that a maintenance demon had in fact died, but that his remains had been cremated, almost immediately, per "family" instructions (though no immediate family could be found). The ashes had already been scattered and the post-mortem had been written under accidental death, insured not at fault. No final details could be verified. The coroner sealed the records.

One thing was for sure – Goethals's penchant for skirting the regs would have to be curbed.

His insuring "plausible deniability" in the defense of Tesla was all well and good, but not good if her suspicions were correct. This time, the experimental schedule of the lab would be posted, with a sector work quarantine in place due to a "potential harmful radiation effects" advisory.

When Goethals found out, he went ballistic. Even though no experimental details were provided, the warning notice would insure he was now open to more layers of scrutiny, and answerable for any mishaps. He was quite livid. And quite calm. For Evelyn, in orchestrating these maneuvers, had secured the permission of Tesla. And it wasn't even hard to do.

All she did was generate the appropriate paperwork with Nick Tesla's signature block, and interrupt him when totally absorbed in his work. She would bat her eyes, and say "Sorry to bother you sir, but these requisitions are urgent, and George is in conference on another deck."

Nick Tesla had no reason to distrust her. So he would invariably sign them, often without even a glance at what he was signing.

Goethals was beginning to feel as if Thomas Edison had sent a spy into his camp, to sabotage the efforts of the team. But with Tesla's signature, good as gold on the key documents, he realized it had been an end run, and he would have to play by the book, at least for the next round of experiments anyway. But the delay really irked him. "No plan ever survives contact with the enemy," he reminded himself and wondered if there were any other ways he could still accelerate the process.

*

Upon learning that a radiation hazard advisory warning had been posted to Tesla's lab, Thomas Edison made a visit to the Director of the Department of Infernal Security, J. Edgar Hoover. Edison relayed the fact that he had been completely cut out of the oversight process on whatever experimentation was going on in Tesla's lab. As Comptroller, this could be used as legal grounds for Hoover to obtain wiretaps or whatever other means necessary to ascertain what devious experimentation was being performed by that archetypal mad scientist

Nick Tesla. Hoover, knowing the extent of Tesla's genius, and the dangerous nature of the work he ranted about near the end of his earthly life, agreed. Hoover looked Edison directly in the eye and said, "Lay low and stay away from Tesla. No need to arouse any suspicions. I'll take it from here."

*

As the latest round of experiments began to draw to a close, the team of experimenters were in high spirits. A block of lightweight steel composite material was brought into the laboratory, and this time, the experiments began varying power, rather than time.

The cold metallic cube rested atop the same laboratory table. But it did not stay cold for long. One milliwatt at one microsecond translated into a point arc of blue-white electric fire, vaporizing a perfectly hemispherical indentation into the surface of the block. Next, a point inside the block was chosen close to its surface for the point of entry. At first, nothing could be seen. If the arc had arisen inside, they would not be able to see the effects, unless they sliced open the cube with a laser to see the internal effects.

This was not the case, however. The internal annihilation of the composite steel within the block created a compressive stress that required relief. The result was an explosive discharge of the thin layer of metal above the region that was vaporized. It melted and splayed out, similar to the effects of a sabot round entering a tank.

Luckily, they had prepared for this type of result, and protective barriers were constructed in the lab, so none of them were hurt. Pieces of the equipment took some hits, but the damage was comparatively minor. Goethals could even laugh about the deadlined boxes this time, saying, "It's like

I've always said – don't worry about the bullet with your name on it. It's the shrapnel marked *Occupant* that'll get you every time."

*

Within weeks of beginning successful controlled experimentation, the excitement within the laboratory could no longer be contained. Additional personnel were recruited, in particular Stanford White, to design an unobtrusive housing for the interferometer antennas to be mounted on the external facade of the DIE HQ Building and a new tower north of the city to be used as a demonstration test fixture to show off the "action at a distance" effects, and bowing to the need for physical security, guards for the lab.

Nikolai Tesla was the happiest he had been in years. He had a visibly renewed vigor about him, a new spring in his walk. This project would be done right. In various stages of conceptual development and testing were a host of wonders: a computer controlled pointing mechanism using simple spherical coordinate techniques, for precision beam pointing and tracking; a scalar interferometer that could create a spatially agile matrix, that in effect would be the equivalent of a solid wall of lightning, for supplying power; non-nuclear electromagnetic pulses of massive power; and access to near-limitless energy potentials.

Worrisome were the point-to-point arcs creating a tear in the fabric of space, and causing relativistic time effects via orthogonal lines of force, depending upon the attitude of the rip. Also puzzling was the ball lightning, with total electrical impulse quenching but no dissipative effects – the mechanism was unclear. Tesla assumed the excess energy was dissipated back into the virtual substructure, with a bleed off occurring, according to Bell's Theorem, somewhere or *somewhen* else.

Goethals on the other hand loved the "new toys" aspect of the leading and trailing edge effects, by phase locking and chaining transmitters together, causing continuous arcs of massive power, looking deceptively like truncated laser flashes (or even old style tracer bullets being fired), but each dot a zone of destructive interference, opening the fabric of space to the virtual substructure.

At this rate, the lab would be forced to move to larger quarters. Tesla could not remember the last time he was so satisfied.

*

Goethals had been deeply immersed in his element for weeks now, the final stages of preparation for practical tests outside the lab. Demonstration for Director Hero was to commence in three days. White had been a very busy man – not only completing the test instrumentation tower in record time on a hill ten miles north of the city, easily in view of DIE HQ, but the modifications to the HQ building to allow the external tests as well.

The fixtures from three industrial road crew light towers were to be utilized in the pre-test experiments. Individual light towers are normally equipped with four 1000-watt metal halide luminaries, with aiming and rotation angles of all luminaries adjustable in all directions, and with variable mounting heights. These three sets were dismantled and reassembled bisecting the center of the test instrumentation fixture at equal intervals vertically.

White had affixed the beam steering scalar interferometers mounted in three pairs, at fixed intervals, around the circumference of the building – at points equivalent to the equator, the Tropic of Cancer and the Tropic of Capricorn. The antenna apertures were created electrically; cavities were controlled by paired sets of computer-driven microcircuits. The test would be simple – no power would be applied to the test tower except that which arose from the ether, as controlled by the beam steering antennas affixed to the giant sphere, ten miles away. The industrial "suns" would be visible from HQ.

The computer so far had been programmed to spatially create and electronically produce power and form for four separate patterns of force: a single point concentration of power; a pulsed form of the same single point, creating ball lightning effects; an overlapping arc of leading/trailing edge point effects; and continuous application of point effects creating the wall of lightning effect.

Though tested within the lab at the lowest powers, it was unknown just how much energy would be unleashed as a result of the extended proximity of the action at a distance effects, and what intensity of time dilation would be experienced.

At the appointed hour after dark, the team assembled for a test outside the confines of the laboratory. Goethals manned the cameras on the observation deck, trained on the test fixtures 10 miles away. Tesla sat at the computer and punched in the coordinates for a single point, spatially the size of a single luminary fixture, and to be projected using a single set of antennas. Nesbit monitored communications and physical plant to insure there would be no chance for any more mishaps or uninvited guests. The lowest power setting was selected and Tesla engaged the controls. Over the open comm link, Tesla said, "And the Lord said *'Let There Be Light'*." Goethals whooped in glee, "and it was." Tesla dialed in a second point and said, "and again." Goethals echoed, "And it was." Tesla dialed in the third pair of antennas, and said,

"And once more." Goethals said, "Congrats sir – initial test successful!" Tesla fully intent on his work, began dialing in the coordinates for phase two of the test – a single line of force using all three sets of antennas.

It was then that Nesbit noticed one of the guards was not at his station and was no longer in view of the security cameras. He had entered the far end of the laboratory, and he was not alone. Thomas Edison was with him, and what he saw was a disheveled cross between an anechoic chamber, a clean room and a warehouse. Packing boxes, transit cases, stands, racks of electronics, fiber-optic cable, wire coils and all matter of test equipment lined and littered the room. Edison carried a laptop, and quickly plugged into the lab network.

Nesbit tried to notify Goethals but the comm system was suddenly down. When she could reach neither he nor Tesla, she got on her hellphone, saying, "George get down here – we have a security breach." Goethals was chagrined to discover that exterior promenade doors had been locked behind him. He quickly informed Nesbit saying, "Listen you've got to warn Tesla. We must shut down the test until we know what the extent of the breach is. Accidents happen, but deliberate sabotage could be biblical – like Sodom and Gomorrah biblical! I will go and manually disable the equatorial set of interferometers. Looks like your being the conscience of the lab has come back to bite us."

Nesbit was unfazed by his remark saying, "You have some nerve talking about conscience. That didn't help the poor bastard that died the last time you cut a corner during testing for the sake of convenience."

If Evelyn could see him, she'd have known that he was visibly shaken. He lowered his voice, saying softly, "Maybe it's time I paid him back."

Nesbit recognized the sound of hurt resignation in his voice. Inside, Goethals still had a soul. She knew it now. It was the warrior's way, the eternal balance between risk and duty, between personal survival and the code of honor that often required the ultimate sacrifice.

Her deal with the devil made, she headed to the lab to warn Tesla, praying she did not meet any intruders on the way.

*

Tesla punched in the coordinates for the second phase test. "Round two, commencing" he spoke into the comm link. But the words fell on deaf ears. Goethals arrived at the antenna at test onset. The light show ten miles away was spectacular – a standing suspended lighting arc. He was not happy with the time dilation effects on his reflexes his reaction time was punctuated by momentary pauses, almost like petit mal seizures, that kept him off balance. With each step he took, he would have to reorient himself, as if he was not there, but only in a dream watching himself. The feeling of disembodiment was unnerving.

But Goethals did not hesitate. He opened the facade and pulled the connectors to the beam steering mechanism for phase-locked operations. A flickering dome of light traced out a massive translucent sphere, dwarfing the *city* by its sheer magnitude.

Tesla checked the comm link when he did not hear Goethals' acknowledgment and found that it was dead. It was then that Nesbit burst into the lab and rushed to tell him of the breach. When he went back to the computer to shut down the experiment, he found to his horror that he no longer controlled the mouse or keyboard, and that the parameters of power and antenna orientation were being filled in by unseen hands. He had been hacked. Then the unthinkable happened – the four corners of the tropics antennas chose their aim points and power was dialed up in continuous mode. The effect was indescribable as a wedge of the city imploded into nothingness.

*

No one is really sure how a third of New Hell disappeared into a retreating wall of lightning that extended ten miles northward. The DIE scientists theorized that Tesla ripped a hole in the fabric of space and created a vortex, consuming the city by dragging it into the virtual substructure. The debris field left behind showed a kind of spatial shearing effect, leaving a cold, smooth almost surgically defined surface behind.

The recoil experienced in the time field left everyone in the city disoriented, and it would take weeks to insure that all time-dependent mechanisms were resynchronized. Zeno of Elea himself, from the Infernal Observatory Department of Apparent Time, was pulled from his duties to oversee these efforts personally. The spherical building that was the point of origin had a slice cleanly sheared out of it, connecting the points of the four antennas. Agents of DIS immediately arrested Tesla and put him maximum security lockup, incommunicado. Hero of Alexandria was also arrested, while Thomas Edison was made Acting Director. Goethals was outside in the field of the shearing effect on the promenade, and assumed vaporized along with a third of the city's inhabitants.

*

Evelyn Nesbit held a private memorial service for her co-worker, George Washington Goethals. She wept openly, saddened by the loss of, in the end, a trusted friend. Evelyn was saddened by the thought that, by the whims of the Undertaker, she might never again see him in the infernal expanse that is hell. For both Goethals the hero, and the nameless tech whose death had not been for naught, she was suddenly somehow lighter in spirit, knowing that, even in hell, the scales of justice still sometimes seek to balance.

AND THE TRUTH SHALL SET YOU FREE

Jack William Finley

Imagine you are in hell.

It's not as easy as it sounds. Lots of people imagine heaven and hell; few can truly imagine their place in either.

Constantine the Great, *Flavius Valerius Aurelius Constantinus Augustus,* Holy Roman Emperor and founder of the Byzantine-Roman Empire could not do it and he had the rather dobious benefit of actually being there.

Try as he might, the greatest general of his time could not come to terms with the reality of his new existence. For what seemed eons he tried with all his heart and mind to come to terms with the nature of his existence and, when failure became inevitable, he chose a different path.

He summoned to him a group of the greatest thinkers the worlds had ever known, seekers of truth, to weave him a lie that would stand the vile and indecent test of this horrible place. He would gather together a great council and together they would find or, if need be, create the shadow of doubt that would release them from this unbearable existence. In the land of the Prince of Lies they would weave a lie greater than all that came before, a lie that would set them free.

'When in Rome, do as the Romans do,' they say, but this was not Rome, this was the land of the Prince of Lies. And in this land of hellfire and damnation Constantine would adapt, overcome and conquer as his predecessors before him had always done. What could be more Roman than that?

*

All of hell's a stage and the damned are merely players in Satan's endless and infernal game

The black velvet curtain falls on the prologue and opens on a stage of many players. Old wise men of learning, famed seekers of truth and knowledge. Poor lost souls who forgot the first rule when seeking knowledge: never ask questions unless you are very sure you want the answers.

Constantine chose to gather his seekers on a stage part ancient amphitheater and part university lecture hall. At the bottom of the terraced stone structure they gathered around tables of wood and stone surrounded by writing boards covered with thousands of years of theories, formulas and maths of a hundred languages and cultures. The knowledge of millennia spread across their surface like a billion stars strewn across a clear night sky.

"We are being lied to. We are being deceived," Constantine's voiced carried an air of authority. It was the voice of a man who was used to giving orders and having them obeyed. It contrasted sharply with the figure of a man withered by the ravages of this hellish land and whose lower half was frozen marble. Frozen on its knees in an attitude of supplication, such were his torments in this place, the nature of which they had all been summoned here to discuss.

"And it is your suggestion that, having acknowledged this, we should now place our faith in you?," asked the Danish physicist Neils Bohr. "What makes you more trustworthy than what we see with our own eyes, what we can touch and feel? If our very own senses are to be questioned then I submit that trust in anything or anyone would be rather hard to come by in these trying times,"

His audience was skeptical, but surely that was to be expected under the circumstances.

"These are as you say trying times," Constantine continued, "but it is not in fact trust that I ask of you. It is your experience and knowledge as seekers of true reality that I wish to partake of. Your reputations as men who seek to know and understand the true nature of existence are why I have summoned you here. We have all heard the lies, the deceptions that this is hell and we are all dead."

"Hell is a fiction," Kierkegard declared loudly. "A fairy tale sold to the morally weak to keep them in line, a tool of the rulers to frighten their subjects. It is merely a sociopolitical tool like so many others."

"The masses must look somewhere for guidance," Voltaire smiled from across the table. "They have neither the will nor the intellect to guide themselves."

Constantine raised a skeletal hand, "that it not the issue at hand. I imagine as learned men that we all agree that this is not, and cannot be the hell it claims. The how and why of it are not our concern. Our concern is not why this cannot be hell but rather where in fact we truly are and, more importantly, how we get back to the places we are meant to be."

"I agree that we are clearly not dead," Schrödinger agreed, "but, if my knowledge of history serves, we should not all be here alive and well at the same time. The fact that we appear to be may call into question all of your perceptions."

"Time as such is an illusion," Bohr explained as if to an ignorant child. "It's a name we give to a totally abstract concept. The temporal vastness of all that is and ever will be is far beyond the capability of any human mind to comprehend. Therefore we invent the concept of time. The so-called time stream. The temporal nature of the universe is not time and it has no borders. It is a vast, unknowable and inconceivable ocean that stretches to infinite horizons. We cannot grasp it, so we create artificial walls in our mental picture of things to reduce this vast abstract thing to a concept our minds can handle. In much the same way a clock is used to reduce the movement of the solar system to a physical thing we can put on the wall or hold in our hand, the human race uses these symbols, both physical and mental, to grasp the ungraspable. We reduce the infinitely vast to mind-sized bits and portions we can study like pieces of a puzzle, that such study may someday lead to a greater understanding of the universe around us."

Voltaire snorted, "Thank you ever so much for simplifying it for us."

Constantine interrupted, "Enough of this pointless musing about things that hold no relevance to the essential question . As we all are painfully aware we are not dead and therefore this cannot be hell. We are, however, somewhere and we must determine where, how and why we got here before we can address the only subject that truly matters."

"And that subject would be…?" Newton asked

"Well that's obvious isn't it," Voltaire replied. "Our over-riding primary concern is escape. This place may not be hell but it's certainly not a place any of us want to stay any longer than we must. The order of the day clearly is to find a way back to where we came from or, barring that, at least someplace far more suitable than our current setting."

Newton smiled, "How exactly are we to achieve this most desirable end?"

"Simple," Bohr responded. "By logic and reason. We study this environment and our place in it. We are all learned men. We study the facts as they are presented to us and, through the process of elimination, we determine the nature of this place and our reason for being here. Surely someone brought us here. We didn't just appear here by random chance. There is a motivation behind it somewhere and behind that motive lies our captor. We determine who he is and what he wants. Then we will know whether it is in our best interest to simply give him what he wants or to somehow oppose and defeat him."

"Surely to defeat our host is hardly an option. He must be vastly more powerful than we to rule such a place as this," Voltaire grumbled.

"Defeat of your enemies is always an option, I assure you," Constantine told them. "It's merely a matter of determining their weaknesses and the proper weapons to exploit those weaknesses. We will begin as we are, pool our collective knowledge and viewpoints and gather others to us if and when it should prove necessary. Any questions?"

He waits. There were no more questions. "Then I suggest we begin our work. Every moment we act brings us closer to victory."

*

High above in the weathered stone seats of the ancient amphitheater two old men in tattered cloaks watch this particular play with some considerable amusement. One of the old men turned to the other and whispered, "I feel sorrow for them I think. I see their futures as surely as I see my own past. No joy and no escape await them, yet, in their innocent arrogance, they run toward a fate as bitter and disappointing as our own."

"No," said the other. "It was their very own folly that brought them here. The truth is what it is and all those who seek to bend it to their own will shall find in the end nothing but pain and sorrow. They deserve sympathy no more than we do. We reaped as we sowed and so shall they."

The brilliant men came and went, scientists, philosophers, theologians, mathematicians, great men and women of science and learning. They bickered and argued and talked of many things and Satan watched from the corner of his eye.

Constantine used all the influence he had gained over the eons in this place to build laboratories and machines so that the great thinkers could experiment and test their many theories and Satan allowed this because their fantasies amused him.

All of this and more the old men watched with seldom more than mild interest, until the flower. A small thing perhaps in the greater scheme of hell but a flower, however small, however brief, a thing of beauty in the midst of hell's desolation. Such things do not go unnoticed in the infernal regions of hell.

First came the flower, then a hole, tiny at first just a pinprick in hell's reality but the pinprick grew and festered and became a hope, a dream. If they could make a flower, and they could make a hole however small, perhaps, just perhaps, they really could make the door to another world they so desperately sought, and Satan was no longer amused, and still, the old men watched.

*

Satan's investigators, Frank Nitti former gun thug and right hand man to Al Capone, current heavy handed investigator for HSM's Department of InJustice and his partner Jack the Ripper followed the directions they had been given and eventually came to the amphitheatre and Constantine's gathering of great minds. The writing that covered the walls and chalk boards meant nothing to Nitti but he recognized it as the kind of scribbling that always seemed to mean so much to brainy types like those around them: men in white lab coats and tweedy sports coats with those stupid patches on the elbows. The very sight of them made Nitti want to punch someone, just for being so conspicuously intelligent.

They sat quietly in the seats near the top of the amphitheater and looked down at the assembled men. Nitti leaned over to the Ripper. "I forgot to buy a program. Who are these guys?"

The Ripper watched the men intently, his face a swirl of gray fog frozen in the shape of a man's head beneath a black silk top hat, white gloved fingers tapping the ivory globe that topped his walking stick as he slowly wathed the activity below them.

"The one with the flowing gray and white locks is Sir Isaac Newton, the original apple genius. Physicist, mathematician, astronomer, philosopher, alchemist, and theologian he was one of the great thinkers of his time. Perhaps of all time. The basis of most of the science of your day started with Newton."

Nitti shivered. The coldness of the Ripper's sepulchral voice gave him goose bumps.

"The one who looks like a snobby poet with a pretty woman's hair is Soren Kierkegaard. He's what he looks like: a deep thinker, a theologian, examiner of Christian morals and other nonsense. Always searching for reasons for things that have no reason. Like so many, he could never accept that some things simply *are*. They all are. The type to drive themselves mad, desperate to explain the unexplainable."

"What are they doing?" Nitti asked.

"Exactly what I said. Trying to explain the unexplainable. Picking the world apart piece by piece on their boards and their papers. Trying to understand what makes the world tick. Clockwork pieces reduced to numbers and formulas."

"Why? What's the point?"

"The point is that if you can take something apart and understand it enough to put it back together again, you needn't put it back together the same way it was. You can, in theory, change it, improve it."

Nitti frowned, "And how is it you understand all this hocus pocus?"

"I am not like you. My spirit ranges freely. I am a legend, a myth. I am as timeless as the ages and, as such, my thoughts and knowledge are not limited to a single life span. My spirit wanders the mists of time. I have seen wonders throughout the ages and have wisdom beyond the understanding of mere mortals."

Nitti stared at the creature of smoke and shadow with whom HSM had partnered him. "I'm so glad I asked," he said with a sneer.

"What about these other egg-heads who are they?"

"More of the same. The older man in the suit is Niels Bohr. He studied atomic physics and quantum mechanics. Thought to be the very heart of the structured universe, or the heart of chaos depending on who you ask. The one with long gray curls and ruffle, who looks like he's meant to be composing a symphony, is the French philosopher, Voltaire. He'll probably slow the others down, incessantly asking 'Why?' like a petulant child. If you find you absolutely must send someone to the Undertaker, send him. He's certain to be one of the more expendable members of the group."

Nitti turned to the Ripper and whispered, "This is going to be a pain in the ass, just wait and see."

Nitti stood brushing off his suit and started down the stone steps.

"Gentlemen, excuse me," Nitti, stood in before the assembled thinkers frowning and scratching his left eye brow. "We hate to interrupt but we need to speak with you for a moment if we could."

Newton smiled at the newcomers, "And what can we do for you gentlemen?"

Nitti wandered in to the cluster of desks overrun with papers and books and gestured to the writing on the black boards that covered every wall. "What exactly is all this?"

It's the sum total of three thousand years of theology, philosophy, physics, genetics, quantum physics, astrophysics," Kierkegard smiled at the dull expression on Nitti's face and smiled. "I'm sorry. To put it more plainly it's math. Elementary differential equations, Calculus, Trigonometry, Fibonacci numbers, Hilbert's infinite hotel paradox, Banach-Steinhoaus's uniformed bounded principle. You do understand math, don't you Mr. Nitti?"

Nitti scratched his eyebrow and smiled, "I must seem pretty stupid to all you smart guys."

Nitti wiped his hand across his face and wandered over to within inches of the old philosopher and bent down close. "Do I look stupid to… never mind I don't give a rat's ass how stupid I look to you. Do I look like someone you really want to call stupid to his face?"

"No," Kierkegaard shook his head, wondering just how badly he had misjudged this situation and his value to this strange man and was now very frightened, "not really."

"Then don't."

"Please forgive our colleague," Niels Bohr tried to calm the situation. "We have so few guests here our manners are rusty. As to what this all is, quite simply put, it is the key."

Nitti looked confused, "The key to what?"

"Everything," Newton answered.

"The universe," the Ripper's raspy voice chilled the room.

"No, not just that," Erwin Schrödinger answered him, "much, much more. What came before the universe, what will be left after the universe? The fabric from which the gods themselves were formed. Everything."

"How's it work," Nitti asked.

They all stared at him as if he were a fool who could hardly be trusted to tie his own shoes without help.

Nitti frowned and tried to stay calm. He reminded himself over and over what the boss would do if he killed them all and tried to be patient with these irritating eggheads. "Use the smallest, simplest words possible. Try not to be too impressive and if it goes over my head I'll have my friend," he gestured to the Ripper, "translate for me."

"Very well," Newton replied, taking on the tone of a lecturer. "Every molecule in the universe is controlled by spirit energy. the life-force all living things possess and radiate. Any living thing can change the universe, but only in respect to its own personal perspective. To change the world in way that affects everyone, that affect reality itself, takes vast amounts of spiritual energy. Gods can do this by tapping into and controlling the spirit energy of every living thing that truly believes in them. Humans could do this but hundreds of thousands of them would have to be thinking the exact same thing – the same to the very last shape, shade, and subtle nuance, at exactly the same time. This, from a practical standpoint, cannot and never will happen so, to change reality, you must find the way to channel the energy of thousands, even millions, of souls to one central spirit that guides and directs all the energy to a single goal, a single focal point. If you can do that you can change anything. You can change everything."

"And you have figured out how to do that? That's what all this scribbling is about?"

Newton grimaced and shook his head, "Not quite yet. We are very close but we still have some small wrinkles to iron out, so to speak, some polishing to do, but we will have the answers very soon, I assure you."

"Yeah, yeah, whatever. Suppose I know a shortcut," Nitti asked them.

"Shortcut," Newton laughed. "There are no shortcuts in science."

Nitti sighed. "Look Bub, I know you guys are used to being the smartest people in the room but shut up and listen a minute. I'm about to make you an offer you really don't want to refuse. The keys to the magic kingdom. Everything you ever wanted to know handed to you on a silver platter."

"Impossible," Bohr sneered.

"How?" Voltaire and Newton asked as one.

"Turns out the guy upstairs," Nitti jerked his thumb toward the heavens, "is a wordy old fart. He likes to write things down.

"God? Are you speaking of God?" Voltaire inquired.

Thunder rumbled in the skies and the ground began shaking.

"Ssssshhhh," Nitti frowned, "we don't much like to use that name around here, but yeah. As I was saying: notebooks to Moses, notes to Noah, books, scrolls, stone tablets. Turns out the Bible was just the tip of the iceberg."

"And how do you come by all these writings?" Bohr asked.

"Lots of ways. Spies, sympathetic angels here and there. Humans who smuggled shit down from above. Who gives a crap how? The important thing is *what*."

"So," Newton asked, "if you have all this knowledge, why are you here talking to us?"

Nitti looked away, shaking his head. This was the part he hated. "Well, we have it all but... it turns out having it and knowing what to do with it are two very different things."

"And you want us to... translate it for you? Make it easier for you to understand?"

Nitti grinned maliciously, "what I *want* is to feed all you smart-asses into a wood chipper."

"Yes," Ripper's cold whisper floated up from behind Nitti. "Our employer would appreciate your assistance. And just think of it. All the mysteries of the world laid bare before you. Can you really resist?"

"It certainly is tempting," Newton mused quietly.

"Of course it is. Temptation is our specialty," Ripper smiled and Nitti had never seen him look more frightening.

The old men watch as the scenery changes and the setting moves to the secret vaults beneath the newly opened Library.

The learned men descended upon the texts like starving children let loose at a feast, devouring everything they could get their hands on: book, scrolls, tablets, parchment manuscripts, all of them covered in words. They drowned themselves in the knowledge of the ages and, before long, they began to choke.

"This, cannot be," Newton objected.

"Impossible," Bohr added.

"Lies, it's all damned lies," Voltaire whined.

"We are clearly being deceived, that much is obvious, but why?"

"Isn't that obvious as well?" Bohr asked. "We are too close for the comfort of our captors. They are seeking to distract us with this rubbish... this madness."

"We are being distracted," Newton said. "A blatant attempt to pull us away from everything we know to be true."

Voltaire looked up from the sacred texts he was reading, "what if it's true. What if we have been wrong all these years. Is there no possibility that we were wrong?"

"Are you insane?" Bohr asked with a sneer. "It's possible we were off in some of our calculations, it's conceivable that we got some of it wrong, but this, this is an outrage. If this is to be believed we never knew anything. Nothing at all. Science from its very beginning was nothing but a lie. *No* reason, no logic, all the feats and thoughts of man nothing more than the meaningless spasms of puppets on the strings of gods."

"No. It's unthinkable," Newton agreed. "Listen to Bohr for pity's sake. We cannot have been wrong about everything. It's utterly unthinkable."

"Then where does that leave us?" Voltaire inquired.

"Right back where we were," Bohr smiled. "The flower, the hole, the doorway."

"Yes, the doorway. It's the only thing that makes any sense. We must have been very close for them to try such an obvious ploy to distract us. We must return to our research at once."

Faced with the knowledge of ultimate truth, the great seekers fled. The very thought of being so totally and completely wrong about everything they had ever believed was simply too much for them.

The old men smiled as they watched the seekers of truth flee back to their comforting lies. They threw themselves headlong into their experiments.

The old men turned to each other and nodded knowingly. They left then. No need to stay; they knew the ending, they had seen it all before, a tragedy in many acts that always ended the same. Escape back to the comforting lies. Betrayal of the truth and everything they said that mattered, because it didn't fit the lies they had come to love and cherish so very much.

On the stage in the shadow of the wise old men, a door was opening. A rabbit hole to the land of madness and delusion. The only place these geniuses of history could ever feel safe and sane again now that they had learned the truth.

*

"This is pointless," the Ripper said as he turned from the cell. "They are all completely worthless."

Inside the stone cell the great thinkers were hung on the walls like pieces of art, their skulls cracked open. All manner of wires, cables, tubes and things infinitely less savory snaked from the jagged holes.

Nitti looked back, "they think they have escaped. Their formulas and equations are as useful as potato chip dip. They mean nothing, they do nothing. Their minds simply refuse to accept reality for what it is: real, painful, unforgiving."

A voice like the sound of infant children being ground into sausage drifted from the shadows, "Oh well. It was worth a try."

Ripper turned toward the shadow, "and what will we do with them now?"

"Oh," said the voice from the shadow, "nothing at all I should think. Humanity's great seekers have been handed the thing they desired most in the world: the Ultimate Truth, and do they embrace it? No. They are so obsessed and devoted to their safe, happy view of things that, when faced with the thing they say they seek above all else, they flee like frightened children into the comforting arms of a delusion. Some of mankind's most enlightened thinkers will spend eternity cowering in the dark like scared rabbits from the thing they sought with such fervor in life. The worst hells are always the ones we inflict on ourselves."

THE ITTT

Michael H. Hanson

Sergei Pavlovich Korolev, former Father of the Soviet Space Program and current President-Elect of The ITTT (pronounced eye-triple-tea) walked through the front entrance of the Pandemonium Hilton. He was the night's after-dinner keynote speaker but the last thing on his mind at the moment was what he planned to say in twelve hours to the five thousand damned souls that comprised the current roster of The Institute of Terrified and Tortured Technicians.

Oh, it was an important conference for sure. The six hundred and sixty-sixth meeting of one of hell's most august bodies, but Sergei, the eminently practical administrator-politician-scientist that he was put little heed in coincidence and superstition. He had twenty secret meetings and rendezvous to orchestrate over the next ten hours, supply transfers to approve, schematics to triple-check, bribes to be paid, equations to process, and a number of annoyances to be quietly retired.

Completing the infrastructure for a gargantuan, fusion-reactor-fed, multi-spectral dark energy projector array was, by every stretch of the word, no small task.

The front desk quickly signed him in and offered to have his luggage delivered to his room.

"No need," Sergei spoke in English with a thick Russian accent, "Smoke, room one forty six. Meet me afterwards at main bar."

On loan from Belial itself, Smoke, a vaporous sentient of unknown and amorphous origins exuded a gaseous tentacle to snatch up Sergei's key card and levitate away with two steamer trunks toward the distant elevators.

*

An hour later, and feeling like a James Bond villain (after Smoke had dispatched a handful of British infiltrators who worked for a wide variety of greater hell's bureaucracies) Sergei and his particulate assassin entered the main concourse of the convention center. It was a huge room filled with a couple of hundred staffed engineering organization tables. Networking, spying, and active recruitment were into full swing as a crowd of one thousand plus souls, and climbing, milled about.

Though a very important meeting beckoned, Sergei felt a sudden urge to tour this grand display of hell's finest engineers, technicians, draftsmen, tinkerers, tinsmiths, and dreamers. Such an opportunity was rare, even for one of his stature.

Stopping near a table of squabbling oceanic engineers, Sergei found himself fascinated by the reverse environmental suits they each wore, throwbacks to the early diving suits of the late eighteenth century, each outfit was filled to the helmet with sea water. The engineers within had red irritated gills and on closer examination Sergei could see that all manner of tiny parasitic fish and sea worm bore and tore into the water logged flesh. Small streams of crude oil would occasionally appear, seeping into the engineer's gills, forcing the man or woman to double over in painful convulsions.

The next table was for chemical engineers. No suits for these guys, the men and women carried small canisters upon their backs from which several small tubes ending in nozzles slithered like live snakes above their heads and continually sprayed all manner of toxic elements onto their faces and shoulders, resulting in a wide variety of visible and nasty skin lesions and cancers.

Circumnavigating the floor, Sergei was shown, quite efficiently, the specific reasons why each of these intelligent and industrious souls was fast tracked to this eternal damnation upon their deaths... each member of The ITTT carried their sins like neon birthmarks.

Sergei's sins were of a more subtle nature, though no less reprehensible, and his damnation was of a more internal nature.

Though perhaps, he thought, *this may soon change*.

The table for genetic engineers was pretty disturbing, as each member had, growing out of their naked chests or backs, deformed appendages that writhed in agony, squirming in a vain effort to detach themselves from their creators as if they could be made whole.

The automobile and aeronautical engineering tables were of course unstaffed, as their representatives had never, in the history of this annual event, ever managed to complete either the flight or drive to Pandemonium, without a major accident due to understaffing, defective labor, or the rampant use of faulty, counterfeit parts.

The computer engineers sported small CAD monitors in their eye sockets and were always running off to the bathroom, never in time by the way, to painfully shit excess pounds of heavy metals and toxic e-waste.

Shaking the odd hand and affirming he would be giving the big speech tonight, Sergei finally started moving to the far side of the great room, where in a small enclosure a group of powerful personages awaited.

*

Thomas Edison, the Comptroller of the Department of Infernal Energy (DIE), and his counterparts (and semi-secret lackeys) for the Research and Infernal Technology Association (RITA), the Corps of Infernal Engineers (CIE), the Department of Infernal Labor (DIL), the Department of Infernal Transportation (DIT), and the Bureau of Infernal Industry and Security (BIIS) waited angrily in the well-secured hotel antechamber. When Sergei and Smoke finally deigned to appear the bureaucrats were incensed.

Sergei raised his right hand to silence the building uproar, and made eye contact with Edison, the true leader of this cabal.

"One word," Edison said, "I utter it, and it is back to the Undertaker for you."

Smoke, not liking such a threat this early in the game immediately hovered over Sergei, expectantly.

Edison's face went white and Sergei smiled. Everyone knew how powerful Edison was within his grand infernal fiefdom. It was a fine reflection of how the great inventor had lived his life, as a crafty bureaucrat who stole the best ideas within reach, without mercy, and exploited them for his own aggrandizement. Merchanteers like Edison had ruled humanity from the shadows for centuries. But to Sergei, a scientist who had risen to the pinnacle of the Soviet space program, and whose every day on the job had been a true life or death struggle, Edison was a blundering buffoon who depended all too much on long-term bribes and threats to maintain his status. Sergei, excellent chess player that he was, could foresee every possible action the former American Bergermeister might make.

"You all came as I requested," Sergei said slowly, "in disguise, unannounced, oh so secretly. In fact, none of your underlings would even think of commenting on or reporting any long-term absence for at least a month."

The effect of this statement was instantaneous and Sergei nodded to the silence.

"Everything you have heard is true," Sergei said. "Tesla was freed and, with collaboration of Madame Marquis Emile Du Chatelet, has laid down theoretical groundwork for project I have been overseeing these past few months."

"Oh yes," Edison sneered, "the vaunted space tunnel that has been whispered about so much. Hell's own escape hatch. And powered by that fraud Tesla, no doubt!"

Sergei smiled coldly, "schematics are on table before you. Prototypes have been tested... and yes, all worked, albeit on very minute scales. When Tesla finishes construction of needed generator we will be ready for great challenge."

"Yes, we all saw the results of the great Tesla's magic zero energy experiment," Edison spat, "half my employees were housed in that corner of New Hell City that was disintegrated."

"Employees who were sycophants that had been forced on you, Edison, and whom you never wanted in your employ. How lucky for you that not only was Tesla's unmatched achievement discredited, but you were also able to simultaneously clean house."

Edison growled and squinted his eyes nervously.

"But this is all shadow play," Sergei said, "your mere presence here indicates you are all... in. Anything but full commitment is of course unacceptable."

This last statement was spoken directly to the Director of the BIIS, William S. Knudsen, former head of U.S. Industrial Production during WWII.

"You're playing both ends, Bill," Sergei said.

"What do you mean?" Knudsen asked nervously. "I haven't leaked a word to HSM."

"HSM is not my worry," Sergei snarled. "Who do you think is actually banking venture?"

Knudsen's eyes opened wide, "he actually knows..."

"I've had you followed," Sergei added, "during your lame attempts to send appeals, communiqués, and even prayers up above. This leak stops now. Smoke."

Smoke, upon this last statement, flew forward and before Knudsen could begin shouting in his own defense, poured into the mouth and lungs of the former president of General Motors. Knudsen began shaking violently. The drama was short-lived, though, as his torso almost immediately exploded. Arms, legs, head, and gore flew in all directions.

Sergei looked across the survivors and saw that his lesson was having its desired effect, "Hoover and Hero are already on board, as well as head of every single engineering society in hell."

Sergei let his latest words sink in for a few seconds.

"You," Edison stuttered, "you really think this daydream has the slightest chance of actually working?"

Sergei smiled and nodded toward the one entrance to the small room. Smoke shot sideways and opened the door. Four men strode in.

"Let me introduce you to lead foremen in each of this grand project's major divisions, whose requests you will soon be fulfilling. Aelius Draco, Roman Emperor Hadrian's former Lead Engineer who is in charge of constructing all foundations as well as the Master Ramp that will mate with leading edge of Heaven's breach; Craterus, Alexander the Great's former mining and hydraulic Engineer is head coolant engineer for main reactors, and renowned physicists Michael Faraday and Rudolf Walter Ladenburg are personally in charge of constructing dark energy array projectors."

Every one made grave but quick introductions all around.

"As I intimated earlier," Sergei said, "prototypes were all a success. Tesla's energy source is stable and controllable. We now need to complete construction of immense projectors needed to part veil of heavens. Other than locating precise site in hell to be used as foundation for mighty arches from which a trestle to freedom will extend, all but one contingency has now been accounted for."

"Which one?" Edison mumbled.

"Well," Sergei added with the slightest shudder, "I must confess inability to calculate accurate *fudge factors* for... the Almighty. But if any of you wish to personally explore and research specific matter..."

There was, of course, no reply.

*

Sergei stood at the main podium and stared down upon the packed Hilton ballroom. Several months of intense efforts and it had come to this. His troops merely waited upon his leadership to set them free. So be it.

"Our plight cannot be viewed too tragically," Sergei said, "and our actions are not predicated upon desire for war, but on justice. If current crisis could be ended with honest prayer and remorse, we would all have been freed from this unholy prison long ago... but such is not to be. This unfair crisis, however, is no shame, but rather an honor. We scientists, we technicians, we engineers are perhaps too educated to put up with injustice… we are too critical. Opinions of fallen waver; the damned fear to have open opinion; we know how that backfires in flames of hell. There are too many sinners down here, who have melancholy repentance at heart."

The entire ballroom fell silent. All eyes were upon Sergei, like a great horde of enthralled disciples who had finally found their savior.

"We members of ITTT, however, have now been given task of conceiving a new public sentiment, and constructing it. Our outrage is too long suppressed, we prefer actions too complex for ordinary people to carry out, and we would put ourselves to service. The ITTT does not look to heaven's judgment, but to its long promised freedom. The ITTT must now collect its forces for positive actions, which have until now been neglected; heaven's unwelcoming borders are not favorable to our need. And remember this, it will not be by speeches and decisions of majorities that this great matter will be resolved, but by ingenuity and hard work of you fine men and women."

Dozens of cheers broke out across the membership as scattered individuals jumped to their feet.

"This wrench," Sergei said, holding the simple tool aloft, "I offer up as symbol of our ultimate redemption. We now engage upon a great project, far outstripping any of humanity's many proud accomplishments. This… gateway, for want of a better word, will be the culmination of endless millennia of human suffering in this intolerable pit."

Sergei paused and everyone fell silent again. He waited but two more heartbeats and then spoke.

"Our slavery is at an end!"

The resulting cheer and shouts of approval nearly brought down the very walls of the Hilton.

SIEGFRIED'S BLADE

Petra E. Jörns

"Ez wuohs in Burgonden ein vil edel magedîn,
daz in allen landen niht schoeners möhte sîn,
Kriemhild geheizen. Si wart ein schoene wîp.
dar umbe muosen degene vil verliesen den lîp."
Song of the Nibelungs
German heroic epic,
Ca. 13th Century, author unknown

"In Burgundian Lands a princess grew
more beautiful the world thitherto knew.
Kriemhild was called this beautiful wife,
therefore many heroes had to give their lives."
Translation by Petra Jörns

Gray.

No above, no beyond.

Just gray.

Where am I?

Coldness crept into Kriemhild's limbs. She froze. And out of the gray, outlines formed. A dusty plain spread before Kriemhild's face. Cold and gray. As cold and gray as the sky which bent above. The air tasted of ashes.

Slowly Kriemhild arose. She took a step without knowing her destination. Was there a destination anywhere? Every direction looked equally forbidding.

Nevertheless, she walked on. Step by step. The cold wasteland appeared familiar, like an old friend. Wind twitched at Kriemhild's long skirt, filled it and hindered her as she trudged along. Several strands loosened from her braided hair and obstructed her sight.

Onward.

What for?

Kriemhild stumbled. The ache of loss seemed far away. Like a dream. The dream of a life which once was hers. Out of her tangled mass of memories a name formed: *Siegfried.*

With the name came the pain.

Only barely did Kriemhild fight back a sob. Siegfried: he was dead. Such a long time now. Nonetheless, it felt as if his dead body had just been thrown before the door of her chamber.

I have avenged him.

Emptiness. So much emptiness.

Cold. So cold.

How shall I live without him?

The earth beneath Kriemhild's feet shook. She stumbled. Her fingers dug in the fine dust. Breathing heavily, she remained on her knees.

Afterlife, she thought. *That is where I will see him again. When I'm dead...*

Dead.

Her sight cleared. The stone beside her hand looked like the thighbone of a human. Kriemhild jerked backward. More stones. Many stones. Her gaze wandered across the rocks surrounding her. Not stones. These were bones.

A skull lay directly in front of her. The empty caverns of its eyes stared at her.

"You have murdered us," the skull said. Kriemhild knew that voice. It belonged to her brother, Gunther. Gunther, who planned Siegfried's death with Hagen. Gunther, whom she'd let be beheaded by Hagen – in revenge.

With a stifled scream Kriemhild jumped up. Trembling, she looked around. Bones. Everywhere. The dusty gray plain was covered with them: a boneyard. Then she saw the river, behind her. There a thick, red fluid ran, beyond a bridge made from swords which she must have passed without noticing. This was Gjoll, the river which formed the boundary of the Orcus, most ancient underworld.

I am in Hel.

*

Hel's hall: it must be here somewhere, Kriemhild thought. *There I will find Siegfried. There Hel will judge me.*

The thought speeded her steps. *But... if Hel damns me? What if...? Even if thousands and thousands of pains await me, I will suffer all – to see him again. Endure everything. For Siegfried.*

As if her thoughts had been heard by someone, she found herself before a great fortress. Huge walls towered before her, reaching for the gray of the sky. Stumbling, Kriemhild went toward it. Her legs ached. Coming closer Kriemhild noticed that the walls were moving. Horror stricken she paced a step backward. Slower now she moved on, until her first inspection was affirmed. Indeed, the walls were moving and crawling, they were formed out of the bodies of thick serpents looping round each other: Hel's hall. At this moment Kriemhild spied another woman out of the corner of her eye;

this woman approached the building from behind and to the left of her.

Kriemhild hesitated.

Then she recognized the other woman: She was Brunhild, King Gunther's wife. Brunhild, who wanted to be better than Kriemhild, the daughter of a king. Brunhild, whose vanity brought Siegfried his fate.

I will never let her *enter first.*

The thought pierced Kriemhild's mind like a spear of light. Touched a memory of bygone days. Impaled her with it.

She remembered another entrance: the huge main gate of the dome in Worms with the round arch above, formed out of several semi-columns; so long ago; so far away. It seemed to her only yesterday that she'd quarreled with Brunhild about who was allowed to pass into the dome first.

I am higher in rank, Kriemhild thought. *I will win again, and be first. Again.*

Brunhild seemed to be aware of Kriemhild's purpose. She gathered her skirts and quickened her pace.

Kriemhild did the same. Panting, she stumbled across stones and bones. Sweat streamed down her face. Her lungs were on fire. Until she reached the porch leading to the gateway at nearly the same moment as did Brunhild, who stood in front of her, gasping for breath.

"I will pass first," panted Kriemhild.

"Never!" Brunhild hurried across the porch, toward the gateway.

With shaking knees, Kriemhild tried to get there before Brunhild. At the gate, she caught up with her. Her fingers clawed Brunhild's braids.

Brunhild fell on her knees. Blood from her scraped knees soaked through her cloth skirt.

"You bear the blame", screamed Kriemhild. "Admit it! *You* incited Gunther to kill Siegfried."

Brunhild grabbed Kriemhild's arm: " Siegfried defeated me under his cloak of invisibility so that I believed it was Gunther who did it. Much worse. He overpowered me under his magic hood on my wedding night. He has betrayed me. He has abased me. *Me!"* With a disparaging sound, Brunhild ripped Kriemhild's sleeve.

"You!" Kriemhild gave Brunhild a kick. "You wanted him. But he loved me. It was Gunther, my own brother, who begged him to do this, because Gunther wanted to marry you. He troubled Siegfried to overpower you and take your magic girdle so that Gunther could fuck you on your wedding night. Dumb twit!"

Brunhild lay on the ground. Gasping, she brought her legs under her body. "That didn't entitle Siegfried to give you my girdle. Or you to wear it in public and debase me in the eyes of all others, forevermore."

"So? Why did you presume to elevate yourself above me? Even now, you must be first through any gate, any door..."

With tears in her eyes, Brunhild arose. "This is your only point, isn't it? To be better than me," she laughed bitterly. "Did it never occur to you that it was *your* vanity that led Siegfried to his death?"

Cold emptiness filled Kriemhild's heart. "No", she whispered. "No... that's *not* true!"

"Are you sure?" With a cold smile Brunhild gathered her blood-stained skirts and passed Kriemhild.

Kriemhild went numb in every limb. She could not move. She could not take one step to stop Brunhild.

Her head high, Brunhild stepped first through the main door.

*

"You are lying," Kriemhild screamed. Her screech echoed off the serpent walls and off the gateway to Hel's hall.

How long had she been there, numb and motionless? A moment. An eon? She didn't know.

It seemed to Kriemhild that the door had barely closed when she shook off her numbness and rushed after the other woman. With a second scream, Kriemhild pulled open the leaves of the heavy gate.

Shocked, she paused.

Here was no hall. No fortress. No Hel. Only the plain, which spread before her eyes behind the door – cold and gray. Now she realized that only the facade of the hall still existed. The rest of Hel's great hall was a field of ruins.

Crushed columns bordered her way down the three stairs.

"Where are you? Brunhild! Come out, sneaky shrew! You have murdered him. It was you. You..."

A movement made Kriemhild pause. She turned around. A shadow appeared out of the ruins. It was Hagen – Hagen of Tronje, Burgundian courtier: grim, implacable, and violent and one-eyed – who came forth from behind the stump of a column. In his right hand he held *Balmung,* Siegfried's accursed sword.

"You", Kriemhild panted, "murderer..." Hatred choked her words.

"Yes, me." Hagen raised the sword and approached Kriemhild. With a dismissive sneer he touched the tip of the blade to her throat. "So, we see each other again," he smiled. "It will be a pleasure for me to kill you. You know where you then will end up? At the table of the Undertaker. And while he disembowels you, I will revel in your screams, strumpet."

Kriemhild raised her head. "You wouldn't dare that. I am a woman. If there is a spark of honor left in you, then you won't harm me, you miserable...."

"A woman?" The tip of the blade pierced Kriemhild's skin. Blood trickled down her neck. "Then it was a woman who killed me. A woman who avenged Siegfried's death. How pathetic! A mere woman, to avenge the great hero Siegfried! What dishonor!"

Kriemhild's knees trembled. "Oh, yes! A mere woman has defeated *you.* What a dishonor for you!" Surprised, she noticed how spiteful her voice sounded.

Hagen snorted derogatorily. "You know you have befouled not only my honor?"

"My honor? Honor means nothing to me. I am woman."

"Not *your* honor, strumpet. With this you have befouled Siegfried's honor. Your beautiful, honorable, victorious Siegfried. A *woman* has avenged him. How low must a man sink, that this could befall him?" Hagen's eyes glowed diabolically.

This is a dream, Kriemhild thought, *a bad dream.* "You are mistaken. It makes no difference if I'm a woman or a man. I have loved him and I have avenged him. And you... you were miserable enough that the hand of a woman was sufficient to kill you."

Slowly Hagen put down the blade. "You know that I am right. Deep inside, you sensed it the whole time, didn't you?"

Tears wet Kriemhild's face. "No!"

"I have no need to kill you. Wherefore? To see you like this is sufficient. You are not worth dirtying my hands, you whore." With a disdainful look Hagen threw Balmung between Kriemhild's feet and turned his back on her. "Get lucky with it."

The emptiness in Kriemhild's chest became burning hatred. With a scream she grabbed Siegfried's sword and pierced Hagen though the chest with the blade.

*

"Are you satisfied now?"

Kriemhild recognized her brother Gunther's voice at once.

Siegfried's sword in her right hand, she turned around to face him. Gunther stood only a few steps away from her, as if he had nothing to fear from her. "No," she panted, "oh, no! I will only be satisfied, when I have killed you with my own hands – traitor."

"Me? A traitor?" Amused, Gunther shook his head. "Don't you remember? It was *you* who betrayed Siegfried. His little secret. The vulnerable spot, where the leaf lay upon him. You told Hagen where to make a lethal strike."

"I trusted him," Kriemhild screamed. With tears in her eyes, she raised the blade.

"And betrayed Siegfried."

"No!" She stepped threateningly toward Gunther.

"Not only then. You have betrayed him so many times."

"That's not true! I loved him."

"Siegfried?" Again Gunther shook his head. "Oh, no. All that you loved was your pride, your vanity and your ignorance. All of this was more important to you than Siegfried. Your pride lured him on to destruction. Your vanity stoked deadly jealousy. Your ignorance made you choose the wrong protector. It was *you* who brought death to him. Only you!"

"No! Shut up!" Tears blurred Kriemhild's sight.

"Because you don't like to hear the truth?"

The blade touched Gunther's chest. Kriemhild's hand trembled.

"Traitor!"

Sobbing, Kriemhild speared Gunther's chest with the blade.

*

When the wind had dried the tears on Kriemhild's face, she stood up, trembling. With Balmung in her hand, she walked away. To where didn't matter to her. Just far away from this place. Far away from Brunhild, Hagen and Gunther. Far away from these truths they had told her. Away.

Her fingers clutched Balmung's pommel a little tighter. Siegfried's sword: all she had left of him. This and her memories.

She stumbled. Her fingers felt cloth. The ground beneath her was soft. Too soft. Horror-stricken she stared at the corpse on which she kneeled. She turned her head: there were other corpses, beside and behind her. Distorted, bloody cadavers. Dead eyes. They stared at her: her son Ortlieb, her brothers Giselher and Gernot, Volker, Wolfhart, Blödel, Rüdiger and all the others. Good men. Innocents. They indicted her. Their murderer. She brought death to them all with her vengeance. Then she saw him.

Siegfried.

A cold wind snatched the scream from her lips. She rushed forward. The sword fell out of her hand when she hugged her beloved. Like a child, she began to dandle him in her arms. Her hands stroked his blond hair, caressed his neck, his face. Her lips met his forehead and kissed it, searched for his mouth.

Cold. So cold.

Under her kiss he opened his eyes. But they weren't blue. They were cold and dark as night. A swoosh of pinion feathers filled the ash-laden air.

"Siegfried", Kriemhild sighed. Her arms were empty.

The body she had held loomed large and dark before her.

"He isn't here," he said.

"Where is he?"

"Where you never will go. In heaven." Feathers swept. Then he was gone.

The plain was again cold and empty. Was just as cold and empty as Kriemhild's soul. Her fingers felt for the sword, the only thing of his that was left to her. A last gift from Siegfried to give her peace. She embraced the kiss of the blade against her skin.

Death. To end pain. Here and now.

Out of the gray sky, laughter drowned the swoosh of mighty wings. "You can't die. Never."

Never.

This insight trickled slowly into her mind.

Forever existing with the knowledge that she had killed him.

Forever without him.

This was her hell.

STAIRWAY TO HEAVEN

Ed McKeown

"Judge me for my own merits, or lack of them, but do not look upon me as a mere appendage to this great general or that great scholar, this star that shines at the court of France or that famed author. I am in my own right a whole person, responsible to myself alone for all that I am, all that I say, all that I do. it may be that there are metaphysicians and philosophers whose learning is greater than mine, although I have not met them. Yet, they are but frail humans, too, and have their faults; so, when I add the sum total of my graces, I confess I am inferior to no one."

– Emile Du Chatelet

Emile Du Chatelet walked up the broad street leading to the massive black fortification that was the abode of Belial, Crown Prince of hell. From a distance she might have been mistaken for a musketeer. She wore a blue coat with lace and ruffles, over breeches and riding boots. A serviceable rapier dangled from her waist. She'd abandoned the imbecilic habits of powdering her brown hair, though she still wore makeup around the eyes that had won Voltaire's heart, if only for a while. Emile knew she was considered a beauty, mixed blessing that it was. Ironically it was only in hell that she had been treated as equal in intelligence and spirit. This made her chuckle bitterly as she passed between two immense demons guarding the main gate, each packing a Russian anti-tank rifle in their immense hands. She walked up the broad obsidian steps to two immense, valved doors which opened at her approach. To her surprise an American cowboy stood there, a tall rangy man with in a vest, dark, broad-brimmed hat and wearing a gun belt. The creature that walked out behind him was hard to focus on, it seemed to be a female shape of dense black smoke; at first she thought it a shadow then saw the glowing white patches of its eyes and knew it for a denizen of hell.

"Evening, ma'am," said the cowboy, tipping his hat. "You'd be Madam Du Chatelet?"

For answer she pulled open her white ruffled shirt to show the pentagram burned on to the whiteness of her right breast.

He grimaced and nodded, "Have one of those myself."

"You are the chamberlain?"

The female shaped laughed.

"Well that's a dollar word for the nickel job that I do around here," he smiled. "The name's Frank Hopkins. This here is Smoke, an evil-tempered creature of no merits I've discovered, who also serves the Prince. But she does come in handy from time to time."

The creature turned to Emile. "You are expected. We are to convey you to our master. Please stay close as it is unsafe to wander these halls unescorted."

Emile followed on their heels as they walked into the huge halls. The entire castle was cut from black stone of various types. It was well lit, though the light never seemed to penetrate very far. Down some of the side halls she saw strange shapes stalking, slithering and humping their way through the distance. Terrible sounds came at intervals, some of rage, some of despair and others of pain. Emile walked on, hand on her rapier.

Hopkins looked at her out of the corner of his eyes and smiled. She straightened her shoulders, took her hand from her weapon and walked on.

The room that Smoke led them too was also vast, dominated by a huge fireplace. Some monstrous skull hung from the mantelpiece. Rugs made from creatures she'd only read of in fantasies dotted the stone floor. A figure stood before the raging fireplace, far too close to the radiant heat for human comfort. Belial, Crown Prince of Hell turned to face Emile. She studied him. He had the appearance of a slender, tall man, the ruin of someone once gloriously handsome. Only his cold, yellow eyes jarred against the genial, intelligent lines of his face. He smiled at her, wolf-like, yet welcoming. "Greeting Marquise, my grim fortress is cheered by the sight of such a lovely flower as you."

Emile swept off her plumed hat and gave the bow of a musketeer.

"Oh," he said. "No curtsey? And you appear before me dressed as a man? Are you one who despises her own fairer sex?"

"No, Majesty," she said. "I am delighted to be a woman. I only resent the restrictions placed on the thoughts and freedom of women. This hell of ours is also a dangerous place for my sex. Complicated weapons often fail. But a good rapier will always pierce the heart of a problem."

"Why do you seek an audience with me?" He walked over to an onyx table and hefted a stone cup of blood red liquid. Emile noted that he did not offer her any.

Emile walked over to a window that overlooked the Great Scar. A full third of New Hell City was gone, leaving only a glassy, utterly smooth surface, as if some giant ice cream scoop had been used to remove part of the city. Aftershocks and secondary effects had done for much of the rest of the city. Building proceeded apace in the haphazard fashion of hell.

"They're gone you know," she said.

The cowboy shifted uncomfortably, as if afraid for her. Smoke gave a low chuckle.

"Do not try my patience," Belial growled.

"They have not reappeared at the Undertakers' or anywhere else in the hells that my contacts can reach. Have your forces learned otherwise?"

Belial stared as if trying to decide if her familiar manner provoked or intrigued him. "They have not, but I cannot say that it has occurred to me to search. Wherever they went they did so in the tiniest of particles."

"True, Tesla is a genius but undisciplined and reckless. He tried this new Dirac power source without understanding it, without checking his math properly. With more intellectual rigor he might have recognized that this is not merely a new power source in hell, like nuclear power was on Earth. He discovered an underlying principle that binds the universe together, but could not control it. I believe that I can."

Belial drained his cup. "Of interest, I admit. Such power could extend my reach in hell; make me more feared by the other powers. Oh, joy. I will have you work with my interior minister –"

"I propose a great mechanism by which we will rip open the dimension of hell and march out of this pit. Perhaps to Heaven itself," Emile said.

Belial stared. Frank dropped his hat. Smoke's form wavered as if in a high wind.

"The audacity of you," Belial said when he could find his voice.

Emile raised a delicate arched eyebrow. "I am a wronged woman and an angry one. I have done nothing to merit hell. In life I defied convention and gave myself to such men as suited me. In a world of arranged loveless marriages, why not? It was a common enough practice for men. Yet G – um, the administering deity, or something, sent me here. I object, sir, I most strenuously object."

"I understand," Hopkins said, "that one can file an appeal in Pandemonium."

Emile snapped her fingers. "Such nonsense, with agents of the same tyranny that banished us here? What hope for justice or answers there? No, if we appear as supplicants we will be treated as such. I do not agree that this power has a right to judge me. I give it no dominion. Let us appear before heaven in arms, in revolution."

Belial laughed long slow and bitter. "Oh, Child. Thank you for the first true laugh I have had in eons. But you see I was there when we faced the legions of heaven at the beginning. Why would it end differently now?"

"Do you not know more of war now? Were you not children then in the beginning of creation? We have weapons now; we have humanity, demons and more. I do not guarantee success, but with Tesla's help, I can create the gates out of here. You may flee out into all creation, or you can join me and face this tyrant creator. As for myself, I am bound to face this so-called creator.

"Why come to me? I am the Crown Prince; why not approach my Master, Satan himself?"

"Machiavelli said that all princes operate the same regardless of where they are from. I believe this to be the case. Your Lord will not want to oppose heaven so openly. He will support us and hope for our success, which will benefit him, or our failure which will amuse he who lives only to ruin others. Either way he benefits, so why should he act in the open?"

"Whereas I, with nothing to look forward to save an eternity as the Crown Prince of this pit, have little to lose and much to gain? Very clever, I must have Machiavelli over for dinner again.

"Meanwhile I must say how you interest me young lady. While I am trying to decide if I will have you for dinner or as dinner, tell me what it is that you want in aid from me?"

"At first I will need your help in freeing Tesla from Hoover and the DIS. With his help I will make a demonstration machine to show you that we can control this power and direct it. Then we will need to create the League of the Damned for it will take every power of hell to create the Great Machine and every weapon to storm heaven."

"Hmmm," Belial said, a wolfish grin splitting his face. "My master runs both the DIS and The Children under his chief operative Welch, who would give anything to discommode Hoover."

"Who you despise as well," Emile said.

"I despise everyone, my dear, but particularly Hoover." He turned to Hopkins and Smoke. "What do you say, my servants?"

"I live only to serve you," Smoke said, bowing.

Frank shrugged. "It's something to do."

"Does your blood not burn with indignation at your fate?" Emile exclaimed, waving an arm.

Hopkins considered. "I get heartburn frequently. Does that count?"

Smoke groaned.

Dinner with the Crown Prince featured the best of what hell had to offer. Belial seemed to genuinely enjoy her company. He dismissed Frank and Smoke and it was only the two of them, along with a legion of demonic servants who flitted about trying their best to be unobserved.

"A fine dinner," Belial concluded, tossing a napkin on the table. I can think of only one thing worthy to follow it." He rose and extended a hand. "The rug by the fireplace will do nicely."

"Alas, no," Emile said.

"You turn me down?" he said astonished. "You who came here seeking my aid?"

"I am a noble and French," she said. "I may give myself to a lover. I may be conquered against my will, but I do not barter myself. Not even to escape hell. For then I would merely take hell with me as part of my soul."

Belial looked at her in astonishment then laughed. "Oh, this is rich. What a break in the ennui of my existence. You are a delightful girl. I think you could give Lucifer himself a lesson on pride. Let's hope you find it less of a dangerous commodity"

"Those with nothing to lose fear little."

"Do not be so cavalier despite your wardrobe," he said a note of true warning in his voice. "There is a wide latitude of experiences available in hell. Yours have been nowhere near as horrible as some."

"And yet if I am consumed by beasts or drowned in acid, what matter?" she replied. "In an infinite existence of suffering are these not the equivalent of a sore foot? With no hope for release or for any future good, why should these things deter me? I do not intend mindless impertinence, your majesty. I must show you that I am resolute and undeterrable, else why would you back the madness that is my course."

He nodded slowly, something like respect in the deadly wolf eyes. "I will have Hopkins and Smoke see you to your new rooms. Servants will bring your other things from your home. I wish to see how rapidly you can turn hell on its head." He bent down and kissed her hand. "Good night, my dear, demons sing you to your rest."

*

Emile rose early in the suite of rooms that Belial allocated her. She found Smoke waiting for her in the hallway. The ghostly demon conducted her to the vast armory in the low regions of the fortress. There she found Frank waiting for her. He was drinking coffee and examining a variety of weapons. "Morning, Ma'am."

"Is there more of that?" she gestured at the coffee. Frank brought the pot over and poured it into a delicate cup for her. Smoke disappeared into a corner, only her eyes glowed at them.

"So what do you think, Frank?" Emile said. "You are the damned. Did you do anything worth an infinite punishment?"

Frank polished away at his revolver for a little before speaking. "I came to hell, or was sent, I don't rightly know, to do something. And yes, when I was alive I was, well, one who could spin a tall tale. Maybe I wasn't the best of husbands or fathers, but I never killed nobody, nor stole much of anything. And I'd say that life was hard enough on me that me and life would have been about even when we called it quits, so no I don't feel I should be here.

"But there's plenty that do. I remember the films of the death camps in Europe. I know of Uncle Joe Stalin, Mao and there were bunch of others. There are some foul bastards down here wearing death's-heads, red stars, and other insignia.

"And punished they should be," Emile nodded. "Yet why should you suffer the same punishment as those barbarians? Even if they should be boiled alive for 100,000 years to return to them all the evil they did, eventually it must end."

"I got no problem with your thinking, ma'am. It just doesn't seem to be the way this works."

"Today," she smiled, "we set about remaking that."

"Well, getting out of hell sounds good to me."

Emile looked him over. "Perhaps when we escape this pit and get to some place where sex can again be joyful we will get to know each other better."

He returned her frank look with a lop-sided grin. "Gives me all the more reason to hope you can make this work."

"What plan would that be?" a new voice called.

Emile turned, "You must be Welch."

The thin balding man simply nodded. "I am under orders to help you with your crackpot idea."

Emile shrugged. "Believe or do not. For now what I need is your best efforts."

"That's what I do."

He looked at Frank and Smoke. "I would prefer my own team. However my boss doesn't want too much of his skin in this game. So I use what I have."

"You use what *I* have," Emile said. "This operation, *mes ami*, is mine."

"Lovely," Welch said.

"Let me show you my plan," Emile said. She walked over to a computer and flicked it on with practiced ease. For once a complicated mechanism started up as it was supposed to. Emile tapped away on keys for a bit; a holographic screen next to her began to glow.

"This is the fortress of Despair," Emile said, looking down at the glowing, ghostly holograph. "Do you recognize it, Frank?"

"Yeah," he replied. "I was alive during WWII. I remember the concrete battleship of Manila Bay."

"I," Smoke said from her corner, "do not."

"It was a stone island that the US Army made into a fortress; it resembled a seagoing battleship, complete with battleship guns in turrets and barbettes," Frank said.

Welch nodded. "It stood against the Japanese until May of 42. It was conquered by lack of water, not force of arms."

"An unsinkable battleship," Emile said, "and Hoover's maximum security prison."

Frank rubbed his chin. "That is a one tough nut to crack."

"It is worse than it looks," Emile said. "The inside is the true danger. It has seven levels and each is guarded by the one of the most powerful of hell's demons. The Seven deadly sins, manifest as demons: wrath, greed, sloth, pride, lust, envy, and gluttony. Each defends his own level. Tesla would be a prisoner in the central level.

"Great," Frank said, "not only do we have to get past naval rifles, we have to tangle with demons of the first rank."

"Impossible," Smoke said.

"Maybe," Welch said, staring narrowly at Emile.

Emile smiled a chilly smile. "I have a way to get on. My working model of the dimension ripper, which I used to prove my theorem, will suffice to put a small party on the surface of the fortress."

"Why not onto the prison level?" Welch demanded.

Emile shook her head, "The device does not have such discretion at close range. It is one of the things that I need Tesla for. No, I can get us onto the fortress but I cannot get us off. That is why we came to you, Welch."

This time it was Welch, who rubbed his chin. “I can arrange for a battleship to take on the fortress. The *IJN Musashi,* 18.1-inch naval guns, 68,000 tons. She came to hell after her own government sent her to her death. Unfortunately the fortress has been up-gunned to the same level, 18-inch rifles, 6-inch casement guns, 12-inch mortars–”

“How will blowing it up with us onboard help?” Frank asked.

“Even the *Musashi* can’t destroy this fortress,” Welch said. “But it can knock off the main and secondary batteries, shatter the guard’s surface barracks, wipe out the nest of antiaircraft guns. That done, well I have the service of the finest helicopter pilot in all hell in Achilles.

“But that is all I can do. About the demons, I can’t do anything.”

“There my Lord Belial has granted us aid,” Emile said.

Smoke shuddered.

“We need only fight our way through three levels and into the fourth,” Emile said. “So we need not battle all seven deadly sins.”

“If you can handle them, then we may have a chance,” Welch said. “When do we go?

“How soon can *Musashi* attack?”

Welch consulted a tablet computer. “Seven days steaming. She’d be in gun range by sunrise.”

“How many in the boarding party?” Frank said.

“The machine can transmit eight, the four specials Belial will send us. Then the four of us.”

“Two amateurs and a petty demon,” Welch said.

“Belial says it is us four. He has faith in Smoke and Frank. He asked for you as you are the best. As for me, I insisted. I am the captain of this expedition. I will not be left behind.”

"This sounds like one of those British polar expeditions that always ended up in disaster," Welch groaned.

"We go before dawn on the seventh day," Emile said. "We will allow ourselves two hours to infiltrate the base and get inside the armor/concrete belt. If we haven't made it by then, we'll be heading for the Undertaker's table anyway."

"You will," Smoke said.

"Do we get breakfast before we go?" Frank said.

"Am I French?" Emile replied.

The days that followed were filled with training and planning. Welch was satisfied with nothing and least of all, Frank's relaxed cowboy demeanor.

*

Fort Drum sat far out in its simulation of Manila Bay, looming dark and forbidding in the early morning hours. The moon was a gibbous line in the sky. Only a few small lights showed here and there. Guards patrolled the fortress' surface but they were few and considered their presence superfluous. The terrible demons, each with its own level, were the fort's true security, though the 18-inch guns and dual-purpose five-inch guns around the "tower" were enough to discourage conventional assaults.

To the rear of the fort stood the water towers and it was there that Emile's Dirac powered transporter placed eight figures: Emile, Frank, Welch, Smoke and four hooded and cloaked figures where simply there, appearing from holes of even deeper inkiness. The instant the Dirac effect released them they moved to deal with the guards. Welch and Frank used silenced pistols to drop their targets. Smoke wrapped herself about her guard the dusky arms snapping his neck.

Welch picked up his mike to the powerful radio he wore on his back and rapped out a few coded words. Out in the darkness, a helicopter lifted from a monstrous battleship, whose guns began to load and elevate.

Emile followed. "This is the entrance to mechanical spaces. We can cut through there to the prison decks." The door wasn't even alarmed and they slipped in. The quartet of robed figures trailed them silently, seeming somehow detached from the expedition yet part of it.

They reached the prison deck, there Welch used a magnesium charge to burn through the lock after dealing with a relatively simply alarm.

"Now begins the danger," Emile said.

A thud sounded from down the corridor

"Didja have to say it aloud?" Frank groaned.

They stepped into a broad hallway; from down the hall lit by the harsh glare of overhead bulbs came something that looked like a sumo wrestler gone on a binge. Gluttony filled the corridor ahead of them, a hulking shapeless male figure with a blob-like head lit by avaricious eyes.

"Food," it said.

"I don't think it's too particular about what it eats," Frank said.

"Can't eat smoke I bet," Smoke said smugly.

"You'd lose," Welch snapped. "There's no end to gluttony.

"Something to fill the vast emptiness," Gluttony said, starting toward them, its massive arms stretched out.

"I think not," Emile said. She turned to one of the four robed and silent companions and ripped the cloak off it. "Starvation, it is your time. Strike now."

Starvation stood before them a naked scrawny female figure with hollow eyes, parchment-like skin stretched over her ribcage, but her teeth were sharp and the narrow body crackled with energy. She spied the immense pile of blubber moving toward them. "Fat," she shrieked, "fat, fat, Fatty. I hate you." She tore through the space between her and Gluttony almost diving into the blobby creatures. The two rolled around on the floor devouring each other's demonic essence, howling and shrieking. The rest of the team held back.

It became hard to tell what they were seeing in the writhing mass of flesh on the floor. Sight seemed to distort. Were two corporeal monsters battling or two concepts; was it a fight or a metaphor? With a last convulsion the glowing mass on the floor disappeared, leaving no trace of either demon.

"It worked," Welch said, shaking his head.

"Of course," Emile returned. "We countered one Vice with another Vice as no Virtues are available to us."

"Don't that beat all," Frank said. "I'll have to tell my pa when I see him that he was a tad off. Looks like two wrongs can make a right."

"We still have three levels to go," Smoke said.

The fortress belled and shook. Dirt shook from the ceiling along with small bits of rock spalled off the ceiling and walls.

Welch checked his watch. *"Musashi."*

Alarms shrilled.

"They'll be busy with the *Musashi* and the special forces attacks on Cavite," Welch said. "All we have to worry about are the demons."

"Oh, is that all?" Frank said.

"You want to live forever?" Welch cracked.

They moved down the corridor, checking Welch's map and finding the stairs to the next level. A sharp crack sounded over them, the vibration drilled through to their bones.

Welch frowned. "Outgoing mail for the *Musashi.* Same caliber she's firing. Only this rock can't sink and she can."

As if to confirm him, a crack and rumble stirred the floor. A different sensation than the massive turrets above them generated.

"More incoming?" Frank said, staring up at the stone walls and swaying lights.

"Yeah, don't worry," Welch answered as he pushed forward. "The original fort stopped 3,000 shells and bombs – none got more than four inches into the stone."

"Were any of those 18-inchers?" Frank asked.

Welch grinned. "No." The walls shook again. "I hope *Musashi* can knock out those guns. There's no way we can survive topside if they're still firing; the overpressure alone would kill us and tear Achilles' chopper to bits."

"Hurry," Emile said. "The naval battle is not our concern. We face greater dangers here.

The next hallway was as different as possible from the bare level above. It was filled with pillows, drapery and divans, as if a New Orleans whorehouse owner has been hired to do interior design.

The level's demon stepped out to bar their way. Lust looked at them. She was a woman with hot sultry eyes and curves that would daunt a Lamborghini. Her body was dusky, gleaming with health and sexuality. "You shall all be mine," she said in a voice that gave Frank and Welch erections and caused Emile's body to throb.

"I think not," Emile managed, the men were beyond speech. "Repression, stop her."

The robed figure stepped between them and the sumptuous female standing astride the corridor. The robe fell and a nun stood there, aged and pale, she held an eighteen-inch golden ruler in her hand like it as a gladius.

"You're filthy," the nun spat, "a disgusting pervert."

"Hah," returned Lust. "You're the pervert, repressing all that is natural, beautiful and pleasurable. You twist desires into damnation." She reached up and drew something seemingly from the very air. The "object" was long, black and would have made a stallion proud. "I know what you need," Lust jeered.

The nun shrieked and charged forward, golden ruler held high. Lust leapt to meet her and the two demons collided, their weapons clashing.

Emile's party with its other robed and concealed vices waited until the nun shoved lust into a side corridor to race past the dueling pair to hurry down a spiral staircase to the next level.

This level looked like a dragon's hoard. Gold and gems winked at them as the four, trailed now by only two cloaked figures moved out.

"Not much doubt about who runs this level," Frank said.

"Why?" came a deep voice, "because I love my baubles?" Greed stepped forward from a cell. He wore an immaculate suit, with every pocket bulging with money or gems.

"We have no time for you," Emile said.

"But I do," said a clear female voice. The cloak fell from an expensively dressed blond woman bejeweled and with money literally falling from her pockets. "I'm Spendthrift, baby. I got money literally to burn, 'cause, after all, what does wealth mean?"

"Fool," Greed shrieked. "Money is everything."

"Well," Spendthrift said, producing a deck of cards. "How about a game?"

Greed pointed at Emile. "I have to destroy them."

"Well, Greed, Sweetie, you can play cops and robbers with them or you can play for some real money with me. Make your mind up or I am outta here."

Greed couldn't take his eyes off the money and gems Spendthrift was literally dripping on the floor. "Oh, fuck it," Greed said. "Despair will take care of these guys. Let's you and me play, honey."

The five raiders slipped past Greed and Spendthrift as the two sat at a table, cards slapping the rich wood between them.

"Quick, down these stairs, this is the prisoner's level," Emile said. "Tesla's cell is number 12."

They found the inventor lying on the floor, filthy and unkempt, his eyes vacant and staring. The cell door wasn't even locked. Emile pushed it open and knelt by the slim inventor.

"Tesla," Emile said gently.

He looked at her with vague eyes. "It's all gone you know"

"What's gone?" Emile asked.

He struggled to focus. "Who are you?"

"Emile Du Chatelet," she replied. "We are here to rescue you. Now what is gone?"

Tears leaked down his face. "My mind, my wonderful brilliant mind. Gone. All gone. I'm merely dull, common matter now.

"Tesla," she said, "you are under the influence of Despair, the demon who haunts this level. Once we get you out of here, your mind will return."

"You can't fight him, you can't win," Tesla said. "There's no escape."

"Ah," Emile said. "People have been telling me I can't win for as long as I have existed. Always I prove them wrong. Come Tesla, rise. We shall escape."

"It won't work," he said but staggered to his feet.

"Then you can come and watch us try," Frank snapped. "It beats sitting on your ass here."

"Something is coming," Smoke said

A figure dressed as an undertaker with a tall hat and gaunt face walked into the light "I am Acedia," the doleful figure said, "self-doubt and despair. You have done well to defeat my siblings above. But all is hopeless when facing me."

"Is that so?" said the last robed figure flinging off its cloak. Arrogance was the image of a Wall Street Broker, the sort that had nearly destroyed the American economy with their free-wheeling disregard for regulation and reason. He lit a cigar and slicked back his thinning orange comb over with one hand. "Your problem, Acedia babe, is that you don't dream big enough. Can't play the big game."

"Die," Acedia said.

"Not hardly," Arrogance replied, blowing a smoke ring at the black clad man.

The battle between them seemed one of wills as they stared at each other and reality around each began to roil and shred, making it hard to see.

Frank and Welch added the fire of their pistols for whatever good it would do. Smoke dashed in slashing with her arms. They needed to finish Despair, and Arrogance was clearly struggling. Emile looked Despair in the eye and unlimbered her Rapier. "Monsieur," she shouted, "I have faced you all my life. I fear you no more here than I did on Earth." She ran forward lunging with the rapier, just as Arrogance gave a great cry and fell to the floor disappearing in a pile of foul-smelling ooze.

Whether it was Emile's spirited attack or the efforts of all of them, Despair fell back, losing much of his shape and size, then he turned and fled.

"Do not pursue," Emile shouted at Smoke and Frank. "It suffices that he is fled. We take Tesla and leave."

The walls shook again, this time they could not tell if the firing was incoming or outgoing, they were too deep in the fortress.

Welch cursed savagely pulling his headset off his head, "Just heard from Achilles."

"What is it?" Emile demanded

"*Musashi* is pulling out. She's down at the bow and on fire. She's retreating out of range. Worse the attacks on Cavite went badly. Paratroops are heading for us. They're going to drop on the base. Our spies say they plan to pour gasoline in and torch the place from outside. Worse yet they didn't blast all the top turrets to bits. Achilles can't land up top."

"A lot of effort to get little old us," Frank said.

"They don't know who or what we are or how many of us are here. They do know we were able to attack their whole operation here simultaneously and that some of the toughest demons around haven't finished us off. They're mostly humans and lesser demons; they don't want to take chances. Hoover would rather see Tesla as a briquette then free."

"Emile," Frank said slowly. "We've used up all our Vices and there are three demons below before we could get down to the boatdock level. I don't see us getting through them."

"No point in fighting our way up, either," Welch said.

Emile put a fist against her head. "Nothing occurs to me."

"Wait," Smoke said. "There was a barbette on this level"

"Yeah," Welch said. "But it's unmanned since they started using this as a prison level and let Despair loose."

"Yes but it opens to the outside air," Smoke continued. "Could Achilles bring the chopper alongside the barbette?"

"He can do anything with a chopper but it will still have to stand off about forty feet with the width of the rotors. We can't jump that."

"Jump no," Smoke said. "Follow me."

The five survivors, led by Smoke raced to the barbette facing the ocean side, as Welch rapped out orders over his headset to the moody warrior and his Blackhawk. In a minute they reached the barbette. Its armored doors were down, closed around the six-inch naval rifle in the barbette. Welch studied the mechanism for a minute then operated the mechanism, the doors cycled open. Cool sea air blew in and the brightness of the sun made them blink. The smell of cordite and burning bit at their noses.

"Call for Achilles," Smoke said. She turned to Frank. "Well Cowboy, time to see if your talents with the lasso are another of your stories."

"What are you talking about?" Frank said.

But Smoke was changing shape, elongating into a snake like shape which got thinner and thinner until she had become a pile of rope, with a small cobra like head and its two white eyes. "I'm strong," she said, "but not enough to take more than one at a time in this shape."

"Son of a..." Frank began.

"Do it!" Smoke said.

Frank picked up the demon rope and quickly tied it into a lasso.

"Here comes Achilles," Welch said. The Blackhawk was racing over the wave tops from astern of the stone battleship. It reached the barbette apparently unobserved or at least unfired on. The chopper rose to their leveled and hovered.

Frank stepped forward, whipping a length of the demon over him and struggling with the weight of the elongated demon. "Smoke, I'm gonna throw you on that front wheel. Can you snake into the cargo compartment?"

"Can you lie like a rug?" Smoke replied.

Taking that for a yes, Frank flung the demon, which looped around the chopper landing gear and promptly crawled into the cargo compartment. Frank hung the other end around the naval rifle. Smoke was stretched across the fifty foot gap.

"She's strong," Frank said. "In her winged shape I used to ride her all over hell. If she were bigger we could have all ridden her out but this will have to do." Frank reached up looped his legs over Smoke and began to go hand over hand to the chopper.

With Achilles holding the chopper steady they made their way over one by one: Tesla, Welch and finally Emile. But they were not to be unmolested. Through the spinning rotors Emile saw a man gesticulating. Shots snapped down but fortunately the rotors stopped most of them. Emile went as fast as she dared having less upper arm strength then the men but being lighter.

A shot stung Smoke, who yelped and let go of the naval rifle.

"I am dead," Emile thought as the demon released from the gun end, but as she fell, Smoke looped around her and Achilles powered off, trailing Emile like a flag. Frank and Welch pulled furiously on Smoke, who thickened and shortened as they did so. In seconds she was gasping on the deck of the chopper, next to Smoke who was rubbing her backside where the bullet had grazed her.

Emile and Frank laughed in hysterical release as Achilles danced the chopper away. They looked over at Welch who was leaning against the bulkhead, strapping Tesla to the floor. He grimaced at them. "Just don't say mission accomplished."

*

Weeks passed and Tesla recovered. He and Emile were closeted day after day. Welch returned to his master. Frank and Smoke stayed to guard Tesla. There were many who would love to rip pieces off the scientist.

On the 28th day after the raid a recovered Tesla and Emile stood facing banks of computers. Frank and Smoke had entered bearing trays of breakfast.

"When the brains get going," Frank had said, "they forget to eat."

Emile thanked them. Tesla merely grabbed coffee and a muffin.

Tesla stared at her latest equations on the screens for an hour, maybe more in silence. Finally he turned to her. "I'd heard you were brilliant but I assumed like so many of the preindustrial dead that you would be useless with computers."

"I have had time to change and to learn," she replied. "Computers were no more in your world than in mine. I learned the mechanics of operating them here, but math is math."

He mused over one glowing screen of abstruse math. "Your approach is novel. To be frank it would not have occurred to me to phrase this equation this way. Still I am dubious of this factor," he gestured at a series of symbols."

Tesla caught Hopkin's expression. "Think of it this way-"

The cowboy raised his hand. "You'd have as much luck explaining it to my horse. My job was to get you here. From here, you're in Emile's hands.

"I hope you can do what you said," Hopkins continued. "I wouldn't want to see Belial disappointed. He only seems like a genial English aristocrat."

"Thank you, Frank. I know this."

Weeks passed and Tesla continued to recover. He and Emile were now locked day and night in the computer room. Frank and Smoke diverted themselves with other tasks for their master. The great gathering for the Olympiad had to managed and Belial was deep in that. It served a dual purpose; there was no other way to gather so many of hell in one place without war breaking out.

Frank found himself summoned one night by Smoke to Belial's hall. When he arrived he found Tesla and Emile there.

Emile smiled at him. "We are ready. It is time. We have the math."

"It will work," Tesla said. "The machine will rip us a path out of here."

"Three days from now," Belial intoned. "You will have your audience before most of hell. Many will be here. Others will have eyes and ears here: some mechanical, some magical. You will reach those that you need to reach. Are you ready to stand or fall with your idea?"

Emile looked back steadily. "I am ready."

*

Emile faced out from the mountain of stone that the ancients had piled in their failed attempt to escape the depths of hell. She knew through Belial's power that her voice would reach all the vast array of beings filling the valley and the hills beyond.

"You assembled legions and powers of hell. Hear me. We are a vast mix, some evil, some victims of circumstance, but many of us do not know why we are here. None of us have lived blameless lives, but it is not given to humanity to do so. Yet we are condemned here to hell forever, with no word of hope or redemption given us. Why? Who calls this justice?"

A rumble of discontent swelled from the multitude.

"Some of you have done true evil and merit your punishment. Yet even the worst of you did a finity of sins and now is damned with infinity of punishment. Who calls this justice?

"Even you most ancient ones, the fallen angels, you were made by this so-called loving deity and you did stray. But what parent never forgives a child for straying? What parent is so cruel and selfish to believe he owns his children as chattel? What parent is it that fears his children will grow and surpass him, so badly, that he must, at their first stumble, cast them down for all eternity? Who calls such a parent just?"

"We are all sinners but we are all made to be sinners in a universe where not to sin is not to survive. This so-called just and loving God seems to have nothing to do but test and punish, raising the bar at each point and yet offering only the back of his hand to those who fail.

"I say enough. It is time for a change.

"You know that the great scientist Tesla discovered a new power source, fantastic in what it can do. In his folly and haste he destroyed a third of New Hell. Yet even this disaster was not in vain for the dead of that disaster have not come back to the Undertaker. They are not in hell anymore."

A beast like a tyrannosaur, with glowing red eyes, spoke in a delicate and female voice, "What profit us to exit hell as stripped electrons or less?"

"No profit at all," Emile replied, "if that was what I offered you. It is not.

"Tesla has been freed and with his knowledge linked to mine we have tamed his equations, and developed a plan for a great machine." She turned to the immense stone ramp behind her. "Primitives before us, realizing the injustice of our fate, piled stone upon stone to escape the pit. But heaven remained out of reach.

"We shall make a new 'Stairway to Heaven,' out of exotic particles and powers that warp the very fabric of all reality. Belial, Crown Prince of Hell, stands behind me as do many others. But it will take the combined forces of all of hell to make the Great Machine possible."

"And then what?" shouted a man in a black uniform with lightening flashes on it.

Emile looked at him in distaste but there was no help for it. "We go before the judge and demand redress for the savagery of our punishment. Surely even for those of you whose ghastly deeds are the stuff of legends, or who filled the 20th century with more slaughter than in all the time before, there must be an end to punishment. A million years may be just, but at a million and one the judge has become an evil tyrant."

The Tyrannosaur cocked its head in an oddly delicate gesture. "So you intend to trouble deaf heaven with your bootless cries?"

"If we are not given justice," Emile shouted, "then as was done in France, it will be time for regicide. If the throne of heaven will sit only on our backs, upend it. It will be time to make Nietzsche correct, 'God' will be dead."

Shocked silence gripped hell.

Emile gripped her rapier hilt. "I say to you that it is time to be bold. There is nothing to lose for the damned of all eternity. The Great Machine will rip open a gate this time. Through it we will flood. Some of you think only to escape hell. Very well, we will not force you to go to the gates of heaven, though how long you will remain free of the pit if we do not succeed, I cannot say.

"For the rest of you," her voice soared. "I say enough. On to heaven's gates, we will gain an audience or we will gain the universe. Who is with me and who wants to stay in this pit forever?

Cacophony broke out, but gradually it gained a name. "Emile, Emile, Emile," louder and louder until it seemed it must be heard in Heaven.

She ripped her rapier out, then stood atop the parapet wall, a tiny figure, but with a promise of power and danger such as had never before been imagined. "Then let the 'Stairway to Heaven' be built," she cried. "Let the great and powerful convene in the Halls of Belial to plan our escape."

The cheers threatened to collapse walls and buildings.

Emile turned to Belial, whose yellow eyes were... were what? Glistening? Filled with the shadow of a hope? Had some vestige of youth attached to them? He waved a hand and the sounds of the vast horde vanished.

"Emile, my dear," he said, his voice shaking slightly. "You take my very breath away...you amaze me. You almost make me... believe."

She looked into the eyes, ancient when homo erectus first lifted a stone ax. "Ah, but you must believe, my Prince. Believe with all your heart. It is only with the most steadfast, unshakeable belief that we have any chance at all."

Belial laughed but it was a wild and bitter laugh full of unshed tears. "Emile, oh Emile, please tell this old devil that you are not asking him –"

"Yes," she said smiling gently at him, "I am asking you to have faith."

KNOCKING ON HEAVEN'S GATES

Larry Atchley, Jr.

But who prays for Satan? Who in eighteen centuries has had the common humanity to pray for the one sinner that needed it most?

– Mark Twain

Anton LaVey floated above what little was left of his body. The rocket propelled grenade launcher that had exploded next to him left him scattered in pieces all over the island of Onogoroshima in hell. Flashing through his mind he saw all the events of his former life, both on earth and in hell with lucid clarity. His last memories were of trying to get the Spear of Destiny back from the traitor, Guy Fawkes, while they were on an expedition together to bring it back to His Satanic Majesty on His orders. The Spear of Longinus, which legend held had pierced the side of Christ on the cross was too powerful an artifact to end up in the wrong hands in hell. Little had LaVey known that he sold it out of his shop in new hell to the Grail Knight Parsival, who used it to slay a powerful demon-spawning entity on the island. Guy had taken the spear with the hope of driving it into The Devil's heart so that he could earn his way out of hell and into Heaven. The fool! There is no way out of hell for damned and irredeemable souls. They had all earned their sentences and now must live with the consequences.

He then moved through a long dark tunnel that seemed to go on for infinity, but moving faster and faster toward a tiny point of light at the end. Suddenly he was surrounded by light and warmth. It was incredibly bright but did not hurt his eyes, and it felt comforting, serene. He perceived a presence in the light and it seemed as if the light radiated from this being. It made him feel the most incredible joy, peace, and love, feelings he had never known before. It spoke to him in his mind: *Anton LaVey, in life you were selfish, egotistical, vain, lustful, and a liar. Even in hell you continue to only serve your own wants and desires. You serve His Satanic Majesty only in the hope of raising your status in the hierarchy of hell. Will you never learn what it means to sacrifice yourself for the benefit of others? This is why you were sent to hell, and why in hell you shall remain.*

The light began to fade away, along with the being of light until all was darkness around him.

"Please don't go! I can change. I can be unselfish, you will see! Wait!"

He felt himself moving rapidly through the black inky formless void, as if being pulled by a tether. A daunting despair like he had never felt came over him in the absence of the light and the radiant being. He felt terribly alone in the cold black void. He realized that the being had spoken true. He had been alone his whole life, even when surrounded by family, friends, lovers. He had never really let anyone inside his protective circle and he had been selfish. How could he change the very essence of what made him who he was? Individualism and self-centeredness was the very foundation of the ideology of the Church of Satan, which he founded on earth. It really had nothing to do with worshipping the Devil, but was more about worshipping the self. He had pissed off both God and Satan, and so had no friends in heaven or in hell. Was he truly irredeemable? Who was the being in the light that placed so much doubt in his mind? Was it an angel? God? He had not needed God before, why would he need him now? But that feeling in the light... oh such joy and love. Was there ever a way to experience that again? And permanently, not in a fleeting moment. Perhaps he could find the answers to these questions.

With a shuddering jolt he found himself back in his body, lying naked on a cold hard metal table. The old familiar sensations of physicality returned. Pain wracked his body and he felt himself jerking with spasms. He was being reconstituted. All the disparate parts of his form were being brought together. It felt like a thousand cuts soaked in alcohol. The stench of brimstone filled his nostrils. Everything was enshrouded in darkness, like his eyes refused to see. He sensed someone leaning over him, exhaling in his face, reeking of shit and decay: hell's Undertaker. He had heard stories from damned souls who had died in hell and gone to the morgue in New Hell to suffer under his painful ministrations and foul breath. This was LaVey's first trip to Slab A, but he had a feeling it wouldn't be his last.

"Welcome back Anton," the Undertaker said. "Fancy meeting you here. Heh, heh, heh. I wish I had more time to spend with the wonderfully torturous process of putting you back together, but His Satanic Majesty is awaiting your report."

Satan will not be amused, Anton thought. *He doesn't look well upon failure, and I have failed miserably.*

He got down from the cold table, his bare feet stepping on bones that littered the floor intermingled with entrails, and made slick by pools of blood. LaVey wasn't squeamish, but it made him want to retch. With nothing in his stomach but bile, all he could manage was dry heaves that felt like he would turn himself inside out as he doubled over in agony. Finally he stood up, his body quivering weakly. He saw some clothes hanging in a wardrobe that was along one wall of the enormous room. He picked out an all black suit that looked to be about his size.

He found a pair of black leather wingtip shoes that fit, and put them on his blood-stained feet. Two demons entered the room and approached him. They had red bodies like salamanders, and horns pointed from their foreheads. They both carried long wicked looking barbed pitchforks that were leveled at him.

"Anton LaVey, come with us," they said, with forked tongues waggling between pointed teeth.

They took him out of the morgue, marching through the streets of New Hell City. Or, more precisely, what was left of it. A huge slice of New Hell City had disappeared. It looked like it had been surgically cut out from the rest of the city by an impossibly enormous scalpel.

"What the hell happened here?"

"Some idiot named Tesla was testing out his latest invention and sucked a third of the city into another dimension. Damn shame it didn't take him with it," replied one of the demons.

Throughout the streets the damned were tormented by demons more than ever before. Demons pranced around on cloven hooves and claws, brandishing tridents, barbed whips, white hot brands, and other insidious devices to torture the irredeemable souls in hell. Here and there, the damned were impaled upon long spikes stuck in the ground, and fires were built at their feet, slowly burning their bodies, making the fat bubble and the skin crispy. Screams abounded and cries rang out from bloodied and burnt mouths.

In the distance LaVey could see smoke rising from the Roman quarter of the city.

"What's going on over there?" LaVey asked the demons.

"Someone blew up Caesar's villa awhile back and it still won't stop belching smoke. No one has claimed responsibility yet, but it is rumored that Erra and the Seven Sibitti are responsible."

A man shambled up to LaVey and the demons. He was dressed shabbily and was wearing sandwich boards with the words 'The end is near' and 'Erra is coming!' painted on them, in what looked like blood.

"The doom of Erra and the Seven is upon us!" the man yelled. "The Lord of pestilence and his personified weapons are striking down the damned all over hell! And His Satanic Majesty punishes the damned for fearing their wrath more than His. Is there nothing that can save us from Satan's retribution and Erra's wrath?"

Some demons, red-skinned, horned and covered in scales, came up behind the man and shoved a pike through his torso, lifting him high up in the air before planting the butt end of the shaft in the ground, impaling him, as he screamed and thrashed about.

Hell, LaVey thought, was really going to hell in a hand basket.

*

They led LaVey to the Hall of Injustice, a colossal tower of red stone, black glass, and blue steel. It stood one hundred and fifty stories high in the middle of New Hell. The demons escorted him up the blood red marble steps and through the massive iron front doors. After going through the security checkpoint in the lobby, which always involved the humiliating process of a strip and body cavity search, they got into the elevator. One of the demons took a key that was on a necklace around his neck and inserted it into a panel under the buttons on the wall. The small door opened up to reveal a brightly lit red button that had the word 'Penthouse' next to it. The demon pressed the button, closing and locking the panel as the elevator lurched upward with a jolt.

LaVey's nerves were starting to get the better of him, now that his appointment with His Satanic Majesty was imminent. Sweat broke out on his brow, and made his bald head glisten in the incandescent lighting. It didn't help that it was hot and stifling in the elevator. Also the two demons reeked of brimstone and it made him cough and choke. After what felt like an eternity the elevator came to an abrupt stop and the doors opened to reveal a spacious lobby with a single black marble desk along the far wall where sat His Satanic Majesty's receptionist. She was an attractive woman, blonde, with subtle makeup on her face and she wore a sensible looking tight white blouse that showed off her bust line. The demons approached the desk with LaVey between them.

"We're here with Anton LaVey. The boss wants to see him."

"Oh yes, of course," she said in a demure voice. "I will let him know you've arrived."

She pressed a button on her desktop phone. "Sire, I have a Mr. Anton LaVey here to see you."

"Ah yes, I have been expecting him. Send him in Miss Braun." The voice from the speaker phone sounded deep, smooth and gravelly, but with a refined accent that was hard to place.

The receptionist led them through two tall wood doors that were stained a dark rusty red color. LaVey didn't want to think about what they had been stained with. Through the doorway they entered a large office on the corner of the penthouse. All the windows had been blown out and gusty hot wind blew throughout the room. A desk carved from a single massive block of blood red marble anchored the far corner of the office, facing the door. Behind it sat the entity known as the Lord of Lies, the Prince of Darkness, the Devil, but first and foremost, His Satanic Majesty. He was smoking a long, fat cigar, blowing smoke rings that the gale from the windows blew apart almost as soon as they left his lips. He was stunningly handsome, beautiful even, with his prominent jaw featuring a well-groomed pointed goatee, masculine nose, and deep black hair swept back from his forehead where two bony red horns protruded. He was quite tall, and wore an all black well-tailored three-piece suit with a blood red tie. It was just as well that he was in his most accommodating visage, because in his true form, merely looking upon him caused one's bowels to loosen in terror and resulted in a descent into gibbering madness. Upon the desk, Satan's familiar, Michael, the hellcat, sat preening its bat-like wings and fur with a tongue that dripped acidic spittle upon the stone desk, scoring it with little pits and sending tiny plumes of smoke into the air. When LaVey walked in with the two demons beside him, he hissed at them spitefully.

Satan waved away the demons, saying: "I will speak with Mr. LaVey alone. You two are dismissed for now." They bowed as they exited the office leaving LaVey to stand alone before Satan.

Anton knelt on the floor, his head bowed, and eyes staring at the jet black marble tile floor. He knew that all damned who appeared before His Satanic Majesty were required to prostrate themselves before him or face terrible, torturous punishment.

"Very well, LaVey, you may rise," Satan said in that cold silky voice that made all damned souls in hell tremble with fear and awe.

"Thank you, Sire," LaVey stood and straightened his jacket and tie.

"So, LaVey, I understand there were some difficulties on your mission. You did not, in fact, bring back the Spear of Longinus, did you?"

"N-no Sire, I did not," LaVey stammered, his throat suddenly very dry. "Our squad wrested it from the entity on the island that possessed it, but we were betrayed by Guy Fawkes, who sought the spear in order to bring the spear back here to slay you. We blew the plane out of the sky over the island with Fawkes and the spear inside. Unfortunately, as the parts of the plane and the spear fell back to the island, one of our rocket-propelled grenades misfired and blew the remaining members of our party to pieces. The Spear of Destiny remains on the island."

LaVey stood before His Satanic Majesty, nervously wringing his sweating hands. He knew the punishment for failure in the Dark Lord's service would be severe, and long lasting. He had been given this one chance to prove himself, and hopefully earn a position in His Satanic Majesty's secret service known as The Devil's Children. He had blown it, quite literally. Now he would probably never earn his way into the intelligence agency, and worse, Satan could make his life a real living hell, much worse than his present mundane lot in the afterlife of tending a shop full of moldering clothes, junk and fake relics.

"That is incorrect," Satan said as he tapped ashes from the end of his cigar into a skull ashtray on the corner of his desk. "The spear is back in New Hell."

"But how, Sire? I saw the plane explode and go down in flaming pieces on the island myself before I was killed."

Satan leaned over to the phone on his desk and pressed a button with a long, sharp pointed black fingernail.

"Miss Braun, have Fawkes brought into my office."

"Yes, Sire."

A few moments later Guy Fawkes walked into the room, in shackles, with two large red skinned demons on either side of him holding the chains to his bonds. Lodged in his chest to the right of his heart, the point sticking outward, was the Spear of Longinus. LaVey thought that for a man with over a foot of metal inside him, he looked surprisingly well. Michael the hellcat looked up from his ministrations and bared its fanged teeth at Fawkes with a hiss that sent corrosive spittle flying across the room.

The demons pulled him down by the chains and forced him to kneel upon the floor between them, pushing his head down as well. He bowed as low as the spear would let him, the tip scraping against the smooth black tile. The muscles in his body were taut with the strain of trying to remain standing against the combined strength of the demons.

"Ah, yes, Guy Fawkes. So nice to see you observing protocol in my presence. Even if you must be forced to do so. Explain to your former associate how you came to bring back the spear to New Hell."

He motioned to the demons. "You may let him rise for now, but do keep a tight grip on him. I wouldn't want him to try anything foolish that either of us might regret."

They pulled the chains up taut and jerked him to his feet.

"Yes, well, I..."

"Yes, *Sire,*" His Satanic Majesty said.

"Yes, Sire," Fawkes said reluctantly. "The last thing I remember was being in the plane, with the spear in my hands, when there was a blinding flash and explosion. The next thing I knew, I was waking up on Slab A in the morgue with the undertaker's foul breath in my face, and a terrible aching pain in my chest. Once the blackness abated and my vision returned, I saw that the spear was sticking out of my chest. A cohort of demons took me from the morgue and threw me into the dungeons below the Hall of Injustice. Not much of a welcome for the one damned soul who managed to bring back the Spear of Destiny that you so badly wanted."

"Perhaps you would prefer a warmer welcome, Fawkes. Maybe we shouldn't wait until the fifth of November to burn you upon the bonfire, for your annual helliday."

Fawkes remained silent, his lips pursed tight. But a defiant glint was still in his eyes. LaVey knew that Fawkes would never rest in his pursuit of trying to get out of hell since he believed he should have been made a martyr for the Catholic Church, and was wrongfully damned to hell. He had even tried to kill Satan by blowing up the Hall of Injustice, thinking that he could escape if hell's ruler was deposed. All it had earned him was a particularly gruesome torture session at the hands of His Satanic Majesty, himself. But now Fawkes possessed the Spear of Destiny; it was a part of him. No one knew the limits of its power, but legend held that whoever had the spear was invincible and invulnerable. That was why Satan had bound him in fetters and thrown him in the dungeons under the Hall of Injustice. He didn't know if the spear could slay him, but he wasn't taking any chances. Also, someone with that much power running amuck throughout New Hell could wreak all kinds of havoc.

"Take him back to his cell," ordered His Satanic Majesty. "Perhaps a few millennia in the dungeons will teach him some humility and he will realize that he belongs here in hell."

The demons escorted Fawkes out of the corner office pulling him along by his chains.

"So, Anton LaVey," Satan mused. "What am I to do with you?"

"Sire... I..."

"Silence! That was a rhetorical question." He puffed on his cigar a bit more, while Michael the hellcat sharpened his claws on his leg. He looked down upon his familiar with disdain, and grimaced, but didn't stop him from shredding his slacks and making long furrows in his leg that welled up with blood. The cat-bat demon was purring contentedly.

"You did indirectly return to spear to New Hell, albeit not in the manner I would have preferred. Still, it is in my safe keeping. I don't think you are ready to join the ranks of The Devil's Children quite yet, however. I do have something else in mind that you can do for me. All this bothersome mess with Erra and the Seven has made the damned souls in hell terribly nervous and distraught. Hell is just not what it used to be, you see, and the denizens of New Hell are anxious. They need something to take their minds off things for a while. I understand you played the organ in your former life on earth. I want you to entertain my subjects, give them a little distraction and a reminder of what hell is really about, and that I still rule supreme here. The rumor is that the damned in hell are building an army, planning a little incursion upon heaven. I want you, through music, to help inspire this force to achieve victory. You will report to the commandant of the HSO, Hellish Services Organization, one week from tomorrow with something in mind for entertaining the troops. I suggest you practice your keyboard skills, LaVey. I want your performance to be flawless. Understood?"

"Oh yes, Sire, of course. As you command, Your Majesty," LaVey said as he bowed low.

LaVey couldn't believe his luck. Not only was he not being punished, he was being given another chance to serve Satan, doing something he loved to do: play music. He wouldn't screw this one up, he swore to himself. He would present the most infernally beautiful performance that hell had ever heard; a musical piece so sublime, even the Devil himself would weep with joy at the sound of it.

"Very well. Now run along, LaVey. I trust you will perform your duties admirably. It's so hard to find good help in hell."

*

Guy Fawkes wasn't having a very good day in hell. The demons who dragged him from the Hall of Injustice back to the dungeons, had made sure to torment him thoroughly before leaving him alone in his dark, dank cell. It had been discovered that since he had the Spear of Destiny inside him, he could not be injured, but could still feel the pain of the attacks inflicted upon him. The various wardens of the dungeon prison made sport of seeing how much they could hurt him. It got old pretty soon, for Fawkes anyway, not for the demons. Eventually they left him alone in the cold blackness to contemplate his misery.

Somehow he must get out of the dungeons, he thought. But how? Security was tighter than King James the Fourth's ass. And to end up in hell in the first place was inconceivable. Why hadn't the Pope and the Catholic Church made him a martyr? And what about God? Had he forsaken him or was this some test of his faith? He had the Spear of Longinus inside him, the spear that had pierced the side of the son of God. There had to be a reason for it, a purpose yet unfulfilled. But what could it be? He had tried to kill Satan before and that hadn't worked. Yet, HSM was apprehensive of the spear, afraid of it even. But what would killing the Devil accomplish? He would still be in hell. There must be another way. There were rumors that others had made it out of hell. If they could do it, so could he. Guy reaffirmed to himself: *I know I am worthy of heaven. This has all been a terrible mistake.*

Fawkes heard the iron door leading to the dungeons open and shut with a loud clanking sound. Booted footsteps approached. It didn't sound like one of the demons, their cloven hooves made a different sound upon the flagstones. Soon a woman came into view in front of his cell. She was tall, and quite beautiful, with makeup accenting her piercing eyes. She was attired in a blue coat that was lacey and ruffled, and she wore breeches instead of a dress that accentuated her slim figure. Knee-high riding boots completed her outfit, and a rapier hung at her hip.

"Guy Fawkes I presume?"

"Yes, what do you want with me?"

"I am Emile du Chatelet. You may not have heard of me as I lived after your time on Earth. I was and still am a mathematician, physicist, and writer. I became known to the world not only for my works, but for being the mistress of the famed philosopher, Voltaire. But I know who you are. The one damned soul who dared to try to kill Satan by blowing up the Hall of Injustice. Your fame as a member of the Gunpowder Plot notwithstanding, you have made quite a name for yourself in hell."

"Fame has its price apparently," Fawkes said as he lifted his shackles up.

"Yes, so I see. Let me get straight to the point. An army of the damned is being formed in hell. I am one of those leading this army. Certain individuals, Nikolai Tesla among them, have invented what they believe to be the means to escape hell. We think that this 'Great Machine' will be able to transport a large number of individuals out of hell and breach the plane of heaven to the very doorstep of Paradise... the pearly gates. We are planning to make an assault on heaven. If God will not grant us salvation, then we will break into Paradise by force. The crux of the problem remains how to get past the gates. Since you have the Spear of Destiny within you, we believe that you are invincible in battle. We need you to lead the vanguard of the assault upon the gates of heaven and bring them down so that the army of the damned can enter heaven. So, Fawkes, will you join us?"

"I am going to have a hard time leading an assault from my prison cell, don't you think?"

"Your release has been arranged, if you agree to help us. His Satanic Majesty is not involved in the plan to assault heaven, the man upstairs would be none too pleased if he found out Satan was trying to upset the balance of the afterlife. His Satanic Majesty has, however, agreed to let you out to aid the efforts of the army of the damned at my request."

"Attack the pearly gates? An assault on heaven? Are you mad? You are going to lead some rag-tag army of damned souls to try to invade Paradise? Even if it could succeed with the help of the spear, what then?" Fawkes said, looking up.

"We are all rebels here, Fawkes, who questioned and defied authority, and were punished for it. Innovative free thinkers, visionaries, dreamers, who wanted to change their world. By our own beliefs, actions and decisions, we chose our fate. Hell was made for us, but that does not mean we deserve damnation. This is our chance to strike back at the heavenly forces that denied us our rightful salvation; make Him answer for damning us to hell and find out why we are denied redemption. This is your one chance to ask him why he has forsaken you, Fawkes. Besides, would you rather rot in this cell for all eternity? And don't forget bonfire night on the fifth of November."

"I always remember the fifth of November. I don't need you or anyone else to remind me of the pain of being burned on the pyre every year on Guy Fawkes Day, or of my torture in this dungeon, Lady du Chatelet. If it will grant me release from this cell and put an end to my torment, then I will join you. After all, I do crave the action of battle again, as I once fought for the revolution in Spain, and tried to overthrow King James in England. So, too, in hell would I embark upon the chance to change the fate of those who are wrongly damned, like myself."

"Very well. I will have the guards release you, then I will take you to our base of operations. You will still be under heavy guard leading up to the time of the assault. His Satanic Majesty doesn't trust that you might not to commit some form of treachery or devastation with the spear while still in hell."

"The Father of Lies, untrusting? But of course he is," Fawkes quipped. "I accept those terms. Anything to get out of this hellhole."

Lady du Chatelet turned from the cell and walked back the way she had come, boots echoing on the flagstones as she went.

Satan is history's first and greatest revolutionary figure, thought Fawkes. If the Dark Lord cannot lead the assault, then perhaps it is fitting that he, one of history's most famous rebels should lead the attack upon heaven. *I want answers to why I was damned to hell. Even if I have to break into heaven, and confront God directly to find out.*

*

Anton LaVey had spent all day at his store, Hellish Curiosities and Clothiers, practicing on the theater organ that sat tucked away in the corner of the back storage room. He was feverishly trying to decide on the perfect musical score to play for the Army of the Damned during the assault on heaven. He could play the notes fine, but the pieces just didn't sound quite right. They didn't have the pomp and flair that he remembered them having when he played then before he had died and gone to hell. Maybe it was a condition of hell itself, LaVey thought. Like everything in the afterlife of the damned you could never achieve satisfaction in anything you did, whether it was sex, eating, drinking, and, apparently, music. Or maybe it was something wrong with him, personally. After all, he had died in hell and been put back together by the undertaker. Perhaps the soul became flawed after dying and being reconstituted in hell. He decided to take a break from the music and contemplate what he was really feeling. Maybe a walk around the shop would help him to put his finger upon the crux of the problem.

"Taking a break, eh maestro?" his assistant Madam Helena Blavatsky asked.

She was an insufferable old biddy, and not much help around the store. She kept lapsing into moments of prophetic vision that kept her from getting much done. Besides, he didn't think she had done an honest day's work in her life, and she hadn't changed her habits in the afterlife.

"Yes, if you must know, I am struggling with the piece. I just can't seem to put the right emotion into it. I've been feeling a bit off ever since I died and was brought back to life in the morgue."

"Oh, a lot of the damned souls who have died in hell feel the same way. I know I did the first time I died here. You should really go see my psychologist, he's quite good at helping you get your mind sorted out after the trauma of dying and coming back," Madam Blavatsky pulled a business card from her purse and handed it to LaVey. It read: William James, Psychologist, Spiritualist, Pragmatist, with an address and phone number to his office.

"Hmmm, maybe it wouldn't hurt to go see this James fellow. Try to sort some things out. I need to have all my faculties and abilities at their best for my performance."

Madam Blavatsky got a faraway look in her eyes, and gripped LaVey's arm tightly.

"I see you performing the music, there is powerful emotion, but also great suffering. You will achieve what you desire, but through much pain."

"Let go of my arm you old hag. And clean this shop up, it's a mess," responded LaVey.

After contacting James's office he was able to book an appointment for the following day as there had been a cancellation. The next morning, LaVey walked from his apartment in the shop to the office of psychologist and philosopher, William James.

"Mr. LaVey, please have a seat; make yourself comfortable," James said. "Would you like a drink?"

"Just a glass of water, please. Everything in hell is tasteless anyway, or worse."

He poured a glass of water from a pitcher on the table next to his desk and handed it to LaVey. "Let us start with why you are here, Mr. LaVey."

"Please, call me Anton," he said, taking the glass. He took a sip and grimaced. As expected it was stale and tasted of sulphur. "The reason I inquired about your services is because ever since I died in hell and was brought back by the undertaker, I just haven't felt like myself. I have this feeling of disassociation with my emotions and with the things that I enjoy, what little there is in hell, especially music. I play the organ, you see, and His Satanic Majesty has commanded me to play for his minions. I have been trying to practice for days and nights on end but I just can't seem to feel the music, to get the emotions to come out in the piece. So I end up giving up and just mope around the shop. I'm moody and angry at myself and everyone around me. I have this terrible sense of dread and fear all the time. What the hell is the matter with me Mr. James?"

"Call me William, Anton. I find that formalities serve only to maintain a barrier between two people. Let us go back to when you died in hell, and discuss what happened," James said as he poured himself a glass of water.

"After dying in hell, I had an event unlike anything I have ever experienced. My entire life flashed before my eyes. It sounds so cliché, I know, but every part of it was shown to me, like watching a film within my mind. Then, I was moving through a cold, dark tunnel for a very long time, toward a pinpoint of light. When I reached this light, it surrounded me with a feeling of warmth, love, and joy like I have never felt. It was a bright light that seemed to be everywhere, but it didn't hurt my eyes. It was soothing, peaceful. Within the light I felt a presence and heard a voice. It told me that I was damned to hell because I was selfish and had never sacrificed my own wants for the happiness of others. Then it left me alone in the cold darkness. I felt more alone and despondent than I can ever remember being. Then I woke up in my body on slab A in the undertaker's morgue in hell to the most awful pain and stench I have ever experienced."

"These post-death experiences are common here in hell," James said. "Hell lends itself to a kind of sickness within damned souls, especially after they have died while in hell. It is theorized that something happens to the soul, when it is reconstituted by the undertaker in the morgue. Some say that it becomes tainted in the process of rebirth in hell. Whether by the undertaker himself, or by the environs of the underworld, no one knows. Perhaps it is both. It fosters within one a sort of psychic alienation. We refer to it as Post-Traumatic Death Disorder."

"But what can be done about it?" LaVey asked, taking a drink of the tepid foul water.

"I have found little to remedy the condition, unfortunately," James said, drinking from his own glass. "But a certain amount of introspection seems to lessen the symptoms. Most damned souls are in denial of the reasons why they are in hell. You need to come to grips with your own shortcomings in life, which carried over into the afterlife. It may not change our fate, but it is some comfort to resolve one's own issues and accept that we were destined for hell. Do you know why you were damned?"

"I understand and accept my fate of damnation," LaVey said. "I know that I am irredeemable by my own actions and beliefs in life. I lived my life in the most self-serving manner that I could, eschewing the sort of compromises that most people make for the sake of relationships. I wanted, more than anything else, to be true to myself at the expense of all others in my life. I even created a religion based on worshiping the self, in the name of Satan. But who is Satan, if not the most self-centered, egotistical, uncompromising genius of all time. He saw what g–"

James held up his hand to cut off LaVey before he could utter the name of the lord which was unspeakable in hell.

"– I mean, the man upstairs," LaVey continued, "was doing, and thought he could do it better. So he rebelled, and many of the angels agreed with him, or were at least swayed by his charisma and intelligence enough to follow him and ultimately be banished to hell with him. It is true that in life I never truly believed in a divine creator upon whom my redemption depended. Nor did I think Satan himself existed, save in the idealism of what he stands for: creativity, intelligence, pride, rebelliousness. Would I have lived my life differently if I had known they were real entities? No, I don't think I would have changed a thing. I made my proverbial bed and now must lie in it. I don't deny that I deserve to be in hell. But I do feel that my station here should be more noteworthy. My talents are wasted, running a second-hand shop in New Hell. This assignment to play the organ for His Satanic Majesty's army is the first real break I've had here; a chance to show off my abilities and do something creative and meaningful once more. But if I can't get over this emotional trauma, I won't be able to play, and I'll lose my assignment and incur Satan's wrath at the same time. Which is why I need your help to get over this disorder."

James thought about this in silence for a while. "What are you ultimately trying to accomplish in performing this music, Anton? Are you doing this for the glory of His Satanic Majesty, or for your own?"

"Look, I want to do Satan's bidding and win his favor, first and foremost, because I know I can better serve him with my true talents. This is my chance to prove to him I am worthy of such a position. If I can't earn an assignment in his secret service forces, the Devil's Children, then maybe I can at least be his official musician. Who knows, maybe if I do well enough at this, then I may get another chance to join his special forces and undertake more exciting assignments which could improve my status in hell."

"So this is all about you then," James said.

"Well, of course. It's always about me."

"Anton, just because we are damned for our sins, doesn't mean we have to continue to embrace them in the afterlife. You can change, and be less selfish, if you choose to. It may help you deal with the PTDD you are experiencing. Try to learn to do things for others who can do nothing for you in return. You may find that there is a certain satisfaction in it. Deep down, I think you want to be a good person, to be unselfish, and loved. Why else would you feel so despondent after the presence of the being in the light left you alone? Perhaps you secretly yearn for redemption, to see the Paradise you have been denied, and to be with your creator who is in heaven."

LaVey stood up abruptly. "That's preposterous. I accept His Satanic Majesty as my lord in the afterlife. I have no wish to be in heaven, or to see God. What has he ever done for me that I couldn't do for myself. If he were a just and loving god, then why are there so many damned to hell, and for that matter, why are you here, William?"

The ground buckled in the throes of a massive hellquake at the utterance of the g-word. LaVey stumbled to the floor, and James' chair was knocked over, throwing him down as well. Plaster fell from the ceiling and pictures dropped from their mounts on the walls. Glasses broke in the cabinet by James' table. After a few long minutes that seemed like hours, the trembling subsided.

"Dammit, Anton, you know you can't utter that word here," James picked himself up from the floor and dusted the plaster from his jacket, then reached out a hand to help LaVey to his feet.

"Sorry. I got carried away," LaVey said, taking his hand to stand, and brushing himself off as well.

"Who knows why I am here," James said. "I lived a decent life, was not a bad person, though I had my shortcomings like any mortal man. It has been postulated that there are countless hundreds of sins we can commit in life that are never atoned for, no matter how hard we may try, even if we could have been cognizant of them at the time. Some say that only saints and infants end up in heaven. Perhaps I'm damned because as a philosopher it was my job to question everything, even the will and mind of the man upstairs. You know, the church believed that the science of psychology was the devil's work. That it was not man's place to delve into the workings of the mind, and try to decipher its secrets. They called it heresy. They said that the only way to cure the ills of the mind was through the redemption of the soul. Perhaps they were right. I tried to balance my belief in science with my faith in spirituality. Maybe it was not enough to get me into Heaven." He laughed a mirthless chuckle.

"Well, you've given me much to think about, William," LaVey placed a few Diablo coins on the plaster-coated table. "This should cover your consultation fee plus enough to get the place cleaned up. Sorry about the mess."

"Good luck with everything, Anton. I hope what we've discussed helps you. And please come back to see me on a regular basis. Treating PTDD is an ongoing process, so follow-up visits will be necessary to help you deal with it."

"I'll be in touch. Thanks for everything," LaVey said before walking out of the office.

I do have plenty to think about, LaVey mused to himself. *What kind of person do I want to be, in this afterlife? Could I really change, and be a selfless person? And would it help me to overcome this feeling of disassociation, this PTDD that*

James spoke of me having? Or did none of it matter in hell? If they were all truly irredeemable, did trying to become a better person even make a difference? *How much worse could my fate be if I was already damned?* He knew there were more sinister hells one could end up in. He'd seen some of them in his journey to try to get back the spear of destiny. *I will try to find a way to deal with this creative block and play the best damned music hell has ever heard. I will make His Satanic Majesty proud, and maybe, just maybe, be promoted to a better position. Come hell or high water.*

*

Guy Fawkes and his commando force, comprised of a platoon of marines who worked as bouncers at the Oasis bar, were transported by the Great Machine, to a lush green grassy plain. A road paved with bricks of gold wound across it near where they had landed. Down the road, in the distance, an impossibly tall wall loomed that shone golden in the bright light that surrounded them, seemingly coming from no discernible point of origin. It was as if the air itself were luminescent with a pure white glow. They set off down the road, moving as silently as their boots would allow on the hard bricks.

Were they really out of hell, wondered Fawkes as they neared the wall. Like the road, it too looked like it had been built of gold. Large smooth stones in this case, instead of bricks. Every few hundred feet a tower with battlement loomed over the top of the wall. In the middle was set a pair of gigantic gates the color of mother of pearl glistening brightly in the light. Sharp spires topped the gates and a massive lock was built into their center where the two gates met.

Could these really be the legendary pearly gates of heaven? Fawkes and the marines scanned the parapets of the wall, looking for any sign of sentries. So far they hadn't seen any, and that worried him. This was too easy, he thought. If these were the gates of heaven, where were the angels that should be defending them?

With a signal, Fawkes ordered the platoon to begin placing the explosive charges on the gates. *This had better work,* thought Fawkes. *I do not want to face His Satanic Majesty if I fail to breach the gates and grant the army of the damned a way into heaven.* He did not want to suffer the pain of the bonfire again, maybe this time for all eternity with no respite. He would complete his mission. It wouldn't be like the Fifth of November in 1605 when he was caught trying to blow up Westminster Palace, Hall and Abbey, the House of Commons and House of Lords, along with the members of Parliament, and James the Fourth to put an end to Protestant rule in England. Perhaps if Fawkes and the conspirators of The Gunpowder Plot had succeeded, he would have been granted a place in heaven for his service to help put a Catholic king on the throne of England once more, as was right and just. Maybe his failure was why he ended up damned to hell. *Whatever the reason, I will get into heaven even if I have to blast my way in. He will have to take notice then, and I can demand an answer to the reason why I, and so many countless others have been damned, with no reprieve or chance at salvation.*

The charges were set. Now the platoon fell back from the gates, and laid low in the green grass of the field. Fawkes held the detonator in his trembling hands. This is it, he thought. He held his breath and triggered the device. Nothing happened.

"Damn these infernal devices," Fawkes said as he thumbed the detonator again and again, still getting no response. "There's been a malfunction. We need to check the detonation caps and wiring."

Fawkes and the demolitions team nervously approached the gates checking over everything to find out what was wrong. While he was concentrating on one of the explosive devices, he heard a sound like the twanging of a bow, and one of the marines cried out. Fawkes turned to see a flurry of arrows that looked like bolts of golden energy being shot at the marines. Some had already gone down, gaping holes seared through their chests. A stray bolt struck one of the explosive charges at the far end of the gates and set it off, starting a chain reaction that activated the rest of them. The remaining marines were blown to bits and Fawkes, still protected by the Spear of Destiny, was launched into the air upon the pressure wave of the blast. He flew hundreds of feet skyward, and when he reached the apex of his flight, began to fall back down and was impaled upon one of the pearly gates' spires. His body came to rest at the top of the gates' cross bar

"Damn that hurts," moaned Fawkes, looking at the thick spire sticking out through his belly. The gates themselves were untouched, except for scorch marks where the explosives had been set. They still stood, glittering in the light. "This is not good."

*

As Anton LaVey approached, he saw the army of the damned assembled out on the plains of the outskirts of New Hell City. Tesla and the others wanted to make sure nothing would be damaged in the event of another accident with the Great Machine, which had transported a portion of the city to even the Devil knew not where. It was comprised of the zero energy engines, and the dark matter array, that were collectively known as the ZEDMA, or Zero Energy Dark Matter Array. It had become popularly known, however, as the

Teslaract. Emile du Chatelet, and Belial, the crown prince of hell, were leading the hordes of more than a million damned souls, along with their generals who had organized the ranks into various armies. They were equipped with every weapon that hell's armories had available, along with the private stores of weapons owned by many of hell's residents. Weapons of death and destruction from every age and level of technology were evident; from stone-headed axes, to automatic rifles and pistols, to huge artillery pieces that fired enormous shells, and rail guns that fired depleted uranium rounds at speeds in excess of mach five. Anything and everything they thought might be needed to blast their way into and through heaven's gates was brought along. The many devices which made up The Great Machine, which was intended to transport the army to the gates of heaven, were being tended by the hundreds of scientists and technicians that operated their complex mechanisms. Nikolai Tesla was overseeing the entire operation with his assistants coordinating everything.

LaVey met with Amducias, arch-demon of music, who was the commander of the HSO, as instructed. Before him was a colossal pipe organ and attached to it were thousands of hell's damned, their disemboweled intestines connected to the pipes. They writhed in agony, their moans and wails of pain filling the air.

"I'm supposed to play this?" LaVey, mortified, motioned to the infernal instrument of torture. "His Satanic Majesty never said anything about this."

"Oh yes," Amducias said. "It's the new and improved Liszt pipe organ. It gives a much richer tone from the entrails pipes than the earlier model which featured hammer upon viscera action. Easier to tune, too. Wouldn't you say so, Mr. Schopenhauer?"

"Life without pain is meaningless. I believe my life in hell is about to become much more meaningful," Arthur Schopenhauer, famous philosopher, said just before a demon cut his belly open and added him to the rows of bodies connected to the instrument.

"I trust you've mastered the pieces you've been studying," the arch demon inquired. "How about you warm up with Johann Sebastian Bach's Toccata and Fugue in d minor ...just to make sure all the pipes are performing perfectly?"

The arch-demon Amducias reached out and grabbed LaVey with one hand around his neck while a wicked forefinger claw on the other hand moved toward his belly.

"What the hell are you doing?" screamed LaVey.

"Oh, didn't you know? When you play the Liszt organ, you must be connected to the instrument. Only from great suffering can great music come into being."

LaVey thrashed around, trying to break free of the demon's grip, but it was like being held in a vise. He watched in horror as his lower torso was sliced open and his intestines, dripping with bodily fluids, spilled out onto the ground with a sickening sound. He bellowed in unimaginable agony. The arch demon shackled him by his ankles to the bench before the instrument's keyboards, then tore open one end of his intestines and attached it to one of the organ pipes. LaVey was wailing and moaning, and saliva drooled from his gaping mouth.

"Now, if you would begin, maestro. The troops are waiting to be roused into their battle fury," Amducias said.

LaVey lay his hands on the keys of the organ and his feet, which had been shacked with just the right length of chain, on the pedals, and the damned who were connected to the infernal instrument screamed in a cacophony of torment and woe like a diabolical choir that could be heard even over the sound of the pipes of the instrument. Every now and then, he would strike the note for the pipe that led to his own intestines and he too would wail in agony. But His Satanic Majesty had decreed that his performance must be flawless, so he couldn't skip a single note. Once he was done with the first piece of music he went on to play Mendelssohn's War March of the Priests as the Great Machine was put into operation and the army of the damned was transported out of hell.

LaVey could see that they were on a grassy plain, reaching as far as the horizon, and before them in the distance stood a massive wall stretching endlessly across the plain that glittered of gold with pearly white gates set in the middle. Were these really the gates of heaven, LaVey thought as he continued playing, the screams and music from the pipe organ carrying over the din of the army of the damned. The vast corps marched forward, closer to the gates. From across the battlefield, Emile du Chatelet was heard to yell, "Fawkes has failed, the gates still stand. Let slip the army of the damned. Attack them with everything you have. Bring down the pearly gates of Paradise and let heaven burn!"

The ensuing sound of weapons fire managed to drown out the music of the organ, and LaVey was witness to an unleashing of firepower unlike anything ever seen by man, alive or dead and damned. Explosions rocked the pearly gates and golden walls as millions of rounds of ordinance was fired into them. Dense smoke covered the plain in a fog of war, but as it began to clear after the first volley subsided, he could see flames that rose up from the gates and sections of the walls as they burned. But they still stood firm. Then he saw winged figures flying out from behind the walls, shooting bows that fired golden arrows like shafts of sunlight. They were hitting the soldiers of the army of the damned with deadly accuracy and with each arrow another warrior dropped dead. Angels, thought LaVey. Thousands upon thousands of them, in all their beauty and splendor, with wings of the purest white, with perfectly formed bodies, lithe and toned with muscle, their skin like unblemished alabaster. They were terrifyingly deadly in their accuracy and the cold emotionless method in which they slew the damned out on the plains of limbo. Hell's damned were fighting back as best they could, but their weapons seemed to have little effect on the angels. The army of the damned was being slaughtered before the gates of heaven. If they died here, where would their souls go? Back to hell and the Undertaker's morgue? Or would they be lost forever in limbo, between heaven and hell? LaVey had little time to ponder the question when an angel's arrow shot through him, ending his suffering.

*

As the pearly gates of heaven burned beneath him, Fawkes could see the army of the damned being decimated by the angelic host of heaven. They were losing the battle, and it was clear that none of them would ever make it into heaven to stand before the Lord and question his authority, his decision of damnation for all those souls deserving of an answer as to why they were judged irredeemable. An angel, mightier and even more beautiful than all the rest, flew before him. He glowed with a heavenly light and in his right hand he wielded a sword of flaming gold.

"Why has our father forsaken us?" Fawkes cried to the angel. "Why will he not answer our prayers and our pleas for a chance of redemption? Why has he abandoned those who are wrongfully damned to hell?"

"It is not you alone that he has forsaken. He has abandoned us in heaven as well," the angel said as it pierced

Fawkes' chest with the tip of the flaming sword, cutting the spear of destiny out of him with a flourish of his wrist and catching it in his other hand. Fawkes' vision went black as death took him and his body crumbled to ash.

HELL BENT

Janet Morris

Their dread Commander: he, above the rest
In shape and gesture proudly eminent,
Stood like a tower. His form had yet not lost
All her original brightness, nor appeared
Less then Archangel ruined, and the excess
Of glory obscured: as when the sun new-risen
Looks through the horizontal misty air
Shorn of his beams, or from behind the moon,
In dim eclipse, disastrous twilight sheds
On half the nations, and with fear of change
Perplexes monarchs.
Darkened so, yet shone
Above them all the archangel; but his face
Deep scars of thunder had intrenched, and care
Sat on his faded cheek, but under brows
Of dauntless courage, and considerate pride
Waiting revenge. Cruel his eye, but cast
Signs of remorse and passion, to behold
The fellows of his crime, the followers rather
(Far other once beheld in bliss), condemned
Forever now to have their lot in pain.
– John Milton, *Paradise Lost*

"Make me eternal with a kiss," pleaded Kit Marlowe, beard shorn, striding across the stage in wig and claret ladies' gown to embrace Shakespeare, armored and sword-girt and plumed, stage right. And kissed him long, with full tongue though none could see.

The play was *Hell Bent*, by William Shakespeare and Christopher Marlowe, held over by Satanic decree and pundits' declaim, perhaps eternally, for all Marlowe knew: their joint endeavor, a fury of creation leaving both men losers, their lives' works carved to shreds by mutual exigency. The only joy Kit could take from this 'play' was that, every night and twice on Sadderday, he seduced Will in front of an audience compelled by His Infernal Majesty to come and clap and laugh and weep when prompted: a hellish parody of entertainment.

He and Will, gone from playwrights to crowd whores... not for the first time.

"Nay, nay, I'll love you not," said Shakespeare, right on cue, "for he that loves pleasure must for pleasure fall." Both lines stolen from Marlowe's *Doctor Faustus*, both hacked into different shapes. Demons swung down as planned, from above the proscenium, and cackled: To suit Satan's pleasure, too many lines from Kit's works had been redacted and redrafted; many more than from Shakespeare's canon. He and Will had argued, fought about the changes endlessly.

For the first time in infernity, here in this corbeled theatre where real lightning and thunder and witches and fiends could be had on demand, where technology spouted gouts of flaming imagery all about them, Kit Marlowe truly feared losing his beloved friend to Satan's scheme – from naught but jealousy, and pride.

Kit should have seen it coming: less of one man's work, more of another's; lines split asunder, characters and story warped beyond forbearance....

"But you'll love Satan," Kit recited in his best stage whisper, tremulous and cutting, looking into Shakespeare's painted face, enduring the slight two-palmed push that sent him staggering backward, toward stage left. "Why should you love him whom the world hates so?"

"Because he loves me more than all the world." These two lines were from Kit's *Edward the Second,* but in this context they cut his heart to pieces nightly and during every matinee.

"Love looks not with the eyes, but with the mind," Kit spoke, this bit stolen from Will's *A Midsummer Night's Dream.* Grabbing his prop, a sword leaning on an azure daybed at his knee, Marlowe prepared to plunge that rapier once, and again, into the heart he loved the best – not for dramatic effect, but for real – and bring death nightly to the man he treasured most. He stage-whispered a line Shakespeare had first written for *Othello:* "Perdition catch my soul,/But I do love thee! and when I love thee not,/Chaos is come again."

"Hell is just a frame of mind," Will gritted.

That line from *Faustus* was Marlowe's downfall, the very line this play, and likely his damnation, hung upon. A line to prove untrue, endlessly: he'd taunted the Devil in life with it; now he paid in hell forever. Kit should have known, should have said a different thing. A clever quip, tossed off for effect, harvested all this misery?

Of course: Satan's plans were made ere time began.

Now Kit must lunge that little distance across the stage, sick at heart but drawing his rapier – not faked but deadly sharp; leap toward Shakespeare, his eyes on that precious, hairy throat.

Hell Bent was their quote game gone rabid and hellacious: every word not newly penned had been worth a fight, a fit, a sulk, a pout – from each of them, or both. In life, it hadn't been that way, although in life they'd oft acted in each other's plays, shared lines, shared thoughts with no care for which would get the credit.

But Satan came here, every night, for each performance; and Will Shakespeare's mind saw nothing else but whitest wings and fallen glory; smelled naught but sweetest breath. And each night, once Shakespeare bled and the curtain came down, the Devil took Will in his angelic arms and healed him; remade him on the spot. Every night. And twice on Sadderdays.

Kit Marlowe never could compete with that.

So now the Old Rogue Theatre's auditorium smelled not only of rancid butter, stale popcorn, and sweat, but of blood and broken hearts and pierced dreams and Kit Marlowe's worst nightmares.

And Will's precious life rests in Satan's hands anew each time the play is staged.

Finally, following the stage directions they two had writ, Kit stabs his best beloved through the heart, then grabs Shakespeare as he crumples. Kit wails again, "Hell is just a frame of mind," his most regretted words.

"Men have died from time to time, and worms have eaten them, but not for love," Shakespeare gasps his own, from *As You Like It*. Then he sighs, proclaiming in newly twisted words: "No, not for love – men die for pride and rage, as sinners show their nature."

In the crowd, without prompting, some gasp, some weep, some moan as Will dies.

Dies real death, for all to see, not play-acting.

The curtain descends behind Marlowe, in his girlish dress and curly wig, hiding Shakespeare's bleeding corpse from view.

Since his part is written and cannot be changed, Marlowe stands tonight as he must for every performance, staring over the audience: "Few love to hear the sins they love to act." And this too is Will's, from *Pericles, Prince of Tyre.* "But hear ye this:" He pauses. They lean forward to hear his words, some sniveling, some coughing, some mewling like kittens. This play is an immorality play, and they are its targets. "Accursed be he that first invented war," he says, as loud and proud as when he'd first said it in his *Tamburlaine the Great.* "And will be, ever. For now our play is done, its battles lost and won. And as we bid you glorious sins unto your measure, recall that we have only acted out what Satan planned and you each bring to life from the potions in your souls."

Then some began to stand, and applaud, and call for more. Fools in hell are the only ones who *ever* call for more. Of anything.

So the curtain rises on Shakespeare's corpse, lying still, and comes down behind Marlowe once again. Then, as is the plan for this curtain call, he tells them: "And recall you this: Our war with heaven isn't over, but just begun."

So they leave, inspired or dejected, these villains of infamous extent, these witnesses to misery and grief and, filing out, take backward glances as the curtain sops Will Shakespeare's blood and, just possibly, Kit Marlowe's tears.

Meanwhile, from somewhere behind that curtain, a smell wafts, sweeter than all the roses on a bier or all the repentance in purgatory.

*

Satan had bent hell itself to accommodate his fools for war. He'd curved a third of New Hell, despoiled by idiots obsessed with power, hatreds, and explosions, into a new dimension, a pocket of space and time just big enough for so many egos and their fiery deaths. This exploded time was a foam, a tiny space, but big enough for souls who thought that wringing power from infinity would make them powerful, that they could overcome fate by force of arms. And there they would remain, for an eternity, where time meant nothing and intent was all: remain until these silly men and women learned, if they ever would, that the fault lay not in their stars, but in their souls. Now that the Hellexandria Library was restored, they had no excuse for folly based in ignorance. But then, ignorant men are legion, and consider their ignorance a holy trust.

The Son of the Morning had made his point thrice over, to those auditors from on high and their masters Above: mankind was demented, foul and unbecoming the light of heavenly grace. Erra and his Seven Sibitti, pitiless enforcers of Almighty will, had learned a thing or two, as Satan's rabble assaulted even the very gates of Paradise.

Or, so they thought, these puny intellects with murder on their vicious little minds.

With Samael on his right, Satan took wing. He flew above his twisted realm, with its new dimension for detaining fans of fiery destruction, and another pocket for those most arrogant souls who attacked the heavens and thought to win salvation by onslaught.

He flew over perdition's vast extent, o'er every hell of humanity's deranged imaginings. Guilty they were, and brought themselves to judgment: This time, last time, next time. Every time.

Samael and Satan flew until they reached His lordly seat in Pandemonium, where they alighted, gliding on alabaster wings now turning black and leathery with wrath. Would the Almighty take heed, and admit that man was flawed beyond redemption?

Satan couldn't know – and in this moment, didn't really care. His doomed herds of unworthy souls were so many, and their punishments so just – especially when self-inflicted as they'd been at the paradisiacal gates – he felt redeemed.

He'd proved his point, whether or not the Host ever admitted this was so.

Adamantine ramparts shimmered under him. Outside his own gates, Akkadians and Achaeans and Spartans and Thebans and Romans and Celts and Nazis and Americans and Chinese and more all gathered: the greatest armies of the damned, each in formation, perfect and glittering with weapons and hubris.

These legions were his stalwarts, whom he and Samael would send among the rapacious rabble who had insulted the highest heavens, there to make judgment, and extract due recompense.

Erra be damned: Witness Satan, disciplining his own.

Almost, the Adversary was pleased. But beyond his farthest battle groups he could see the deep; the dark; the cold of displeasure from on high. And it was roiling, while above the vault was rowling.

Something up there had turned an eye, pricked an ear, to what Satan and his damned had wrought.

So? Dare the auditors and those who ruled the heavens blame him? For what? How was Satan shamed by humankind, that mass of flaws and failings too long overlooked? Blame him for enticing man to do his best and thus show his worst? Blame him for trying to wrest fairness from the firmament?

Satan barked to himself, almost laughed: a third of the stars from the sky were with him here; yet the deep was always dark, and he'd spent so very long there.

Samael came to him, wings black and furled, head cocked, eyes coruscating with the fury of Death ready to unleash. "Sire? Your will?"

Purposely misunderstanding, Satan said to Samael, "Yes, bring me Shakespeare. We shall see what the newly resurrected bard thinks of Pandemonium, and thereby take another slice of Marlowe's hopes away: Bring him too. Not since Adam and Eve have I had such a pair to play, the one against the other."

The angel of death searched the Deceiver's baleful eye, seeking more deliberate instruction. Then Samael nodded, bated, and took wing back to New Hell, the worst of all hells, to make the city just one whit worse than it had ever been before.

This being hell, and he being Satan, and Samael being the angel of death, and humanity being the fools who had just stormed the gates of Paradise and been repelled, Satan had his own work before him: so many overweening souls to be punished.

His armies awaited. Nearly time to set them marching. Now that the puny damned had assaulted heaven, he had wrongs innumerable to right. Fresh torments would he and his inflict, now that humanity had challenged the Almighty. And lost.

Satan spread wide his wings and, in the glow from Paradise, they slowly changed to white. His fury curled around his spine; then vanished as he admitted that he'd won this battle against humankind and its divine supporters.

Now down the ramparts came a howling and a yowling and a flurry of fur and claw and fang and bushy tail as Michael, his familiar, launched at him in a rush of wings. And landing on his shoulder, Michael commenced gnawing Satan's flesh. The cat/bat/thing dug its claws into him so that red blood dripped from his wounds onto his beauteous white feathers. Then Michael butted him in the face and began purring so that the fundament thrummed beneath their feet.

Even the Prince of Hell needs a friend.

*

Comes a Command performance in Pandemonium, Satan's lordly seat. The stage will be dark at the Old Rogue Theatre in New Hell tonight, and perhaps on the morrow. Marlowe knows what is afoot, but cannot stay it. Satan would wind his whitest wings round Shakespeare, and Will would think of nothing else. Shakespeare might be in love, but he was not stupid. Naïve, perhaps. But more, selfish. 'Shall I be tempted by the devil thus?' Will had penned for *Richard III*, writ to most indite Marlowe: 'Conscience is but a word that cowards use.' So now Will would prove this true for himself, as authors always have their characters for company.

Never had Kit faced such foes, adversaries who could wing him whither only fallen angels go. With Will under one arm and himself tucked in the other, Samael, the angel of death, soared over hell's despair far below.

And never said a word. Nor did Will, aloft in the cold, high in the air of perdition – nor afterward, when Pandemonium came into view, surpassing grand, beyond all expectations.

Now here they were, two playwrights to perform their new, grotesque and ugly farce again, to fret awhile upon the stage; to kill again and die again for the infernal pleasure of the Lord of Lies. *Hell Bent* they'd named this tragedy, and hell bent it was; full of vile and bony plot and the Devil's dark divining.

Samael deposited them backstage at the Pandemonium Theatre, a cavern of a venue that looked more grown than built. Letting go of them, the fallen angel disappeared. That left Kit with Will, alone, beneath meagerly lighted rafters, without even a stage manager to help them find their way, their props, their dressing rooms, their proscenium....

Thence, a chance that might never come again, or not come soon enough to suit Kit's burning need to save his only love in all of hell's extent.

"Will, let's change these lines. And exchange our roles: I'll play the hero tonight, and you'll kill me – this time, next time, every time until my breast is as pierced as yours. It breaks my heart to pierce yours nightly and see you die, but in another's arms."

They were backstage, if such a place had a true stage, front and back; and if that cathedral of sin could be called a playhouse, or the back of one: more like the backside of damnation it was, with real skulls and bones of ages hung on pegs; with staffs to spit lightning and piles of human skins flayed off entire, so you could step into any one as into hose and doublet, and be other than you were.

"What? No, Kit. 'The poet's eye, in fine frenzy rolling,' as in *A Midsummer Night's Dream*. I wrote that for you, once you were dead and gone from me. I have had these hurts. I have lived these pains. I have wished hell upon that Ingram Frizer who killed you dead, and his helpers, both. And none of that availed me. 'The lunatic, the lover and the poet/ Are of imagination all compact: One sees more devils than vast hell can hold.' So here we are, with devils lesser and devils greater all around. You tire of my manly self? You tire of your skirts and counterfeited breasts and shaving that winsome face and throat to softest white each night? I'll not put you in my place, to face that rapier from Hades, hot and burning in my breast. You stay the woman, I'll be the man – it suits us both." Will Shakespeare bared his teeth amid the carcasses and skeletons and props made from human hide, then stepped into a manly skin, tanned and more muscled than he'd ever be, and pulled it up over his hose. "What think you?" He put one arm above his head and twirled full around, then struck a martial pose, as if he held a spear: "Am I fearsome?"

"You are fearsome, but not because you wear some dead Achaean as your raiment. Is that Odysseus, great liar among men? Or some nameless hero? See, it matters not: a man's skin is not the man."

"Then be you the woman for all these nights, and I'll caress you like one, after the play is done. You know you like that, and Satan only holds me for a little while once the curtain falls...." Now Shakespeare bares his teeth until his goatee wobbles and bristles like the hackles of a frightened dog.

Desperate scheme, hatched aloft: For every time Will dies and awakes to Satan's hot embrace, the bard's mind is further clouded, his love for aught but Satan withered more. And every time Kit Marlowe must kill his best beloved Shakespeare, both hearts are pierced, both souls shriveled.

"Will, please. Just tonight, let me be the man, and you the murdering whore. It will freshen both our parts, both our eyes, and give Satan a good surprise. 'Come live with me and be my love' – again, 'and we will all the pleasures prove,' – again, once we buck the Son of the Morning off our backs, convince him to find new inducements for his depravity, and leave this play to close and be forgot."

"I cannot disappoint great Lucifer, Kit, even for you." Will still remembered him, then, and what they'd been to one another. Sometimes Kit thought Will no longer loved him – before the play's curtain rose, on each and every day. Afterward, when footlights faded and the Adversary dissolved into nightmare, Shakespeare and Will would huddle. Then Will did shiver under Marlowe's arm. But too often, lately, Shakespeare eyed him dully before the houselights dimmed. Then Kit saw a man facing his executioner, hopeless of reprieve.

If the light went out of Shakespeare's eyes, then Paradise might cease to shine, and all hell's vault go black as Satan's blasted heart, which was not riven nightly – had never been riven at all, if the Great Deceiver even had a heart or blood to pump or flesh as Marlowe understood the terms. Kit wondered if Satan had thought of that: no Shakespeare, no Marlowe: this was little loss to hell. But the light in Shakespeare's eye was the light of creation, of inspiration.

"Let me be the man. You must, Will, or this damnation will never end. And because..." – Marlowe pleaded, adding (since their quote game had brought them to this perilous estate in hell, and of all Shakespeare's words, these apostrophized him best – "'And as imagination bodies forth/The forms of things unknown, the poet's pen/Turns them to shapes and gives to airy nothing/A local habitation and a name.'"

Shakespeare's mettle raised enough to join the game, if weakly: "So, you want to prove this pleasure? I don't recommend you try it. To play this part? Only a fool would volunteer."

Marlowe shrugged as if to shake off a fly: he'd eluded many a plot, from the Privy Council on down to jealous reavers, before he'd died of one. He knew the smell of treachery so well it barely caught in his throat: man's infinite connivance. Is there nothing lower than a man, who will sell his lovers, parents, all his brothers for a moment's glory?

"Fine. So be it." Kit could not ask Shakespeare to understand, not now: Satan was not a man, and what lust those two shared, no part of love. But by these means, Shakespeare's precious soul was being torn asunder before Kit's eyes. "It's decided. I'll try the death of fools, and you'll kill me with your pointy blade: apt, a little death at your hands, and penetrating my shamefully unriven breast." His earthly death, by knife and knave, had been through the eye and into the brain. He'd dreamed of that pain and suffering every night, until those dreams were replaced by nightmares of stabbing Will's hairy chest between the nipples. Not again. Not one more night. "Now where's that sword? I need to show you how to pierce me quickest, kill me best...."

Trapped was Will Shakespeare, and he knew it. After Kit had died, when Will had written *Richard III*, he'd put Marlowe in it. So Marlowe said, to continue the quote game and raise Will's courage more: "'So wise so young, they say, do never live long.'"

And Will gave back, "As you like it, then." And grinned once more until his billy-beard wriggled: "'Bloody thou art, bloody will be thy end.'"

So they rehearsed their parts and rewrote some lines, redrafted pages... even sneaking barefoot upon the murky stage in Pandemonium.

They were still there when Satan found them. And he was steaming, twice the size of any man; leathery.

"Infernal Majesty," said Kit before Shakespeare had the chance to quail or whine or weep. "We've rewritten these lines, and changed our parts around, the better to please you and keep *Hell Bent* fresh and stirring."

Satan's eyes shone with all the ire of hell as he said, "You have? My play? Which I pronounced fitting? You've changed it? It's no longer as I liked it?" Smoke issued from ebony ears. Something black and furry misshaped his neck and wings, growling, and a tail lashed around his awful neck.

"Sire," said Will, "we must. I'll be the killer tonight, and Kit the victim. I want to see how it feels, to truly kill a man onstage. As in *Richard III*, 'Since I cannot prove a lover... I am determined to prove a villain.' And then, of course, once we've both learned what we can from this, swap our roles right back."

"So, the eternity of thy discontent sets in, dishonest souls?" The hump on Satan's shoulder yowled as if an inquisition were under way. The satanic horror of the Devil's presence changed, and shivered, and shimmered and became... beauteous. The yowling faded as if a cat were thrown down a well.

Damned fiend, prepared for all and exultant even in Marlowe's momentary triumph: "Thou sayest my *Faustus* once amused thee. So remember this I said there : 'Fiendful fortune may exhort the wise,/Only to wonder at unlawful things.'"

Now whitest wings bated here in the Pandemonium Theatre. Now the houselights raised enough to make pinions gleam. Now that face more beautiful than creation looked earnestly at Shakespeare, and words issued from lips made for kissing: "Do what you will, my poets. But don't expect me to personally bring our Marlowe back to life tonight. I have a... pressing... engagement once the play is done. As you famously said, Marlowe, "'*Terminat hora diem, terminat auctor opus:* the hour finishes the day, the author finishes the work.'"

Over Satan's glorious shoulder, Kit spied Shakespeare's face, drawn and white. But he thought he saw mischief and mystery and illustrious knowingness twinkling in his beloved bard's_eyes.

28894806R00278

Made in the USA
Lexington, KY
06 January 2014